A SHOT AFTER MIDNIGHT

ALSO BY TODD E. CREASON

A Shot After Midnight

A TWIN RIVERS NOVEL

TODD E. CREASON

MOON & SON PUBLISHING CO.

A SHOT AFTER MIDNIGHT
A Moon & Son Book

Published by Moon & Son Publishing Co.
Fithian, Illinois

Copyright © 2012 by Todd E. Creason
ISBN 13: 978-0-9831156-1-8

Book design by Brion Sausser

Printed in the United States of America

FOR MY MOTHER
JANE S. CREASON

*This novel wouldn't have happened if
you hadn't convinced me to continue.*

"*The world is weary of the past,*
Oh, might it die or rest at last."

—Percy Bysshe Shelley

"*I arise in the morning torn between a desire to*
improve the world and a desire to enjoy the world.
This makes it hard to plan the day."

—E. B. White

Prologue

"60 . . . 80 . . . AND 100," LINDA DARBY SAID AS SHE FINISHED COUNTing the money out to the customer at her teller window. As Lucille Garvey counted the money back to her, Linda winked at the little boy sitting on the counter beside his grandmother. Grinning broadly, he looked at Linda expectantly with his huge blue eyes. She knew what he wanted, but Lucille had raised him to be polite.

When Lucille finished counting, she said, "Thank you, Linda."

"Would somebody like a cherry sucker?" Linda asked the little boy. His face fell slightly.

"Or would you rather have a grape one?"

He beamed. Linda knew his favorite was grape.

"Yes, please!" he said.

She handed him a sucker, which he quickly unwrapped and stuck into his mouth.

"I'm gonna be three tomorrow!" he announced around the sucker.

"No, you're going to be four tomorrow," his grandmother said with a laugh.

"Will you come to my party, Miss Darby?"

"That sounds like fun, but I have to work tomorrow."

As Lucille turned to leave, Linda glanced at a group of men who'd just entered the bank. When she looked at them again, she couldn't believe what she saw. It took the shrill scream of a woman in the lobby to give it reality. Three men, wearing ski masks, were spreading out across the lobby and coming towards the teller windows. One had a shotgun and a canvas bag slung over his shoulder. Lucille Garvey backed up to the window and held the little boy tightly as the masked men quickly approached.

The one with the shotgun walked towards Linda's end of the counter, but he didn't seem to be paying particular attention to her. Linda froze before remembering the silent alarm button under the edge of the cashier's station. In the fifteen years she'd been working as the head cashier at the First National Bank of Calloway, nobody had ever robbed it. She'd always known it could happen, but after so many years, she'd come to believe it wouldn't.

"Hands up! This is a robbery! Stay calm, and nobody gets hurt!" the man with the shotgun bellowed.

There were a few more screams, but the chaos quickly subsided as everyone in the bank realized there was no way to escape.

When Linda slowly moved her hand towards the silent alarm switch, the man with the shotgun jumped right in front of her—the barrel of the shotgun hovering in front of her face.

"I said hands up!" he shouted again right at her.

She looked down the barrel of the shotgun, her hand frozen just inches from the silent alarm. A tremendous explosion boomed through the bank as he fired the shotgun into the air, bringing down plaster and other debris from the ceiling. Linda's heart leaped into her throat. Suddenly finding the ability to move, she raised her hands and stepped back from the counter.

"Everyone, take a step away from the drawers and don't trip the alarms," Linda ordered her cashiers. She looked at the man and said firmly, "We're going to cooperate with you fully. I promise you that. Take what you want, then leave."

"Very good," the man with the shotgun said through his mask.

He pumped the empty shell out of the shotgun, took another from his pocket, and pushed it into the receiver. He was obviously the leader of the group since neither of the other two men had spoken.

"We don't mean anybody any harm, but it would be a mistake to trigger a silent alarm," he said.

Linda shook her head. "We won't do that."

Once all the people in the bank had their hands up and the cashiers had stepped back from their stations, the leader handed the shotgun to another robber, who covered the cashiers and the customers in the lobby. The third robber jumped over the far end of the teller's counter and began cleaning out the drawers, stuffing the cash into a pillowcase.

It was obvious to Linda they knew what they were doing, and as long as everyone cooperated, the men would be gone in minutes. When she heard the young cashier next to her sobbing, she whispered, without looking at her, "Don't worry, Helen. They aren't going to hurt you. They just want the money. They'll be gone in a minute."

The lead robber heard Linda's advice. "That's right, darling. We're just after the cash. Be a good girl, and you'll have a great story to tell your grandkids one day."

He quickly climbed over the half-door that divided the lobby from the cashier stations and disappeared inside the vault. Hearing loud banging coming from inside the vault, Linda wondered what the leader was doing in there.

Linda had never dreamed she'd ever need the robbery training the bank required all employees to take periodically. The employees were doing everything they were supposed to do—cooperating. But another part of the training taught them to notice anything about the robbers that might aid the police later. There was little to tell about the leader or the man now covering everyone with the shotgun. They were both wearing nondescript clothes and shoes as well as gloves.

The leader's voice wasn't familiar to Linda, but there was something odd about it. She wondered if he was trying to disguise it. Linda also made a mental note of the military-style canvas bag he had over his shoulder. That detail might be useful to the police.

Linda looked at the third robber who was cleaning out the drawers behind the tellers' stations. Judging from the way he'd leaped over the counter, she guessed he was younger than the other two. He also appeared to be less experienced. The other two were calm, but his hands were shaking as he cleaned out the cashiers' drawers, and he was the only one not wearing gloves. On his right hand was a ring with a purple stone and a stylized comet on the side. She tried not to gasp as she thought, My God! He's a local!

Years ago, she'd worn a ring just like it, with the shank wrapped tightly with angora yarn—back when she'd gone steady with a boy from nearby Twin Rivers High School, back when she was a student at Calloway High. Generations of Twin Rivers High School boys had worn that very same distinctive ring. She tried to see the other side where the year of his graduation would be deeply engraved, but she couldn't see it from her position. She could only hope that one of the other cashiers would note that small detail.

Only minutes later, the lead robber returned, the canvas bag slung over his shoulder again. Under his arm, he carried a single safety deposit box, which he handed to the man covering the lobby as he took the shotgun back.

The robber cleaning out the drawers hadn't yet made it to Linda's station at the end when the leader yelled at him, "That's enough! It's time to go!"

The young robber quickly leaped over the counter with the pillowcase, landing in front of Lucille Garvey, who was still clutching the $100 she'd just withdrawn from her account. Her grandson was looking at him from her hip with wide blue eyes. As the robber reached for the money, he glanced towards the other two who were near the front door. When he saw that they weren't looking his way, he shook his head and ran after them, leaving Lucille Garvey with her money.

As he left, Lucille glanced at Linda, who understood exactly what that look said. Lucille had come to the same conclusion. At least one of the robbers was a local boy, probably somebody they both knew.

The second the men left, Linda triggered the silent alarm. She watched the robbers through the glass doors, running towards the edge of the street where a dark green Impala suddenly rolled to a stop in front of the bank.

The little boy began crying, still clutching his purple sucker.

"It's okay," Lucille said as she held him, rocking him in her arms. "They're gone, Levi. Everything's fine. Bad guys can't hurt a brave boy, and you were a very brave boy."

* * *

Enjoying his day off, Deputy Jim Mathis had just finished lunch at Pete's Diner in Calloway.

"You want another cup of coffee, Jim?" Lynette asked as she passed his table with the coffee pot.

"No, I'm ready for the ticket," he replied, digging his wallet out of his pocket.

Lynette set the pot on his table and flipped through her ticket book. "Two dollars, Jim," she said, laying the ticket down.

He laid three dollars on the table. "Let's call it even," he said as slid out of his booth.

"Thanks," she said, smiling broadly. Jim was always a good tipper. "Shouldn't you be fishing today? You always fish on your day off."

"My fishing partner called in sick this morning. I wasn't too happy about it, but it's probably for the best. I don't want to get too far from home. Marian could have that baby just about any time now, so I guess I'll go home and mow the yard. It needs it."

"You make sure you let us know when that baby comes," Lynette said.

"In this town? You'll probably know before we even get to the hospital," he said with a grin.

"True," she said, picking up the coffee pot. "I'll see you later, Jim."

He'd just stepped out onto the sidewalk when he saw the three masked men running out of the bank towards the street.

"Holy crap," he muttered under his breath.

A green Impala rolled to a stop in front of the bank, and the three men ran towards it. The driver was also wearing a mask, but he was wearing short sleeves. Jim recognized the skull and crossbones tattoo on his arm. It was Bruce Franklin. He'd had his share of run-ins with Franklin, who was a dangerous man to tangle with.

Jim pulled his revolver out of a shoulder holster and ran towards them, closing the distance as the robbers began piling into the car.

One slid into the front passenger seat and one into the backseat on the driver's side. The robber with the shotgun had lingered behind to cover their retreat. Since he was looking for pursuers from the bank, he still hadn't seen Deputy Mathis approaching. Once everyone else was in the car, he lowered the shotgun, crossed behind the car, and began to climb into the back seat on the street side.

Jim Mathis had closed to about forty feet.

"Stop! Police!" he shouted as people on the sidewalk took cover as best they could.

Bruce Franklin's arm, holding a revolver, suddenly appeared out of the window of the getaway car. He fired twice, missing both times, but the second round stopped Mathis' advance when it broke out a shop window behind him.

Deputy Mathis dropped to one knee and fired two rounds. The first shot missed, hitting the solid door of the Impala, but the second bullet found its mark through the driver's window. It hit Franklin in the chest. He slumped over as his revolver clattered onto the curb beside the car.

Mathis began running towards the getaway car again, thinking he'd stopped it. The robber with the shotgun climbed out of the back seat and rounded the trunk of the car in a defensive crouch. Mathis couldn't see him. Suddenly, the robber jumped from behind the car, dropped to one knee, and shot Mathis twice in the chest at close range. With a grunt, Mathis fell backwards to the ground as the robber with the shotgun turned to flee. Though badly wounded, Mathis was able to level his revolver and fire again. The round hit the robber in the back of his thigh. His leg folded, and he fell to his knees, dropping the shotgun, but he was able to get up and limp back to the car.

"Go! Bruce! Go!" he shouted as he pulled the back door closed behind him.

"I'm hit," Bruce said weakly, leaning over the steering wheel.

"So am I! Put your foot down, and let's get the hell out of here," he yelled.

Two more rounds slammed into the car as Deputy Mathis continued to fire, trying to hit a tire.

"Go!" the leader yelled again.

The Impala lurched forward, banging first into a parked car and then into another car as it squealed around a corner.

"Help him steer, Joe! He's going to kill us all," the leader snapped as he peeled off his ski mask and used it to the staunch the blood flowing from his thigh.

"Oh my God . . . oh my God . . . oh my God . . ." the third bank robber repeated, holding his head in his hands as he rocked back and forth with the pillowcase full of cash in his lap. "You said nobody was going to get hurt."

"Shut up, Andy," Joe hissed from the front seat as he tried to help Bruce steer.

"I knew it was a mistake to bring this moron on this job," the leader said as he held the ski mask tightly to his leg with a shaking hand. "Didn't I tell you it was a mistake, Bruce? And what the hell was Jim Mathis doing in town? He always fishes on his day off. Just my luck."

Then looking at Andy, he said, "Where the hell are your gloves?"

Andy looked down at his hands, his face going pale. "I don't know," he said, reaching into the pockets of his jacket and coming up empty.

"You dumb son-of-a-bitch, you probably left your fingerprints all over those drawers at the bank," he said as he grabbed Andy around the neck with a blood streaked hand and banged his head against the window. "If I still had that shotgun, I'd shoot you right this minute. Do you have any idea who you're working for?"

Andy had a look of terror on his face. The furious leader slapped him, leaving a bloody handprint on his face.

"Let's focus on getting the hell out of here. We got what we came for," Joe shouted as he tried to keep the car on the road as Bruce Franklin slowly bled out behind the wheel with his foot down on the accelerator. The car suddenly lurched towards the edge of the road and snapped a stop sign off its post. The sign crashed into the windshield, spider-webbing it, as Joe pulled it back onto the road. Bruce moaned.

"We got to pull over for a minute. Bruce is going to pass out," Joe yelled.

"Keep going! We stop now, and we're caught," the leader snapped from the backseat. "Head to the River Junction Road. We'll go to the cabin as planned and get everyone patched up. Then we'll decide what to do with Andy here."

"What do you mean?" Andy said, his eyes wide, as he rubbed the side of his face where he'd been slapped.

"You know exactly what I mean."

"You're going to kill me," he sobbed.

"You can bet on it."

"Oh, crap," Joe shouted from the front seat as Bruce went limp and slumped over the steering wheel. The Impala veered towards the edge of the road. When Joe tried to crank the wheel, the car began to skid toward the iron frame of the Calloway River Bridge. They barely had a chance to brace themselves before the Impala slammed head-on into the concrete skirt of the bridge at high speed.

Steam hissed from around the edges of the crumpled hood as the blaring of the horn pierced the quiet of the woods surrounding the bridge. There was nobody moving in the car. In the distance, police sirens wailed.

Chapter One

Levi Garvey was sitting on the porch swing with his feet up on the porch rail, cuddling a cup of steaming coffee in his hands. He looked out from under the brim of his Panama hat at the expansive front yard of the Garvey house, where he'd grown up. The old Victorian house, which had been in his family for generations, sat on a six-acre estate on the edge of the small town of Twin Rivers. After returning home nearly two years ago, the best-selling novelist had taken up residence in his grandmother's old house with his new wife, Tori.

It was late March, the first day that hinted that spring was near. While the last piles of snow melted away under the elm and oak trees in the warm golden light, the first leaves were beginning to show on the trees. The American flag mounted on the porch post flapped slowly in the gentle breeze as fluffy white clouds skated across a clear blue sky.

Levi smiled as he watched a squirrel scamper down the trunk of one of the large oaks in the front yard. He began nearly every day the same way, summer and winter, on the front porch of the Garvey house with a cup of coffee. He'd had the same morning ritual on the porch of his massive townhouse on Pulaski Square during the ten years he'd lived in Savannah, Georgia. It seemed now like that life was a totally different one, but his morning ritual had remained. Morning was still his favorite time of the day, his time to think.

He was having some problems with his current novel, problems which were keeping him up late at night. The novel just wasn't coming together the way his first four novels had—actually, it wasn't developing at all. As he sat sipping coffee, he was thinking about the story he wanted to write but couldn't yet get started.

A small noise distracted him. He glanced over towards the side of the porch where the sound had come from. He listened for a moment before he heard it again—a little metallic jangle.

Relief washed through him. He knew exactly what that sound was. It meant the end of what he'd been more worried about over the last few days than the problems he was having with his novel.

"Is that you, Rosco?" he called sharply over the side of the porch. There was no answer, but he heard the jangle again.

"I can hear you, Rosco. You'd better get up here now," he said sternly.

A dog slowly crept in front of the porch and climbed the stairs. The German shepherd sat down at the top of the stairs and looked at Levi expectantly with his big sad brown eyes, his muzzle lowered and his ears laid back in shame. He knew he was in big trouble.

Levi glanced at him and shook his head.

This wasn't the first Rosco but the most recent in a long line of German shepherds Levi had owned and named Rosco. The first he'd gotten from his Uncle Ed as a birthday present when he was ten years old. The first, Rosco the Hunter, and the last, Rosco the Brave, were buried under the elm tree beside the driveway. And there were several in between. But because this Rosco was young still, he hadn't yet earned a nickname. It might very well turn out to be Rosco the Explorer.

This newest Rosco, who was just two over years old, was already the largest of the bunch at just under a hundred pounds. He was a mess—covered in mud, his fur matted, his ears and haunches covered in cockleburs. A familiar scent in the breeze indicated that Rosco had also managed to get sprayed by a skunk—again.

"Where in the world have you been?" Levi scolded as Rosco whined. "Tori is going to have a fit when she sees you—and smells you. You've been gone three days this time. That's a new record."

Rosco plopped down exhausted and put his muzzle on his front paws. Levi knew he had to be starved—he always was when he returned home.

"You know what's going to happen if you keep running off, don't you?" Levi said. "It's going to be a trip to the vet for you. Snip. Snip.

You're lucky Tori didn't take you the last time you did this."

Rosco whined at the word *vet*, but Levi couldn't help but crack a slight smile. When he did, Rosco's ears perked up a bit. Rosco was smart enough to know that the brief smile on Levi's face meant he wasn't in as much trouble as he thought.

Whenever Rosco ran off, Levi and Tori were both afraid some farmer was going to mistake him for a coyote and shoot him. Coyotes were a problem in River County, and every time they heard a shot late at night when Rosco was missing, they both feared the same thing.

Rosco's ears fell flat, and his head dropped back down on his paws when Tori stormed through the screen door and stared down at him. She never said a word. Her arms were crossed, and her toe tapped on the wooden porch floor.

"Now you're in for it," Levi said with a chuckle as Rosco blinked up at her.

Levi was easy, but even Rosco knew Tori was the one he had a problem with. Rosco began slowly sliding backward towards the stairs as he looked up at her stern face.

"Where do you think you're going?" she said.

Her green eyes were flashing, and a single ringlet of her kinky blonde hair hung in front of her face. Levi knew it was a show. He knew what she really wanted to do was hug that dog. She'd been driving all over the county looking for Rosco. Actually, he thought it might be kind of entertaining if she did hug the dog since she wasn't yet aware that he'd been sprayed again.

"I don't know what I'm going to do with you," she said, shaking her head.

Rosco whined.

"Carriage house! Now!" she ordered, pointing towards the large round building that sat off the back of the house.

Getting up slowly, Rosco walked down the porch steps and crept towards the carriage house. He stopped half way up the driveway and glanced back briefly, hoping for a reprieve.

"Go on!" Tori ordered, pointing again.

Rosco finished walking up the driveway, slipped through the open gap between the two sliding doors, and disappeared inside.

As soon as Rosco vanished, Tori looked at Levi and smiled, the relief on her face was obvious. She was stunningly beautiful—the kind of woman that men couldn't help but notice. Strong and independent, she was also the kind of woman most men would describe as "a handful." She was happiest when her hands were dirty in the garden or when she was swinging a hammer.

She sat down next to him on the swing, took his hand, and kissed his cheek.

"Morning," she said as if nothing had just happened. She brushed her fingers through the graying blonde hair at his temples. "About time for a haircut, isn't it, hippie?"

"I'm getting one today," Levi said. She'd dropped two hints earlier that week. "Are you going to kill my dog?"

"I haven't decided yet," Tori said thoughtfully. "Did he get sprayed again?"

Levi nodded slowly.

She sighed. "Is your stupid dog ever going to learn about skunks?"

Levi thought for a moment, then shook his head. "That seems unlikely. When you're a dog, that's a lesson you learn the first time, or you never learn it at all."

Tori took Levi's cup and sipped the coffee. She didn't hand the mug back.

Levi glanced at her sideways. "You know, I've never actually had a full cup of coffee out here."

Ignoring him, she took another sip and handed the mug back.

"More than half a cup left," he said. "That's a change. You usually drink it all."

"It's been giving me heartburn," she said.

Glancing at her, Levi noticed, not for the first time, that she looked tired. He knew saying something would get him nowhere, so he let it go. But he was worried about her. She'd been putting in long hours.

After their experience with Doug Malone, Tori had never returned to her job as president of the First National Bank of Calloway. What she loved was historic restoration. Years before Levi had returned to Twin Rivers, she'd bought and restored the Comet Theatre in town, an art deco theatre dating from the 1920s. As kids, they'd spent a lot of time together in the old run-down theatre, but now the Comet Theatre looked as it had when it'd first opened.

Tori had looked at historic restoration as a hobby at the time, but she was good with her hands, and she'd loved the process of bringing something old back into use again. It was something they shared. Levi and his Uncle Ed worked on restoring old Ford trucks while Tori worked on a slightly larger scale—restoring entire buildings.

After they were married, Levi had encouraged her to do restoration for a living, and it wasn't long before she was approached about restoring the old Majestic Theatre in the nearby town of Olton. The project had taken eighteen months. Now the people in Olton were doing the same thing with their restored theatre that Twin Rivers was doing—showing classic movies twice a week. The profits went towards community improvement projects. As with the Comet Theatre in Twin Rivers, the Majestic in Olton had become a huge success story.

Tori had just finished the Majestic Theatre when Levi was elected Worshipful Master of the Twin Rivers Masonic Lodge. The lodge members decided to hire Tori to restore the hundred-year-old building to its former glory. It was particularly challenging because the Twin Rivers Police Department was on the first floor. The lodge rooms upstairs were in very bad shape due to a leaky roof that had been ignored for decades. The building, however, was solidly built, just badly neglected. She'd gutted it down to the rafters, studs, and floor joists. It would be a long process restoring all the woodwork, antique furnishings, and the stained glass windows.

"Your book isn't going very well, is it?" Tori said after a few minutes of silence.

"How can you tell?"

"You slept in the den again last night. That's the third time this week."

"It's beginning to come together," he said.

"I checked on you this morning when I got up," she said. "Your computer was on. You've been working on that novel for two or three weeks now, so I was a little surprised when I read over what you've written so far."

Levi laughed. "You like it?"

"It's a great start, Levi. I'll never forget your opening. . . 'Chapter One.' Is there going to be more?"

The truth was, Levi hadn't written one word yet.

"Most of the work goes on right in here," he said, tapping the side of his head.

"Well, if that's the case, you're screwed."

Levi laughed.

"So what seems to be the problem?" Tori asked.

"This is the first novel I've written that hasn't come from real life experience. It's proving to be a little more challenging."

Levi's first three books had been based on the same theme—his ten years of experience after college as an Illinois State Police officer. His most recent book, *The Devil Within*, was based on the events surrounding Doug Malone. Levi and Tori had stumbled onto a secret two years ago—a decades-old murder. As it turned out, it wasn't just one murder and not just one killer either. The Twin Rivers Police Chief, Doug Malone, and his deputy, Alan Haig, both of whom Levi and Tori had known in high school, were serial killers.

Levi and Tori had barely survived the experience alive. Doug and Alan hadn't. Levi's Uncle Ed, a former Marine sniper during the Vietnam War, had killed Doug to save Levi, and Levi had killed Alan weeks later to protect Tori when she'd figured out that Doug couldn't have acted alone.

The story had been national news as car after car—each containing the body of one of their victims—was pulled from Kingery Pond. Levi's novelization of the story had been a run-away bestseller. Just as with his first three novels, Hollywood was already working on a screenplay. There were rumors in the tabloids that Clint Eastwood might direct the film. Every time the subject came up, Levi whistled the haunting melody from *The Good, the Bad, and the Ugly.*

Tori looked at Levi and sighed. "Why are you driving yourself nuts? You're past having to write on deadlines. You don't have to put out a book a year. If you're not ready, give yourself some time. The story always comes on its own, doesn't it?"

Levi nodded. Tori was right. His fans would wait. It might even work in his favor since the longer it took, the more anxious they would become.

Tori got up from the porch swing and stretched. "I'd better get that stupid dog cleaned up and get over to the lodge."

"What's going on today?" Levi asked.

Tori frowned and glanced up at the brilliant blue sky. "I sure hope the weather forecast for this week is right. The roof is coming off today. The crew will be there at eight to start work. Bob said it'll take two days to rip the old one off and three or four days before the new roof is on, but I'm thinking that's optimistic. It's a huge job. I'm thinking more like ten days. If it rains . . ."

"It won't rain," Levi said, finishing his coffee. "You know our meeting is this week. We'll be able to use the lodge, won't we?"

"You'll be meeting under a starry sky, but you'll be able to have your meeting," Tori said. "It might be kind of cool, actually. Your mysterious secret society with all its ancient knowledge, holding a meeting under a moonlit sky."

"If it doesn't rain," he said. Then when Tori glared at him, he hastily added, "I mean, it won't rain this week. No chance."

"I suppose the Freemasons control the weather, too," Tori said teasingly.

"I can't talk about that." Levi winked as he stood up and stretched. "Come on. I'll help you get Rosco cleaned up. You still have the ingredients for the secret de-skunking formula—baking soda, hydrogen peroxide, and dishwashing detergent?"

"I buy peroxide by the gallon now," she said as they walked down the porch steps. "Your stupid dog."

Levi laughed. "I sure hope that doesn't become his nickname—Rosco the Stupid."

"About time you made that appointment for Rosco, isn't it?" Tori said as they headed towards the carriage house, swinging their joined hands between them.

Levi winced.

"We can't have Rosco running all over the county," she said. "You know that, right?"

"You let me run all over the county, and you haven't had me fixed yet."

"I'm thinking about it."

"I'll call," he said

Tori had heard that story before—the last two or three times Rosco had gone missing.

Chapter Two

"Rosco, there are two windows in this truck," Levi said, pushing the dog off his lap. "This one is mine, and that one is yours. I even rolled it down for you."

Levi fired up Old Blue, his 1960 Ford F-100 which he and Uncle Ed had restored even before he'd gotten his driver's license. He'd driven it all through high school. Then Ed had kept the truck after Levi left Twin Rivers. Levi hadn't returned home, even for a visit, for more than twenty years because of Tori Buchanan, whom he'd loved since they were kids. But he'd never told her. When she married another man, he was heartbroken. Finally, he returned after his grandma died. At his twenty-fifth class reunion, he found that Tori was no longer married. Old Blue was still waiting for him, too. The rest was history.

As he rolled out of the carriage house, Levi glanced at their latest project, Tori's truck. It was up on blocks in the corner of the huge carriage house, easily visible in the light streaming in through the cupola windows above. The truck was in pieces, scattered everywhere, but looks were deceiving. The truck was nearly finished. In a week, possibly less, it would be ready for paint.

Uncle Ed had been calling that truck "Pappy" because, according to him, it was Old Blue's daddy. Pappy was a 1949 Ford F-1 with a V-8 flathead. The real war would begin when they started painting it. Tori had said from the beginning that if it was going to be her truck, she wanted it to be purple. Ed and Levi had been thinking from the beginning that it would be red.

Old Blue rolled out into the bright morning sunlight. Levi headed to Harv's Diner in downtown Twin Rivers where he went every morning for coffee and pie. It was a short drive. When he rounded the corner of Main Street, Rosco climbed into his lap again and stuck his head out Levi's window.

"Rosco, dammit," he said as he tried to steer, mash the clutch, and shift the three-on-the-tree while trying to push the nearly one-hundred-pound dog off his lap.

Then deciding it wasn't worth the effort, he said, "Rosco, if anything ever happens to you, I'm seriously considering never owning another dog."

Rosco licked his face and then stuck his head out the driver's side window again as Levi looked through the windshield over his back.

"You still smell a little like skunk," Levi remarked as he swung into a spot in front of Harv's. "You stay here and no barking. You got it? No barking!"

Levi climbed out of the truck and looked across the street when he heard the sound of hammers. Workers were on the roof of the Twin Rivers Police Department three stories up. The top two stories of that building belonged to the Masonic Lodge. Actually, the entire building belonged to the lodge. The restoration project was being financed by the rent the police department had been paying to the Masonic Lodge for more than eighty years. Since the lodge had spent very little of the money, it'd been collecting interest for decades.

There was a huge orange tube hanging down the front of the building. The old shingles and plywood the workmen were throwing into the tube crashed into a dumpster three stories below, ruining the usual peace and quiet of the small town morning.

As Levi walked towards Harv's, Rosco began barking out the window of Old Blue.

"I'm warning you, dog," Levi said, turning back towards the truck. "I'll roll up those windows!"

Rosco's head quickly disappeared inside.

* * *

THE BELL JINGLED BRIGHTLY OVER THE DOOR WHEN LEVI WALKED IN.

"Morning, Levi," Harv's wife, April, said from behind the coffee counter.

"Good morning, April. Morning, Harv."

The massive man standing in front of the coffee pots with a mug in his hand grunted his usual greeting. Harv and April had owned the diner for over forty years, and Harv's father had owned it for fifty years before that. Back when Levi was in high school, his friends, a group known as "The Zoo Crew," had hung out there. He'd been a morning regular ever since he'd returned to Twin Rivers. It was the pie that lured him in. April Jenkins had a reputation for making the best pies in River County. In the years before Levi had returned, she'd gotten out of the habit of making pies regularly. But when Levi expressed his love of her pies, she'd begun making them every day again. They'd brought the morning business back to the diner.

April's pies were so popular, the regulars no longer called the days by their names. Instead, Monday was Coconut, Tuesday was Lemon, Wednesday was Banana . . . Levi's favorite day was Chocolate. That was Friday. But today was Lemon, very disappointing—Levi's least favorite day. He could deal with Butterscotch, but he never could get to liking Lemon. He generally skipped the pie on Tuesdays.

April had set a cup of coffee down at the counter in front of his favorite stool even before he'd reached it. The familiar form of the Twin Rivers chief of police was on the stool next to his.

"Morning, Chief Craig," Levi said, setting his Panama on the counter next to the chief's flat-brimmed trooper hat and taking the stool beside him.

"Good morning, Levi," he said, swiveling on his stool and offering his hand. "We were just talking about you."

Chief Clifford Craig was short and stocky with his silver hair cut in a military-style buzz. He always seemed tan, summer and winter, and his face was lined deeply with age. His silver mustache and goatee were meticulously trimmed. He was a likeable man, but somehow you knew that, even as he approached seventy, he could probably beat the crap out of you. Maybe that's why almost everyone in town called him Craig or Chief Craig or just Chief. There were very few who called him Clifford or Cliff.

Chief Craig had been the chief of police when Levi was a kid. When he retired, Doug Malone had taken over. After Doug was killed, Craig had been asked to come out of retirement until a permanent chief could be found. He'd been perfect for the job the first time and was still perfect. But Chief Craig had made it very clear that since he was pushing seventy hard, he had no interest in doing the job for more than a few months. The search committee for a new chief hadn't had much luck in finding a replacement, and a few months had become almost two years. Fortunately for the chief, nothing much happened in Twin Rivers.

"I think you may know my new deputy here," Craig said, indicating the man on his other side.

He was in his late thirties, tall and muscular, with chiseled features. He looked like he belonged on a Marine Corps recruiting poster. Levi recognized the boy the man had once been—mostly because of a deep scar on his chin.

"You were a little younger last time I saw you," Levi said, smiling. "I went to high school with your brother. You're Mark Walker's little brother, Ben, right? Last time I saw you, you were playing Donkey Kong at Hillbilly Bob's Convenience Store and trying to bum quarters from all of us."

"Good seeing you again, Levi," Ben said, reaching behind Chief Craig to shake his hand.

April set a piece of pie in front of Levi. He looked down at it and then up at April.

"Hey, I thought today was Lemon—this is Chocolate!" he said, a huge smile on his face.

"Strangest thing, Levi," April said, leaning on her elbows on the counter in front of him and peering over the top of her readers. "I went to Norm's Grocery to buy lemons after work last night, and somebody had gone in there yesterday and bought every fresh lemon in the place."

"Well, isn't that odd," Levi said, digging into the pie.

"I think it might have been on purpose," April remarked.

"No?" Levi said, washing the first bite down with coffee. "Some kind of citrus conspiracy, do you think? Right here in Twin Rivers? Did you report it to Chief Craig?"

"She sure did," he said with a chuckle. "But although April thinks screwing with the pie schedule at Harv's Diner should be considered a felony, it's really not."

"He wouldn't even take a report," she said, frowning at Chief Craig. "I even got a description of the perpetrator from Norm. Blue eyes, blonde hair graying a little at the temples, and somewhat overweight."

Levi glanced down and pulled his belt up without thinking.

"I knew it!" she exclaimed.

"What?" Levi said.

"You bought those lemons so I couldn't make lemon pie today, didn't you? You mess with my pie schedule again, Levi Garvey, and I'll take chocolate out of the rotation completely. We'll have butterscotch on Fridays in here," she said wagging, a finger in his face.

"Nobody likes butterscotch either," Levi argued.

"I like butterscotch," a man drawled slowly from the big farmers' table behind him.

Levi spun around on his stool and looked at him harshly. "Shut up, Floyd!"

Laughter erupted throughout the diner.

"I'm warning you, Garvey," April said, poking him on the forehead with her finger. "You do that again, there's going to be trouble."

"Did you see that, Chief? Aren't you going to do anything about this. That's a threat! And she just assaulted me, too!" Levi said, rubbing his forehead where she'd poked him.

"Actually, Levi, I always come in on Tuesdays for the lemon pie. It's my favorite," he said, giving Levi a look that reminded him that, even pushing seventy, Chief Craig wasn't somebody he'd want to piss off.

"Oh, I see. I'm sorry, Chief."

"Every crime has unintended victims," Craig said. "You need to remember that."

"I take it that when you said you'd just been talking about me, that's what it was about. Me buying some lemons—a freakin' felony in Twin Rivers apparently," Levi said loudly towards April, who was circulating around the diner with the coffee pot.

"Nope, that wasn't it," Ben said.

"Ben has been hired as a temporary deputy," Craig said, "but he'd like to be permanent, so I've given him a case to solve to prove his worth—a cold case."

Levi looked at Craig with his eyebrows raised. "A cold case in Twin Rivers?"

April walked by with the coffee pot. "The case of the 'Bikini Bandit.' I'm sure you remember the crime, Levi. My thought on that crime is he's probably a repeat offender. Could even be the Lemon Bandit."

Levi laughed. "I told you nearly thirty years ago I didn't have anything to do with that. Somebody put that bikini on the war memorial statue in the park that Halloween, but it wasn't me."

"You told me a lot of interesting things during that period," Craig said, sipping his coffee. "Of course, most of them weren't true. Even when I caught you red-handed, you always had a story. But I still have the original photos, footprint casts, and the like, and if Ben here can solve the crime, he's got the job. It was the only unsolved case I had open when I retired the first time. Before I go this time, Garvey, I'm going to know how you did it. It's bugged the crap out of me for years."

"I'll be coming over to talk to you at some point," Ben said, almost as an apology.

"You're wasting your time, Ben."

Turning to Chief Craig, Levi said, "You know what surprises me the most?"

He shrugged.

"There's evidence? You took castings and photographs back then? Are you kidding me?"

"Oh, yes. I've preserved all the evidence—including the bikini. It was a brilliant prank, obviously conceived from a twisted mind," he said, looking squarely at Levi. "That statue sits on top of a thirty-foot pillar. There's no way to climb it. There are no overhanging tree branches or anything. There was no way you could have driven Old Blue out there with a ladder in the back. It'd rained earlier that night, and the ground was soft. There were no tire marks and no ladder impressions. There is, however, a wide sidewalk about twenty feet away, and I thought you'd parked Old Blue on that sidewalk and leaned a ladder over the bed to the base of the statue. But I did the math and it would've taken a fire department ladder truck to reach that statue from the sidewalk."

Craig paused, then added, "I've always wanted to know. How the hell did you get up there and tie a bikini on that statue?"

Levi sighed. "Did it ever cross you mind, Chief, that maybe the reason I can't give you an answer is because you are still chasing the wrong suspect?"

"Not once," Craig answered with a smile. "You did it."

"And I'll figure it out," Ben said. "My brother has told me stories about you. You may be smart, Levi, but I'll figure it out."

"He's a smart guy," Craig said, cocking a thumb at Ben. "I don't mind admitting he's smarter than me, and I have every confidence he'll solve it. I can't wait until he does."

"And when he does," Levi said, "what's the penalty for the crime?"

"If you didn't do it, you shouldn't be worried about it," Craig said, "but back in 1982, that offense carried a $25 fine."

Levi laughed as April refilled his coffee cup. He knew that if Ben was a good officer, solving that old prank wouldn't matter. Craig would hire him anyway. It was nothing more to Craig than a character exercise—to see if Ben had what it took to solve the little meaningless problems law enforcement in small towns dealt with. And to satisfy his own curiosity.

"So how is the search for the new chief going?" Levi said, changing the subject.

"We interviewed one last week that didn't work out," Craig said. "He had all the right experience, but he wasn't right for Twin Rivers. It's hard to find a guy with the right attitude to work in a small town. We need to have a chief with a more relaxed attitude in law enforcement. A small town cop has to understand there are different ways of enforcing the law—more than just writing tickets and making arrests. There is a human aspect to law enforcement that most of our candidates so far just haven't understood."

"And you've got to make sure you get it right, especially after the last chief," Levi said tightly.

Craig nodded. "Malone was hired against my recommendation. The town wanted a local guy, and he was the star football player and all. I knew it was a mistake when they did it. I knew he was a jackass, but I sure didn't know he was a killer."

"Nobody did," Levi replied.

"But we've got a guy who's highly recommended coming in this afternoon for an interview. He's recently retired with thirty years experience, in his mid-fifties, and very laid back. I've talked to him a couple of times, and I think he could be the guy we're looking for."

Levi pushed his pie plate away and drank the last swallow of coffee. "Well, good luck. I hope he works out."

"Me, too," Craig said. "I'm looking forward to getting back to my fishing."

Levi stood, picked up his Panama, snugged it on his head, and turned to leave.

"I'll be seeing you, Levi," Ben said. "Before it's all said and done, I'm going to write you that $25 fine."

"You're wasting your time, Ben. Think about it. Where did that bikini come from? There was only one woman in the house I grew up in at the time, and that bikini sure didn't belong to my Grandma Lucille," Levi said with a smile.

"Is that a clue?" Ben asked.

"It could be," Levi said, as he paid Harv for his ticket.

"Lemon on Friday, Levi," April called as he pulled the door open.

Levi paused for a moment, mumbled something under his breath, and walked out.

Chapter Three

Lawrence Swaney pulled his construction truck into a space in front of the Twin Rivers Police Department and climbed out. He looked up towards the sound of hammering on the roof three stories up and saw the workers on the roof of the Masonic Lodge. Seconds after he pulled his toolbox out of the back of his truck, a huge crash rang out as old shingles and plywood crashed down the refuse tube and fell into the dumpster nearby.

Slowly, Lawrence walked down the narrow alley between the Masonic Lodge and the barbershop and entered the building through the lodge entrance at the back of the building. He climbed the long staircase to the second floor, pausing at the top to rub his knee with its new titanium joint. Since he was sixty-eight, it was taking a little longer to recover from the surgery than what he'd expected.

Although the building was three stories tall, most of that third floor space was occupied by the towering, twenty-foot vaulted ceiling of the main lodge room on the second floor. There was only a small kitchen and dining area on the third floor—a low-ceilinged room large enough to seat about thirty at narrow wooden tables. After lodge meetings, they'd all climb the stairs to the third floor kitchen for refreshments and, more often than not, a few hands of euchre.

Lawrence dropped his toolbox off on the second floor and climbed the narrow flight of stairs up to the kitchen for a cup of coffee. He expected to find Tori, but the kitchen was empty.

The sound of hammers was deafening up there. He grabbed a coffee mug from the sink drainer, poured himself a cup, and walked back down the stairs. He picked up his toolbox in the Tyler's room and walked into the enormous room, which seemed even larger with the plaster ceiling gone and the inside of the roof rafters visible two stories above. There were three rows of theater-style seats along the walls on the north and south sides which provided enough seats for about a hundred and fifty Masons. It had been a long time since the lodge had needed that many. All of the heavy wooden furniture was covered in plastic, and sunlight was streaming down through holes in the roof where the workmen had already pulled off the sheeting.

Tori was sitting on the bottom step of the Master's dais at the east end of the lodge room, her head on her knees. She looked tiny in the massive room.

"You okay, Tori?" Lawrence Swaney asked, looking down at her over the tops of his bifocals.

Tori jumped. She hadn't heard him come in. She looked pale.

"I'm fine. Just praying," she said, looking up at the ceiling.

Lawrence chuckled. "It's not going to rain, Tori. And even if it does, that old roof had so many holes in it, it's not like this old lodge hasn't been wet before. You saw that plaster ceiling in here before we pulled it down. Part of it was sagging from the water damage. It wouldn't have been long before it would've come down on its own. Last time we had a meeting during a rainstorm, we used every pan in the kitchen to catch all the drips. Levi presided over his first meeting as Master with a roasting pan sitting on his lap to catch the leaks over his chair. Don't worry. We have all the furnishings covered in plastic. It'll be fine."

Tori smiled at him weakly. He'd first noticed the dark circles under her eyes a few days ago. Yesterday, he'd seen her hand shaking when she took a drink from her water bottle.

"Something else bothering you?" Lawrence asked.

Tori sighed. "This project is the biggest one I've ever done. Every time we crack into a wall, we find a new problem."

"Yup," Lawrence said. "It needs a lot of work."

"It's going to run thousands more than I originally thought," Tori said, shaking her head. "The wiring has to be redone. The plumbing is bad. The furnace is shot, and the duct work wasn't done right when it was converted from steam heat to gas."

"We did that back in the early '70s. The guy was cheap, but you get what you pay for."

"Well, it's got to be fixed," Tori said. "That's why in the winter it's ninety degrees in the Tyler's room and fifty degrees in here."

"Let's just add central heat and air while we're at it," Lawrence remarked. "It's bad enough freezing through the winters up here, but the summers are worse. I get tired of trying to hear what people are saying over the noise from the window air conditioners—not that they do much good in a space this size."

"You know what central air will run in a building this size?" Tori said, looking at him in surprise.

"Ten thousand, maybe," Lawrence nodded.

"Or more," Tori said.

"Don't you worry about the money, Tori. We've got it. We all agreed in the beginning that if we were going to have you restore this lodge, we were going to do it right. There will never be a better chance to do it. I'll bring it up in the meeting, but let's get some bids on it."

Tori smiled and nodded. "You know, since we're going to have to redo the wiring. I had some ideas about some different lighting in here, too."

Lawrence nodded. "Now you're talkin', Tori."

"And that bathroom is disgusting. It needs a new toilet and vanity," Tori said.

"Let's add a urinal while we're at it—a big wide floor urinal. They sure as hell can't hit the toilet," Lawrence said with a chuckle. "Let's give them a bigger target to aim for. We can shove that bathroom wall out three or four feet into the preparation room to make space for it."

Tori stood up and kissed Lawrence on the cheek. "Thank you, Lawrence. I needed to hear that."

Lawrence's face reddened.

"Will you tell me something if you can?" Tori asked.

"Sure," Lawrence said.

Tori pointed along the south wall where they'd moved some of the lodge furnishings out of the way.

"I'm curious. What are those long spears for?" she asked, pointing to the four seven-foot long maple rods, each capped with a silver spear tip styled like a Masonic symbol and standing upright in separate holders.

Lawrence laughed. "Those aren't spears. They're called rods."

"What are they used for?"

"There are four rod officers in the lodge," Lawrence said. "The Senior and Junior Deacons and the Senior and Junior Stewards. The Senior Deacon sits at the base of the dais at the right hand of the Worshipful Master in the East, and the Junior Deacon sits on the right of the Senior Warden in the West. The two Stewards sit in front of and on either side of the Junior Warden's dais in the South."

"So what do they do with those rods?"

"Well, the rod officers are messengers and kind of represent guards, too. They carry those rods during the Masonic rituals for opening and closing and during our degrees. There's a right way and a wrong way of handling those rods. We call it rod work, and it is part of our ritual traditions. I used to teach rod work before my knee went out," he said, walking over and pulling one from its stand. "Wanna see a little?"

Tori nodded.

Lawrence walked over and sat down in the Senior Deacon's chair with the rod. "When the rod officers do their jobs right, the way they use these rods is very precise, almost like a military drill."

With that, he turned, facing forward, and stood sharply, his hand gliding up the rod as he rose so it never left the floor. He paused and stepped out from his chair, tucking the rod under his arm in one smooth movement. Then he walked around the lodge, doing a series of sharp turns with his feet and shifting the rod from hand to hand in a series of precise maneuvers. Finally he returned to his chair, turned and sat, sliding his hand down the rod as he lowered himself."

Tori clapped.

"I used to do it better," Lawrence said, rising. He walked over and placed his rod back in its holder. "You can imagine how impressive that is when you've got two rod officers, sometimes all four, working in perfect tandem with each other."

"Very impressive," Tori said.

"It's one of my favorite parts of our traditions," Lawrence said. "Years ago, we had a bunch of guys in this lodge that were really good at rod work. When we'd have our public installation of officers each year, those four guys would do a little rod drill for those attending. We used to pack this place back then. Everyone who came really enjoyed that part and gave those guys a huge round of applause afterwards."

"You don't do that anymore?" Tori asked.

"No, not for a long time," Lawrence admitted. "You missed our installation."

"Yeah," Tori said. "Levi really wanted me to be here when he was installed as Master, but Olton planned the opening of the Majestic Theatre the same Sunday."

Lawrence nodded. "Well, other than the twelve officers that were installed, we probably didn't have more than another dozen guests. Things have changed. We used to have standing room only. Probably two hundred would pile in here. We'd have a nice meal afterwards at the park. It was a big deal in town."

Tori rubbed her chin and looked around the lodge. "You install new officers in June?"

Lawrence nodded.

"Think we could have this done by then?"

Lawrence smiled. "About four months from now? Maybe. Why?"

"It'd be a good time to show the town the restored lodge," Tori said.

Lawrence smiled. "Maybe get a rod team back together for a little exhibition?"

"That's what I'm thinking," Tori said.

"Me, Floyd, Ed, and one more . . ." Tori could tell his wheels were turning.

"What about Levi?"

Lawrence rolled his eyes and shook his head.

"What?"

"Levi is the worst rod officer I've ever seen," Lawrence said. "No hand-eye coordination at all. You see that rod with the bent tip?"

Tori glanced over at the rods and nodded.

"Levi did that," Lawrence said with a chuckle. "You know how when I stood up, I let my hand slide up the rod as I rose?"

Tori nodded.

"Well, one night Levi was filling in for a missing Senior Deacon, and he wasn't paying much attention. When he was supposed to stand, it caught him off-guard, and he clamped his hand down and stood up, raising that rod high in the air."

Tori snickered.

"That would've been okay," Lawrence said, "if it weren't for the ceiling fans. He drove that rod right up into the metal blades."

Tori laughed.

"It made a hell of a noise and brought down about thirty years worth of dust on his head besides. That was the last time anybody let Levi fill in for a rod officer."

"That's what we should shoot for," Tori said, after she quit laughing. "We should have the grand re-opening of the Twin Rivers Masonic Lodge for the officer installation. And we'll invite the whole town."

"Good idea," Lawrence said.

"I think I'll go over to Calloway. I've got some ideas about carpet," Tori said.

"Why don't you take the whole day off," Lawrence suggested. "That can wait. If you don't mind my saying so, you're not looking very well today. You weren't looking well yesterday either. You're working too hard and worrying too much. I've got a couple of guys coming over to pull out the old carpet, and I'm going to set up a couple of sawhorses and begin refinishing doors today. It would be a good day for you to take off and get a little R & R."

"I don't know . . ."

"Go home," he said. "Watch some TV, take a nap, relax a little. You're tired."

Tori finally nodded. "Thank you, Lawrence."

She began walking towards the door.

"And don't be watching the Weather Channel either," Lawrence called after her. "A little rain isn't going to hurt this old lodge."

"That's very good advice, Lawrence. I won't."

As Tori descended the steps, she was overcome by a wave of nausea. She leaned against the wall halfway down the stairs as sweat ran down her neck. The stairwell seemed to tilt to one side as she gripped the handrail. She didn't want to grip it too tightly, because, like everything else in the old lodge building, it needed repair, too. She sat down on a step until the nausea passed.

She'd felt like this for about two weeks. She hadn't told Lawrence, but she wasn't going to Calloway to look at carpet—she was going to see Dr. Jackson. She hadn't told Levi either. Each time she was hit by the dizziness and nausea, she thought of her mother who'd died when she was three years younger than Tori was now—and her grandmother who'd died at about the same age.

Tears came unbidden when she thought of Levi and all the years they'd wasted when they could've been together.

Chapter Four

"COME ON, COME ON," ED GARVEY SAID AS HIS TOW TRUCK LURCHED up the road in jerks and starts. He should've fixed it a week ago when it started acting up, but he and Levi had been too busy working on Pappy.

The truck sputtered and shuddered until Ed finally had to stop. If it died, he'd never get it started again. He'd have to call Dickerson Towing to haul his tow truck another two hundred yards to the Garvey house, and Scott Dickerson would never let him forget it.

That jackass, Ed thought.

Unable to stand the thought of that kind of humiliation, he popped into neutral gear, revved the engine a few times, and continued up the road. Slowly, he turned into the driveway of the Garvey house and headed towards the carriage house. He was just about there when the tow truck finally died, and the check-engine light came on.

"No shit?" Ed said, banging on the steering wheel as he looked at the glowing light.

The carriage house doors were open. Old Blue was gone as well as Tori's white Chevy Impala. "Chevy girl." That's what Levi sometimes called Tori, but it wouldn't be long before Pappy would be running, and they'd purge the Garvey house of the wretched Chevys once and for all.

Ed reached under the dash, released the hood latch, and climbed out. After pushing up the hood, he pulled off the air filter and peered down into the carburetor with his blue eyes. It was a mess. He ran his fingers through his white hair and shook his head.

"Oh boy, that's going to take some time," he muttered.

Ed was in good shape for a man of seventy-two. After losing about thirty pounds in the last two years, he was back down to what he jokingly referred to as his "fighting weight." He'd curbed his drinking—learning late in life that even he had limitations. There were parts about getting old he didn't mind so much, but there were other things, like the aches and pains, that bothered him to no end. Those he'd noticed much more since he'd limited his drinking—alcohol was a pretty good pain killer.

While Ed was in the garage getting a few tools, he heard a car pull up. He figured it was Tori since Levi spent almost every morning at the Twin Rivers library—after pie at Harv's, of course.

Ed searched for the little screwdrivers he needed and then walked out of the carriage house. A man was leaning under his hood, peering into the carburetor. A rental car was pulled up next to the tow truck.

Another damn Chevy, Ed thought.

"Carburetor is shot, huh?" the man remarked in a low, slow drawl. He was obviously not from around the area.

"Yeah," Ed said. "I've got a new one over at my shop. I've just been putting off installing it. Now it's stranded me."

"I can give you a ride over to your shop if it's nearby. I'm early for my appointment," the man said slowly as he stood upright next to the truck. "I've got nothin' better to do right now."

He was a big man and in good shape. He was well over six feet tall, with a shaved head and a mustache, the likes of which Ed hadn't seen since he was a kid—a handle bar mustache, curled up and waxed at the ends. It looked like something from a photograph of an old Civil War general. Ed figured him to be in his late forties or early fifties.

"I'd appreciate that," Ed said. "It's five minutes away."

Ed didn't know the man, but there was something about him that seemed familiar.

"Do I know you from somewhere?" Ed asked, looking at him closely.

"You just might. Is this Levi Garvey's house?"

The remark put Ed on the defensive. Levi was a best-selling author, and there had been a few times when overly admiring fans and members of the press had intruded on his privacy.

After the episode with Doug Malone, the press had hounded Levi for months. Levi had hired a security company to erect a massive wrought iron fence along the front and sides of the property and to install a huge electric metal gate at the end of the driveway. For the most part, it'd been a waste of money since, as the months passed, fewer and fewer people had come looking for the famous writer. Besides, that, the gate didn't work out so well. Levi and Tori were impatient people. They got tired of waiting for the gate to open up so they could drive in. As a result, the gate had been open most of the past year.

But with Levi's new book recently released and talk of another movie deal . . . well, they'd be showing up again. Suddenly, Ed felt stupid for falling for the act. This was just the kind of tactic some of them had used to get close to Levi Garvey.

"Who are you?" Ed said bluntly.

The man smiled broadly. "Not a fan or a reporter, I promise you that. I know Levi, and I know who you are too, Ed. It's funny, but I recognized this house as soon as I saw it because of Levi's descriptions of it in his last novel. Now that's the sign of a good writer," he said.

"That he is," Ed said, looking him over carefully, "but he didn't get that talent from me."

"Does Levi still sit on the porch every morning, wearing that stupid Panama hat and sipping coffee?"

Suddenly, Ed knew who the man was. There couldn't be two bald-headed giants with handlebar mustaches in the world.

Ed held out his hand. "I know who you are—"

"Good to meet you, Ed. I'm Ray Billings," he said, shaking his hand.

"Levi's cop friend from Savannah. What are you doing here?"

"Well," Ray said, looking down at his boots, "Levi and Tori have been bugging me for two years to come visit. I retired about six months ago, but I don't like it very much, so I decided to visit."

"Levi never mentioned you were coming," Ed said.

"Levi doesn't know. Tori arranged it," he said with a chuckle.

"That's just like her. We're going to have to figure out a clever way to surprise Levi," Ed said.

"Oh, he's going to be surprised all right," Ray remarked. "I'm not here just for a visit. I'm here for a job. Tori told me that Twin Rivers is still looking for a chief of police. I've got an interview with Chief Craig in a couple of hours, and I've got a good feeling about it already."

"Well, if you win over Clifford Craig, you've most likely got the job. The hiring committee didn't listen to him last time, and we wound up with Doug Malone. They'll go with anything he says this time around."

Ray nodded. "I figured it was a good sign when he asked my hat size and measurements."

Ed laughed. "Craig is so anxious to get out of that job, he's probably got your uniforms ready. But why would you leave Savannah? Levi sure loved it there, and you've lived there your whole life, haven't you?"

"I guess I'm not ready for retirement yet. There's only so much fishing I care to do, and I've done all I want in the last few months. I thought it was time for a change. To be honest with you, other than my job, all I have in Savannah is ex-wives."

Ed laughed again. "How many?"

Ray shrugged.

"You lost count?" Ed said.

"Four," Ray admitted.

Ed whistled low.

"Levi and I were good friends. I'm the kind of guy that makes very few friends, but the ones I do make—"

"You marry?" Ed said with a snort.

Ray glared at him before a broad smile crossed his face.

"I know what you mean," Ed remarked. "I'm the same way though most of my friends are gone now. Levi is the same way, too. Besides you, he's got only two close friends here, other than Tori, and he met both of them in kindergarten." Ed paused, then added, " I think you'll make a hell of a police chief, Ray."

"I sure hope so since I know how you Garveys deal with bad cops," Ray said.

It was Ed's turn to glare at Ray. Then ignoring the remark, he said,

"Let's go grab that carburetor. Then you can get ready for your interview here. Levi's usually gone all morning."

"Sounds like a plan," Ray said as Ed followed him to his car.

"You mind if we take the long way to the shop instead of driving through town?" Ed said. "I don't want to be seen in a Chevy."

"Didn't Levi tell me once you had a Cadillac?" Ray said as they climbed into the car.

"It was Mom's," Ed said. "That's different."

Ray smiled as he started the car. He knew he'd just made a fast friend.

Chapter Five

WARDEN STEPHENS WAS SITTING AT HIS OAK DESK, LOOKING OVER A massive file, when his intercom buzzed. It was technology from three decades ago—out-of-date like everything else at the prison.

"Prisoner 8-9-1-2—" she began.

"Don't give me a number," he hissed as he pushed up his wire-rimmed glasses. "Give me a name!"

Warden Stephens was a man who believed in rehabilitation. Nothing annoyed him more than referring to prisoners as numbers. They were human beings. There was a long pause as he heard her turning pages.

"Andrew Miller is waiting to see you, sir," she said.

At thirty-two, Stephens was young for a warden. He'd never had a real job before graduating from college. His father, a wealthy businessman and an important political financier in the Chicago political machine, had helped to elect several governors. One of those governors had gotten Stephens his overpaid job. Later, that governor had wound up as an inmate in Stephens' prison for a time, and it wouldn't be long before another of the governors his father had helped elect might find a home in his prison as well.

"Send him in," he replied shortly.

Warden Stephens wasn't liked by his staff. Both arrogant and condescending, he was thought to treat the inmates better than he treated those who worked for him. He frequently broke with the standard safety measures when dealing with prisoners and did whatever he wanted to do. He had little regard for his employees' safety when he broke the standard operating procedures. Many of the staff silently hoped that one day one of his precious "rehabilitated inmates" would shive him with a sharpened toothbrush handle.

The prisoner, Andrew Miller, walked in, wearing an orange jump-suit, his wrists and ankles cuffed. The prisoner was escorted on either side by two large prison guards. The warden wasn't concerned about his own safety since Andrew had been a model prisoner at the facility for thirty-eight years without so much as a single bad mark on his record. Such a record was indeed rare.

"Hello, Andrew," Warden Stephens said.

"You can call me Andy."

"Uncuff him," the warden ordered.

The guards glanced at each other. There were rules about that—prisoners were never to be uncuffed in the warden's office—but they reluctantly complied.

Once Miller's hands and legs were free, the warden directed the prisoner to the chair in front of his desk. Then looking at the two prison guards, he said sharply, "You can leave."

That was definitely against policy, but once again, they did as the warden ordered and left the office.

Warden Stephens studied Andy, whose deep-set brown eyes had large dark circles beneath them. Having just looked at the picture taken of Andy when he'd first arrived, the warden could see how much he'd aged. The sixty-one-year-old had been in prison longer than Stephens' lifetime.

"What's going on, sir?" Andy asked directly. He was long past pretense.

Warden Stephens admired directness. "You were involved in a bank robbery thirty-eight years ago with three other men. One, who died from a gunshot wound, was found in the crashed getaway car. One was found unconscious and badly injured at the scene of the crash. You may not know that he has been serving his sentence in this very same prison."

Andy nodded. "Bruce Franklin died at the scene, and Joe Bailey survived. I've seen him here a couple of times over the years. There's little that goes on in a prison that the inmates don't know about. I also know Joe died a few weeks ago. Cancer, I heard. And I've never denied I was one of the four who robbed that bank."

Andrew Miller had been questioned many times over the years. He knew the drill. He'd heard that Warden Stephens was the kind of man who thought that everyone else on earth was a moron compared to him and that, after a brief glance at a prisoner's file, he could solve any crime. Andy had been patiently awaiting his turn with the man his fellow inmates sarcastically referred to as " the amazing detective."

"I'm familiar with every detail of your record," Warden Stephens said, patting the thick file sitting on his desk. "It seems you got in with a bad crowd when you were young."

"And I pay the price for that every day."

"You've been a model prisoner since you came here," the warden said, glancing down at the file. "You're a trustee. I've never seen such a perfect record in this prison."

"I knew from the beginning I'd never see the light of day again, so why fight the reality. I accepted that fact. I realized I could do things the hard way or the easy way. I chose to keep my nose clean. It's made life in here a little better. I appreciate the praise, Warden, but what's this about?"

The warden laughed at that directness again. "You don't pull any punches, do you, Andy?"

"I've been here a long time, and I've learned it's best to be honest and direct."

"You're right," Warden Stephens said with a nod. "Let's get right to it then. You know why you've been in here so long?"

"A cop was killed during the robbery," Andy said. "And there were a few parts of my story the cops never bought. They think I'm lying, but I'm not. I've told this story many times before."

"I know you have, but there are a couple of points I want to talk about one more time," Warden Stephens said, patting the file. "You didn't kill the police officer, we know that. But it's a little hard for me to believe you didn't know the fourth bank robber—the gunman."

Andy sighed. "I never knew who the gunman was. I've told this story over and over again. I met him the day of the robbery when they came by my mother's house to pick me up to do the job. I saw his face. I described him the best I could, but I never heard his name, didn't recognize his face, and don't know where he was from. And that's the truth."

Warden Stephens looked across the desk at Andy for a long moment, then adjusted his glasses and glanced back down at the file.

"Your gang was after a safety deposit box. According to your story, you never knew what was in it."

Andy smiled tightly. "You're trying to trick me, Warden. I know exactly what was in that safety deposit box. I went through it after the crash. I just never knew what was supposed to be in it. There was nothing in that box but papers. It was obvious that whatever was supposed to be there wasn't."

"Or maybe it was about the papers in there?" Stephens said.

Andy shrugged. "I thought about that later on. I've had a lot of time to think. It may well have been about what was in those papers, but I never took anything out of there, and the cops have had the contents of that box for decades. If that's what it was about, they've sure never figured it out."

"But you saw a name on those papers, didn't you?" the warden remarked.

"Alex Patton. All those papers belonged to Alex Patton." He leaned back, crossing his arms in front of him. "I knew it was his safety deposit box."

"And you knew who Alex Patton was?" the warden asked.

"I did. He owned a jewelry store in Calloway."

"So you went to see him after the robbery."

Andy sighed. "He was pretty well off. I knew I was going to get caught, mainly because I'd forgotten to wear my gloves. I got wondering about what was supposed to be in that box, and I figured whatever it was we were trying to get must've been worth a fortune to risk an armed bank robbery."

"That makes perfect sense, Andy, but it went badly when you went to see him. He wouldn't tell you what was supposed to be in that box, would he? You got angry and nearly beat him to death, trying to get him to tell you."

As tears welled up in his eyes, Andy looked at the warden. It seemed like a lifetime ago.

Andy nodded. "I was a heroin addict at the time. That's how I wound up in so much trouble with Bruce Franklin. He was my connection, and I'd ripped him off. That's how I ended up in the bank that day. I did a lot of stupid things back then, a lot of things I can't believe now I was ever capable of."

"Tell me how you got involved in that robbery in the first place, Andy," the warden said, leaning back in his chair and tossing his glasses on his desk.

"As I said, Bruce was my drug dealer. I got behind, I needed my fix, and I wound up making certain deliveries for him. Then I stole one of the packages I was supposed to deliver to an address in Champaign. I holed up in a motel in Kankakee. Sold some of the heroin. Used the rest. Spent two weeks as high as a kite before Bruce caught up with me. The only way I was going to get free and clear was to do the robbery. Even back then, those guys didn't play around. If I hadn't done that robbery, they would've found me with a bullet in my head most likely. As bad as I thought Bruce Franklin was, he was nothing like the guy that went on the robbery with us, the fourth guy—he was terrifying. Even Bruce Franklin seemed to be afraid of him."

"He was the leader?" the Warden asked.

"Without a doubt," Andy said. "He set up the whole operation. He knew exactly what he was doing."

"Who do you think he was?" Warden Stephens asked.

Andy shrugged.

"You think he was a mob guy or something?"

"I don't know. There were a lot of drugs running through Twin

Rivers and Calloway back then. They didn't get there by themselves. Somebody was trafficking them. And it wasn't just heroin. There was cocaine, pot, pills, LSD—you name it. It wouldn't surprise me if that guy wasn't higher up on the food chain than Bruce Franklin."

"You've been honest about all that from day one. But there's still part of the story that's problematic," the warden said.

Andy nodded. He knew what the warden was talking about. "I know—how I got caught. They never believed that part of my story."

"Andy," Warden Stephens said, leaning forward with his elbows on his desk, "that part of your story doesn't make sense, and in my experience, if something doesn't make sense, it's most likely not true."

"I told the truth," Andy said. "Don't you think if I knew more, I would've traded that information a long time ago for better accommodations? Maybe a nice minimum security prison somewhere?"

"Maybe," he replied. "What I do know is that a few hours after you beat the hell out of the jeweler, Alex Patton, you were arrested in a local bar in Twin Rivers for getting into a fist fight. The coincidence is what I have a problem with. The guy you were fighting with was one of the first suspects the police had as the fourth gunman."

"Ed Garvey was not the gunman in the robbery," Andy said. "I've said that over and over again. He had nothing to do with the robbery."

"You went directly from beating up Alex Patton to the Beer Chaser, where you were arrested after fighting with Ed Garvey."

"It was unrelated," Andy said.

"It seemed to the investigators that Alex Patton may have told you something after you beat him up. You left there and made a beeline to Ed Garvey."

Andy shook his head. "I've explained all this over and over. When I left Alex Patton's house, I heard my name on the car radio. The police had identified me. My guess is somebody at the bank figured out who I was. There were two people in the bank that morning who knew me— Linda Darby, the head cashier, and Lucille Garvey. The day before I'd been at the Garvey house, mowing her yard and burning branches. I'm not mad at them for identifying me. In fact, looking back, they probably saved my life. But when I heard my name on the radio as 'armed and dangerous,' I knew I had to get away. Since Ed Garvey owed me money, I went to get it, but he refused to give it to me."

"But Ed Garvey didn't seem to know anything about that money when he was questioned, and he either didn't know what the fight was about, or, like you, he refused to say what it was about," Stephens fired back.

"Think what you like," Andy said angrily.

He was tired of the interrogation. He just wanted to go back to his cell.

"I think there's more that you aren't telling me," he said.

"Warden, I'm telling you the honest truth," Andy said. "I still don't know why we robbed that bank. I still don't know what was supposed to be in that safety deposit box. Alex wouldn't tell me. I went to see Ed Garvey to get the money he owed me so I could get out of town. That's the truth."

Warden Stephens was silent for a bit as Andy stared at him. Then he said quietly, "Would you like to know what it was about, Andy?"

Andy looked at him blankly. "After thirty-eight years? It doesn't matter anymore."

"It was diamonds, Andy. They were delivered to Alex Patton the day before the robbery. If you'd looked in his freezer the night you beat him up, you'd have found twenty grand in diamonds hidden in a bag of ice. Alex usually stored items like that in his safety deposit box, but he got into a fender-bender on his way to the bank. The bank was closed by the time he got there, so he hid the diamonds in his house. That's why they weren't in his safety deposit box when you robbed the bank the next day."

Andy sat, stunned. Because of the tortured look on Andy's face, the warden almost wished he hadn't told him.

"Diamonds?" Andy said. "Twenty grand in diamonds?"

The warden nodded his head. "Alex Patton pulled them out of the freezer and showed them to the police hours after the robbery. Those diamonds were obviously the objective of the robbery."

Andy was shaken.

"You thought it was more than that?" Stephens said.

"I don't know what I thought," Andy said. "I've just learned I've spent thirty-eight years in prison for a measly twenty grand. Why didn't Alex Patton just tell me? Surely they weren't still in his house. I went to see him a couple of days after the robbery. He could've told me about the diamonds and that they were locked up in the bank vault. I just don't understand that. He was a wealthy man. I could've killed him."

"Alex Patton wasn't as well off as you think, Andy," the warden said. "He'd gone through a divorce and was having some serious financial problems. And there's a good chance those diamonds were still in his house. Remember that he'd gotten into a fender bender a few days before, so he didn't have a car that week."

Andy sighed. "You can't change the past. I wish you hadn't told me. Now I have to spend the rest of my life knowing I threw it all away over twenty grand."

"Well, sometimes we get second chance," the warden remarked. "Your brother Steve is here."

"Stevie?" Andy said as his head snapped up. "Why?"

"Because you've served your time, Andy," the warden said. "You're no longer considered a danger to the community if you ever were. It seems like you were more of a danger to yourself back then."

"I'm being paroled?" Andy asked. He couldn't believe it.

"No, Andy, you're not being paroled. You're being released," the warden said. "The Illinois Department of Corrections is done with you. It's time for you to go home. Make a life for yourself. It's not too late."

Andy stumbled to his feet as the warden rose and reached over the desk. As tears welled in his eyes again, Andy took the warden's hand.

"I don't know what to say."

"You don't have to say anything," the warden replied. "You've earned it. We'll have you processed out within the hour, and you'll be on your way home."

"My God," Andy said as the reality of freedom sank in.

"And besides," the warden said, looking at him earnestly, "we need the room. Illinois just elected a new governor in November, so it won't be long before we'll need your cell."

Andy looked at him blankly as a small smile crossed the warden's face.

Then Andy smiled when he realized the warden was joking with him.

"I doubt former governors serve their time in a place like this," Andy said, wiping a tear from the corner of his eye. Then when he saw the hard look on the warden's face, he quickly added, "Not that this facility isn't lovely. It's like living in heaven."

The warden chuckled as he rose from behind his desk and headed for the door. "Come on, Andy. Unless you want to stay here in heaven, your brother is waiting to take you home."

Chapter Six

"YOU HAD A PERFECT RECORD UP UNTIL THREE YEARS AGO," CHIEF Craig shouted across the table in the tiny interrogation room in the Twin Rivers Police Department as the other three on the committee consulted the paperwork in front of them.

Something crashed onto the floor just over his head, and Ray Billings jumped. It sounded like there was a bowling alley upstairs.

"We got a new captain three years ago," Ray shouted back as the lamp over the interrogation room table swung back and forth. His interviewers didn't seem to notice it. "The new captain was young, and one of those touchy-feely sorts—a college boy with a head full of new ideas about how a law enforcement officer should conduct himself."

Craig smiled. "And you didn't fit into that mold very well, did you?"

"Not really," Ray said as the sound of splintering wood filled the air. "I was pretty much set in my ways after thirty years on the force. I stuck with what I knew worked—kind of old school. Captain Harper wanted me gone. He even called me a dinosaur once. He wrote me up a couple of times those last two years—it was complete bullshit. He knew I had my time in, so he was kind of pushing me towards the door. The first time he wrote me up was after I broke up a fight outside a bar at two in the morning. One guy was happy to see us show up and quickly surrendered. The other guy was the problem—he had a knife."

"You were written up for excessive force," the woman on the committee shouted.

"Yeah," Ray admitted as his jaw tightened. "Captain Harper felt I should've used my pepper spray or my tazzer. He was big on these non-lethal weapons. They do work in some situations, but that wasn't one of them."

"What did you do?" the woman said loudly over the hammering overhead.

"I don't have a lot of faith in pepper spray or tazzers, especially when there are a lot of innocent bystanders around. You never know how a guy that's been pepper sprayed is going to react, especially if he's waving a knife around. And tazzers are nice, but the way that nutjob was thrashing around, I knew there was a good chance I wouldn't have nailed him with the leads where I needed to. Either way, using those gadgets could've gotten somebody hurt on a crowded sidewalk in downtown Savannah on a Saturday night."

"So what did you do?" the woman repeated.

"I did what always works," Ray said. "I stepped in quickly, grabbed the hand he was holding the knife in, and punched his ass out. Then I cuffed him and dragged him to the car."

Chief Craig laughed out loud. "That's a non-lethal weapon that always works."

Ray felt a wave of relief wash over him. He'd promised himself to tell the honest truth, and he'd thought that question was going to end the interview.

"Like I said," Ray remarked. "I'm kind of old school. I tend to stick with what I know works."

There was some shouting upstairs, followed by a crash as something fell over.

Craig looked around the table. "Anybody have any more questions?"

"What?" the woman shouted back.

"More questions, Eve?" Craig shouted at her. "For Ray?"

She shook her head.

"Give us a minute, Ray," Chief Craig said.

Ray didn't hear him and shrugged.

"Leave!" Craig said, pointing at the door.

Ray left, pulling the interrogation room door closed behind him. He waited in the office outside the conference room—what might've been called the squad room in a larger police department. There were a couple of desks for the deputies to do their paperwork. A receptionist was typing on her computer. She probably served as a dispatcher as well. The largest room was in the back where there were two holding cells. In the corner of the squad room was an office that said Chief on the door. Ray was hoping that would be his office soon.

It wasn't five minutes before Chief Craig opened the door and waved him back in. There was a stack of neatly folded uniforms, a flat brimmed hat, a Glock in a holster, and a gleaming gold badge sitting on the table. All four of his interviewers were smiling broadly.

"Congratulations, Chief Billings," Craig shouted as he extended his hand. "I'll hang around for two or three weeks to get you settled in and to familiarize you with the town, but that shouldn't be too difficult, Ray, since nothing ever happens in Twin Rivers."

"Thank you," Ray shouted, reaching over the small table to shake hands with the search committee members. "When do you want me to start?"

Chief Craig stood up, reached in his pocket, and tossed him a set of keys. "You started five minutes ago, Ray, when we made our decision. Those are the keys to your cruiser, the Police Department doors, and your office."

"You have any questions for us, Chief Billings?" Eve asked.

"Yeah, just one thing."

"What's that?" the woman shouted back.

"What the hell is going on upstairs?" he asked, pointing towards the ceiling and the swinging light over the interrogation room table.

"Tori Buchanan!" Craig shouted back as the other three nodded. It was as if that name alone provided a complete explanation for the noise.

Ray Billings chuckled. They'd never met face to face, but he knew a lot about Tori Buchanan although her name now was Tori Garvey. And from what he knew, her name did provide a complete explanation.

Chapter Seven

STEVIE MILLER WAITED WITH SOME TREPIDATION FOR HIS OLDER brother, Andy, in the waiting area at the penitentiary. He hadn't seen Andy for over thirty years. Stevie had visited him in the prison only once. At that time, Andy had made it clear that he didn't want to see Stevie again. Andy wasn't mean about it, but since he'd never get out of prison, it would be too hard to be reminded of the life he'd once had. He hadn't accepted any letters from home, and he'd never sent one.

Andy was ten years older than Stevie, and when Stevie was a kid, he'd thought his brother walked on water. Andy had taken him to movies at The Comet, let him hang around with him and his friends, and even given him money for candy and sodas. But when Andy got into drugs, he changed. During the two years before Andy went to prison, Stevie had been terrified of his brother. Andy had become short-tempered, unpredictable, and viciously violent.

Stevie's heart leaped into his throat when he heard the electronic buzz of the heavy steel door at the end of the waiting area and the loud metallic clunk as the lock on the door released. He stood up slowly. Andy, carrying a large duffel bag, walked out with Warden Stephens. Andy was still thin and lanky, but his hair had turned completely white, and his face was deeply lined. The brothers looked at each other for a long moment.

"Hello, Stevie," Andy said. A wide smile crossed his face and tears clouded his eyes. "I never thought I'd see you again."

Andy walked over and hugged his little brother. As Warden Stephens watched the reunion, he had a few tears in his eyes as well.

"Is there anything else we need to do?" Stevie finally asked the warden.

"No, he's been processed out. You're free to go."

Andy and Steve walked to the doors where they waited until the deputy in the booth behind bullet-proof glass buzzed them out. Moments later, they climbed into Stevie's car and drove towards the outer gate. Stevie was nervous as the guard carefully looked over the paperwork he handed him. The guard finally motioned to another guard in the gatehouse, and the massive gate, topped with razor wire, slowly rolled open.

"Never thought I'd pass through these gates in anything other than a hearse," Andy said as tears ran down his face.

They were quiet for some time as Stevie drove to the interstate. Andy was just looking out the window, smiling as he watched the scenery roll by.

"Mom still alive?" Andy finally asked.

"Yeah, but she's not very well, Andy. She's got Alzheimer's. She has good days and bad days. More bad days lately. Sometimes she knows me, and sometimes she doesn't. I told her you were coming home. She smiled, but I don't know if she understood. She hasn't said anything for a couple of weeks now. The doctor said sometimes Alzheimer's patients forget what words mean, and they stop talking."

Andy nodded.

"So what do you want to do when we get back home?" Stevie asked. "I took a few days off work. I thought, if you wanted to, we could go fishing over at the river junction like we used to when we were kids."

Andy nodded. "I'd like to go visit a few old friends first."

With a worried look on his face, Stevie asked, "Like who?"

Andy chuckled.

The sound of that chuckle set the hairs up on Stevie's neck. It was an unpleasant sound which reminded Stevie of his brother the last couple of years before he went to prison.

"Please tell me Ed Garvey is still alive," Andy said, looking at Stevie.

Stevie's head snapped towards him. "Andy—" he started to say.

"Is he still alive?" Andy said sharply as he looked back out the window.

"Yes."

"I've got a little unfinished business with Ed Garvey, but don't worry about it, Stevie. I'll take care of it, and then we'll go fishing, just like you said."

Stevie's heart was hammering in his chest. "I think that's a bad idea, Andy. You need to leave it alone."

"It's a small town, Stevie. I'm going to run into him eventually. It's best we get it sorted out right up front. He has something that belongs to me."

"Ed's not a man you want to screw around with," Stevie said. "Maybe you didn't know it, but a couple of years ago—"

His face full of rage, Andy slammed his fist on the dash. "That's where you're wrong, Stevie," he shouted. "I'm not a man you want to screw with! I never thought I'd get out of there or get a chance to meet up with Garvey again. Well, things have changed, and we're going to have us a little chat."

Stevie's knuckles were white from clutching the steering wheel. Andy wasn't any different now from when he'd been arrested.

"Is that a liquor store?" Andy said, pointing to a small shop on the corner.

"Andy," Stevie said.

"Pull in," Andy snapped.

When Stevie pulled to a stop in front, Andy held out his hand. "I need some money."

Stevie pulled out his wallet and handed his brother some cash. Andy stepped out of the car and disappeared inside the store.

As Stevie waited, he considered calling Warden Stephens, but what would he say? He also thought about calling Chief Craig to warn him. In the end, the fear of his brother left him paralyzed, just like when he was a boy. It was surprising just how fast that fear had come back after so many years. After a bit more thought, Stevie figured it was better to let Andy do what he was going to do. In all likelihood, it wouldn't be long before Andy would be heading back to prison. Stevie's only hope was that nobody would get hurt before that happened.

Chapter Eight

WHEN LEVI PULLED INTO THE DRIVEWAY AT THE GARVEY HOUSE, HE saw Mrs. B's Lincoln Continental parked in front.

"Look who's here, Rosco," Levi said with a smile as he pulled up next to the Lincoln.

Mrs. B.'s German shepherd, Roxanne, barked at them through the window of the car. Rosco barked back, his tail wagging. Mrs. B. had been the librarian in Twin Rivers since Levi's grade school days. Now, Levi and Mrs. B. worked together on the Young Author program at the library. A couple of years earlier, Mrs. B. had been so impressed with Rosco the Brave that she'd gotten a female German shepherd whom she'd named Roxanne after her favorite movie.

After climbing out of Old Blue, Levi walked over to the Lincoln and rubbed Roxanne's ears as he looked around the house. Ed's tow truck was parked in front of the carriage house with the hood up. Apparently, the carburetor had finally gone out. He'd really expected to find Tori here since she wasn't at the lodge, and Lawrence said she'd taken the day off. Wherever she was, she wasn't answering her phone. Levi didn't see any sign of Mrs. B. either, other than her car and her dog, but she was obviously somewhere.

"Come on, Rosco," he said as he climbed the porch steps and walked into the foyer of the Garvey house, the screen door banging shut behind him.

Mrs. B., who was just closing the pocket doors on the den, startled when the door banged. Something's up, Levi thought. First, they never closed those pocket doors; in fact, he'd kind of forgotten they were there. Second, it was strange that Mrs. B. had just walked into the empty house. He smelled a rat.

"There you are," she said. "I was going to leave you a note."

She was a tiny lady with snow-white hair, pulled back tightly in a bun. She looked up at him with her pale blue eyes, smiling gently, but looks were deceiving. He knew Mrs. B. was a tough old bird, and he wouldn't be fooled by that sweet-old-lady routine again any time soon. She'd coerced Levi into being involved with the Young Author program at the library over a book Levi had failed to return when he was in high school. But as formidable as the old woman was, there were few people in Twin Rivers for whom Levi had more respect.

"Well, you don't have to now. I'm right here. What's going on?" he said, looking at her suspiciously.

"I brought you something," Mrs. B. said, smiling brightly.

Suddenly, Levi became aware of thumping noises coming from inside the den. As he walked towards the pocket doors, Mrs. B. stepped out of the way. He glanced at her, suddenly curious.

Then he smiled. He knew who was in the library—the children from the Young Author program and probably Tori, too. They were just about done with the program for the year, so Mrs. B. had probably arranged a little surprise party for him. He pulled the pocket doors open, expecting to hear a dozen little voices shout, "Surprise!"

Instead, five German shepherd puppies tumbled through the opening between the doors and began to romp in the foyer. His jaw dropped.

"Oh, no," Levi said.

"Oh, yes," Mrs. B. said. "There are three Roscos and two Roxannes, and they are six weeks old. Congratulations, Levi. They are all yours now."

"Are you saying," Levi began, glaring down at Rosco whose ears fell back as he looked up at him.

"Yes, I'm saying that. Rosco is their daddy," Mrs. B. said cheerfully.

"Oh, crap."

"That's what happens, Levi, when you let your dog run around town unleashed."

Levi shook his head as he watched the five puppies play. He could just hear what Tori would have to say about that.

One of the puppies was trying to pull the skirt off the drum table in the corner. Picture frames and knickknacks wobbled as they moved slowly to the edge of the antique table.

"Stop that," Levi said, scooping up the puppy.

When a car door slammed in the driveway, Rosco started barking as did all the puppies, including the one Levi was holding.

Tori walked in, looked at the puppies, and said, as she walked towards the stairs, "Oh, good, you've figured out where Rosco has been going."

When she started up the stairs, Levi said, "Is that it? That's all you've got to say?"

Tori stopped and looked back at him and the puppy that was chewing on the sleeve of his jacket. "Well, if you'd done what I asked you to do over a year ago, you wouldn't have this problem now, would you?"

"I think I'll be going," Mrs. B. said with a chuckle as she walked out the screen door.

"Thank you, Mrs. B.!" Levi shouted sarcastically.

"You're welcome, Levi," she called back sweetly.

"Tori, where the hell have you been? I've been trying to call you."

He set down the puppy he was holding. Then he yelled, "Get off me, you little monster," to another that was biting his pant leg.

"I had a doctor's appointment," she said with a shrug.

"Everything okay?" he asked, suddenly concerned.

"I'm fine. It's a simple case of too much work and too little sleep. And a mild case of dehydration," she said, raising the water bottle in her hand. "I'll be on light duty for a couple of weeks."

There was a crash as two of the puppies managed to pull the skirt off the drum table with all the stuff on top. Tori shook her head and started back up the stairs. Levi was right behind her.

"What are we going to do with these five little terrors?"

"What do you mean 'we'? Levi, this is your problem."

Levi followed her through the bedroom and into the bathroom.

He looked around. The vanity mirror was steamed up. A towel lay on the floor, and the shower stall was wet.

"Did you take a shower?"

Tori looked at him, puzzled. "What do you think? I just got home. You didn't take a shower?"

"No, I just got home, too."

Levi noticed something else on the floor—a very large pair of dark green boxer shorts.

"And whose are those?" he said, pointing.

"Well, they're obviously not mine," Tori said with a snicker. She hadn't seen Levi this rattled in a long time.

Suddenly, there was a loud knock on the door downstairs. Rosco and the five puppies started barking.

"Hello," somebody shouted as the door banged shut. A few seconds later, the same voice shouted, "Help!"

"What the hell?" Levi said as he started back towards the stairs.

From the top, Levi saw Ben Walker standing in the corner of the foyer with his hands over his head. Rosco was standing in front of him, growling, and the five puppies were attacking his shoelaces.

"What do you want, Ben?" Levi called down.

"I told you I'd be by to talk to you about the statue thing," Ben said nervously, looking down at Rosco's sharp teeth.

"I'm not in the mood right now," Levi said.

"Believe me," Ben said as he tried to squeeze more tightly into the corner to escape Rosco, "I'd leave if I could."

"Rosco!" Levi said firmly. "That's enough!"

Rosco ceased growling, walked to the center of the foyer, and sat down, panting and wagging his tail, as the puppies continued to attack Ben's shoelaces. Ben slithered along the wall towards the screen door, his eyes never leaving Rosco.

"I'll come back another time," he said.

Levi couldn't help but grin as Ben struggled with the door, trying to keep the puppies in the house as he tried to get out and nervously watching Rosco the whole time. Tori walked up behind Levi, wrapped her arms around his waist, and kissed the back of his neck as they watched Ben stumble out the door.

"I'm going to put a lock on that door," Levi said.

"There is a lock on that door. We just never use it," Tori said.

"Do I have a key?"

"It's on your keychain."

"Which one is it?" Levi said, digging his keys out of his pocket.

"The pristine one—the one you've never used."

"Until today . . ." Levi said.

Levi looked down into the foyer as two puppies wrestled with a throw pillow from the den. As their sharp little teeth tore the fabric, the stuffing began to fly, and the other three joined the tug of war. Levi sighed and sat down on the top step as Tori sat next to him. They watched the puppies shred the pillow.

"What the hell am I going to do with those puppies?"

"We'll buy a couple of baby gates and corral the puppies in the kitchen where they can do the least damage," Tori said. "They're thoroughbreds. We won't have any trouble finding homes for them."

"And who left the underpants on my bathroom floor?" Levi asked.

"Now, you've got me on that one, but whoever it was used your electric razor, too."

Tori laughed when Levi sighed.

"What's so funny about this?" Levi said, looking at her.

"It sucks being the victim of chaos rather than the source of it, doesn't it?"

He took off his Panama and shook his head, trying not to smile.

"What comes around goes around, Levi," she said, kissing his cheek.

"I think I'll go work on Pappy for a while," he said, climbing to his feet.

"I think that's a good idea." Tori laughed. "You seem a little rattled."

"You think?" Levi said sarcastically.

"I'll lock those little monsters in the pantry until I can get the gates,"

Tori said. "I've got to run back up to the lodge. I've got some carpet samples I want Lawrence to look at."

Levi started down the stairs and then turned back to Tori. He looked at her carefully.

"You sure you're okay? You'd tell me if something was wrong, wouldn't you?"

Tori smiled at him. "I haven't been feeling well recently. I was worried, and you know why, right?"

Levi nodded. He knew her family history well, and he'd had the same worries when he'd noticed she was looking tired.

"But it wasn't what I thought," Tori said. "I'm fine. Better than fine, actually. I got a clean bill of health."

"I'm surprised you even told me you went to the doctor," Levi remarked.

"I had to," Tori said with a grin. "I ran into Christine White at the doctor's office."

"Oh, how fun," Levi said.

"She was the last person I wanted to see."

Christine White was the biggest gossip in River County. They'd all graduated in the same class—the Twin Rivers High School Class of '85.

Levi snickered. "Oh yeah, I'd have found out for sure."

"Go work on my truck," Tori ordered. "It's about ready for paint, isn't it?"

Levi broke eye contact with her.

"Pretty soon," he said.

He walked down the stairs and worked his way through the puppies as the stuffing from the throw pillow swirled around his legs.

Tori laughed after Levi walked through the door. She hoped Levi and Ed were smart enough not to paint that truck purple as she'd suggested two years ago when Ed had shown up with the old heap on the back of his flatbed—the same day he'd given Levi another German shepherd puppy, the current Rosco. Tori had suggested purple only to drive Levi and Ed nuts. Apparently, her plan was working. Levi couldn't even look at her when the subject of Pappy's color came up. She wondered if they were leaning toward black or red. She was guessing Pappy would be red when they finished.

Chapter Nine

THE SUN HAD GONE DOWN HOURS BEFORE, BUT THE LIGHTS WERE burning brightly in the carriage house as they did almost every evening. The carriage house was older than the Garvey house. It was a throwback to the age of horses and carriages. The interior of the massive round brick building was large enough to hold at least ten cars, and years before, it had stabled not only carriages but also the ten horses the Garvey family had used for transportation and for working the fields as well as all the equipment they'd used for both purposes. There was a loft in the back where hay had once been stored and where lumber was now kept, much of it left over from the construction of the Garvey house back in the 20s. The area under the loft, where horses had once been stabled, was now where Ed and Levi worked on old Ford trucks on the flagstone floor. The round roof above towered into a windowed cupola that during the day illuminated the carriage house. For night work, Levi and Ed had installed bright fluorescent fixtures under the loft.

"Quit shoving on it," Levi shouted from under Pappy as he pulled his hand back quickly. He was on his back trying to feed bolts through the frame to attach the bed of the old truck. "You're going to pinch my fingers."

"They've got to match up," Ed argued.

There hadn't been a bed on the truck when Ed had brought it home. It hadn't been easy, but they'd finally found a '49 Ford pick-up bed that was in good shape.

"The holes don't match up," Levi growled. "They aren't even close. I say we set the gap between the cab and the bed, mark it, and drill new holes in the frame."

"There's something wrong," Ed said. "They should match up. I just don't get it."

"Any chance that truck had a flat-bed on it?" a voice said.

Since Levi was under the truck, he couldn't see who'd spoken.

"You know what," Ed said, rubbing his chin as he examined the bed they were trying to attach. "I'll bet you're right. The frame is the right length, but if there was a flat-bed or if it had a box on the back, like a delivery truck—"

"The holes wouldn't match up," the voice replied.

"Who is that?" Levi said from under the truck.

Then when he saw the shoes and ankles of the man—the highly polished black shoes and the khaki pants—he knew who it was.

"Not a good time, Ben," Levi said.

"It's not Ben," Ed said. "It's our new chief of police."

Levi didn't know they'd hired a new chief. He slid out from under the truck and climbed to his feet. When he looked across the bed of Pappy, his heart pounded.

For a split second, he thought he was seeing Doug Malone, who always wore the full police uniform. The man was looking down, and the flat brim of his hat covered his face. He was the same size as Doug, his badge gleamed from his pocket, and he wore a Glock on his hip—probably the same one that had put the slug in Levi's shoulder two years earlier.

Levi's heart pounded harder as the man's head slowly rose. Levi knew it wasn't possible. Doug was dead, but just like in the dreams he'd had during the past two years, he expected to see the face of Doug Malone looking back at him from under the brim of that hat.

Instead, Levi stared blankly at the face of his old friend, Ray Billings, who was grinning broadly from under his handlebar mustache. It took a second for it all to sink in.

"Ray? You're the chief of police? In Twin Rivers?" Levi said, both stunned and relieved at the same time.

Ray nodded.

"Does this town have no standards left?"

Ray laughed.

"How in the world did you wind up—" Levi started to say, and then it all clicked. He shook his head. "Tori. It was Tori, wasn't it?"

"Does everyone in this town say her name as if it's an explanation for something?" Ray asked.

"It was Tori," Chief Craig said as he walked in through the sliding doors. "She recommended him, and I owe her big time." He was wearing a plaid shirt and blue jeans. "I was beginning to think I'd never get back to my quiet retirement."

Levi walked around Pappy and shook hands with Ray in the certain way Masons do when they meet. "I think you left your boxers in my bathroom," he said.

Ray grinned. "I used your razor and your washrag, too."

"I'll buy new washrags tomorrow," Levi said with a chuckle.

"I think this calls for a beer," Ed announced.

"Everything calls for a beer with you," Craig said.

"To the Beer Chaser," Ed shouted with a finger pointing in the air.

It was as if Batman was calling them all to the Bat Cave after seeing the Bat Signal over Gotham City. There were no arguments.

As they started towards Old Blue, Ray yelled, "Shotgun!"

"Crap," Ed said as he climbed into the bed.

"You know it's against the law to ride in the back of a pick-up," Craig said.

"Get in, Craig," Levi said. "You can write me a ticket later."

As he climbed into the bed, Craig said, "I don't write tickets anymore. I'm retired."

Levi fired up Old Blue as Ray pulled the passenger door closed. Levi reached up and knocked twice on the ceiling of the cab. Two raps came back from the bed.

They were ready.

Levi pulled out of the carriage house, stopped beside the porch, and honked. Tori ran out, skipped down the steps, and jumped into the bed. Levi rapped twice more. Two raps came back.

Ready again.

Old Blue headed to the Beer Chaser.

Chapter Ten

Joyce brought Levi and Ray another beer. Chief Craig didn't drink, and Tori was sipping on a bottle of water. Ed was a few feet away, sitting on his barstool on the corner called "Liar's Corner."

"And there I was, standing with six broken bottles at my feet as beer soaked into my socks, watching her little naked butt jiggling up the stairs." Ray wiped tears out of his eyes as he continued laughing.

"I made him drink cans that night," Levi said as Ed laughed behind him. "He was distracted for hours. I'm not sure he'd ever seen a naked woman before."

"Not like that one," Ray admitted. "Wow! I was thinking so hard about her as I walked home I walked right into a damned lamppost. Put a giant goose-egg on my head."

They'd been at the Beer Chaser about an hour, and Tori's side hurt from laughing so hard. She hadn't heard that story about the last of Levi's many girlfriends—all beautiful according to the tabloids, all empty-headed according to Levi. Levi and Ray had been talking as old friends do—so close they seemed to have a routine between them. She patted herself on the back for bringing Ray here. He was perfect for the job, and Levi needed somebody like Ray in Twin Rivers. Ray was the only thing Levi seemed to miss from his old life in Savannah.

They were still laughing when Ben Walker returned from the bathroom and sat down at the table. He waved his empty can at Joyce, and she brought him another. Ben had pulled Levi over on Main Street for having passengers in the bed of his truck. When he saw one of the passengers in the back of the truck was his old boss, Chief Craig, and the passenger in the cab was his new boss, Chief Billings, he figured that since he couldn't beat them, he might as well join them. His shift was over anyway.

"Levi has never told me how you two met," Tori said to Ray.

Ray and Levi looked at each other and became suddenly quiet.

"Now that must be a good story," Craig said with a chuckle.

"He arrested me," Levi finally admitted.

"For what?" Ben asked.

Levi and Ray looked at each other again. They both answered at the same time. Ray said, "Public urination," and Levi said, "Solicitation."

Tori exploded into laughter. "What, Levi? You peed on a hooker?"

"Thanks, Ray," Levi said, sipping on his beer.

"What? I had your back. You're the one that told the truth," Ray said with a laugh.

"I'd met this young woman at the Crystal Beer Room, and we got talking," Levi said.

"To make a long story short," Ray said, "I came up on this car in the parking lot of the Crystal Beer Room, and the windows were all steamed up, so I knocked."

"I think I know where this is going," Tori said.

"I was innocent," Levi said, glancing at Tori. Then he grinned, "Well, at least I was innocent of the legal charges."

"I know all about you," Tori said, looking at him with her deep green eyes.

"He wasn't charged, and neither was she," Ray said. "She had a record of providing certain services—"

"I can imagine," Tori said as she continued to look at Levi sharply.

Suddenly, Levi seemed to be interested in the college basketball game on the television mounted high up over the bar.

"But she didn't have any money on her, so I figured Levi was telling the truth."

"Unless he used a credit card," Tori said, still looking at Levi.

"It's not like she had a credit card machine in her purse," Levi said. "Where would I have swiped my card?"

Ed laughed from Liar's Corner. "I'll bet I know where he swiped it!"

"Let's not go there, Ed," Tori said as she glared at him.

"I ran into Levi a couple of days later," Ray said.

"And we got talking," Levi said.

"Then fishing," Ray said.

"There was some beer drinking involved, too," Levi added.

"And then Levi joined my Masonic Lodge in Savannah, and we spent a lot of time there."

"I know how that works," Tori said. "I'm a Masonic widow. One meeting a month soon became once a week, then sometimes twice a week."

"We do a lot of good work," Levi said, "and raise lots of money so that out-of-work contractors can have gainful employment."

"Well, one of us needs to have a real job," Tori said as the group exploded into laughter.

When the door of the Beer Chaser opened, Levi turned to see who'd come in. He didn't recognize the old man. He glanced at Ed, who'd also turned towards the door. At first, it seemed that Ed hadn't recognized the man either, but suddenly Ed's face went slack as if something had just clicked.

The man quickly crossed to the bar and kicked the stool out from under Ed, who went down hard. The guy was on top of him in a flash, punching him repeatedly.

Ray nearly knocked the low table over when he stood up. He quickly grabbed the guy by the back of his collar and pulled him up, wrenching his arm behind him and slamming him over the edge of the bar. Levi noticed with some anger that Chief Craig had backed away from the scene—clear over by the jukebox, his face turned away from the fight.

Levi and Ben pulled Ed up off the floor. Ed violently pulled himself free of the two—angry that he'd been caught off-guard and even more angry that they thought he needed help. Ben and Levi backed away from Ed as he straightened his jacket, set the stool upright, and sat down at the bar again. He calmly took a sip from his beer bottle and then looked at the man lying half across the bar in front of him with Ray holding him down. Ed's eyes were blazing, but a playful smile appeared at the corners of his mouth.

"Hello, Andy," Ed said casually. "How you been?"

"I've been in prison for thirty-eight years, you son-of-a-bitch!" he hissed.

He winced as Ray wrenched his arm up higher on his back. His eyes were red-rimmed, and he reeked of bourbon.

"You might be on your way back there, my friend," Ray said, pushing him tighter against the side of the bar.

Ed wiped blood from the corner of his mouth. "You know, Andy, if I'd recognized you one second sooner, you'd be on your way to the hospital right now."

Andy laughed. "You'll get another chance, Ed. I'm not done with you yet."

"Well, you are tonight," Ray said. "You'll be cooling off in jail. Then I'll figure out what to charge you with."

"Let him go," Ed said. "It was just a little misunderstanding."

Ray looked at Ed questioningly, but Ed stared back resolutely. The intensity of Ed's expression was chilling, so Ray released the man.

Andy rubbed his arm and shoulder as he glared at Ed. For a minute, Levi thought Andy was going to charge Ed again, but Andy knew another attack would be a mistake because Ed was ready for him now. Levi had never seen that look on his uncle's face before, but he instinctively knew at that moment that all the rumors he'd heard about his uncle over the years were true.

"We'll talk later," Ed said to Andy, looking at him icily.

"You're damned right we will," Andy said.

He glanced at the group surrounding him, paying particular attention to the two cops in uniform. Then his eyes lingered on Craig, who was still cowering over by the jukebox, looking as if he'd like to disappear.

"I sure picked the wrong night to come in here," Andy said as he walked to the door. "I'll be seeing you, Ed."

Andy paused in front of the door then looked back at the group as if he'd just remembered something. He looked at Levi for a long moment, a small smile on his face. Andy seemed familiar to Levi, but he couldn't quite place him. I should know who he is, Levi thought.

Then Andy opened the door and walked out of the Beer Chaser.

After he left, Ray said to Ben, "Make sure he's not driving."

Ben walked to the window and watched as Andy crossed the parking lot and headed towards town.

"He's on foot."

Ray nodded. "Anything you want to tell me about this, Ed?"

"I can't think of anything," Ed said, picking up his beer bottle and taking a sip.

Ray knew he could ask more questions, but he figured it would be pointless because Ed wouldn't answer them.

"I've had enough fun for one evening," Tori said. "I think it's time to go."

Everyone seemed to agree.

"I think I'll stay a while longer," Ed commented.

"You don't have a ride," Levi said. "Your truck is still dead in my driveway."

"I'll walk home later."

Levi started to say something, but Ed shot him an angry glance. "I've done it many times before, Levi," he growled.

Levi looked as if he'd been slapped. Ed had never used that tone with him. "He could come back," Ray remarked.

"He's not coming back tonight," Ed said. "But if he does, I've got a little something for him. You all go on."

Chapter Eleven

"... AND THEY FOUND THE GETAWAY CAR CRASHED INTO THE SIDE OF the Calloway River Bridge," Chief Craig said, sipping coffee. They'd gone back to the Garvey porch after leaving the Beer Chaser.

"Bruce Franklin was dead at the scene. Joe Bailey was badly hurt. After a month in the hospital and then a trial, he went to prison, of course. They found the safety deposit box—nothing of value in it. The other two bank robbers survived the crash and escaped into the woods. They knew the shooter had a gunshot wound in his leg from the deputy, but they never learned his identity. It wasn't long before the witnesses at the bank figured out that the younger suspect was Andy Miller. They picked him up a couple of days later at the Beer Chaser, doing the same thing he was doing there tonight."

"Beating the hell out of my Uncle Ed," Levi said, sipping his beer.

Craig nodded. "Actually, it was the other way around. He kicked the stool out from under Ed, and Ed hit the floor like he did tonight, but Ed managed to kick Andy's legs out from under him, and Andy left the Beer Chaser in an ambulance."

"So that's why Uncle Ed said what he said tonight."

"I sure never heard this story," Tori said, "and I was the president of that bank for more than ten years."

"It was a long time ago," Craig said. "I wasn't even on the force yet, but it was big news. I read all the police reports later—I've got copies of all the case files in my office. It was a fascinating case. In fact, Levi, I'm surprised you don't remember the story."

Levi laughed. "I'm only forty-three, Chief. I was what, three or four years old at the time?"

"I meant because you were there," Craig said. "You and your

Grandma Lucille were in the bank the day it was robbed."

Levi looked at him blankly.

"It's true," Craig said. "Lucille was the first one who suggested that one of the robbers was Andy Miller. She had the money she'd just withdrawn in her hand. When he didn't take it, she realized it was somebody she knew. Andy Miller used to mow your grandma's yard. It didn't take Lucille long to figure out who he was."

"What does Ed have to do with all of this?" Tori asked.

"Now, that's a damned good question," Craig said. "Nobody knows."

"And they never figured out who the gunman was?" Ben asked.

Craig shook his head. "Andy saw his face, but said he didn't know him. He'd met him only the day of the robbery. Joe Bailey said the same thing. They both agreed that he was the leader of the group though, which matches what the witnesses at the bank said, too. It was a well-planned heist. If Jim Mathis had gone fishing that day as he always did on his day off, they'd have gotten away with it. Of course, they didn't get what they'd come for because it wasn't in the safety deposit box."

"What was that?" Levi asked.

Craig chuckled. "About twenty grand in diamonds, if you believe that," he said. "They normally would've been in Alex Patton's safety deposit box, but he didn't get to the bank before it closed. I can't remember why now, but he pulled those diamonds out of his freezer and showed the cops after the robbery."

"What did you mean by, 'if you believe that'?" Tori asked.

"That was a pretty small take for such an organized robbery," Craig said. "They knew a lot about Alex Patton's habits. They knew not only his safety deposit box number but also his routine. Not to mention they cracked that box like it was a bubblegum machine. There was always a suspicion that the robbery was about a lot more than diamonds and was organized by more than just a group of local thugs."

"You talking about the mafia or something?" Ben asked.

"That was the rumor at the time," Craig said. "The Chicago Outfit is what they called it, and it's still around—it was started back in Al

Capone's day. There were rumors that Alex Patton might have had 'connections' back then to the Chicago Outfit."

"Really?" Levi said.

"He had a rather tarnished reputation," Craig remarked.

"So if it wasn't the diamonds, what was it?" Ray asked. He'd been sitting quietly, taking it all in.

"I don't know, but the robbery was a big risk to take for such a small prize," Craig said. "And the police had a feeling there was something Alex Patton wasn't telling them when they questioned him. They thought there was something else going on besides those diamonds."

"You're leaving something out, Craig," Ray said.

"Ed Garvey," Craig said, glancing at Levi briefly.

"He was a suspect?" Ray asked.

"He was. At first, they thought he was the fourth bank robber."

"Oh bullshit," Levi huffed. Tori put her hand on his arm.

"Then another curious thing made them take an even closer look at Ed. They learned that after the police questioned Alex Patton the day following the robbery, Alex went to see Ed at the Beer Chaser. They either talked at the bar or maybe left together," Craig said. "That was never very clear."

"That doesn't mean anything," Levi snapped.

"They never learned much about that meeting between Ed and Alex. Joyce was the only one in the bar when they met, but one of the customers saw Alex come in as he was leaving. The customer heard Alex start talking to Ed. And Joyce was standing right there on the other side of the bar, but she wouldn't answer any of the questions the police asked her about what went on between them. She was nearly charged with hindering the investigation. In fact, she spent a night in jail over it."

"Those two have been friends a long time," Tori said.

"They pulled Ed in and questioned him for hours," Craig said. "He had an alibi for the robbery, so he couldn't have been the shooter. He'd broken his wrist the weekend before, water-skiing at Olton Lake. The investigators even had that wrist x-rayed at the hospital to make sure it was actually broken—it was. And they also knew the fourth bank robber was wounded in the back of the leg. Ed wasn't wounded."

Ray chuckled.

"What?" Levi said, looking at him.

"I think I know where this is going. They knew he didn't do the crime, but they thought Ed might've planned it."

"That's exactly what the investigators thought," Craig said.

"Ed knew Alex obviously," Ray said. "They probably thought he'd learned something about what Alex was into and planned the heist."

"To rip him off? That's insane," Levi said derisively.

"The facts are clear," Craig said. "Two days after the robbery and a day after Alex Patton and Ed met at the Beer Chaser, Andy Miller went to Alex's house and beat the hell out of him. Then Andy left Alex's house, drove straight to the Beer Chaser, and went after Ed. He was arrested at the Beer Chaser and went to prison. He gets out thirty-eight years later, and what is the first thing he does?"

Levi didn't want to accept that all this made his Uncle Ed look suspicious.

"You've got to admit it, Levi," Ray said. "It's odd that Andy Miller went after him again after so long."

"Maybe he blamed Ed for being in prison," Tori suggested.

Levi seized on that. "He had a long, long time to think about how he got caught."

"That's true," Craig said. "They investigated Ed for a long time but came up empty. The case went cold. Nobody has ever learned the identity of the fourth bank robber or the real motive for the crime."

"Unless it was really about those diamonds," Ray remarked. "You know, people have done a lot more for a lot less. There are a lot of assumptions here. I take it there is no solid evidence that the Chicago Outfit was involved?"

Craig shook his head. "I think a few of the members were brought in and questioned, but there was no motive found there either."

"Do you think Uncle Ed was involved?" Levi asked.

Craig shrugged. "Your uncle was a different man back then. It took him a long time to find himself again after getting back from Vietnam. He hadn't been home long when this happened, and his engagement to April Jenkins had just dissolved."

Levi couldn't believe what he'd just heard in passing. He looked at Tori. She had the same surprised look on her face—she didn't know about Ed and April either.

"Ed drank. He got into fights. He wrecked cars. He was involved in a few questionable business dealings. He had a pretty impressive arrest record back then. Hard to imagine him being involved in anything like that now, but back then, the police had every reason to suspect him."

"You didn't answer my question," Levi pressed. "Do you think Uncle Ed had anything to do with that robbery?"

"I never did," Craig admitted. "I'll tell you what I've always thought, Levi. I think Alex Patton was involved with the Chicago Outfit. I think he took something from them, God only knows what, and they wanted it back. They planned that heist to do just that—to get whatever it was back from him. The investigators always assumed it was about cash or valuables, but I've always wondered if it couldn't have just been information Alex had—maybe information he'd collected during his dealings with the Chicago Outfit."

Levi nodded. "That sounds a little more reasonable."

"Maybe Alex went to Ed for help after the robbery when he realized the mob was coming after him. It's anybody's guess. What I do know is that Alex Patton committed suicide about a month later, but there have always been rumors that his death wasn't a suicide."

"Mob got him?" Ray said.

Craig shrugged. "That's what some say, and it fits, too. Whatever it was they were after, they must have gotten it. It ended with Alex Patton's death."

"That doesn't explain Andy going after Uncle Ed tonight," Levi said.

"Yeah, it does," Craig said. "Andy beat Alex badly. Alex was a skinny little jeweler with thick glasses, and he probably would've said anything to get Andy to stop beating him."

Ray continued with Craig's theory as he looked at Levi, "He threw your Uncle Ed under the bus. Probably told Andy he'd given Ed whatever it was that was supposed to be in the safety deposit box. Ed probably didn't know anything about it. He probably still doesn't know anything about it."

"Ed would've never gotten involved in something like that," Tori said, reaching over and taking Levi's hand. "But Andy spent thirty-eight years believing Ed had the one thing he'd wasted his life trying to get."

"That's right," Ray said. "And over decades of thinking about it, he's convinced himself that Ed still has something that belongs to him. He probably doesn't know Alex Patton was possibly murdered, and the bad guys got what they were after in the end."

They all sat silently for a moment, thinking about the complicated unsolved case.

"It's sad," Craig said. "It's often said the mistakes of youth are soon forgiven, but some aren't. Just ask Andy Miller."

"And the fourth bank robber—the shooter?" Levi asked.

"My theory has always been that he was a pro. He was sent down from the Chicago Outfit to plan and pull off the heist."

Ray nodded. "That's exactly what I think. We'll never know who that guy was."

"What are you going to do about Andy Miller?" Levi said.

"Don't ask me. Ask the chief of police," Craig said with a chuckle, cocking a thumb at Ray.

"I'll talk to Ed," Ray said. "Maybe I ought to arrange for Ed and Andy to sit down and talk—the sooner the better. Andy needs to know the truth. He's been living a lie for nearly forty years. It's time he learned the truth. Maybe once he comes to grips with it, he can get on with his life."

Craig stood up. "That's a good plan, Ray. It's hours past my bedtime, and I'm tired. I'll be by in the morning to take you on a driving tour of Twin Rivers."

Ray glanced at his watch. "It's eleven, Craig."

"You just wait, Ray. Old age will catch up with you one day," he said as he walked down the stairs.

"I'm tired, too," Tori said. "I'm going to bed."

After the squad car left the driveway and Tori disappeared into the house, Levi glanced over at Ray.

"Now that the cops and the wife are gone, you want another beer?" he said. "I got some in the fridge."

"What do you mean the cops are gone. I'm the chief of police, Levi," Ray said with a laugh. "Whatever," Levi said, getting up. "You want one or not?"

"Just one," Ray said.

Levi rolled his eyes. "I've heard that before. Last time I heard it, you walked into a lamppost. Where are you staying, anyway?"

Ray grinned.

"Oh, no," Levi said, pausing at the screen door.

"I'd like to have my breakfast served by six."

"I'll let Tori know," Levi said.

"Oh, don't do that."

"You're not afraid of a girl, are you?"

"That's no ordinary girl, Levi," Ray said with a chuckle.

Chapter Twelve

Even though he was off duty, Ben made a few rounds through town in the cruiser. All was quiet. He'd driven by the Miller house on the edge of town, too. It was quiet there as well. He saw Andy through the picture window in the flickering light of the television, pacing the room with a bottle in his hand. By the way he was weaving, it was clear that Andy was in for the night.

When Ben stopped at the park, he spent a few minutes gazing up at the statue on top of the War Memorial. "If I were going to put a bikini on that statue, how would I do it?" he muttered to himself.

He thought about it for some time before sighing. It seemed impossible without a ladder or some kind of lift. The pedestal was a smooth column thirty feet tall, and the statue stood on top of it. The statue itself was probably five or six feet tall. He knew he needed to look more closely at the evidence Chief Craig had preserved. The answer was there somewhere.

He started the car and drove to the Twin Rivers Police Department. Through the window, he saw Amber dozing at her desk. He opened the door carefully and sneaked in. He stood in front of her desk, looking down at her. She was in her twenties with jet-black hair and piercing dark eyes. They'd been dating secretly for a couple of weeks, but since their relationship was beginning to get serious, they wouldn't likely be able to keep it secret for long.

Suddenly, Ben pounded his fist down on the desktop. "You sleeping?" he shouted.

Amber jumped, throwing the paperback book she'd been reading straight into the air. It hit her in the head when it came down.

"Ben," she said, looking at him with wide eyes, one hand on her chest and one rubbing her head, "you're going to give me a heart attack."

"Stop falling asleep on the job," he said with a laugh. "Anything going on?"

Amber sighed. "Nothing ever goes on in Twin Rivers after ten o'clock."

"Are you off at one?" Ben asked.

Amber nodded.

"That's about half an hour," he said, glancing at the clock on the wall. "Why don't you come by?"

She smiled.

"We got a key to the Masonic Lodge upstairs?" Ben asked.

Amber slid open her desk drawer and pulled out the key box. "I think so," she said. "Why?"

"I noticed a light on up there, and I thought I'd check," he said as she tossed him the key.

He glanced back at her. "Half an hour, right?"

"I'll be there," she said.

Ben walked up the alley and climbed the steps to the second floor of the Twin Rivers Masonic Lodge. The light he'd seen was coming down from the top of the third floor steps. He went up to the kitchen and found it empty. He turned off the light and walked back down the stairs, using his flashlight.

He checked all the smaller rooms to make sure there were no intruders before walking into the enormous lodge room. He'd been there before, but what he saw made him gasp. With the huge vaulted ceiling gone, the room was lit by the pale blue light of millions of stars. The effect of looking up into the Milky Way was dizzying.

He walked to the dais in the East and, with some satisfaction, took a seat in the Master's chair. I'm sittin' in your chair, Garvey, he thought.

He gazed up at the sky in wonder. He'd never seen anything quite so beautiful. He wasn't sure how long he'd been sitting there when the lodge room door creaked open.

"Oh, my God," Amber said, looking up at the sky. As she crossed the lodge towards Ben, her eyes never left the sky. "Have you ever seen anything so beautiful?"

Ben looked at her in the starlight. "Actually, I have."

She climbed the dais, sat on Ben's lap, and kissed him.

"Claire come in early?" he asked, glancing up into the sky again.

She nodded, kissing him again more deeply.

"You lock the door downstairs?" he asked as he ran his finger down the center of her back.

She nodded as she peeled her shirt off.

"Claire know we're up here?"

She shook her head as he kissed her neck and popped the top button on her jeans.

"I'm going to tell you this now, Amber. One of these days I will tell Levi Garvey what we did in his chair," he said as she unbuttoned his uniform shirt.

She giggled when his gun belt fell to the floor.

As they kissed under the stars, a sharp explosion split the night's silence.

"What was that?" Ben said, pausing for a moment.

"Rifle," Amber said breathlessly in his ear. "Coyotes."

He nodded and kissed her neck. Then he stopped again. "But did that sound close to you?"

She stopped sucking his earlobe and sat up in his lap. "Yeah, actually, it did," she said, frowning.

"I should check, right?"

"Do you have to? It was probably further away than we think."

"Yeah, you're right. It was probably nothing," Ben said, burying his face in her hair.

"But," Amber said, placing her hands on his shoulders.

He sighed. "I should check. It's my job."

She nodded as she picked her bra up off the floor.

"Can I have that?" he said as he buttoned his shirt.

"My bra?"

"Yeah," he said.

After he'd straightened his tie, he took the bra and shoved it down into the crack of the Master's chair, leaving a strap hanging out.

Amber laughed.

"I'll go check this out. I'll be at the house in fifteen minutes," he said.

"I'll be wearing nothing but a smile," Amber said.

* * *

"Uncle Ed was pissed when we pulled him up off the floor," Levi said.

"You should've let him get up himself," Ray said. "He was caught off-guard and got sucker punched. He was already angry about that. Then you two idiots nurse-maided him off the floor like he was a senior citizen while the guy that did it watched."

"I'm not the only idiot," Levi said. "You should've let Andy go as soon as Uncle Ed sat back down at the bar."

Ray shook his head. "I thought about that, but I knew Andy would've charged him again. You think Ed could've taken him?"

"Uncle Ed could take you," Levi said with a chuckle as he sipped his beer.

"I'll tell you one thing," Ray said. "That look in Ed's eyes when he was talking to Andy was intense."

Levi nodded. "They were kind of glowing, weren't they? I've never seen that side of him before." Levi was rattled by what he'd seen and heard that night. He'd had four beers at the Garvey house to Ray's one, which was sitting full and warm on the porch rail.

"I'd never seen it before tonight," Levi repeated. "I've heard about Uncle Ed my whole life—the fact he wasn't somebody you wanted to get on the bad side of. I've done a lot of things in my life that should've made him angry but didn't. I've sure never seen that look on his face before tonight. I know about what he did in Vietnam now, but I never knew much about that before a couple of years ago. I've never seen Uncle Ed hurt anyone. But if you'd let Andy go and he'd charged

Uncle Ed again, there's no doubt in my mind Andy would be in the hospital tonight."

"And that side of Ed saved your life a couple years ago."

Levi nodded.

"I didn't see it," Levi said, "because I was drowning in a mine shaft with a bullet in my shoulder. I never expected to survive. But when I heard the rifle crack, I knew he hadn't missed. I just knew it."

"I guarantee that when he pulled the trigger, he had that same spooky calm he had tonight. There's a dark side to Ed," Ray said.

Levi slowly forced a grin and began to whistle the familiar refrain from *The Good, The Bad, and the Ugly*. Ray had seen that Ed Garvey look before—Clint Eastwood couldn't have done it any better. There were a dozen movies where Clint Eastwood had given somebody that same look Ed Garvey had given Andy Miller earlier that night.

It seemed to Ray like a good opportunity to change the subject.

"Is Clint Eastwood gonna direct your movie?"

"It's not my movie—it's just my book. But if he does, he's going to have to shoot part of it here," Levi said, smiling broadly. "There's not another site on earth like Kingery Pond. And thanks to round-the-clock coverage by the news media a couple of years ago, every American knows exactly what Kingery Pond looks like. It'll have to be a location shoot. They'd have a tough time reproducing Kingery Pond in Hollywood."

"Beers with Dirty Harry?" Ray said.

"Right here on the Garvey porch," Levi said.

"I thought they bulldozed Kingery Pond—filled in the old mine shaft after they pulled all Doug Malone's victims out," Ray said.

"That was the plan, but Illinois went bankrupt," Levi said. "They put the project on hold. River County is doing better than some counties, but they couldn't afford the ten million dollar tab to fill it."

"So it's still there," Ray said.

Levi nodded.

"I'd like to see it some time," Ray remarked.

Levi started to say something when a loud crack filled the air.

Ray stood up. "That was a rifle."

"Where's Rosco?" Levi said, quickly looking around.

Hearing his name, Rosco raised his head from where he'd been sleeping at the top of the porch steps.

Levi relaxed. "That happens all the time," he said, taking another drink from his beer bottle. "There are lots of coyotes around, and farmers often take pot shots at them."

"That came from town," Ray said.

"Nah," Levi said.

"What's over that way?" Ray said, walking to the edge of the porch and pointing towards where he thought the shot had come from.

"There aren't any farms over there," Levi said, "just a few cornfields and the Kingery Mining Property."

"It came from that direction," Ray said.

"It was probably an echo," Levi said. "It's hard to tell where shots come from out here. You'll get used to that."

"I think I'll go check it out," Ray said, walking to the top of the steps.

"You just want to drive around in your new ride," Levi said, motioning towards the cop car sitting by the carriage house.

"Well, yeah."

Levi stood up, too. "I think I'll go stare at a blank computer screen for a few hours."

Ray walked to the steps and leaned over to scratch Rosco's head. "I'll catch up with you later."

* * *

STEVIE HAD BEEN TOSSING AND TURNING FOR HOURS. HE'D JUST glanced at his alarm clock—it was nearly one in the morning. He could hear the television on downstairs and his brother's restless pacing. Andy had been furious when he got home. He'd had some kind of fight with Ed Garvey. Stevie knew there was going to be more trouble before all this was over. He'd been torturing himself, trying to figure out what he should do. Andy was dangerous. He might've been fine when he was safely behind bars, calmed by the knowledge he'd never see freedom again. But when Andy was released, he'd quickly reverted to the same animal he'd been before he was locked up.

Stevie heard a shot, which wasn't uncommon since almost everyone in Twin Rivers had at least one rifle or shotgun, and they weren't shy about using them. But that shot had sounded close.

He climbed out of bed and crossed to his bedroom window. The light from the stars was so bright he could see clearly the street in front of the house and the field on the other side. His eyes searched carefully, but he didn't see anything outside.

Wondering if Andy had heard the shot, he walked into the hall and started down the steps. He was half-way down when he stopped suddenly.

"Oh, my God," he said, stumbling backwards up the steps.

Andy Miller was lying sprawled on his back on the living room floor. In the flickering light from the television, Stevie could see his neck all covered in blood and his eyes staring blankly at the ceiling.

Stevie ran back to his room and grabbed his cell phone off the nightstand with shaking hands. He took a deep breath to steady himself and then dialed the three digits.

"This is Stevie Miller," he said, his voice shaking. "My brother Andy has been shot. I think he's dead."

Chapter Thirteen

CHIEF RAY BILLINGS WATCHED AS THE MEDICAL EXAMINER FINISHED with Andy Miller. Chief Craig was examining the bullet hole in the picture window.

"There's not a lot of blood," Ray remarked.

"He was dead before he hit the floor," the medical examiner said, snapping off his gloves and dropping them into his kit. "Once your heart stops beating, you stop bleeding. Single shot through the throat, severing the spinal chord. Judging by the wound and the size of the hole in the wall over there, I'd guess it was most likely a .308. Jeff will recover it, and we'll run the ballistics."

Turning towards the crime scene investigator who was standing near the front door, he said, "I'm finished here, Jeff. It's all yours."

Ray walked over to the wall to look at the hole the round had made. There was some blood spatter and some bits of what he assumed was bone from the spinal column on the wall as well. Ray turned around to examine the bullet hole in the window on the other side of the living room.

"You got one of those little laser lights?" Ray asked the CSI.

Jeff nodded, then dug through his box and handed him one.

"Don't touch the wall," Jeff said sharply.

Ray held the laser light in front of the hole in the wall and pointed the red beam through the hole in the window.

"Can you see where that's pointing, Craig?"

Looking down the red beam and then out the front window, Craig said, "I think I know where to look."

Ray turned off the laser light and handed it back to the Jeff. Then he joined Craig at the window.

"You see that tree out in the middle of the cornfield?" Craig said. Ray nodded.

"That's where we should look."

"You mind if we have a look, Jeff?" Ray asked the CSI.

"If you find anything, don't touch it," he said.

"How many times a day do you say that, Jeff?" Ray said, chuckling.

"Say what?" he said, looking up at him.

"Don't touch that," Ray replied.

Jeff rolled his eyes and pulled a digital camera out of his kit.

"You remind me of my first wife," Ray said.

Craig laughed.

"Where's Ben?" Ray asked.

"I'm here," Ben said, walking down the stairs. "I was getting Stevie's statement."

"He see anything?" Ray asked.

Ben shook his head. "He heard the shot and looked out the window upstairs, but he never saw anything even though it was a clear night. He didn't think much of it at the time. He's heard shots at night before. But when he went downstairs to check on his brother, he saw him dead on the floor. I guess Andy was drunk as a monkey."

"I can't believe he was standing when he was shot," Jeff said from the floor where he was squatting in front of the body, taking pictures from various angles. "He smells strongly of liquor. There was a Jack Daniels bottle in his hand when he died that was mostly full." He pointed to the large stain on the carpet around the bottle. "There's another Jack Daniels bottle empty in the trash can in the kitchen and a few beer bottles over by the recliner in front of the television. This guy was probably loaded. Blood test will tell us for sure."

"He'd been locked up thirty-eight years," Ray said. "He got out and decided to tie one on to celebrate. He cut a big 'ol hog in the ass."

Jeff looked up at Ray questioningly.

"It's a Southern expression," Ray said. "He was on a bender."

Jeff nodded. "I know that one."

"There's a lantern in my trunk," Craig said, tossing his keys to Ben. "We're going to go find out where the shot came from."

The three of them left Jeff to his work and walked out the front door. Craig went to the front of the house and peered up at the bullet hole in the picture window. Ben headed for Craig's cruiser.

"Hey, Ben," Ray said, motioning him back.

"Yeah?"

Ray leaned over and whispered, "Fix your shirt."

Ben looked at him and then looked down at his shirt.

"It's buttoned wrong," Ray said with a chuckle. "Funny, I didn't notice that earlier this evening."

Even in the starlight, Ray could see Ben's face flush. Ben turned and walked towards the car, fumbling with his buttons as he went.

* * *

THEY WERE STANDING A FEW YARDS AWAY FROM THE TREE IN THE field, which was covered in bean stubble from the fall harvest. Even without the lantern, they'd clearly seen the glint of brass on the ground as they approached the tree. The shooter had picked a spot just under the shadow of the tree. Even in the bright starlight, he would be well hidden from view if somebody had happened to look towards the sound of the shot.

"Hand me that lantern," Ray said to Ben.

Ray squatted to look at the shell, trying not to get too close to it. There was a good possibility Jeff would find evidence at the scene.

"The medical examiner was right. It is a .308," Ray said.

He held the lantern out and examined the ground around the shell casing carefully.

"That's something," Craig said, pointing. "There's an indentation on the ground."

"Two indentations," Ray said, pointing at another one.

"And the stubble behind the shell is flattened," Ben said. "The shooter was lying down on the ground, and those two indentations are from a rifle tripod."

Craig patted him on the shoulder. "That's good work, Ben. You're right. See that mark there to the left of the shell?"

Ben looked at it carefully and tried to imagine the shooter lying on the ground. He turned towards the Miller house, then held his arms out as if he were holding an invisible rifle.

"Ah, I know what made that one. That's an elbow mark from his left arm. His right elbow would've left a mark, too." He looked closely at the ground. "Right there!" he said, pointing at another area of flattened stubble.

"This is the spot," Ray said.

He turned to look back at the light shining through the window of the Miller home. The Miller house sat in the middle of a block, on the last street on the north side of Twin Rivers. The houses on that street were very close together. The Miller house looked small from the middle of the field.

"That's a hell of a shot. How far do you think that is?" Ray asked.

Scratching his chin, Craig looked for a moment. "I'd say it's a little more than a quarter of a mile."

Ben nodded. "I'd guess about 500 yards."

The three walked a few feet away from the shell, so they wouldn't compromise any evidence at the scene. Then they gathered in a circle to compare thoughts.

"Why the hell would the shooter pick a spot to shoot from so far away from the target?" Ray asked. "He could've shot him from the street right in front of the house—could've rolled down the window and popped him from his car. Andy wouldn't have seen him pull up since the light from the television reflected on the inside of the window. All Andy could see in that window was himself."

"That's why you had the lights turned off when we got there," Ben said, suddenly understanding Ray's request earlier to recreate the lighting of the living room when Stevie had come down the stairs.

"I can think of a couple of reasons," Craig said. "People are used to hearing gunshots at night around here. But if you fire off a .308 close to town, or even a revolver, somebody is going to notice that. They might look out the window and see you. They might recognize your car. And even if they don't see anything, they'll call that in. The phone at the Twin Rivers Police Department would ring off the hook. Happens all the time—somebody will blast a raccoon or a possum in town with a shotgun, and we're flooded with calls. The shooter knew that. Not one person called that shot in tonight. If anybody heard it, and I'm sure a few did, they just figured another coyote had bit the dust."

"You said you could think of a couple of reasons he'd make a long shot like this," Ray said.

"He knew he could make that shot," Craig said.

Ben pointed towards the tree. "And I think he had an escape plan in mind, too. Another hundred yards beyond that tree is a farm road. I'll bet the shooter used that road to get here and then walked back to it, using this big oak tree to cover his retreat. We didn't see any footprints coming out here from the house. He walked in from the back."

"He knew what he was doing," Ray said, "and he was a damned good shot, too."

Ben and Craig glanced at each other knowingly, and Ray caught it.

"What?" Ray said.

Craig sighed and shook his head. "If I was looking at this scene, not knowing what I know about events that took place earlier this evening, I can think of only one person who could've made that shot."

"Who?" Ray asked even though he had a sinking feeling that he already knew the answer.

"Me," a voice said from behind them.

All three turned together. Ed Garvey was standing a few feet away with his hands in his pockets, looking down at the ground.

Nobody said anything for a long moment. Ben finally broke the silence.

"Ed, is that shell casing and the slug in the wall of the Miller house going to come back from ballistics as coming from the same rifle that killed Doug Malone? Your rifle?"

Ed looked up at them, his face calm. He nodded. He pulled his hands out of his pockets and held them out in front of him.

Ray's stomach flipped when he realized what was going on. He glanced at Craig, whose face was set like a stone statue.

Ray knew what he had to do. He nodded at Ben who took Ed's wrists, cuffing them behind him. Then Ray walked over to stand in front of him.

"Ed Garvey," Ray said, looking into Ed's blue eyes, which looked so much like Levi's, "you are being held on suspicion of murder in the first degree. You have the right to remain silent—"

"I know my rights, Ray," Ed said. "This isn't my first rodeo. Let's just get this over with."

* * *

"Hi, Ed," Claire said from behind her desk at the Twin Rivers Police Department when Ed walked in.

"Hey, Claire," Ed said cheerfully.

When Ben walked in closely behind him, Claire's face fell as she realized Ed Garvey was handcuffed. Chief Craig came in next, followed by another man who Clair assumed by the uniform was the new Twin Rivers chief of police.

"Claire, this is Chief Ray Billings," Craig said, nodding toward the tall bald-headed man.

Ray smiled briefly, and she nodded to him.

"Can you put some coffee on?" Craig asked.

Then the group passed her desk, went into the interrogation room, and shut the door.

"Walk us through it, Ed," Craig said, taking a seat.

Ben removed Ed's cuffs and took a chair next to Craig with Ray on Craig's other side. Ed sat down across from the three of them, rubbing his wrists where the cuffs had dug in.

"I was going to tell you I did it since you've already decided I'm guilty," he admitted with a sigh. "Then I'd let you figure out for your-selves I couldn't have."

"I haven't decided anything," Craig said, "but are you telling me you didn't shoot Andy Miller?"

"That's right. I didn't shoot Andy Miller," Ed replied.

"What time did you leave the Beer Chaser?"

"You can check with Joyce, but I think it was about quarter after midnight."

"Tell us everything that happened, and don't leave anything out," Ray said.

"I walked home. It's a long ways. The Beer Chaser is on the south edge of town, and my house is on the east side—a good twenty-minute walk, but it probably took me a little longer because my knee has been giving me fits, and I had to stop a few times. I was a couple of blocks from the house when I heard the shot. I didn't think much of it, other than it was odd. It sounded like it came from the north, but there aren't any farms north, just the Kingery Mine Property.

"A few minutes later, I saw flashing lights cross the intersection of Main Street, and a few minutes after that, as I was climbing the steps of my house, I saw another cruiser cross that same intersection."

"How did you happen to notice those lights, Ed? You would've been walking away from Main Street, right? Probably several blocks away from that intersection," Ray said.

"There aren't a lot of street lights in Twin Rivers, just one on the corner of each intersection, and the light doesn't reach very far. It's pretty dark as you're walking. Those cruiser lights are bright, and even blocks away, I saw them flashing red, white, and blue up on the houses and trees along the street. I turned around and looked."

Ray nodded.

"When I got to my door, it was locked," Ed said. "I haven't locked that door more than a couple of times in the last forty years—usually when I go out of town for a few days. I didn't have my keys. They're hanging out of the ignition of my truck over at Levi's. It's still sitting over there dead. So I broke the window out of my back door with my elbow, reached through, and unlocked the door. I knew somebody had been there before I went in.

"I turned on the lights and looked around but didn't see anything disturbed, so I figured it was kids looking for beer. They swiped beer out my garage refrigerator so many times, I quit keeping any out there. I started to go to bed, but when I walked by the gun cabinet, I saw the empty spot. One of my rifles was gone—the good one."

"Just one?" Ben said.

"I keep eight rifles and shotguns locked up in that cabinet, none loaded. There is a .38 revolver locked in the bottom drawer of that cabinet that is kept loaded. There's also a 12-gauge double-barrel in my bedroom closet and Levi's .455 Webley in my nightstand—Levi didn't want it in his house after . . . Anyway, the only gun missing is the .308 Remington."

"They break the glass in the gun cabinet?" Ray asked.

"That's the weird part," Ed said. "The cabinet door was locked. It's still locked now. The key for that gun cabinet is also hanging from the ignition of my truck."

Claire tapped on the glass window of the interrogation room and held up the coffee pot. Craig waved her in. She quickly poured coffee into four foam cups and left the pot on the table. Sipping on the coffee, Ed looked at Ray.

"I always keep two rounds for the .308 sitting upright on the inside edge of the gun cabinet behind the rifle butt, just in case I need to get to them quick. Other than that, I don't keep any ammo in the gun cabinet. Those two rounds were gone, too."

"You sure that rifle was there when you left this morning?" Craig asked.

"I used it this morning. I took that rifle and two others out to the Sportsman's Club and fired a few rounds first thing this morning. I do that once or twice a month. I love to shoot, and that's a great range."

Ed's face softened as he recalled the events of that morning.

"It's a perfect range for zeroing your rifle at various distances. First station is set up with targets at 100 yards, and as you go down the line, each station pushes out another 100 yards. You get to the far end, and you're looking 1,000 yards. There's not another range where you can shoot at those distances in this part of the state. I usually go out early in the morning, so I've got the place to myself. This morning, there were a couple guys playing with a .45 Henry open-sight at the two-hundred-yard station. We traded off, and I fired that Henry a couple of times, and they fired my Marlin .30-.30 a few times. I gotta admit that Henry rifle was fun to shoot. I might have to get one of those. You ever shoot one of those, Ben?"

Looking confused, Ben shook his head and said, "Not the .45. I had a Henry .22 I used to squirrel hunt with when I was a kid."

When Ray glanced at Craig, he knew both of them were thinking the same thing. Ed Garvey sure didn't act like a man who thought he was going to be charged with first degree murder.

"Anyway, when I was done at the range, I went back to the house, locked up the rifle, and headed to my shop. This kid had called me when I was on my way back to the house. He was looking for a bumper for an '86 Chevette. Can you believe there's still a Chevette in this world that runs? But my stupid tow truck started acting up, sputtering and spitting, and I knew I'd never make it, so I headed to Levi's house instead. It's closer than my shop."

"Okay, back up a little bit," Ray said. "You realize your rifle is gone—what did you do?"

Ed's face got dark. "I knew when I saw my rifle was missing that Andy Miller was dead. I'd heard the shot earlier, and those police cars were headed north. It all clicked. I knew it was my rifle. I went out and got in Mom's Caddie, but it wouldn't start—dead battery. I don't think I've driven that car since fall. I hate Chevys. Anyway, I jumped it off my battery charger and drove over to the Miller house. When I saw you all out in the field and the bullet hole in the window, I knew what had happened. And here I am."

"I thought your keys were hanging out of your truck ignition over at Levi's," Ray said, looking at Ed with his steely blue eyes over the top of the steaming coffee. "How did you start that Cadillac without your keys?'

"Oh, you're good, Ray. If you check in my left front pants pocket, Ben, you'll find a single key. That car's got electric locks. I was always locking myself out of that damned thing, so I keep a spare key in a little magnetic tin stuck under the tire well."

Ray leaned back in his chair, stretching is arms behind his head. He looked at Ed for a long time.

"So let me run this back," Ray said. "Somebody entered your house and unlocked the gun case without a key. They took your rifle and two rounds that were sitting on the back edge of the gun cabinet. They relocked the gun cabinet without a key and then locked your door when they left."

Ed nodded. "That's what I'm telling you."

"And you're forgetting part of it," Craig said, leaning forward on his elbows. "Whoever took it was a hell of a shot, too. He hit Andy Miller in the throat at about 500 yards. 'One shot. One kill.' Isn't that some kind of saying with Marine snipers, Ed?"

When Ed glared at Craig, Ray saw a glimmer of the intensity he'd seen on Ed's face earlier when he'd looked at Andy Miller. Suddenly, Ed exploded into laughter, sounding like a mule.

"What's so funny," Ray said.

"He was hit in the throat?" Ed asked, shaking his head.

"Severed his spinal chord," Craig said coldly. "He was dead before he hit the floor."

Ed put one index finger in the center of his forehead and the other on his Adam's apple.

"That was a lousy shot. The shooter missed by eight or nine inches. If I'd made that shot, or any Marine sniper had," he said, looking sharply at Craig, "he would've been hit right between the eyes. I fired my last three rounds off this morning with that .308 at about four hundred yards at a target about the size of a quarter. I hit it with the first round dead center and put the next two through the same hole. Whoever shot Andy Miller sure as hell wasn't a very good shot. And he was certainly no trained sniper. That was slop. The fact he hit him at all is more a testament to the quality of the rifle and scope than to the skill of the man behind the trigger."

"Your whole story doesn't make sense, Ed," Craig said, looking at him darkly.

"You're right, it doesn't," Ed snapped back. "If I'd shot him, I certainly wouldn't have used the .308 I used to take out Doug Malone. I sure wouldn't have popped the brass out of that rifle and left it lying on the ground, probably with my fingerprints on it. There's two other rifles in my gun case I could've easily made that shot with at that range—a Remington .243 and that Marlin .30-.30. Neither of those guns would have a ballistics record in your database like my .308 does, and I could've dropped either of those rifles in the river on my way home, and nobody would've known I ever owned them."

Ray glanced at Craig and shrugged. Ed had a point. It was beginning to look to Ray as if somebody had gone to a lot of trouble to make it look as if Ed Garvey had murdered Andy Miller.

"Ben," Ray said, "get that key out of Ed's pocket and have Claire drive you over to the Miller house. Have Jeff, the CSI, go over Ed's car, and when he's done, have Claire follow you in Ed's car. Park it in his garage. Then have Jeff come over here to examine Ed."

Ed stood as Ben quickly found the single key in his pocket and left the room.

"I'm going to hold you, Ed," Ray said. "I have to. And I'll have a lot more questions to ask you about what went on back in 1971."

Ed nodded.

"I'm also going to have Jeff go over to your house and go over it with a fine-tooth comb. I'm going to talk to Joyce, too. We'll figure out what's going on here."

"I appreciate that," Ed said.

Chapter Fourteen

APRIL ALWAYS WALKED THE FIVE BLOCKS TO WORK WHEN THE weather was nice. She'd have everything ready to go when Harv rolled in an hour later. That morning, she was digging through her purse when a truck swung into a parking space in front of the diner. She knew who it was without looking—Floyd was always the first customer of the day. For thirty years, he'd eaten breakfast at the diner before opening his hardware store at six. Last year, he'd closed the store and retired. The store was gone, but the habit had remained.

"Mornin', April," he said as he climbed out of his truck.

She sighed. "I forgot my keys."

"You sure?" Floyd asked as she continued to dig through the large purse.

"Yeah, I'm sure. Can you give me a lift back to the house? I think I left them sitting on the counter."

Floyd walked over to the door and wiggled the knob. It was locked.

"I don't think that'll be necessary," he said, dropping to one knee.

He pulled a penknife out of his overalls pocket and began tinkering with the lock as April continued to sort through her purse.

"I don't think that's going to work. It's a fairly new lock, Floyd," she remarked as he stood up. "It was worth a try," he said as April patted him on the shoulder.

Grinning broadly, he turned the knob and pushed the door open.

April smiled. "You never cease to amaze, Floyd."

"I learned a thing or two in the hardware business," he said as he followed her into the diner. "Of course, I first learned how to get into my dad's desk with one of my mother's knitting needles when I was a kid."

"I'm almost afraid to ask."

"Dad had served in France during World War II, and one of the things he came home with was this huge stack of postcards."

April turned on the lights and adjusted the thermostat as Floyd walked behind the coffee counter.

"And he kept those postcards locked up in his desk?"

"Well, I don't know if they were actually postcards, but they were about that same size, and they were absolutely filthy," Floyd said with a grin, "even by today's standards."

April laughed.

"I don't think Mom knew he had them. I saw them one time when I went in his den to kiss him goodnight. He tossed them into the drawer and closed it, but I saw something I couldn't stop thinking about."

"I'll bet," April said.

She tossed her purse under the counter and walked through the swinging doors into the kitchen to turn on the grill so it would be hot when Harv arrived. Floyd began making the coffee. He helped her open just about every morning. She returned moments later with two pies, which she sliced, placing the wedges on small plates and putting them into the carousel.

"So you figured out how to get into your dad's desk, didn't you?"

"Of course, I did," he said with a broad smile.

They quit talking for a bit, the gurgle of the coffee the only sound in the diner. Floyd noticed how tired April looked as she worked at the counter, and he knew why. The phones in Twin Rivers had been ringing all night with the news of Andy Miller's death. The silence lengthened as they avoided the topic that was on both their minds.

Finally, April said, "You think he did it?"

"Ed?" Floyd said, his bushy gray eyebrows going up. "You don't, do you?"

"No, of course not, but who would've wanted to kill Andy Miller after all these years?"

Floyd shrugged as he stood with a mug in hand, watching the coffee pot fill. His face was tight.

"What's bothering you?" she asked.

"I've always had the feeling Ed knows more about that robbery than he's ever said. Has Ed ever told you why Andy Miller came after him at the Beer Chaser after the robbery?"

April shook her head.

"I think that's very strange. That part of the story has never made any sense to me, and to be honest with you, it made him look guilty back then, and now that it has happened again, it makes me really wonder what was going on. He never told Joyce either. I asked her one time."

April bristled at the mention of Joyce's name, and Floyd caught it.

"Was it Joyce that broke you and Ed up?"

April's eyes flashed angrily, then softened almost immediately.

"The Ed Garvey I fell in love with in high school never came back from Vietnam. There was another woman towards the end, a meaningless affair he had, but our relationship was pretty much over by then. And it wasn't Joyce—that was later."

Floyd poured himself a cup of coffee after the stream finally stopped running. "I had no right to ask you that. I'm sorry. I've always wondered, and it just slipped out."

"I know a lot of people probably think that same thing," April said. "They've been together for a long time."

"They're not really together," Floyd said. "That's not quite the right way to describe it. I mean they don't go out to dinner or go see a movie together or take trips."

"What is that phrase they use now?" April said, pausing to think. "Ah, yes, I believe they call that friends with benefits."

"That's closer," Floyd said. "Or maybe a booty call?"

April glared at him as he grinned back at her over the top of his coffee cup.

"Shut up, Floyd.

* * *

"Morning," Tori said as she climbed over the baby gate into

the kitchen. It was just past six.

"Well, good morning," Ray said, glancing up at her.

Ray was sitting at the table in the breakfast nook as the golden light of morning streamed in through the bay window. He was wearing his uniform as he sipped coffee and looked over the morning paper, the *Twin Rivers Gazette*, which he'd heard smack the Garvey porch from the arm of a talented newspaper boy on a bicycle. There were five very well behaved puppies looking up at Ray expectantly.

"Did you drug those puppies?" Tori asked.

Ray chuckled. "I have a way with animals. We've all been outside already, and we have all pooped and peed in the yard. I'm glad I don't have to mow there. It's like a mine field out back."

Tori walked over to the kitchen island and grabbed a banana.

"There's coffee," Ray said. "But I'm not very good at coffee. It's like motor oil."

"No, thanks," Tori said, pulling a bottle of juice out of the refrigerator.

She poured a glass, then took a bottle out of the cabinet over the dishwasher, popped two capsules into her mouth, and washed them down with the juice.

"What are those? They look like horse pills," Ray said.

"Vitamins," Tori said, peeling the banana and taking a bite. "I'm working too many hours at the lodge. Got dehydrated, so I'm on light duty. Doctor Jackass said I can't have any coffee or beer until I get my electrolytes back in balance."

"Dr. Jackass?" Ray said with a chuckle.

"Dr. Jackson, sorry," Tori said.

"Must be related to Captain Hippie, I mean Harper."

Tori laughed.

"Did these puppies leave any messes this morning?" Tori said, chewing the banana and glancing around the kitchen floor.

"No, it was just like you see it now. They didn't even use the paper," he said, pointing toward a corner of the kitchen where Tori had laid out newspapers. "But they couldn't wait to get outside. They were standing at the back door, yipping with crossed legs, so I let them out. One of them didn't make it to the bottom of the steps."

"Six weeks and they're housebroken?" Tori said.

"You get one to learn, and they all pick it up fast though I'm sure there will be a few accidents," Ray said. "We raised beagles when I was a kid."

Tori walked over to the trash can, opened the lid, and glanced inside before closing it.

"Looking for something?" Ray asked.

"No."

Ray looked at her suspiciously. "I've been married a few times. I know what you were doing."

"What?" Tori said.

"You were looking to see how many beer cans are in the trash. Something going on with Levi?"

Tori sighed. "He slept downstairs again. He never came to bed. He's crashed out on the settee in the library. Thought maybe he'd polished off a twelve pack. He's done that a few times lately. I'm a little worried about him."

Ray looked at her in the morning light. She was beautiful with her kinky blonde hair and stunning green eyes. Even as pretty as all the young things Levi had dated in Savannah were, Ray had known Tori would be something special since Levi had never gotten over her. For a woman in her early forties, there was only one way to describe her—Tori was a knock-out.

"So what's wrong?" Ray asked.

Ray was the kind of person people instantly trusted. Levi had always said that. His size, his mustache, and his shaved head gave him an intimidating presence, but when he smiled, you could see the kindness in his eyes. That's what Tori saw at that moment.

"As I said, I'm getting worried about Levi," Tori said. "He's written only one book since we've been together, but that one took a lot out of him. He knew the story he was going to write, but he stared at that blank screen for weeks. He didn't eat right. He didn't sleep well. He was disconnected from everything. He just seemed to shut down as he thought over how he was going to tell the story about Doug Malone and the murders. I didn't think he'd ever start writing.

"Then one afternoon, I heard him start typing. Day and night for two or three weeks, he banged away—hours and hours at a time. When he was typing, he never stopped. He never paused to think. He never seemed to back up and correct anything. It was as if he was putting something down on the page that he'd memorized. He'd type twelve hours straight, sleep three or four hours, and then get up and begin typing again."

"So what's going on with this one that's different?" Ray asked.

"I don't think he has an idea. He's up all night, but I don't hear any typing. He either sits and stares at the screen, or he sleeps on the settee."

Neither one spoke for several minutes.

"What if he doesn't get an idea?" Tori asked finally. "Last night at the Beer Chaser was the first time I'd seen the Levi I know in a long time. This time isn't like last time at all."

"If he doesn't get another idea, you'll need to talk to him, Tori," Ray said.

"I just wish he'd leave it alone," Tori said, scooping up one of the puppies and stroking his head as a tear slipped down her cheek. "He doesn't have to write another book right now. He just thinks he does."

"Tell him that," Ray said.

Tori wiped the tears off her face with the back of her hand and kissed the puppy she was holding.

"There's more," she said.

"What?"

"His behavior has been erratic this time, too. He's done a few things recently that make no sense at all. When I bring them up, he doesn't have any explanation."

"Like what?"

Tori sighed. "Well, yesterday or the day before, I can't remember which, I came back from the lodge for lunch, and Levi wasn't here. But there was a sack on the kitchen counter," she said, wiping more tears from her cheeks with the back of her hand. "I really think Levi's mind is beginning to crack under the pressure."

"What was in the sack?" Ray said.

"Lemons. He bought an entire sack of lemons at the grocery store," Tori said as another tear slid down her face. "The receipt was in the sack. Twenty-two dollars worth of lemons—that's all he bought. And he doesn't buy lemons. He doesn't even like lemons."

Ray was suddenly more concerned about Levi than he'd been before.

"I mean, if it was limes," Tori said, "and I'd find a case of Mexican beer in the refrigerator . . ."

"True, that would make sense. But why lemons?" Ray said mostly to himself.

Tori shrugged, and neither spoke.

Finally, Ray said, "There's something you have to know, Tori."

"What?"

"Ed Garvey is sitting in holding on suspicion of first degree murder," he said bluntly. "Andy Miller is dead. One shot at five-hundred yards with the same .308 rifle that killed Doug Malone."

"Oh my God!" Tori said. "Levi is already on the edge—"

"Let's wait to tell him. Let him sleep. I don't think Ed did it, and I'm going to be checking out his story this morning," Ray said. "Let me get a few more details together, and then we'll talk to Levi once I know a little more."

Tori nodded.

"You realize we're talking about Levi as if he were a mental patient, but he's not. He's way stronger and way smarter than either of us, Tori. We're not giving him enough credit. He seemed fine last night. I think he's figuring it out on his own. He's either got an idea or he's realizing he doesn't, and he's trying to figure out what to do about it. I'm sure there's a reason for the lemons, too," Ray said with a smile.

"Let's plan on having lunch at Harv's," Tori said. "I'll go work on the lodge. Then about eleven, I'll call and invite Levi. We'll talk to him after we eat."

"You sure he won't find out about Ed before then?" Ray asked.

"He was still staring at the computer at two when I checked on him. If I know my husband, he'll be out until noon. He's off his usual schedule, or he'd be drinking coffee on the porch right now."

Ray got up from the table without mentioning that when he'd gotten back to the Garvey house well after four in the morning, Levi was still staring at his computer, oblivious to the fact Ray was watching him from the doorway.

"I'll be at Harv's at noon," he said. "Oh, by the way, where is Harv's exactly?"

"Directly across the street from your office," Tori said in a tone implying that he wasn't very smart.

"Hey, I just got here yesterday. And, by the way, Tori, weren't you the one who said, 'Come on, Ray. Take the job in Twin Rivers. Nothing ever happens in Twin Rivers'?"

Tori smiled. Normally that was right. Nothing ever happened in Twin Rivers—except when Levi came back two years ago and now when Ray Billings had arrived.

"Where's Rosco?" Ray said, changing the subject and looking down at the puppies. "He seems to be avoiding this situation he's created."

"The last Rosco was my dog, but this Rosco is Levi's. He's probably in the den, sleeping on the floor next to him. It's rare when they aren't together. I'm shocked he didn't take Rosco to the Beer Chaser last night."

"A man and his dog," Ray chuckled. "I was good friends with ol' Rosco the Lethargic—he sure surprised everyone in the end, didn't he?

Tori nodded—it was still a painful subject.

"He might have bonded to you once Levi came back to Twin Rivers, but Levi and Rosco were a team in Savannah. I sometimes thought that either that dog could read Levi's mind or he could understand English perfectly. But I've never seen a lazier damn dog that wasn't a beagle or a blue tick hound."

Tori smiled. "That's what Levi used to say, too. I told him that Rosco the Lethargic wasn't lazy—it was just that Levi was boring."

Ray chuckled at that. "I miss that lazy damn dog, and this Rosco is completely different from the last one. Have you come up with a nickname for him yet?"

Tori waved towards the puppies. "I think we're going to have to call this one Rosco the Naughty," she said.

Ray laughed. "You know, that nickname would have fit Levi nicely when I first met him."

"Yeah," Tori said with a chuckle. "They are a lot alike, but at least Levi never chased skunks."

"Nope, not skunks . . ."

"You really want to go there, Ray?" Tori said, regarding him with the hard edge of her mesmerizing green eyes.

"Nope," Ray said quickly.

His father had once given him good advice—when you find yourself in a hole, stop digging.

Chapter Fifteen

THE DREAM STARTED DIFFERENTLY. SOMETIMES HE WAS AT A MOVIE at the Comet Theatre. Sometimes he was at a baseball game at Wrigley Field. Sometimes he was back in high school at a dance in the gymnasium of Twin Rivers High.

But the dream always ended the same way . . . The floor of the theatre would rip open. Or the pitcher's mound at Wrigley would cave in. Or the gymnasium floor of Twin Rivers High School would suddenly collapse. Levi would struggle to get away, but he always fell into the bracingly cold water with a black abyss opening out under him. Something grabbed at his ankles, trying to pull him down into the depths of the putrid pit. He was drowning in Kingery Pond.

Levi sat up suddenly on the settee, covered in cold sweat, the smell of sulfur from the pond lingering for a moment even after he awoke. Rosco was licking his hand.

He'd fallen asleep again while writing. No, that wasn't quite accurate. He'd fallen asleep again, staring at a blinking cursor on a blank page. There was no writing. There were no ideas. There was no story. There was no novel. There might never be.

He glanced at the sunlight streaming into the window of the turret room, which had been his favorite place to think as a kid. The same chair he'd sat in for so many hours reading Sherlock Holmes stories was there now with the same crocheted blanket lying over the back. He didn't remember walking into the library, which adjoined the den, but he wasn't surprised he had. He'd awakened on the settee a lot the last couple of weeks.

It wasn't the first time the desire to write had seized him. It was the fifth. The urge usually came slowly with a single image that stuck in his mind. The story would soon follow. He'd be unable to think about anything else but the story once the urge struck. He'd begun to think of it as "the rapture." It took him out of the real world and threw him into a world that didn't exist—the world of fiction, where he told the stories that haunted him.

This time, the desire to write had come but with no image and no story. The cursor wasn't blinking as he worked out the story in his head. The cursor just blinked, marking off the seconds and minutes. His mind was empty of new ideas.

While Rosco stared at him expectantly, Levi pulled his phone from its holster on his belt. It was 8:30.

Tori would be gone, and Ray, too. Levi smiled. His best friend was here. Maybe having Ray around would help.

Levi hadn't been able to focus the last few weeks. He couldn't keep up with the things he was supposed to be doing at the lodge—like the event they'd had there the other night. The Master had missed it—Levi had totally forgotten. He knew what the problem was—he was consumed with the desire to write but about what?

"I gotta figure this out," Levi said aloud.

Rosco's tail thumped against the hardwood floor as he looked up at Levi, anxious to begin their day.

There were several places where Levi had gone to think in Savannah. Though a famous author, he was, for the most part, anonymous in that large city. He couldn't be anonymous in Twin Rivers, population 2,500. Levi used to the spend time at the Gryphon Tea Room in Savannah, where he was rarely disturbed. He sure couldn't do that at Harv's. Another place he'd gone when he needed to think was Bonaventure Cemetery.

Suddenly, Levi realized there might be a place in Twin Rivers where he could go to work a few things out. He'd avoided the place for a couple reasons since he'd been back, but perhaps, this was as good a time as any to go.

He used the same words he used back in Savannah with Rosco

the Lethargic.

"Wanna go for a ride?" he said, looking down at Rosco.

Rosco did.

* * *

LEVI WAS SITTING ON A BENCH AT OAK HILL CEMETERY WITH THE morning sun shining in his eyes. He zipped up his light jacket against the chill of the early spring morning. The nearly two-hundred-year-old Oak Hill Baptist Church rose up in the distance, its spire invisible in the glare of the sun. Between him and the church were hundreds of gravestones and markers, studding the rolling hills—some going back to the beginning of the town's history.

Nearby was a sandstone mausoleum built for the man who'd founded the town of Twin Rivers. Two columns rose, one on either side of the gate, each with a globe over it. The initial "B" was engraved in one and the initial "J" in the other—mysterious engravings for the uninitiated but well-known ancient symbols amongst Freemasons. The heavy iron gate with a thick padlock on the door protected the vaults within.

Engraved in the sandstone above the mausoleum's entrance, in letters large enough to be read from the road that ran in front of the church, was the name Garvey. His great-great-great-grandfather Charles was the first to homestead in what was now River County. He and his wife Margaret were interred in the mausoleum. They'd had six children, all but one of them buried near the mausoleum. It was one of those children, William, who was credited with founding the town of Twin Rivers.

William had served in the Union Army during the Civil War under General Winifred Hancock. Wounded at Gettysburg, he'd returned home after the war a hero. William was soon married, and he and his wife Sarah had nine children. As Sarah raised their children, William built his empire, and the town of Twin Rivers rose around it.

It was William who built the brickyard, then the lumberyard, and finally the foundry. It was William who brought the railroad through the growing town of Twin Rivers to carry those goods to Chicago, where they were used in building that city. And when the lumber was gone from the woods surrounding the rivers, it was William and his partner, Edward Kingery, who began mining coal from those same hills which had once provided lumber for the lumberyard. William died a wealthy man. It was his money that built the mausoleum where he and his wife, Sarah, rested beside his parents, Charles and Margaret.

It was one of William's children, Levi's great-grandfather Abe, who'd built the house he now lived in and who'd brought the Webley revolver back from World War I—the same gun that had saved his great-grandson's life and Tori's nearly a hundred years later. Abe and Mary rested in the ground nearby along with their seven children and their families, too. One of his sons was named William. He was Levi's grandfather.

Levi had never known his grandfather William, who'd died before he was born, but he knew his wife very well. Grandma Lucille had raised him. She was the newest addition to the expansive Garvey plot in the Oak Hill Baptist Church Cemetery. There was rarely a day when Levi didn't think about his Grandmother Lucille.

"Good morning," a voice said from behind him.

Levi turned. An old black man with a cane was shuffling towards him, the gold ring on his left ring finger gleaming in the morning sun.

"Reverend Guy!" Levi said, holding his hand out.

"How you been, Levi," Reverend Guy said, shaking his hand and taking a seat on the bench beside him.

Levi looked him over and smiled broadly.

"What?" Reverend Guy asked.

"You got old," Levi said with a chuckle.

"I was just thinking the same thing about you," he shot back.

"Put a pair of sunglasses on you, and you'd look just like Ray Charles."

Guy smiled. "Well, with that Panama hat and gray hair, you're only a pair of round rimmed glasses away from being Harry S Truman."

Levi laughed again. "It's good to see you."

"Come to talk to Lucille?" Guy said as he stroked the head of the dog that had just run up to him.

"Yeah. And to think."

"Could it be that you're lost, and in need of advice or spiritual guidance?"

"I came out here to get away from people—it hasn't worked out so well."

The old man laughed.

"You might not realize it, but you did come here looking for me. Come on, Levi, I'm an old man, and it's chilly this morning. It's not the first time we've sat on this bench. Why don't you just spit it out?"

Levi thought about that for a moment. Maybe Reverend Guy was right. It wasn't the first time they'd talked on that bench. Maybe that's why he'd gone to Bonaventure Cemetery in Savannah so often—maybe some part of him was looking for Reverend Guy.

"I think my writing career is coming to an end," Levi said. "I'm having a tough time coming to grips with that. I'm out of material, and the creative well seems empty."

Guy's eyes widened. "That's terrible. What would you do for a living if you didn't write? Maybe you could get a job working at the Home Depot in Calloway?"

"That's funny," Levi said. "It's not useful, but it's funny."

"People are often bothered by things they have no control over. Because you can't force an idea now, you think you'll never get one. And so what if you don't? You're a wealthy man. You don't have to write. You can quit forever if you want to." He pointed towards a headstone nearby. "And Lucille left you some farm ground, a house, and probably some money, too."

"She did."

"So give it a rest and enjoy life," Reverend Guy said simply. "Garveys seem to think in absolutes. It's either now or never. Can't you just enjoy where you are right now and worry about tomorrow when it gets here?"

Levi shrugged.

"And, Levi, you'll get another idea. Maybe today or tomorrow or next month or next year, but you'll get one."

"I just don't understand why there's nothing there now," Levi said.

Guy smiled. "I know why. You're happy, Levi. For the first time in your life, you're happy. I've read all your books. In the first three, you wrote about pain and adversity. You wrote about rising above challenges. I just loved those books—all three of them. Even so, the last book about Doug Malone was your best, but it was very different. You wrote a true story like a novel—and it was chilling how you managed to climb into Doug Malone's head. It was brilliant. But you know what I think?"

"What?" Levi asked.

"You're married to the woman you've always loved. You cruise around in Old Blue with your dog. You enjoy the best pie and coffee in America every single day. You and Mrs. B work with those kids at the library. You and your Uncle Ed are back to doing the two things you enjoy the most—rebuilding old Fords pickups and arguing with each other. Seriously, Levi, have you ever been this happy in your life?"

Levi considered the question, then shook his head. Reverend Guy was right. Life had been good the last couple of years.

"So is it any wonder you can't write the kinds of dark novels you've written before?" Guy asked.

"I guess not."

"So either give it a rest or find something else to write about."

"Like what?"

Guy glanced at the Garvey plot. "You know, I could tell you a story that I'll bet you've never heard about your great-grandfather Abe and that Webley revolver of his."

"Yeah?" Levi asked. "Tell me."

"See, there is still some part of you that wants to write," Guy said with a grin. "I'll make you a deal. When I see you and Tori in church some Sunday morning, I'll come over to the Garvey house that very afternoon. We'll sit on the porch, and I'll tell you the whole story. But you'd better hurry because I've decided to retire. This year's Christmas service will be my last sermon, and that's only about nine months away."

Levi sighed.

"That's the deal. Take it or leave it. But I promise that when you hear the story, it will be your next book. You'll have to write it."

Levi did want to hear the story. He extended his hand and said, "Thanks, Reverend Guy."

As Reverend Guy turned to go, Levi stopped him and said, "I noticed your ring earlier. I didn't know you were a Mason."

Reverend Guy glanced down at his left hand, and smiled as the solid gold triangle surrounding the number '33' gleamed in the morning sun.

In Levi's ten years as a Mason, he'd known few who'd been given the privilege of wearing that particular ring—it represented the fraternity's highest honor.

"For four or five generations now, all the Garveys in Twin Rivers have been Masons, Levi. The Garveys founded two lodges in River County, one white and one black."

"Are we related?" Levi said. "I've always wondered."

"If you've always wondered, then why haven't you asked before?"

Shifting uncomfortably, Levi looked at him.

Guy smiled. "Yeah, you're getting it now, aren't you? That's a tough question for a white guy to ask an old black man, isn't it? You know, only one other person has ever asked me that question?"

"Who was that?" Levi asked.

"I don't think the name will surprise you."

Levi glanced at Lucille Garvey's stone.

"That's right, Levi. Lucille asked me many years ago. You know why nobody else has ever asked me?"

Levi nodded. He knew exactly why.

"Go on. Go ahead and say it."

Levi shifted on the bench again. "It's because there are only two ways we could be so different and yet have the same last name, and for a long time both of them have been subjects that make polite small town folks very uncomfortable. Either we're blood relatives, which means a long time ago one of your relatives and one of mine got together," Levi said.

"And the other way?"

"At some point, my family owned your family," Levi said.

Reverend Guy nodded. "And that's exactly why nobody asks."

"Did you tell her?" Levi said as he nodded toward Lucille's headstone.

"I sure did."

"You gonna tell me?"

"Just as soon as I see you and Tori in church," he said with a grin. "It's part of that story I promised you."

Reverend Guy paused to sniff the air. "You smell that?"

"Oh no," Levi said, rising quickly. "Rosco!"

Rosco ran up from the brush bordering a small creek beside the cemetery. As he got nearer, the smell became overpowering.

"I think your dog got sprayed by a skunk," Reverend Guy said.

Levi glared at him. "If I had to guess, I'd say we're related by blood because you certainly seem to have my Uncle Ed's comic talent of stating the obvious."

"I gotta go," Guy said with a laugh as he waved his hand in front of his face. "That's nasty. Good luck, Levi."

Chapter Sixteen

Tori was sitting in their usual booth at Harv's Diner, nervously sipping a glass of water. A picture hung over the booth, a picture of the Zoo Crew taken outside the diner back in 1983. The Zoo Crew was the group of friends she and Levi had run around with when they were in high school. It chilled her to see Alan Haig standing and smiling with them. Even now, she could hardly believe the dark secrets that would come to dominate Alan's life.

Tori looked toward the door, hoping to see Levi. She'd forgotten her phone that morning. When she'd gone back home to get it, she'd expected to find Levi still sleeping on the settee, but he was gone. She'd been surprised, considering how late he'd been up.

Levi hadn't been answering his phone. She knew he'd most likely show up for lunch. He was a creature of habit, and they ate lunch at Harv's almost every day. She only hoped he hadn't heard about Ed.

Minutes later, the bell over the door jangled, and Levi walked in, wearing his Panama hat. He smiled when he saw Tori. As he crossed the diner, he stopped to exchange barbs with one of the farmers at the large center table. Then he slid in across from her.

"I've been trying to call you," she said curtly.

Levi chuckled. He obviously hadn't yet heard the news about Ed. He pulled his phone off his belt and set it on the table. It was dead.

"I need a new phone. This one got wet."

"That's your third phone in three months. You lost one. And somehow, the next one got chewed up in the snow blower."

"It fell off my belt," Levi said defensively. "I told you that holster you got me was a piece of crap."

"Well, the holster didn't survive the snow blower either. Now how did that happen?" Tori said sharply, pointing at the dead phone.

Levi shrugged. Then he looked at her questioningly. Tori usually wouldn't be too concerned with something as insignificant as a dead phone.

"What's wrong?"

"There's something I have to tell you," Tori said.

Suddenly, April was at the table, sliding a cup of coffee in front of him. "You want to order now?"

"We're waiting for one more," Tori said.

"We are?" Levi said.

"Ray will be joining us," Tori said.

"I should've called Uncle Ed," Levi said. "He and Ray have sure hit it off."

April looked at Levi. "Oh, good! I was hoping Ed—"

Tori glared at her, and April abruptly stopped talking.

"Hoping Ed what?" Levi said.

But April was already walking back to the counter.

"What the hell is going on, Tori?"

"I don't know how to tell you this," Tori said. "So I'll just tell you. Last night—"

The bell over the door jangled. Ed Garvey walked in with Ray Billings right behind him.

Tori sighed as Levi looked up and waved them over.

"Well, this is more like it," Ray said, looking around the diner as he slid into the booth next to Tori and Ed slid in next to Levi. "I have to tell you, Levi. That tea shop where we used to meet in Savannah was a little on the girlie side. This is a little more my style."

April appeared with two more cups of coffee. Ray picked up the mug and took a sip. A broad smile crossed his face.

"I hear you have pie," Ray said to April.

"You must be Chief Billings," she said, beaming. "I'm April, and that big clown behind the cash register is my husband, Harv."

Ray smiled and took her hand. "It's nice to meet you, April. And you too, Harv," he added with a wave in his direction.

Harv grunted in his usual way.

"I'll be right back," April said, winking at Ray.

"What did you want to tell me, Tori?" Levi asked.

Ed leaned away from Levi. "What in the hell did you get into, Levi?"

"What do you mean?"

"You're not very . . . fresh," Ed said, wrinkling up his nose.

"Yeah," Ray remarked. "What's that smell?"

Tori instantly knew how Levi's phone had gotten wet.

"Rosco," she said, glaring at Levi.

Levi sighed. "He got sprayed again. At the cemetery. I used your magic formula, Tori."

"Not very well, obviously," she said, waving a hand in front of her face. "I'm going to kill that dog."

"Wait a minute," Levi said. "You were going to tell me something?"

April returned with three plates of pie. "Here you go, Chief," she said, sliding a piece of chocolate in front of Ray. "And Ed." She smiled as she set chocolate in front of Ed. "And Levi," she said coldly, placing butterscotch in front of him.

"What the hell?" Levi said as he looked first at his pie and then at theirs.

"I had two pieces left from yesterday," April said. "You started this, Garvey."

Levi sighed and pushed the plate away. "Nobody likes butterscotch, April."

"I like butterscotch," one of the men at the farmers' table said.

"Shut up, Floyd," Levi snapped.

Everyone laughed.

"Let me out," Levi grunted, nudging Ed towards the end of the booth.

"Gladly, skunk boy."

Levi stormed across the diner and out the front door. Moments later, he returned with a sack in his hand.

"Here, April," he said, handing it to her. "I'm sorry. I'll never do that again."

April glared at him before a small smile appeared on her face. She knew the apology was about the pie and not her feelings, but she forgave him anyway. She kissed him on the cheek.

Levi returned to the booth, but before Ed let him back in, he took a big bite in front of Levi and licked his lips theatrically.

"Ass," Levi muttered as Ed stood to let Levi back into the booth.

"Do you know what your husband did?" April asked as she refilled coffee cups.

Tori shrugged. "Hard telling."

"He doesn't like lemon pie, so he bought every lemon in town, knowing that if I couldn't get them, I'd probably make chocolate pie instead—his favorite. He almost got away with it, too."

Tori and Ray exchanged a brief look of relief. Levi picked up on the glance that had just passed between them.

"What?" he demanded. "There seems to be a lot going on this morning that nobody is willing to tell me about."

"It's nothing," Ray said, taking a big bite of chocolate pie and washing it down with a slug of Harv's coffee. "Oh, this is so much better than the Gryph."

"Wait until you try the cheeseburgers, Ray," Ed remarked.

Levi was looking at them all suspiciously. He hated the feeling that he was missing something.

"What were you going to tell me when I first came in here, Tori? It seemed like it was important at the time. You couldn't tell me fast enough. And now all of you are trying to steer me away from it."

"Oh," Ed said nonchalantly, wiping the corners of his mouth with a napkin, "I know what it was. She was probably going to tell you Ray arrested me last night on suspicion of first degree murder."

Levi dropped his mug, and coffee ran all over the table.

* * *

Levi looked stunned, the fresh cup of coffee April had brought him untouched, as Ed recounted in detail the story from the night before. They knew everyone in the diner was listening. When Ed finished, there was a long moment of silence.

"He couldn't have done it," Ray said finally, pushing his pie plate away.

"You want another piece of chocolate pie, Chief?" April said as she refilled his cup.

Ray nodded.

"What do you mean *another* piece," Levi said, pointing at the untouched piece of butterscotch in front of him. "I thought there were only two pieces of chocolate left?"

"You're not getting a piece of chocolate today, Levi. Get used to the idea. I don't reward bad behavior," she said as she walked off.

Levi handed his piece of butterscotch to Ed, who handed it to Floyd at the next table.

"Thanks, Levi."

"Shut up, Floyd."

Ray continued the story where Ed had left off, not caring who heard the details of the case. In fact, he spoke loudly enough for everyone to hear. It was a good opportunity to stop the gossip that had undoubtedly been circulating around town already. Harv, his massive form covered by a white apron, came out from behind the counter, pulled up a chair from an empty table, and sat down to listen even though a couple orders hung waiting for him. Nobody cared.

Ray said, "I checked with Joyce at the Beer Chaser. Ed was the only customer left at midnight. He bought his last beer at 12:03, according to her register tape, and after her last customer left, she locked the door and joined him for one more on the house before he headed home, like they do every so often."

"Yeah," Ed said with a chuckle, "every so often—like three or four times a week for the last forty years."

There were chuckles around the diner.

Ray grinned. "She thought it was after 12:30 when Ed left. Even if he hadn't walked home, if he'd driven or gotten a ride, there wasn't enough time. By the time he got to his Cadillac—if it'd started right up, which it didn't—he still couldn't have gotten out there and killed Andy Miller a few minutes before one in the morning.

"I timed it from Ed's house. That farm road is a mile out of town, and it takes about ten minutes to get down it to the place where we found the tracks—it's a grass lane, but it was obvious it was a large vehicle, like a truck, not a car. It would take another ten or fifteen minutes to walk to the tree in the middle of that field and set up the rifle. We found boot tracks in the field. Ed is a size eleven, and those were about a size 9. Ed didn't do it, so I released him this morning."

"What about the ballistics?" Tori asked.

"As expected," Ray said, "it was fired from Ed's gun, which was registered in the ballistics database at the lab because it was the gun that killed Doug Malone."

There were murmurs around the diner.

"Well, duh," Ed said. "I knew that."

"Wait, here's the interesting part," Ray said. "Ed's prints were on the shell casing. Thumb and forefinger right side up, and another set, thumb and forefinger, upside-down."

Ed nodded and laughed.

"I don't get it," Tori said.

"I pulled those two shells out of a brand new box, where they are packed upside-down in a foam block. I turned them over and placed them right side up on the back edge of the gun cabinet. That's one set upside down and one set right side up."

"And let me guess, there are no other prints on the round," Levi said.

"Two sets," Ray said, "that's all."

"Wait a minute," Floyd said, looking up from his last bite of pie. "That can't be right. There should've been a print on the bottom of the round. There's no way to load a bolt action rifle without leaving a thumbprint on the bottom of the casing."

Ray and Levi exchanged glances. Floyd had figured it out, too.

"Aren't you going to tell me to shut up?" Floyd said, looking at Levi.

"Not this time, Floyd, because for once you're right."

Ray continued. "No thumbprint on the bottom of the shell, where he'd pushed it into the receiver. Whoever loaded that round into the rifle was wearing gloves."

"And why would Ed wear gloves and not wipe the other prints off the round?" Tori said.

"He wouldn't," Ray said.

"What about the locks?" Levi asked.

"Jeff, the CSI, found nothing at Ed's house of interest," Ray said. "The knob on Ed's door was a thumb lock. No prints, not even Ed's. He found the broken window in the back door which Ed said he broke out to get in. He found tiny shards of glass on the elbow of Ed's flannel shirt—consistent with Ed's story."

"In other words, I told the truth," Ed said as he smiled at Levi.

"I'm following this just fine without your help," Levi growled. He was still mad about the pie.

"I don't know when I last locked that knob," Ed remarked, "but I don't know how long fingerprints last either."

"According to Jeff, they can last a long time on metal. It's hard to say if that means anything or not, but it could mean that whoever turned that lock was also wearing gloves and wiped your prints off in the process."

"And the gun cabinet?" Tori asked.

"Jeff took that lock back to the police lab to have it examined," Ray said. "There are no scratches on the inside indicating it'd been jimmied, so whoever unlocked and then relocked the gun cabinet had a key."

Ed looked at him. "That's not possible. The only key was hanging out of the ignition of my truck at Levi's house."

"Yup," Ray said, pulling some keys out of his pocket and tossing them on the table in front of Ed. "I took these keys with a warrant."

Ed shrugged. "That's fine. And what did you learn from them?"

"No fingerprints on your keys other than yours, Levi's, and Tori's," Ray said.

"So who killed Andy Miller with Ed's rifle?" Levi asked.

Ray shrugged. "Ed said he didn't know—but you do know, don't you?" Ray said, looking squarely at Ed.

There were murmurs around the diner.

"Why don't you enlighten us then," Levi said, obviously annoyed by Ray's suggestion that Ed knew something he wasn't saying.

Ed nodded. "Tell 'em," he said.

"There's only one person left with a motive—the fourth gunman from the '71 bank robbery," Ray said. "The shooter."

There was a collective gasp in the diner and then a buzz of conversation. All seemed to agree that the fourth bank-robber was back.

As the buzz around the diner ramped up to a dull roar, Levi asked Ed, "Who was it?"

"I wish I knew. I thought he was long gone."

Ed leaned toward the center of the booth, his voice low. "But there's another possibility. It could be whoever originally planned the heist. They killed Andy because of something he may've known that could tie that crime back to them."

"The Chicago Outfit? Levi suggested.

Ed nodded. "They thought he could be a problem, and they took him out. If that's true, Andy Miller was dead before he set foot outside that prison gate. Andy knew a lot more about that crime than he ever admitted. He never told the truth about why he came after me. He probably kept his mouth shut about what he knew because if he told, he knew he'd wind up dead."

"Why did Andy come after you the first time?" Ray asked Ed.

"You'll have to figure that out on your own," Ed said.

"Were you involved, Ed?" Ray asked.

"Not criminally. I have very good reasons for not telling you yet." Ray looked at Ed for a long moment.

"You're just going to have to trust me on this, Ray," Ed said.

"One thing seems certain," Levi said. "Andy Miller's murder is tied to the bank robbery. It's either the fourth bank robber who killed him or those that planned it originally. He was either killed to protect the fourth bank robber's identity—"

"Or he was killed to protect those who planned the heist," Tori added.

They all looked at each other. Levi and Tori had summed it up exactly right.

* * *

"WHAT ARE YOU THINKING ABOUT, TORI?" RAY SAID AFTER ED AND Levi left with Rosco in Old Blue.

They were standing on the sidewalk in front of Harv's. She'd seemed preoccupied for the last few minutes.

"I'm thinking about locks," Tori said.

"What about locks?" Ray remarked, pulling off his flat-brimmed hat.

It'd been warm in the diner, and there had been nowhere to park his hat on the small booth table. His bald head was beaded with sweat under the felt hat. As he wiped the sweat off the top of his head, he looked across the street to the roof of the Masonic Lodge where workers were banging away feverishly with their hammers.

"Whoever did this knew something about locks," Tori said. "They unlocked and re-locked Ed's gun cabinet without a key."

Ray nodded.

"And that fourth bank robber?" Tori said.

"Yeah?"

"He cracked a safety deposit box," she said. "Wouldn't that take a special tool?"

Ray looked at her. He'd seen a few movies where bank-robbers had used a tool that forced open the locks. Tori might be on to something.

"Is there a locksmith in Twin Rivers I could talk to?" Ray asked.

Tori shook her head. "But there's one in Calloway, C & S Locksmiths."

"Maybe I'll go over and learn something about locks," Ray said, walking to his cruiser.

Ray climbed in and started the cruiser, but before he started to back out, the passenger door swung open, and Tori leaped in.

"What are you doing?" Ray said.

"I'm going with you," she said.

Ray started to argue, but when he saw the determined look on her face, he realized it was useless to argue with Tori.

"Okay then, to the locksmith shop," he said, backing into Main Street.

"Actually, you go to the locksmith shop. I want to talk to my old buddy Bill," she said.

"Who's Bill?"

"Bill Patton—he's Alex Patton's son."

Ray glance at Tori. He couldn't place the name, although it was very familiar to him.

"You remember the jeweler from the bank robbery?"

"Oh, yes," Ray nodded. "They were after his diamonds."

"I became friends with Bill Patton when I was president of the First National Bank of Calloway. He still lives in his father's house." She looked at Ray. "Are you just going to sit here idling in the middle of Main Street, or are we going to go?"

"I'd go, but I don't know where the hell I'm going? Where is Calloway exactly?"

She chuckled. "Go straight, then turn left at the Beer Chaser. Calloway's eight miles up the slab."

"I didn't realize Alex Patton had a living heir. You know, Tori, he could very well be a suspect since he may've held Andy Miller responsible for his father's suicide."

"Unlikely," she remarked. "He's a paraplegic—a veteran of the first Gulf War."

Chapter Seventeen

"THIS DOG STILL REEKS," ED SAID, PUSHING ROSCO OFF HIS LAP AS Levi turned the corner by the library.

"How was that pie?" Levi said sharply.

"Well," Ed said, sucking air through his teeth and making a smacking sound as if trying to dislodge a bit left over, "the crust gets a little soggy the second day, but it didn't taste too bad after I spent the night in jail."

Levi snorted.

Ed looked out the window towards the park. "Isn't that Ben?"

Ben was standing in front of the war memorial, looking up at it. Levi swung Old Blue into the park entrance and pulled in next to the cruiser parked beside the pavilion.

He and Ed got out with Rosco following. Rosco got to Ben first.

When Ben saw Rosco, he backed up a few steps, remembering his first encounter with the dog in the Garvey foyer. But Rosco was wagging his tail, so Ben offered the back of his hand which Rosco licked. Ben was rubbing Rosco's head when Levi and Ed walked up.

"How did you get up there, Levi?" Ben said bluntly.

There was a ladder leaning against the column.

"You ever see lumberjacks climb trees," Ed said, scratching his chin. "They use a strap which they wrap around the trunk. Then, using cleats, they shinny up the trunk, flipping the strap higher and higher as they go. You could do that on a column like that, using those Nike tennis shoes Levi was so fond of back in the early 80s."

Levi shot Ed a look. "You can stop helping me any time now."

"It was muddy. Only a few tracks," Ben said. "Nothing Levi's size, which back then was a size seven."

Ed chuckled. "Levi's smart. He could've washed those tracks out with a bucket of water. There's a spout over at the pavilion."

Levi shook his head. "Boy, you're helpful. I am smart though, at least smarter than you," Levi said. "Of course, it's not a huge challenge to be smarter than you. I used to steal your truck and your beer on a regular basis, long before I got my driver's license."

Ed frowned at him.

"I saw the pictures Chief Craig took at the time," Ben said. "I don't think he erased the tracks. I'd thought that same thing, but the ground was undisturbed. And there's a small granite platform on top of the column the statue sits on that comes out over the column. Maybe he gets to the top of the column, but he can't get any higher than that. And the neck of that statue is still more than six feet over his head. Even if he could get past that platform, there's no place to stand up there while he ties on the bikini, and it was tied."

Ed, Ben, and Levi stood for several minutes, looking up at the statue on top of the column.

"How the hell did you get up there, Levi?" Ed finally asked.

Levi shook his head. "You know, that statue was made by a local sculptor back in the 1920s. There are actually two statues, identical in size and dimensions, that were cast in bronze. One is up there on the top of that column to commemorate the Twin Rivers veterans of World War I. The other sits at the base of the stairs at the Twin Rivers Library."

Ben's eyes lit up. "Is that how you worked it out, Levi? You spent a lot of time in that library—you still do. You worked it out there, didn't you?"

Levi shrugged.

"You sure know a lot about this statue," Ben said accusingly.

"I wrote a paper about it in the 5th grade," Levi said with a smile. "My great-grandfather, Abe, was drafted for that war, along with about twenty more in River County. He was one of six from Twin Rivers who returned alive. They raised the money to build the memorial and commissioned the sculptor—the same artist who made a bust of Abraham

Lincoln that is on display at Lincoln's Tomb in Springfield. I saw it when I went over there for a jamboree with the Cub Scouts."

"I'm going to figure it out, Levi," Ben said. "It's only a matter of time."

"Good luck with that, Ben."

* * *

AFTER DROPPING TORI OFF AT THE PATTON HOUSE, RAY DROVE BACK to the shop she'd pointed out when they'd pulled into town. It was one of several shops on the first floor of an old sandstone building on Main Street in Calloway. Ray swung into a space in front, crossed the sidewalk, and walked in. The shop, which was dimly lit, smelled of grease and oil, graphite powder, and metal that was ground on a wheel.

There was nobody behind the counter.

"Hello?" Ray called.

He heard someone shuffling in back. "I'll be right there," a voice called out.

A moment later, a man stepped through the doorway behind the counter. He was in his thirties with long hair and glasses so thick his dark eyes seemed to swim behind them. His arms were covered with tattoos.

"Oh," he said when he saw Ray in his uniform. After looking him over, he held out his hand and smiled. "Russell Martin. You must be Clifford Craig's replacement over in Twin Rivers. I heard they hired a new police chief. You can just call me Russ."

"Ray Billings," Ray said, taking the man's hand.

"What can I do for you, Chief?"

"You can call me Ray."

"Okay, what brings you here, Ray?"

Ray looked him over again. He looked young, probably just answered the phone and watched the store. Ray wasn't sure he'd be able to provide the information he'd hoped to get.

"How long you been doing this, Russ?"

Russ laughed. "Since I was born. I own this joint. My dad bought this shop back in the early 80s when we moved here from Cincinnati. I grew up in here with dad teaching me everything he knew about locksmithing. Got me in a lot of trouble when I was younger, being able to get into anything I wanted—the teacher's desk, the principal's office, the candy store over on Cannon Street. I took the shop over about eight years ago when my dad retired."

Ray laughed. "I can imagine what kind of trouble you got into. Lucky you didn't wind up in juvie hall."

"They'd never have been able to keep me locked up," Russ said with a grin.

Ray took off his hat, ran his hand over his scalp, and tossed his hat on the counter.

"What's C & S stand for? It certainly isn't Martin."

"I don't really know. Since the shop had been around so long, Dad kept the name. It's been here since this building was built at the turn of the last century. I don't know if you noticed the mosaic tile outside the door when you came in, but it has C & S spelled out in it. It's original to the building."

"Interesting," Ray said, "but what I came for is an education about locks, Russ."

"You came to the right place. Ask away."

"I'm thinking about stealing my friend's rifle, but it's locked up in a gun cabinet," Ray said. "How could I do that. I obviously don't have a key."

Russ's eyebrow went up from behind his thick glasses when he realized Ray was probably investigating an actual crime and didn't want to give him any details.

"Gun cabinet or gun safe?" Russ asked.

"Cabinet."

"Glass front?"

"Yes."

"I could do that in kindergarten," Russ said. "That's a pretty weak lock."

"I can't leave any marks inside the lock," Ray said. "I don't want to get caught. And I'll need to relock it after I steal the rifle."

Russ knew what that meant—the police lab hadn't found any signs of tampering.

"The tools we'd use now for a lock like that are made of plastic or vinyl. They wouldn't leave a mark."

"And you could relock it, too?" Ray said.

Russ nodded. Then he disappeared through the doorway. He came back moments later with a small gray cash box—the same kind of little box the Masonic Lodge in Savannah had for pancake breakfasts. Russ also had a small leather pouch in his hand.

"This is the same kind of lock you'd find on a gun cabinet. Behold," Russ said as he pulled a small plastic pick out of the pouch, inserted it into the lock, and, in seconds, opened the lid.

Ray stepped forward and inspected the box.

"Lock it," he said, sliding the box back to Russ.

In a couple of seconds, Russ pushed the box back towards Ray. The lid was locked.

"No marks?"

Russ shook his head. "Twenty years ago, we'd use a little metal pick which might leave marks because the metal in the pick is stronger than the metal the lock is made out of, usually brass or cheap stamped metal. These newer picks won't leave marks, but more importantly for us, they won't damage the locks."

"How long would it take me to learn how to do that?" Ray asked.

"Not long," Russ said. "You have to understand how locks work and how keys work. Once you do, you basically mimic what that key does with a pick. I can teach you in about an hour, and with a little practice, you can do it. This is a very simple lock, like you'd find on an old desk drawer. You can open a desk drawer, if you know what you're doing, with a paperclip. Dad could open one with a wooden matchstick. When you get working with more complex locks, it gets a lot trickier. But I can open about any standard lock on the market today in less than a minute. I've had a lot of practice."

"And training," Ray said.

"Absolutely."

"You know," Ray said. "My friend also has some stuff in his safety deposit box I'd like to get my hands on."

Russ grinned broadly. "Oh, Ray, that's way harder. You'd need a thumper there."

"A thumper," Ray repeated.

Russ disappeared through the doorway again. He returned with a heavy tool that was about eighteen inches long. It looked like a metal pipe with a screw on one end and a cap on the other. There was a large iron piece that slid freely up and down the length of the tool.

"Breaking into a safety deposit box is not about lock-picking expertise. It's about brute force. And this is the tool we use."

"How does it work?" Ray asked.

"You use this tool to shatter the lock and pull the whole lock core out." Russ pointed to the end of the tool, which had a screw on the end of it. "You screw this end directly into the lock. This heavy iron piece, the slider, slides up and down the center rod, and there's a cap on the end that makes the slider stop suddenly. Once you have the tool screwed into the lock, you pull back sharply on this iron slider so it bangs against that end cap. When that slider hits the end cap, it stops suddenly, transferring all that energy into the screw, and if you do it right, it breaks the whole core of the lock out and all the parts that keep that door closed."

"So when you get done, the core of the lock is screwed to the end of that tool," Ray said.

"That's right."

"Sounds simple enough," Ray remarked.

"It's not. I do this often over at the bank, usually when somebody dies. The next of kin want into the box, and they can't find the key. If you don't hit that core just right, you break the metal screw on the end of the tool, and the safety deposit box wins. Then you have to replace the screw on the end of the tool, dig the broken screw out of the lock, and try again. You've got to pull it just right with just the right amount of force to break the lock without breaking the screw. It takes a lot of practice."

"But there are two locks on a safety deposit box," Ray said. "When you're breaking into a safety deposit box at the bank's request, you're dealing with only one lock. The bank has its key."

Russ nodded. "That's right. And that makes it way easier. You see, one tab on a safety deposit box locks into the bottom of the frame, and the other lock tab runs into the side of the frame. When you have one key, there's a little play in the door, and it makes it easier to break the second tab off."

"What if I'm breaking into the bank, and I don't have either key?" Ray asked.

"That's a bitch," Russ said. "When both locks are locked, there's little play in the door which means there's little room to work with to snap it loose. You've got to hit it just right to bust that first one."

"You ever have to do that?" Ray asked.

"Yeah, I did," Russ said. "A few years ago, a bank master key came up missing. Tori Buchanan—she was president of the bank—called me to break into twenty-five boxes and replace the locks. It took me four hours. I'd never done that before. The first one took me thirty minutes and a dozen screws. I kept breaking them off, and I'd have to dig them out and try again with a new one. Once I cored that first box, it got easier, but I bet I went through forty screws all told. But, by the time I got to the last four boxes, I'd gotten much better. I busted those last four open in ten minutes and never broke a screw. I'd have made my daddy proud."

"What if I told you that I know a guy who went into a bank vault, busted into both locks of a safety deposit box in five minutes, and walked out with the box in his hand," Ray said.

"I'd say you knew my father. He could do that. And I could do that now but not before a few years ago. That takes some serious skill and experience."

"Where would I get a tool like this?" Ray said, hefting the thumper.

"These days, you can get one on the internet just by saying you're a locksmith, the same with lock picks and slim-jims to break into cars," Russ said. "That's where I got this thumper—on the internet with no questions asked. But until the last few years, there was just a handful of locksmith supply places where you could purchase locksmith tools, and you'd have to prove you were a licensed locksmith to get them. You even had to sign for them. Those tools had serial numbers, and they kept close track of who owned them."

"So the standards aren't what they used to be," Ray remarked. "But even if I got my hands on this tool, it's unlikely I could open a safety deposit box."

"You want to try?" Russ said with a grin. "I bought a bank of thirty-six safety deposit boxes and keys when the old Olton Bank closed. I keep certain information in them that local residents have entrusted to me—master keys, electronic codes, stuff like that. I have them in the back if you'd like to give it a try."

Ray grinned as he picked the thumper up off the counter. "Are you a gambling man, Russ?"

"Five minutes, like your friend?" Russ asked.

Ray nodded.

Russ reached into his pocket and pulled out his wallet. He laid a hundred dollar bill on the counter.

Ray laid five twenties on top.

"Tell you what, Ray. That's not a fair bet. I don't want to take your money. I'll give you an hour, and I'll even tell you exactly what to do. I'll bet you won't be able to bust one box open in an hour with me helping you."

Ray rubbed his hands together and picked up the thumper. "That's a bet."

* * *

"YOU SURE YOU DON'T WANT SOME COFFEE, TORI?" BILL PATTON SAID as he wheeled his chair out of the kitchen with a cup of coffee on a tray mounted on the arm of his wheelchair. He was a handsome man in his mid-fifties with deep-set brown eyes. The scars from shrapnel wounds he'd gotten in the Gulf War were still visible on his hands, arms, and neck.

"I'm fine," Tori said, examining some of the items hanging on the walls of the living room.

"I know this isn't a social call," Bill said. "This is about Andy Miller, isn't it?"

"Did you know he was getting out of prison?" Tori asked.

Bill shook his head as he sipped his coffee. "No, I didn't. I was a surprised when I read this morning that he'd been released and then murdered. Are you helping with the investigation?"

"Not officially. Our new police chief, Ray Billings, is a friend of Levi's from Savannah. I rode over here with him. He's over at C & S Locksmiths, getting educated about locks, and I thought I'd stop by to ask you about your dad."

"So Andy Miller's murder is connected with the bank robbery," Bill said. "I kind of thought it had to be."

"Is this your dad's work?" Tori said, tapping on the glass of a shadow box mounted on the wall. It was full of various bronze and brass metals and medallions.

"He was good, wasn't he?" Bill said. "He loved creating art a lot more than running a jewelry store. And he loved working with bronze. He created award medals for the school, the Cub Scouts, and the Daughters of the American Revolution. He created commemorative coins, too. All the towns around here celebrated their centennials, starting in the late sixties, and Dad created the coins for all of them. He had an impressive workshop in the garage with metal presses and stamps. And, of course, he designed custom jewelry."

Tori moved to another display. "I've seen these before. These are

Masonic symbols." She was looking at a collection of large bronze medallions that were about three inches across. "The Twin Rivers Masonic Lodge has these same medallions embedded in the wood backs of all their officer chairs."

"Most of the lodges around here do," Bill said. "Dad made three of those originally, representing the Master of the Lodge and the Senior and Junior Wardens. After he put them in a case in his store, it wasn't long before he was getting requests for them. He eventually created medallions that represented all the officers in the lodge. They became very popular, and he made many castings of them."

"They're beautiful. Your dad was remarkably talented. I'd assumed they were old when I saw them at the lodge. They're stylized in almost an art-deco design. Was your dad a Mason?"

"No, he just loved working with the symbols. He did work for the Shriners, too, because he liked working with the Egyptian-based symbols they use," Bill said, pointing to another display on the other side of the room.

Tori walked over to look at the collection of bronze medallions featuring pyramids, sphinxes, and scimitars.

"There's something you want to ask me," Bill said.

"We've known each other a long time," she said as she sat down in the chair next to him. "I don't want to drudge up anything you'd rather not . . ."

"It was a long time ago, Tori. We're friends."

"Why do you think your dad was targeted in that robbery?"

He'd had a feeling that was what she wanted to know. "It sure wasn't those diamonds in his freezer," he replied.

"Why do you think that? They were worth a lot of money."

"Sure, they were," Bill said, "but why rob a bank for them? Dad had a large jewelry store. On any given day, he had ten times that amount of diamonds, gold, silver, platinum, and stones in his shop. Why not rob the shop if that was what it was all about? At night, he locked up all that merchandise in an old vault behind the counter at the store. It looked like Fort Knox, but you could pry that safe open with a screwdriver. It would've been a lot easier to knock over the jewelry shop."

"So you think it was something else?" Tori said.

"I do," Bill said. "After Mom and Dad divorced in the early sixties, Dad had some financial difficulties. He was paying mom a king's ransom in alimony. I think he got involved in some things he shouldn't have."

"Any ideas about what that robbery was actually about?" Tori said.

"No, but I think he got in over his head with a rough crowd. There was a lot of money going through that shop, and I've always wondered if all that cash was legit."

"You think maybe he was laundering dirty money?"

"I think that's a distinct possibility," Bill said. "I just wonder if those bank robbers weren't after records of those transactions or the names he may've had. I don't know for sure, but it wasn't diamonds. I'll never buy that."

"Your dad went to see Ed Garvey after the robbery," Tori said. "Any idea why?"

"He was scared. My dad was this little bald guy with thick glasses. Maybe he went to Ed for help since Ed was known as one tough son-of-a-bitch. And Dad knew him. Even then, Ed had a reputation for being somebody you could trust."

"Andy Miller beat up your dad pretty badly," Tori said. "Then he went straight to Ed Garvey, got into a fight with him, and was arrested. Yesterday, the first thing Andy did when he was released from prison was beat up Ed again."

Bill first looked surprised, but then he smiled.

"I think Dad probably lied to Andy Miller. I think Andy came look-ing for the goods they'd failed to get in the robbery, and my dad, after being beaten, told him Ed Garvey had the goodies. He knew Ed could defend himself. Dad was an artist. He couldn't defend himself against an old lady with an umbrella—let alone somebody like Andy Miller."

"And not long after that your dad committed suicide," Tori said.

Bill shook his head. "I never believed that either."

"Why?"

"I took care of Dad while he was recovering from that beating," Bill said. "I'd taken him to a doctor's appointment about a week after the beating. I'd just gotten my driver's license. Andy Miller had broken two of his ribs, and he was having trouble breathing. He was admitted to the hospital for a couple of days. When I got back home that evening, there was something wrong. I wasn't sure what it was at first, and I thought it was because I wasn't used to being home by myself. Then when I was lying on the couch watching TV, I noticed that desk over there."

Tori glanced over at the old roll-top desk.

"One of the drawers was open just a little bit, which was odd because that desk was always kept locked, so I got up to close it."

Locks again, Tori thought.

"Then I walked around the house, looking at everything carefully. I noticed another drawer in Dad's bedroom dresser open a little bit, and things inside had been shifted around a bit. I wouldn't have noticed it at all if I hadn't put clean t-shirts in that drawer that same day. Like I said, I'd been taking care of Dad. Somebody had been in this house and had been very careful not to leave any signs of their entry, but they'd been in every room."

"That's odd," Tori remarked. "That was long after the robbery. They surely didn't believe those diamonds were still here."

Even after all those years and twenty-five years in the Army, Bill's face looked haunted at the memory. "Like I told you, it was never about the diamonds. There was something else they were after. Dad was dead a week later."

"And you never believed it was suicide," Tori said.

Bill shook his head.

"Why was he murdered?" Tori asked.

Bill shrugged, his face pale.

"You found him?"

Bill nodded slowly. "The house was locked when I got home from school. There was no note or anything. And the thing is, Dad had started acting like himself again. He wasn't depressed."

"You think the killer got what he came for?"

Bill shrugged. "I've thought a lot about this over the years, and I can come up with only one reason why Dad was murdered."

"Tell me your version of what you think happened," Tori said.

Bill nodded. "I think that fourth bank robber came here and searched the whole house, looking for whatever it was they robbed the bank for—and I don't believe it was the diamonds. When he didn't find what he was looking for, he came back to get it from Dad. I think Dad probably gave him what he wanted because that was the end of it. But there's only one reason he would've killed Dad once he got what he'd come for."

"Your dad knew the man who killed him," Tori said.

Bill nodded. "That's exactly what I think."

Tori sat for a few moments, thinking it over.

"And I'll tell you one more thing I'm sure about, Tori. Dad lied to the police about those diamonds. I never knew him to lock up stones in his safety deposit box. I never knew him to bring valuables like that home either. He got stones to use in the jewelry he made at the store, where he had insurance against theft. I think he brought those stones home after the robbery and put them in his freezer because he knew the police would want to talk to him, and he could pull the diamonds out of the freezer. Dad knew exactly what that robbery was about, and it was probably something illegal. Those diamonds were his cover story. Like I said, the robbers were after something else."

Chapter Eighteen

"YOU GOING TO TELL ME WHAT HAPPENED TO YOUR HAND?" TORI ASKED.

She'd headed back towards C & S Locksmiths when she was done talking to Bill Patton. Since she'd been there a long time, she was surprised that Ray wasn't waiting for her. When Ray saw her walking along the sidewalk, he picked her up in his cruiser. His right hand was wrapped in gauze.

"I won a hundred dollars," Ray said. "I also met Dr. Jackson and got four stitches on the side of my hand. But I did learn something. Whoever the fourth bank robber was, he was a trained locksmith. There's no way, even with the right tool, somebody could bust into a safety deposit box in under five minutes without experience. There are only two men in this area who can use that tool to open a safety deposit box in under five minutes. Back then, one was living in Cincinnati, and the other wasn't born yet. But I won a hundred dollars."

"And how much did Dr. Jackson charge you?" Tori said, suppressing a grin.

"You want to tell me what you learned before I leave you at the side of the road?" Ray asked.

"Alex Patton was murdered," Tori said.

Ray nodded. He knew that.

"You get any idea how Ed was involved?" he asked.

Tori shook her head.

"He is involved somehow," Ray said as he looked at her.

She sighed and said, "I don't know how, but I think he was, too. Levi is going to freak out."

"Ed either knows something about the robbery, or he's protecting someone."

Tori's head snapped towards him. "I hadn't thought about that, but you're right. He could be protecting someone. That makes more sense than anything I've heard so far."

"But who?" Ray said.

Tori shrugged. "Ed has a reputation around here as somebody you can trust. In fact, they call him the patron saint of lost causes. Bill Patton thinks that might have been why his dad went to him. Alex Patton needed help."

"You think that's it?"

Tori nodded. "Ed's not a wealthy man, but he's refused Levi's offer of any part of the Garvey inheritance, unlike his brother, Larry, who's Levi's dad. He's begging for money, even threatening to sue Levi over Lucille's will, which left everything to Levi."

"Yeah," Ray said, "Levi's dad and mom are real gems."

"But for decades, Ed has had a reputation for helping people. He's paying the rent and utilities for the old woman who lives in the house next door to his. She's in her nineties now. Her son, Buck Taylor, was Ed's best friend all through school. They wound up drafted together, in basic training together, and later, in the same unit in Vietnam. Buck Taylor was killed by a Vietnamese sniper as they defended some forgotten hill in 1967. Ed, who was out searching for the sniper, killed him when he took the shot that killed Buck. To this day, Ed won't admit he takes care of Mrs. Taylor, but Levi knows he does. That's the kind of guy Ed is."

"I've got to investigate Ed," Ray said.

"Are you sure that's not what Ed wants?"

Ray smiled. "I think that's exactly what Ed wants."

"So where do you start?"

Ray was pulling back into Twin Rivers.

"Maybe with his oldest friend," he said, glancing at the Beer Chaser as they passed it.

"Oh, Ray, she's not going to tell you anything. You're an outsider. You may be friends with Levi, but understand one thing—even if you live here the rest of your life, you're always going to be the new guy in town. And Ed and Joyce go back decades. She's not going to help you investigate Ed's involvement in a robbery. Even if she knows something about it."

"No, Tori, I think she will."

Chapter Nineteen

THE MONTHLY LODGE MEETING WAS WINDING DOWN, AND LEVI WAS about to begin the closing. The meeting had been routine, other than a long discussion after Lawrence Swaney brought up the subject of the lodge renovations, which ended with the members voting unanimously to whatever repairs and improvements Tori thought were necessary to prepare the building for another hundred years of use—regardless of the expense. And that included central air and heating that all of them were looking forward to. The days of either freezing or sweltering during meetings were nearly over.

The brethren of Twin Rivers Lodge No. 400 had been unusually distracted that evening, including their Master. They'd had a tough time getting through the ritual opening of the lodge, which was something they all knew well. Considering the distraction, it was no wonder. It was another cloudless night, and, other than the altar lights, the lodge was brightly illuminated by the Milky Way, which stretched out above them, and the moon. Halfway through the opening, they'd all stopped to watch a meteor shower. It was unlikely anyone would soon forget the night Twin Rivers Lodge met under the open sky in their own lodge room.

"Anybody got anything else?" Levi said as he adjusted his fedora, which had once belonged to Tori's grandfather.

The secretary raised his hand from behind his desk and rose.

"Yes, Floyd, you have something else?" Levi said.

"Yes, Worshipful," he said. "Even though we can't vote him in until next meeting, I'd like to once again welcome Brother Ray Billings to Twin Rivers Lodge No. 400. And I'd also like to congratulate him on his new job as chief of police in Twin Rivers."

The lodge applauded.

"Anything you'd like to say, Ray?" Levi said.

Ray nodded and stood. "Although Twin Rivers Lodge has questionable judgment when it comes to electing Masters, I'd like to say I'm looking forward to joining you."

The lodge erupted into laughter.

"And I'm looking forward to serving as the chief of police, but I thought I was applying for a gravy job since I was told nothing ever happens in Twin Rivers."

Laughter again.

Floyd stood up again. "Well, Brother Billings, we may have questionable judgment at times," he said, nodding toward Levi as a few members snickered.

"Watch it, Floyd," Levi said.

"But you obviously have excellent judgment," Floyd continued, "since the first thing you did as chief was to arrest a Garvey."

More laughter.

The Senior Warden, Ed Garvey, stood up from his chair in the West and regarded Floyd. "You'd better remember who's going to be Master of this lodge next year, Floyd. I'll put you out of that chair."

More laughing.

"You can't fire me, Ed. I'm not appointed by the Master. I'm elected by the Brethren. And besides that, nobody else wants my job," Floyd said.

Laughing, Levi leaned back in his chair as the exchange continued. This was the part of being a Mason he enjoyed the most—watching men from all walks of life, who have genuine affection for their Brothers, rip on each other in good fun.

Suddenly, Levi realized he was sitting on something. Reaching behind his back, he pulled it out. The insults stopped as the lodge went instantly quiet. Levi sat there, staring at the pink bra hanging from his hand.

Suddenly, the lodge exploded into waves of laughter.

"This kind of thing never happened when our old Master was in the East," Harv Jenkins said.

"That's because Floyd is seventy-three years old," Levi said, tossing the bra onto the secretary's desk. "You even remember what this is?"

"I sure do," Floyd said, picking it up. "It's a double-barreled sling-shot."

"I think I'll have Tori re-key the doors of this lodge while she's at it," Levi said. "There's obviously all kinds of interesting things going on up here at night."

"I'll just lock this up in my desk out of your reach, Worshipful," Floyd said, tucking the bra into a drawer. "I wouldn't want it to turn up on the war memorial statue."

"Shut up, Floyd," Levi said as snickers came from around the room. Then turning to the others, he said, "Anybody got anything else?"

The lodge members glanced around. They were done.

"Then we'll proceed to close," he said as he picked up his gavel and snapped it once. "Brother Senior Warden . . ."

Ed Garvey rose.

* * *

THE LODGE ROOM QUICKLY EMPTIED AFTER THE MEETING. LEVI, ED, and Ray stayed behind to put everything up and to cover all the lodge furniture in case of rain. Floyd finished up his work at the Secretary's desk, picked up his briefcase, and walked to the lodge room door.

"Don't forget to call the Cub Scout Master and ask him if he needs any financial assistance getting his boys to the jamboree again this year," Levi said.

"It's on my list," Floyd said. "And stay out of my desk, you pervert."

"I never liked you, Floyd," Levi called after him.

"Shut up, Levi," he called back, laughing as he descended the stairs.

"Good group of guys," Ray said after the door downstairs banged shut.

Ed nodded. "I'd trust any one of them with my house key, my credit card, or my life."

"You let them have their fun, don't you, Levi," Ray said. "You remember how a meeting in Savannah could be about as much fun as going to a funeral?"

Levi nodded. "I sure do. We do things a little differently here. If these guys quit having fun, they'll stop coming. Sometimes I just lean back and let them go. We look forward to this meeting because we enjoy it."

"How's your investigation going, Ray?" Ed asked, changing the subject.

Ray finished covering the altar with a piece of plastic and sat on the dais steps in front of the Master's chair.

"Not that well," he admitted. "I know Andy's murder ties back to that bank robbery, but there aren't any leads. I also know that the fourth bank robber was a trained locksmith."

"A locksmith, huh?" Ed said.

Holding up his bandaged hand, he said, "You don't bust into a safety deposit box without training. Then there's your gun cabinet. And another little piece of information came up that involves locks. Alex's son, Bill, is certain that somebody entered their home and searched it after the bank robbery. The robber not only opened the front door but also unlocked a desk. Then he locked the door when he left. It's probably the same guy who came back later and murdered Alex, and I'm convinced he was murdered."

"That's good investigating, Ray," Ed said. "I never doubted he was murdered, and it was probably the fourth bank robber."

"But, Ed," Ray said, looking at him squarely, "I know there's something you're not telling me. Either you know something about the robbery, or you're protecting somebody. I've also learned that Alex Patton came to see you right after the robbery. You've not been very forthcoming about what that was about. Then Andy Miller came after you twice. I think you're holding the missing piece of this puzzle."

"You're going to have to find that out for yourself," Ed said, crossing his arms.

"I think you want me to investigate you," Ray said.

"Now why would I want you to do that?"

"I don't know, Ed."

"You're partially right about one thing. I am looking out for some-body."

Levi couldn't believe what Ed had just said. Ed did know more.

"Who?" Ray said.

"Jim Mathis."

Ray had heard the name, but he couldn't place it.

"The cop that got killed during the robbery," Levi said.

Ed nodded. "I grew up with him here in Twin Rivers. We went all through grade school and high school together. We weren't best friends, but we played football together, even dated some of the same girls. After high school, he went to college, and I went to Vietnam. When I got back, he was a deputy over in Calloway. That's when we got to be good friends. On his day off, we fished over at Olton Lake or at the river junction just about every week."

"He was off the day of the robbery," Levi said.

"Yeah, we were supposed to fish that day, but I'd gotten hammered at the Beer Chaser the night before. Wound up in an ugly game of pool with Randall Malone."

"Doug's dad," Levi said.

"I told you that story once," Ed said, rubbing the scar at the edge of his hairline. "Randall was mean as a snake. When he lost the game, he cracked my head with a pool cue—a real poor sport. I eventually stumbled home drunk. I was living with Mom back then. I got up the next day with a three-alarm hang-over. When I came up from my room in the basement to the kitchen the next morning, Mom took one look at the gash in my head and insisted I go to the doctor in Calloway. You didn't argue with my mom. I called Jim and told him I couldn't fish that day. Then you and Mom and I headed over to Calloway. Your mom and dad were on a trip somewhere again."

"Like always," Levi said with a sneer.

"She dropped me by the doctor's office while you two went to the bank. Your birthday was coming up, Levi, so she stopped for some cash to buy you that red bike. You remember your first bike?"

Levi smiled and nodded.

"Anyway, if I'd gone fishing with Jim like I always did on his day off, he wouldn't have been in town during the robbery, and he might still be around today," Ed said.

"What did Alex Patton want with you?" Ray said.

When Ed looked blankly at Ray, it was obvious Ed wasn't going to say.

"Did he give you something?" Ray pressed.

Ed shrugged.

"I'm going to have to find out what it was, Ed. I just hope it doesn't come back to hurt you," Ray said with irritation.

"You do what you have to do. And Levi, don't get angry with Ray," he said when he noticed how rigid Levi's face had gotten. "Ray is doing exactly what he's supposed to be doing. I've been waiting for this to happen for thirty-eight years. Whatever happens, this needs to be resolved."

Levi knew his Uncle Ed. Either he was involved somehow, or he was putting himself in extreme danger, perhaps setting himself up as the next victim of the fourth bank robber. Levi feared it was the latter.

"Why didn't you want Andy Miller arrested after he assaulted you at the Beer Chaser?" Ray said. "He'd still be alive today if he had been."

"I sure didn't see that coming, Ray," Ed said with a pained expression on his face. "I misjudged him. I just want to know who killed Jim Mathis. I thought if it got out that Andy Miller had been released, it might just bring out the missing bank robber—if he's still around, that is. Andy was the last person alive who could identify him."

"It did bring him out," Levi said.

Ed shook his head. "I knew he'd try to kill him, but I didn't think it would happen that fast. I'd planned on watching Andy to find out who was stalking him."

"Nobody in Twin Rivers knew he was getting out of prison," Ray remarked. "The prison never called the Twin Rivers Police Department. They should have, but they didn't. I checked with Claire and Amber. But somebody knew well in advance of his release."

"Somebody planned to murder him even before he stepped into the Beer Chaser," Ed said. "Andy Miller was dead before he left the prison. The plan was to murder Andy and frame me since I was a suspect originally. That was a professional hit, not a last minute plan."

Levi glanced at Ray, whose eyes said he agreed.

"To be honest," Ed said, "I don't really care about what happened to Andy Miller. I just want to know who killed Jim Mathis. His wife was expecting a baby any day when he died. Jim never saw his son or his three grandkids that followed. His son's oldest boy, James, is married now, and they're about to have a baby. If Jim had lived, he'd very soon be a great-grandfather. I want to know who killed my friend."

The tone of Ed's voice sent a chill up Ray's spine. "There's still a dangerous secret out there that is worth killing over," Ray said. "What do you think, Ed? We talked about two possibilities earlier. Do you think it's the fourth bank robber, or do you think this hit was planned by the architects of the original robbery?"

"I don't know for sure," Ed said. "My money is on the fourth bank robber. But it could very well be one and the same. That fourth bank robber could be a mob guy sent down here to set that whole thing up. If you could knock a few things loose in the investigation, we just might know for sure."

"If I have to investigate you," Ray said, "you could be setting yourself up as a target."

Ed nodded. "That's right, but I can take care of myself. I think you're already on the right track."

Ray sighed. "If I can resolve this, am I going to wind up cuffing you again, Ed?"

Ed chuckled. "I sure hope not. You arrest me again, Ray, and next month when we're voting on your membership petition, I just might drop the black ball on your ass."

* * *

"You want a beer?" Levi asked as Ray followed him up the porch steps after the meeting.

"No, I'm tired," he said as he stretched. "I've got a lot to do tomorrow. I think I'll just go to bed."

Ray had spent the first night in the guest room upstairs. Then he'd found Ed's old basement room which had its own bathroom. It had not only an entrance up into the kitchen but also one to the outside as well. He could come and go as he needed to without disturbing Levi and Tori.

Once inside, Ray walked down the narrow hall beside the stairs towards the kitchen. "I'll catch up with you tomorrow," he said.

Levi heard him climb over the baby gate in the kitchen and the cacophony of whining, yipping puppies. The noised stopped as soon as the basement door closed.

Levi went upstairs. Tori was sound asleep. It was about 10:30, but Levi wasn't tired. He went back downstairs and sat down at the antique roll-top desk. Resisting the urge to have a few beers, he stared at the blinking cursor.

When the words didn't come, he leaned back in his desk chair and looked at the collection of framed photos on the top of the desk. One always seemed to capture his attention, a small black and white photo of two young boys, sitting on the porch steps, with a German shepherd between them. The boys were smiling broadly, holding up their Pepsi bottles as the picture was taken by Grandma Lucille. He'd found the photo in a drawer after he'd moved back into the Garvey house. It was the only clear picture he had of the first Rosco—Rosco the Hunter. But in the back of his mind, Levi wondered if there wasn't another reason he'd framed that photo and kept it where he could see it every day.

He stared at the other boy as he so often did, thinking back thirty years to the adventures they'd shared and looking for some missing clue.

But he was just a young boy—Levi's first close friend. It didn't matter how many hours he spent looking at that young boy's face, there was no clue of the evil he would later do.

Shaking off his nagging thoughts about the photograph, he turned back to his computer. Levi decided to make a rare appearance in the fan forum on his website. For an hour, he'd messaged back and forth with a few of his fans, who held regular conversations about his books there.

Suddenly, he heard a noise, which he thought came from outside the window of the den. He glanced at Rosco, who was snoring from the wingback chair. Levi walked to the window and looked out. The old house made noises at night. It creaked in the wind, the air conditioning ticked, and sometimes pipes in the walls gurgled. But this sound wasn't one of those sounds. Levi's heart was thumping. He didn't see anything in the bright moonlight, so he returned to his chair behind the roll-top desk. Moments later, he heard the noise again—and he froze. It definitely came from outside. There was something familiar about the sound, but he couldn't place it.

I'm freaking myself out, he thought as he glanced towards the window. It's nothing.

Rising, he kicked the wingback chair. Rosco's head popped up, and he looked at Levi. Levi nodded towards the window. Rosco jumped out of the chair, ears up, and followed Levi to the window. Putting his paws on the sill, Rosco looked out the window as Levi peered out from the edge of the curtains. For a moment, Levi thought something moved in the shadows under the trees, but maybe not. There was a gusty wind blowing, and the branches of the trees were rocking back and forth, casting odd shadows on the ground in the moonlight.

Rosco was growling, most likely because he sensed that Levi was anxious about something.

"You see anything out there, Rosco?" Levi asked.

Rosco whined and wagged his tail. Obviously, he didn't.

"Yeah," Levi said, scratching Rosco's head. "It's the wind."

Then Levi jumped when he heard a loud crash in the kitchen and something running towards him. He snatched a heavy bookend off a bookshelf—ready to protect himself. When five puppies bounded into the den, Rosco leaped up onto the chair.

Laughing, Levi scooped up one of the puppies, which began licking the side of his face and his ears. Levi set the bookend back on the shelf.

"You little monsters," he said. "You scared the crap out of me. That must've been what I've been hearing. You were trying to knock down that baby gate, weren't you?"

The puppies gazed up at him expectantly, circling around his legs.

"You need to go outside?"

One of the puppies yipped. They already knew what that meant.

"Come on. Let's go outside," Levi said. "You need to go out, too, Rosco?"

Rosco put his head down on his paws. He didn't think very much of fatherhood. In fact, he worked hard to avoid those little rambunctious fur-balls that had so disrupted his quiet life in the Garvey house.

Chapter Twenty

THE BAR WAS EMPTY. JOYCE WAS SITTING ON A STOOL WITH A CUP OF coffee and the TV remote. She lit a cigarette and reached for an ashtray. It was against the law to smoke in a bar in Illinois, but the Beer Chaser had gone rogue. Stupid rules were made to be broken, she believed. She was watching a morning news program when the door opened and Chief Billings walked in.

"Ah, crap," Joyce said. "Somebody report me again for letting my customers smoke?"

Ray looked at her and shrugged. "You can't smoke in a bar?"

"Welcome to Illinois, Ray," Joyce said.

Ray hadn't noticed it before, but Joyce, with her coifed black hair, was much older than he'd originally thought.

"This is twice you've come to see me early in the morning. You want some bacon and eggs?" Joyce asked.

"I'd go for a cup of that coffee."

Joyce pointed at the coffee pot behind the bar.

Ray smiled as he walked behind the bar, took a cup off the shelf over the pot, and poured himself some coffee with his left hand. His right hand was still wrapped in bandages—the result of his lessons in locksmithing the day before.

"What brings you this time?" Joyce said. "More questions about what time Ed left the night Andy Miller was murdered?"

Ray walked up to her, still behind the bar, and set his cup down across from hers.

"No, I want to know if you knew Alex Patton?" Ray asked, leaning over the bar.

"Sure," Joyce said, pointing to the corner of the bar.

Embedded in the dark wood under layers of shellac was a bronze medallion featuring two beer mugs being clanked together in a toast. Ray glanced down the bar. A dozen medallions were embedded in the oak bar every few feet from one end to the other.

"Was he one of your regulars?" he asked.

Joyce shook her head and held out her hand. On her ring finger was a beautiful ruby ring.

"Alex was a talented jeweler, and I like jewelry. He wasn't one of my regulars, but I was one of his. He made me several custom rings. This stone belonged to my dad. Alex made the medallions when I replaced the old bar in '68, I think."

The phone on the wall behind Ray rang.

"You want to get that?" Joyce said, sipping on her coffee and glancing up at the television.

Shrugging, Ray picked up the phone.

"Beer Chaser."

"Who is this?" the voice said on the other end.

"Ray," he answered.

There was a long pause. "You didn't arrest Joyce, too, did you? You've sure been busy the last twenty-four hours."

"No, I didn't arrest Joyce," Ray said. He thought he recognized the voice, but he couldn't place it. "She's right here. You want to talk to her?"

"No, this is Floyd. Just ask her if I left my cell phone on the bar last night."

Ray looked at Joyce. "Floyd leave his cell phone?"

She nodded.

"It's here, Floyd."

"You know, Ray, I'm on the town council. If the chief's salary is so poor that you have to bartend to make ends meet, I can discuss it with the council."

"Shut up, Floyd."

Ray heard Floyd cackling on the other end as he hung up the phone.

"So he wasn't a regular here," Ray said, turning to face Joyce again.

"I saw him in here, maybe twice."

"With Ed?"

When Joyce frowned at him, he thought the conversation might be over.

"Ed admitted Alex came here to see him," Ray said.

Joyce stared at the television, but Ray wasn't done asking questions yet.

"Was Alex with Ed the other time he was in here?"

"No, he wasn't," Joyce snapped as she snubbed out her cigarette in the ashtray.

"Just stopped in for a beer?" Ray said.

Joyce sat staring at the TV with her jaw clamped shut.

"Well, if you don't remember," Ray said. "It was a long time ago."

"Oh, I remember," Joyce said. "And the first time he was in here, it didn't have one thing to do with Ed Garvey. It was years before Ed started coming in here. I didn't get to know Ed until after he came back from Vietnam—that's when he became a regular."

"So when did Alex first come in here?" Ray said, turning to pick up the coffee pot. He refilled Joyce's cup and then his own.

Joyce glanced away from the television. "We didn't have a color TV yet. I'm thinking it was like '62, give or take a couple of years."

"What was he doing?" Ray said.

"Alex met someone here," Joyce said. "He got a PBR from the bar, took that table over in the corner next to the jukebox, and waited."

"You remember a lot about it considering Alex wasn't a regular, and it was nearly fifty years ago," Ray remarked.

Joyce smiled tightly. "Oh I remember it well because everything about that meeting was unusual. You know what they say, Ray—nothing ever happens in Twin Rivers."

"Yeah, I've heard that," Ray said with a chuckle.

"So anyway, then it starts getting interesting. It wasn't long before this guy came in and joined Alex. He was wearing a black suit, a fancy silk tie, and a gray fedora. No one around here dressed like that in the

60s. He ordered scotch. Then he bitched about it. I'd given him the only brand I had. Nobody in Twin Rivers drinks scotch."

"My dad told me a long time ago never to trust a scotch drinker," Ray remarked.

Joyce smiled. "He was right. I knew the guy was bad news. A couple minutes later, this giant thug came in wearing a gray suit and a fedora. He sat right where I'm sitting now. Never ordered a drink, just sat watching Alex and the guy in the black suit at the table over by the jukebox. When I tried to serve him a drink, I saw he was wearing a shoulder holster under that suit."

"Bodyguard?" Ray asked.

"Yup," Joyce answered as she sipped her coffee.

"How long did Alex and the guy in the suit talk?" Ray asked.

"Three scotches probably, and he complained every time. I'd say it was well over an hour."

"What do you think they were talking about?"

"I don't know," Joyce said. "They were leaning so far over the table their heads were almost touching. I couldn't hear what they were talking about, and I was trying."

"So the bodyguard is why you remember the meeting so well?"

"No, that's not all. The suit talking to Alex slid a small package across the table a few minutes before he left. Alex glanced around, nervous like, before tucking it into his pocket."

"Wonder what was in the package," Ray said.

Joyce shook her head. "I have no idea. It looked like a little cloth bag. I've wondered about it for years."

"You think it could've been the same thing Alex gave Ed Garvey after the robbery?" Ray asked.

"It looked like the same kind of bag," Joyce said.

"So Alex did give something to Ed Garvey?" Ray said with the shrewd grin.

"I didn't say that!" Joyce snapped.

"You kinda did," Ray said. "Alex gave Ed a little cloth bag, just like that same bag he'd gotten years earlier from the man in the suit."

"I didn't say that," Joyce said again, but she knew her denial was too late. "You're a very tricky man, Ray."

"I know you spent a night in jail back in '71 to protect Ed. You never told the police about what went on between Ed and Alex Patton when he came in here after the robbery. But Ed knows I'm here. I think he wants me to figure out what happened. I'm guessing he's never told you either."

"Over the years, Ed's been in here too many times to count—sometimes drunk, sometimes not," Joyce said. "I've asked him over and over again about what was in that little bag, but he's never said a word. Is Ed involved somehow?"

Ray shrugged. "I don't know, Joyce. But I think Ed wants to know who killed his friend Jim Mathis even if he sets himself up as the next target."

Joyce stared at Ray over the end of her long narrow nose. Her face was unreadable.

"Any idea who the suit was?" Ray said.

Joyce's face hardened, and she reached for her cigarettes.

"Joyce, I've got to know. I think Ed knows only part of this story, and I think you hold another piece. You've got to tell me."

"I never told Ed this because I knew what he'd do," she said. "I didn't know who that suit was back when I first saw him, but I figured it out almost thirty years later. I never forget a face."

"And you saw that face again."

"I'll make you a deal," Joyce said.

"I'm listening."

"I'll tell you who that guy was on one condition," she said. "If you ever find out what was in that bag that passed between the suit and Alex Patton, you'll tell me. It's bugged me for years."

Ray smiled. "That's a deal."

Joyce climbed off her barstool and went behind the bar. At the far end, she began opening and closing the drawers.

"I kept the paper. I just don't remember where I put it."

"It was in the newspaper?" Ray said.

Joyce nodded. "I hope I didn't throw it out," she said as she searched the drawers.

"Oh, wait," she said, snapping her fingers. "I know what I did with it."

She disappeared through the doorway behind the bar back into the kitchen. Ray heard her opening and closing drawers in the back where he assumed she had an office.

"Got it!" she exclaimed.

Joyce walked back out with a newspaper under her arm. She slapped it down on the bar and stabbed a finger at the picture right in the center of the front page.

"That's who met Alex Patton in here back in the early sixties. I never forget a face."

When Ray looked down at the newspaper, his mouth went dry and his eyes widened. They'd talked about it, but it'd seemed improbable until that moment.

"You kidding me?" Ray said as he wiped sweat off his forehead.

"It's no joke. That's who he was."

"Holy shit, Joyce. Are you telling me that Alex Patton had a meeting in here with Anthony 'The Shotgun' O'Malley?"

Ray had seen TV shows about Tony O'Malley, whose father had been one of Al Capone's lieutenants. Tony had grown up in the Chicago Outfit, and since the early 70s, it was believed he'd headed it."

"That's who was here," Joyce said.

"This paper is from '92. He wasn't exactly young when he was indicted then. Surely, he's dead now or in prison."

Joyce shook her head. "Shotgun O'Malley is old, but he's still alive. And he's never spent a single day in jail. Witnesses against him seem to disappear."

"Are you sure? This guy is still around?"

"I couldn't be more sure. Don't you watch History Channel or True

TV? He's still alive, and he still runs the Chicago Outfit."

Ray looked down at the newspaper. When he glanced up at Joyce, her face fell.

"You're not thinking about—" she started to say.

"What do I owe you for the coffee?"

"Nothing," Joyce said, a frown line between her brows. "I know what you're thinking, Ray. That would be really, really stupid. That's why I never showed this to Ed. Don't do it."

"Thanks for the information, Joyce," Ray said as he walked towards the door.

"Ray," Joyce said, stopping him.

He glanced back.

"It's not worth it," she said.

"It's my job," he said, turning.

"It was nice knowing you, Ray," she said as he pulled open the door.

Ray paused with his back to her for a moment. Then he stepped out.

* * *

TORI AND LEVI WALKED INTO HARV'S TOWARDS THE END OF THE breakfast rush and sat in their usual booth. The diner's part-time waitress, Nichole, was ringing tickets at the register while April rushed orders back and forth. She still managed to set two cups of coffee in front of them before they'd even gotten settled in. Harv could be heard whistling from the kitchen over the hiss of sausage, hash browns, and eggs on the grill. He was never happier than when he had a full grill.

"Oh, shoot," April said as she picked up the coffee cup from in front of Tori. "I forgot. Would you like some orange juice, maybe?"

"Sure," Tori said.

"You're kind of cranky in the morning without coffee," Levi said with a chuckle after April left.

Tori glared at him as he set his Panama hat on the table.

It was a dark morning with low-hanging gray clouds threatening rain. Tori hadn't said two words since she'd gotten up. She'd never been a morning person, but Levi knew what was on her mind that morning—the lack of a roof on the Twin Rivers Masonic Lodge. Bob's crew had been working since first light, setting the new rafters, but the work was going slowly.

"It's not going to rain," Levi whispered to her across the table. "You know the Masons control the world, right?"

Tori glanced at him, the slightest hint of a smile on her face.

"We voted last night," Levi said, looking around to make sure nobody was listening. "There won't be any rain until next Tuesday."

"Is that what you decided?" Tori said, gazing at him. "I've always wondered what you guys do up there."

Levi glanced around again and then nodded, tapping the side of his nose conspiratorially.

"You're so full of shit."

"Would I lie to you?" Levi said, crossing his heart.

Tori smiled. She didn't know what had happened exactly, but Levi seemed like himself again.

Suddenly, a shadow fell across their table.

"Morning," Ben Walker said from the end of the booth. He was in uniform.

"Hi, Ben," Tori said cheerfully.

"Ben," Levi said with a curt nod.

"I've got a question for you, Levi," Ben said.

"Sure."

"Where were you last night between ten and about two?"

"Well, I was at the lodge until after ten. I got home about 10:30, worked for a while, and went to bed around one."

"Tori can vouch for that?" Ben said, looking at her.

"Actually, no," Levi said. "She was asleep when I got home."

"I did wake up when Levi came to bed," Tori remarked. "It was more like 1:30.

"That's kind of what I thought. I'll be seeing you, Levi," he said, looking sharply at Levi.

After Ben left the diner, Levi glanced at Tori and shrugged his shoulders.

"What was that all about?" Tori asked, looking at Levi closely.

Levi sipped his coffee nonchalantly.

"Have you been up to something again?"

Levi grinned as April came to the table. "I don't know why you antagonize Ben like that, Levi," she said. "You two want breakfast or pie?"

"I'll just stick with the juice," Tori said, "and maybe two scrambled eggs, bacon, hash browns, and two slices of white toast."

Levi looked at her, his eyebrows raised. Tori rarely ate breakfast.

"I'll just have pie," he said.

"And what do you mean about Levi antagonizing Ben?" Tori asked.

"Oh, you don't know?" April said. "I'll be right back."

"What have you been up to?" Tori said, her chin resting on her hand.

"I don't know what she's talking about," Levi replied, smiling at her over the top of his coffee cup.

"Here you go," April said, sliding a piece of chocolate pie in front of him. She had a newspaper tucked under her arm.

Levi smiled broadly as he looked down at the pie in front of him. "I had a nightmare last night, April. I dreamed you were going to punish me with an entire week of lemon and butterscotch."

Levi spun around and pointed towards the farmers' table. "Don't say it, Floyd!"

Floyd cackled.

"I just can't stay mad at you, Levi," April said, "but I seriously thought about using those lemons last night."

Levi smiled. "I'm glad you're no longer upset with me, April. I don't like it when people get upset with me."

"I'm no longer mad at you, Levi," April said, "but I can't say the same thing for Ben Walker."

She laid the morning paper down in front of Tori.

"Levi!" Tori said in amazement. "Are you ever going to grow up?"

"Not if I can help it," he said, taking the paper.

After looking at it, he laughed loudly.

The front page of the *Twin Rivers Gazette* was splashed with a banner headline—"The Bikini Bandit Strikes Again!" Beneath it was a color picture of the war memorial statue, wearing a bikini. Whoever had written the tongue-in-cheek story had enjoyed it a great deal.

Levi read an excerpt of the story out loud. ". . . and just when the community was beginning to believe they could put the monstrous defacement of one of our town's most beautiful landmarks nearly thirty years ago behind them, the villain struck again in the night . . ."

Tori laughed.

"Oh, brother," Levi said, chuckling as he read through the rest of it.

It was a funny, well-written piece. The article included mug-shots of six of the suspects in the case: Lex Luther, Ming the Merciless, The Joker, Boss Hogg, Darth Vader, and Levi Garvey.

"It's a good picture of me," Levi remarked. "It's pretty clever how they pasted my picture over the height chart and added a number at the bottom. It does look like a mug shot."

Tori rolled her eyes. "That *is* your mug shot, Levi. Remember when you and I were arrested two years ago?"

"Oh, yeah," Levi nodded. "It's a good likeness though. I could use that picture on the back of my next book, but maybe it's a little serious for a book cover."

Tori snatched the paper out of his hand. "It was serious at the time, Levi. We were being charged with assaulting a police officer."

"Oh yeah," Levi said as he nodded.

The bell over the door jangled. Chief Craig walked in, wearing jeans and a windbreaker.

"Just couldn't leave it alone, could you, Garvey?" he said as he grinned at Levi.

"I told you the first time, Chief. I didn't do it."

"Yeah, I know. It wasn't you," Craig said, taking a seat at the coffee counter. "Maybe it was the one-armed man."

"Well, he wasn't mentioned in the article, but there are five other suspects," Levi said, waving the paper at him.

"Ben is questioning Darth Vader right now. But you know what I think, Levi?"

"Hard telling."

"I think you did do it the first time, and I think you did it last night, too. And I think you did it the exact same way so that Ben would have a fresh crime scene to investigate instead of trying to recreate a thirty-year-old crime from old photos and evidence. I don't think you're going to make it easy for him, but I think you did it as a favor. You like Ben. You want him to solve the case because you want him to get the job. You did it, knowing he'll catch you because you're a big softie."

Tori smiled at Levi.

Levi shrugged.

"And I think I'll go talk to Deputy Walker," Floyd said, rising, "because I have some evidence for him. I know when you got the idea to do it, Levi. It was last night during our lodge meeting when you found that pink bra stuffed in your chair."

Tori looked at Levi. "What the hell do you guys do up there?"

"It's another Twin Rivers mystery," Levi said.

"Seems like we've had a lot of those lately," April said. "There is the lemon bandit, the bikini bandit, and now the appearance of a pink bra. You seem to be right in the center of them all, Levi. You know, before you came back to Twin Rivers, this used to be a quiet little town."

"A quiet, boring little town," Harv added from the order window. "Keep up the good work, Levi."

Chapter Twenty-One

RAY WAS SWEATING PROFUSELY AS HE SAT IN HIS CRUISER AT THE speaker box. He was beginning to realize he'd wasted a trip. There was no way one of the most notorious gangsters in Chicago's history was going to see him. Joyce was right. It was a stupid idea—possibly even a suicidal one.

Even if I can get in, will I ever be able to get out again? he thought.

He'd told the truth when the voice had come over the speaker box. "I want to talk to Tony O'Malley. My name is Ray Billings, and I'm the chief of police in Twin Rivers, Illinois."

And he'd been sitting since. According to the clock on the dash of his cruiser, more than ten minutes had passed. Just when he was ready to back out, the huge gate began to open slowly.

"Pull up to the front of the house," the voice buzzed from the speaker box.

This is a bad idea, he thought. He put the car in reverse, but as he started to back out, he thought about Ed Garvey and his friend, Jim Mathis. He put his foot on the brake because the answer might be right here. Steeling his resolve, he shifted the car into drive and pulled through the gate.

The estate was enormous. As Ray rolled up the winding driveway towards the impressive mansion, he saw three gardeners raking leaves out from under the bushes along the road. They looked a little old to be gardeners, and one was wearing shiny black dress shoes. Ray waved, but they didn't wave back. As he drove on by, he noticed the familiar bulges under their jackets.

Shit, he thought. Those guys are armed, and they're certainly not gardeners.

He stopped in front of the main entrance and climbed out of the cruiser, leaving his flat-brimmed hat sitting on the seat. The sun glared off his bald head as he walked to the front door in the morning sun. He rang the bell.

Ray was a big man, but he had to look up at the man who answered the door. The man was in his seventies with a nose that had obviously been broken numerous times. He wore a tuxedo like you'd expect to see a butler wearing, with the notable exception of the bulges under his left arm and his right ankle.

"Chief Billings," the man said, inviting him in.

As nice as his clothing was, it was obvious from the way he spoke that he wasn't the kind of butler a British lord might have. His heavy Chicago accent sounded more like the brogue of a Wrigley Field hotdog vendor than that of a butler. As the man closed the door, Ray stood in the towering marble-floored foyer, looking up at the massive chandelier hanging from the ceiling and the winding staircase rising along one side to the second floor. He wondered if he'd ever walk through that door again.

"My name is Carl," the big man snarled. "I'll need your gun."

Ray removed the Glock from his gun belt and handed it to him.

"And the other one, too."

Ray looked into his eyes for a moment. Then he removed his ankle holster and handed it to Carl as well.

"Mr. O'Malley is a very sick old man," Carl said. "He's not long for this world, but he's intrigued by why you want to see him."

"Is his interest related to the fact I'm from Twin Rivers?" Ray asked.

Carl's face tightened. "I don't ask Mr. O'Malley questions. I do what he tells me, and he told me to find out what you want."

"I believe he knew a man named Alex Patton."

There was a glimmer of recognition on Carl's face that quickly vanished. He motioned Ray through a side doorway into a large library with high ceilings and a fireplace on one end. Tall windows let in the bright spring sunlight.

"You'll wait here," Carl said.

It wasn't a request. Ray's pulse raced when, seconds later, the door behind him closed, and he heard the lock engage.

Ray walked around the room. The shelves were filled with books about history. In a small alcove were photos taken in the 1940s, all of sailors. Ray recognized Tony O'Malley in most of the pictures. One photo in particular showed a group of smiling sailors on the deck of a naval destroyer with palm trees and several other naval ships in the background. One of those ships was the *U.S.S. Arizona*. On the fireplace mantel was a display of ribbons, all naval decorations, including a Purple Heart.

The library door opened. "Chief Billings?"

Carl motioned for Ray to follow him out of the library and up the winding staircase. They walked down a long hallway to the door at the end.

Before knocking, Carl said, "He's unwell. Don't upset him. If you do, I'll make you very sorry."

Ray's heart skipped a beat as he nodded.

Carl tapped twice, then opened the door. Ray stepped into the large bedroom. On a massive four-post bed lay an old man. The tomblike room was full of hospital equipment—a wheelchair, oxygen tanks, IV bags. The only sound was the quiet beeping of a heart monitor. Sitting in a chair beside the bed was a young woman, taking a blood pressure reading. When she saw Carl, she quickly finished and left.

The old man was lying on his back. When Ray started to walk to the chair next to the bed, Carl's massive arm shot out and stopped him. A frail, shaking hand touched a switch, and the bed began to rise slowly. Suddenly, Ray was looking into the rheumy blue eyes of the notorious gangster, Tony "The Shotgun" O'Malley. He had an oxygen tube under his nose.

"So what brings the Twin Rivers chief of police here," he said, his voice surprisingly strong, considering the weak body it came from.

"I want to talk to you about your friend Alex Patton," Ray said, his voice shaking.

"That's what I understand," the old man said as he motioned towards the chair next to the bed.

Ray looked at Carl, who nodded. Ray sat down. There wasn't much left of the infamous gangster. His flesh hung where muscle once was.

"I knew Alex," Tony said. "We had some business dealings back in the sixties and seventies. He was a very talented man."

"I think he had something that didn't belong to him," Ray said, figuring there was no sense in gilding the lily at this point.

The constant beep of the heart monitor quickened momentarily and then returned to its previous rhythm.

"I think whatever it was Alex had you wanted it back, and you organized a little bank robbery in Calloway in '71 to get it," Ray said.

Again, the heart monitor's pace picked up before returning to normal.

The old man chuckled. "Carl, you want to turn that damn thing off," he said, flicking a finger towards the heart monitor. "I think the chief here is using it like a lie detector."

Ray smiled as Carl walked over and flipped the switch. The beeping stopped.

"My name is Ray," he said, extending his hand.

"Tony," the old man said, offering his hand, which was ice cold and covered with what appeared to be burn scars. "I'm an old man. I'm dying. Maybe today. Maybe tomorrow. But it won't be long now. I'm tired. But I'm wondering why you want to know about Alex now."

The old man coughed deeply. Carl took a couple of steps forward before Tony waved him back.

"Why are you looking into this, Ray? It was forty years ago," Tony said. He stopped and shook his head. "See what I mean? I'm slipping. I'd have never made that mistake a few years ago. I just admitted I know something about it, didn't I?"

"You did," Ray admitted. "They say confession is good for the soul."

Tony closed his eyes and lay motionless. Ray waited. After several minutes, Tony said quietly as he opened his eyes, "It's true. I hired Alex to do a job, which took him a number of years to accomplish. Then our relationship ended badly because he took a certain item from me, and I wanted it back."

"So you organized the bank robbery."

Tony nodded. "I hired a young thug named Bruce Franklin to pull it off. Franklin had worked for me for years. I told him what I wanted him to do, and he hired three associates to help him."

"That would be Joe Bailey, Andy Miller, and a fourth guy that was never identified," Ray said.

"I don't know who he hired," Tony said, leaning back with his eyes tightly closed.

He was obvious suffering a wave of tremendous pain. When the spasm passed, he looked back at Ray.

"If you've come to ask me who that fourth guy was, you're going to be disappointed. I never knew any of the names until after the arrests were made. Of course, that whole robbery went to shit, and a cop got killed. I pretty much decided I was out of it when that happened. It wasn't worth it, even considering what I was losing. But you never answered my question—why now? Why are you looking into this now?"

"Andy Miller was released from prison," Ray said.

From the surprised look on Tony's face, Ray knew he didn't know that.

"He was murdered less than twelve hours after he was released— shot dead through his living room window at 500 yards. He never even had a chance to unpack his bag. One of the locals that was a suspect in the original crime was framed for the murder, but he didn't do it. He couldn't have."

"Sounds like a professional hit," Tony said. Then his eyes lit up, and he smiled briefly. "Ah, so that's why you're here! It looked like a professional hit, and I'm a professional."

Ray nodded.

"Go ahead," Tony said. "Ask me the question you came to ask me."

"Did you have Andy Miller killed?" Ray said.

Tony chuckled, then fell into another coughing fit. Carl walked up beside the bed, pulled some tissues out of a box on the nightstand, and handed them to him.

"I wrote that Twin Rivers problem off a long time ago," Tony said weakly. "I lost a fortune on the deal, but I didn't kill this Andy guy, and I was questioned about the death of Alex Patton, too, years ago. One of the few times in my life I was ever questioned about something I didn't actually do."

"So this item of value that you were you trying to get back—was this property or information?" Ray asked.

Tony stared at him. Suddenly, Ray saw the gangster instead of the dying old man and wondered briefly if he hadn't gone too far. The intensity in the old man's eyes was chilling. Ray was aware that Carl was standing just over his shoulder. Ray was waiting for Carl to grab him and eject him from the room.

But Tony flicked a finger, and Carl stepped back to the door.

Ray's heart was thumping in his chest, and sweat ran down his face.

"I think if I hooked you up to my heart monitor right now, Ray, you'd short the damn thing out," Tony said with a chuckle.

"I don't want to wind up in Lake Michigan, wearing a pair of concrete shoes."

Tony chuckled again. "We don't do that anymore. It's been a long time since we've done anything like that. What's it been, Carl? Ten? Maybe fifteen years now since we dumped a guy in Lake Michigan?"

"Well," Carl said, thinking back, "there was that deal last year—"

"Oh, that doesn't count," Tony said. "That was a politician."

Carl smiled briefly. Ray saw the affection between the two men. They'd obviously been friends for decades. Ray guessed that Carl and the three gardeners he'd seen had been with Tony for a long time. He also wondered if Carl wasn't the thug Joyce had described who'd accompanied Tony to the Beer Chaser fifty years ago.

"I can't fault you for that," Ray said with a weak smile.

"Ray, you can relax. You'll leave this house alive. Right, Carl?" Tony said.

Carl shrugged.

"That's reassuring," Ray commented.

Tony smiled at Carl, and again, Ray noted the friendship between them.

"You'll leave alive, Ray," Tony said. "I won't. Next time I leave this house, I'll be in a hearse. But you seem like a decent guy, even if you're a cop, and you're trying to do the right thing. That's something I haven't done myself very often."

He was silent again as minutes ticked by.

Then he said, "You ask me any question you want. I'll either answer honestly, or I won't answer you at all. Either way, you're leaving here safely today."

Ray thought for a moment about how to ask the question, finally deciding that Tony was a man who appreciated bluntness.

"Like I asked before, what was the robbery about? Were you after property or information?"

"Kill him," Tony said to Carl.

Carl pulled a revolver as Ray rose suddenly to face him. There was a long moment as Ray waited for the bullet.

"Just kidding," Tony said.

Carl laughed, something Ray thought him incapable of, and holstered his gun.

"Sorry, Ray, just a little mob humor," Tony said.

"That wasn't funny," Ray said, settling back in the chair. "I'm not a young man anymore. I could've had a heart attack."

"I've had four," Tony said. "Suck it up, Ray."

"So I take it that's not a question you're going to answer," Ray said, pulling a hankie from his pocket and mopping his head.

Tony shrugged, then said, "You see that picture over there?"

Ray walked over to look at the painting of a naval battle between two tall ships, their sails full of wind.

"You know any history, Ray?" Tony asked. "That was a famous naval encounter."

Ray shook his head. It was a test he knew he couldn't pass.

"I don't know much about history."

"It doesn't matter," Tony said with a laugh. "There's a hinge on that picture, and behind it is the answer to your question."

Ray reached over and pulled the edge of the painting. It swung open like a cabinet door, revealing a wall safe with an electronic keypad on the front.

"Six digits, Ray," Tony said. "Three chances before the lock shuts down for twenty-four hours. I'm guessing you don't want to spend the night here so you can try again tomorrow."

"No, not really," Ray said.

"Your answer is in that safe," Tony said, "if you can open it."

Ray looked at it and then at Tony.

"If it's the date of the event in this painting, then I'm screwed," Ray said.

Ray looked at the keypad, then back at Tony lying on his death-bed—his face impassive. Suddenly, Ray knew exactly what the six digits were. Each time he touched the keypad, it beeped. When he pushed the last digit in, nothing happened at first, but seconds later, there was clunk as the lock released.

Tony was shocked. He'd thought there was no chance Ray could open the safe, even with three tries at it. Ray smiled as he pulled the safe handle down, and the door swung open.

"I don't know much about history," Ray said, "but I know the date of Pearl Harbor."

Tony looked down at the scars on his hands and arms. "Don't touch anything else in there, Ray," he said sharply, "but there's a velvet jeweler's bag on the top shelf. Bring it here."

Ray reached into the safe, pulled out the velvet bag, and held it up. Tony nodded.

Ray took the bag back to the edge of the bed and sat down.

"You know, Ray. You took a big risk coming here. You had to think there was a good chance you wouldn't leave this estate alive."

"It was worth it, if for no other reason than learning you didn't have Andy Miller killed, and you don't know who did. And I don't think you had Alex Patton killed either."

"A famous American once said, 'Those who will not risk, cannot win.' That's why I instantly liked you, Ray. You have a lot of guts coming here. And that's also why I like that painting?"

Tony pointed at it.

"During the American Revolution, that tiny ship, the *Bonhomme Richard*, went up against a much larger ship, the *Serapis*. The captain of the small ship was a Scotsman named John Paul Jones."

"I have not yet begun to fight," Ray said.

Tony smiled. "The British ship *Serapis* had blasted Jones' ship, *Bonhomme Richard*, to pieces. She was burning as fast as she was sinking. But instead of giving up, John Paul Jones turned his doomed ship into the wind and rammed the *Serapis*. It was a suicidal ploy—so insane and unexpected the British never saw it coming. John Paul Jones lost his ship in the end but not before he captured the *Serapis*. He sailed it home, becoming a legend in the process.

"You did that same thing today, Ray. The cop from the little town of Twin Rivers rolls through the gate to talk to me. I figured that you're either stupid or brave. You're not stupid. I sure didn't figure you'd get my damn safe open. Today you win."

Ray looked down at the velvet bag.

"The answer is in your hand," Tony said. "But before you open that, I want to tell you just one thing. I never meant for a cop to get killed. That wasn't supposed to happen. I'd really like to know who did that myself. I should've let my boys handle the robbery instead of leaving it to Bruce Franklin. Nobody should've been hurt."

Ray nodded.

"Open it," Tony said. "You may not know what it is, so I'll tell you."

Ray loosened the drawstrings, opened the mouth of the pouch, and slid the contents into his hand. At first, he thought it was a joke, but when he saw the grim look on O'Malley's face, he looked again, more carefully. Suddenly, he realized what he held in his hand.

"You've got to be kidding me?"

"It's no joke, Ray."

"My God," Ray said. "This is priceless."

Tony snorted. "Nothing is priceless. Everything has a price, Ray. In this case, however, the price is millions."

Chapter Twenty-Two

"You've done a good job on this story, Regan," Levi said, handing the notebook back to the blue- eyed girl,whose blonde hair was blowing in the spring breeze. "You're doing much better at explaining what's going on in your story now."

There were a dozen children between eight and ten sitting around two picnic tables under the oaks and elms beside the Garvey house. Mrs. B. was at the other table, reading stories and helping the kids.

"I added more to the story about the baby bird by making up another story about why the mother bird was late getting back to the nest," Regan said as she smiled brightly.

"That's what we were talking about last week, wasn't it?" Levi said.

The children around the table nodded.

"Sometimes a story has more than one story in it," a little boy named Justin said.

"And what do you have to do with those different stories?" Levi asked.

"You weave them together," Katelyn said, holding up her hands and meshing her fingers together, "so that the two little stories become one big story."

"When we watched *The Wizard of Oz* last week, we talked about how it was a lot of little stories, didn't we?"

"Dorothy had a story—she wanted to go home," Regan said.

Levi nodded.

"The scarecrow wanted a brain," Katelyn said.

"And the tin man wanted a heart," Justin added.

"And then there was the Wizard of Oz himself, and he had a story, too," Levi said.

"And there was the witch, and she had a story," added Katelyn.

"That's right. So the real story was a bunch of little stories woven together. After reading your stories, I think you all learned something last week. You're all doing really well," Levi said.

"What should we do this week?" Regan asked.

"Just keep working on adding more details to your story. Describe things that are happening in your story," Levi said. "Justin, why won't the werewolf in your story cross the river?"

Justin shrugged.

"I'll bet you can figure out a reason if you think about it, can't you?" Levi said.

Justin smiled.

"I think we're done now because here come the cookies," Levi said as Tori crossed the yard with a huge tray.

Mrs. B. grinned as the mob of children swarmed around Tori.

"You enjoy this," Mrs. B. said, walking up beside Levi.

"I actually look forward to it. Did you read Regan's story?"

"I did. She's going to be a good writer. But, of course, she's working so hard at it because she wants to impress you."

"Well, she's managed to do that. Excuse me for a minute," he said before walking towards the house.

Tori walked up to Mrs. B. "You know, Katelyn reminds me of Levi," Tori said.

"How's that?"

"Her troop had Girl Scout cookies left over. When she came to sell me some last week, I reminded her I'd already bought some from her. Then she reminded me that the Young Authors group was meeting here today. I bought ten more boxes."

Mrs. B. laughed. "Yes, I can see some Levi Garvey influence there. I saw that Levi has re-released his first three books in a boxed edition."

Tori laughed. "There's a new movie in the works, and Levi is selling his old cookies, too."

Tori glanced down at her phone and frowned.

"Is something wrong?" Mrs. B. asked.

"Probably not, but Ray Billings, the new police chief, said he'd drop by to meet the kids and their parents. Seems a little odd he didn't show up or call. That's out of character for Ray."

"Something probably came up," Mrs. B. remarked.

Suddenly, excited shrieks went up as five puppies plowed into the children's midst. Levi followed with Rosco at his heels.

"Are these your puppies, Mr. Garvey?" Regan asked, hugging one as it squirmed in her arms.

Levi nodded.

"Can I have one?" she said.

"You'll have to ask your mother," Levi said.

"Does he have a name?" she asked.

"That's a little girl. The boys are Roscos, and the girls are Roxannes," he said, glancing at Mrs. B. who looked back at him sternly. "But you can name her whatever you want."

Tori and Mrs. B. looked at each other. They both knew what he was doing. Levi was treading on shaky ground.

A huge Ford Expedition pulled into the drive. It was Regan's mother, one of Levi's least favorite people in Twin Rivers. The feeling was mutual. Christine White wobbled out of the huge vehicle on high heels, her cell phone in one hand and a cappuccino in the other. She was forty-three but trying to look twenty-five with her style of dress, her make-up and hair, and her impressive store-bought boobs. Tori had once commented that she suspected that Christine dyed her hair the same shade as her daughter's for added believability.

Regan ran up to her mother, holding out the puppy. Levi grinned as the phony smile Christine White always wore cracked into a look of horror. Her eyes were blazing as she glared across the yard at Levi Garvey.

Levi waved pleasantly at her.

Christine stormed towards him.

Tori leaned over and whispered, "Run, Levi, run!"

Mrs. B. laughed.

"What do you mean by telling Regan she can have a puppy?" Christine hissed.

"I didn't tell her that," Levi said innocently, "but they are free to a good home. I'll go ahead and let you have one anyway. If you don't want one, just go tell her."

Christine glanced back across the yard at her daughter, who was kissing and hugging the wiggling little dog, and sighed.

"They are so cute," Levi said.

"Are they housebroken?" Christine said, still glaring at Levi.

Tori shrugged. "They're getting there, but I'd leave them on linoleum for a while."

"We don't have linoleum," Christine said with a sneer.

"Well, then leave them on the Corinthian tile?" Levi suggested, trying to maintain a straight face.

Christine pointed at Levi with a purple acrylic nail that matched her dress perfectly.

"Not cool, Levi," she said.

Then turning quickly, she stormed across the yard. Regan cheered after her mother leaned down and spoke to her. She waved at Levi as she skipped to the Expedition with the puppy in her arms.

"You're a very bad man, Levi," Tori said.

It was something she said often.

"That's one down and four to go," Levi said as the Expedition backed out and a blue Chevy pick-up pulled in.

Justin ran across the yard with a puppy as his father, Jerry Davis, one of Levi's oldest friends since grade school, climbed out. It was Jerry, they'd discovered, who'd written the hilarious story about the Bikini Bandit for the *Twin Rivers Gazette*. Neither was surprised by the news.

"Oh, no," Levi said as Justin said something to his father and Jerry suddenly looked directly at him.

"Garvey!" he roared.

"I think I'll take your earlier advice," Levi said, turning suddenly and running towards the house.

Jerry raced across the yard to cut him off, but Levi was a little faster and cut around the side of the house. Jerry tripped over a bush, taking down a yard gnome as he fell. The children laughed hysterically as the two men chased each other around the house, through the carriage house, up the porch steps, and over the porch rail at the other end. They wound up chasing each other around the trees and the picnic tables where the children were.

They paused for a moment on either side of one of the picnic tables.

"We're getting too old for this," Levi said, holding up his hand as he breathed heavily and wiped sweat off his face.

"Well, then quit running, old man, and take what you've got coming," Jerry panted as they looked at each other across the picnic table.

Levi picked up a cookie and bounced it off Jerry's head. Jerry's eyes narrowed as he climbed over the picnic table. More cookies flew everywhere. The children laughed. The chase began again around the trees and picnic tables. Suddenly, Levi made a break for the carriage house with Jerry right behind him. Both disappeared inside. Then there was some loud banging and a few blood-curdling screams before it became dead quiet. The children exchanged looks.

"I think your dad got him," one of the boys said to Justin with wide eyes.

The sound of a motor starting came from the carriage house. Wearing a scuba mask, Levi came through the double doors on a golf cart with Rosco riding shotgun, his tongue hanging out. Waving a badminton racket, Jerry was in hot pursuit behind him on a riding lawn mower. The children shrieked with laughter.

"Now they're just putting on a show for the kids," Mrs. B. said with a chuckle.

"Those two are kids who never grew up. And it is a good show," Tori said, wiping tears from the corners of her eyes.

As Levi rolled by on the golf cart, he held up two fingers to Tori and then three. Tori knew the meaning—two puppies down and three to go.

Chapter Twenty-Three

RAY BILLINGS LOOKED DOWN AT THE COIN IN HIS HAND AND THEN into the sunken eyes of the old gangster.

"Where on earth did you get this?"

The old man's laugh turned into a coughing fit. Carl stepped towards him, but Tony waved him back.

"I found it," he said after he'd regained his breath.

"This is one of the rarest coins in the world," Ray said. "A 1933 $20 Double Eagle."

Tony smiled. "You know anything about the history of that coin?"

"Not much, other than a few have turned up over the years. I think I read that one sold for over seven million dollars."

"Let me tell you the story," Tony said. "In 1933, Franklin Roosevelt took the United States off the gold standard, so gold could no longer be used as currency. At that time, the United States Mint had already produced about 450,000 gold 1933 $20 Double Eagles to be released to banks that year. Roosevelt ordered them all to be melted down with the exception of two that were put into the National Numismatic Collection for posterity. As far as anybody knew, they were all gone, except for those two. But a few years later, one 1933 Double Eagle turned up and then another. It was pretty obvious that not all of those coins had been destroyed."

Looking down at the small coin again, Ray said, "Somebody at the United States Mint had swiped a few."

"Yes, probably a cashier at the Mint. Knowing they'd be worth a lot of money later, he stole a few before they were destroyed. He was very clever about it. It's likely he swapped them out for the earlier minted 1932 $20 Double Eagles just before the 1933 Double Eagles were destroyed. About twenty of those coins have turned up over the years, and every one, so far, has ties back to the same guy, a jeweler named Israel Swift."

"Is that where this one came from?" Ray asked.

"Probably, but I never learned the details about how it came into the possession of the Chicago Outfit," Tony said. "My father, Frankie O'Malley, worked for the Outfit during prohibition as one of Al Capone's most trusted lieutenants. When Capone went to prison in 1932, he left Frank Nitti in charge although the real power was with one of Nitti's underbosses, Paul Ricca. Like I said, I'm not sure how, but Ricca came into possession of that coin. He kept it in his headquarter's safe. Ricca began to suspect my father was skimming profits from some of the rackets they were running at the time. He was right. My father was ripping Ricca off. I think he was planning to make a run for it because he knew Ricca was onto him. It would be only a matter of time before he'd catch a bullet. My father stole that coin out of Ricca's safe, and he got caught shortly afterwards."

"That wasn't good," Ray said.

Tony shook his head. "My father vanished. It wasn't hard to figure out what had happened. I never learned the details, but Ricca never found his coin. That was in 1937."

"But you found it," Ray said.

Tony nodded. "It was years later, after I came home from World War II. I moved out of my family home into this one. I was working for Ricca, who was always good to me. He never held me responsible for what my father had done. He even paid for my college education. I think Ricca was sorry about leaving me without a father—you know, mob family values."

Tony paused for a moment. A single tear ran down his cheek, which he wiped away with a bruised, liver-spotted hand.

"Anyway, I was moving some old books from our old house on the north side into the library downstairs when one book caught my eye—*Dollars and Sense* by P. T. Barnum."

"The circus guy?" Ray asked.

"Yeah," Tony said. "It was a 'how to' book about getting ahead in the world. There are a lot of books like that now, but his was probably one of the first ones ever written. I sat down behind the desk in the library to look at it. When I opened it, guess what rolled out of the spine onto the desk blotter?"

"A priceless coin," Ray said, smiling.

Tony nodded. "I could almost see my father grinning at the irony as he hid that coin in a book entitled *Dollars and Sense*."

"What did you do when you found it?"

"I'm not stupid," Tony said. "I took it straight over to Paul Ricca. You should've seen the look on his face."

"And your career was made."

"There had never been a trust issue between us before that, but returning the coin certainly demonstrated I was not only honest but also faithful," Tony said. "That's when Ricca started to rely on me, and I climbed the ladder quickly."

"It's a good story, but what's all this got to do with the Calloway Bank heist?" Ray asked.

"Ah, yes," Tony said. "One of the things I did for Ricca was launder his ill-gotten gains. I worked with a lot of small businessmen, and one of my associates was running some of this dirty cash through his jewelry store."

"Alex Patton," Ray said.

Things were beginning to click together.

When Tony pointed up over his head, Ray leaned forward to look at the headboard. A bronze medallion was embedded in the center of the headboard.

"Alex was very talented," Tony remarked. "That's the O'Malley family crest that he made for me. I worked with Alex for years. When I visited Alex in his store, I saw these amazing art pieces he was creating in bronze, and I started getting this idea."

"I bet it had something to do with Ricca's coin," Ray said.

More of the pieces were falling into place.

Tony's eyes lit up, and a crooked smile crossed his face.

"When I mentioned it to Ricca, he gave me the original coin, which I took to Alex. I wasn't sure Alex could do it, and neither was he at first, but he sure was excited about trying. He went to work at once, but it was a great challenge. He started working when Eisenhower was in office and finally finished when old Tricky Dick was in office. He was well compensated as he worked all those years. We gave him a very generous cut of the money laundering, and he was promised a generous percentage of what we made on the counterfeit coins."

"Was he able to do it?" Ray asked.

Tony smiled. "The job wasn't easy. He had to not only reproduce the coin but also make it from some unique metals. Those coins were about ninety percent gold and ten percent copper alloy. What that copper alloy consisted of exactly and the exact percentage of gold to copper alloy was a well-guarded secret of the United States Mint. Ricca spent a small fortune just getting that information. And once Ricca had it, Alex had to create a perfect counterfeit die, meld the metal perfectly to get it to measure and weigh correctly so it could pass an expert's examination. Alex wasn't creating a copy. He was creating an exact duplicate in every way, including that coppery luster Double Eagles get over time because of the unique metal content. Once he mastered the coin and the metal, it took him a long time to figure out how to age the coins in order to match that honey-colored patina."

"But he finally did it," Ray said.

Tony nodded. "I had an expert numismatist checking his work. In the end, he created five duplicates so perfect my expert finally couldn't tell the original from the duplicates. If you're a collector shelling out millions for a rare coin, that coin is going to be put under tremendous scrutiny."

"I know what Alex did now," Ray said. "He didn't give you back the original, did he?"

"There was a tiny little scratch on the edge of that original coin,"

Tony said. "Alex had noticed it, of course. He gave me five perfect counterfeit coins and the one he said was the original, which had that little scratch on the edge. However, my expert had measured and photographed that original in stark detail before we ever gave it to Alex. After careful examination, the expert knew the coin Alex had returned as the original wasn't actually the original. He'd given me a counterfeit to which he'd added that tiny scratch. I didn't let on to Alex that I knew since he'd have hidden that original well—like my father had. So I let some time pass by. I figured once he thought he'd gotten away with the scam, he'd put the original in his safety deposit box for safe keeping."

"So you stole his safety deposit box and got it back," Ray said, holding up the coin. "It all makes sense now."

Tony shook his head. "Except that's not the original either."

Ray's face fell. "What do you mean?"

"I never recovered the original," Tony said.

Ray sat for a moment looking at the coin in his hand.

"The original is still out there?"

"It is," Tony said. "Ricca decided to let it go. We'd made one try, and Franklin was killed during the robbery. He was the only one who could've tied the robbery back to the Chicago Outfit. And we didn't exactly walk away empty-handed. Actually, at that point, Ricca didn't care about losing the original. He was happy to have perfect duplicates of the coin, each worth millions and one of which he gave to me," Tony said, nodding toward the coin in Ray's hand. "You could take that coin to the Smithsonian right now, and they'd never be able to prove it wasn't an original. In fact, I know there are two of Alex's coins that have passed the tests of the experts in museums today."

"So what's the rest of the story?" Ray asked.

"Ricca was an old man by then," Tony said. "In fact, he died not long after the robbery. I don't know what he did with those coins, other than the two that wound up in museums on display as originals. The others never turned up with the estate. I'm sure they're in private collections today—the owners completely unaware that the rare coin they shelled out millions for is a clever counterfeit."

"No idea what ever happened to the original?" Ray asked.

"I thought for awhile that fourth bank robber took it out of the safety deposit box and disappeared with it, but then Alex Patton wound up dead."

"And you knew his death wasn't a suicide?" Ray asked.

"I knew Alex," Tony said. "He didn't have the guts to kill himself."

"Did Bruce Franklin know what he was stealing?" Ray asked.

"Of course not," Tony said. "He thought it was a ledger he was after. His instructions were to simply deliver the entire box back to Ricca unopened."

"So that's the end of it," Ray said.

Tony shrugged. "Of course, I thought I knew who might have the original at one time."

"Did it have anything to do with a man named Ed Garvey?" Ray said.

Tony's eyes quickly flicked to Carl, whose face went hard.

"You thought Ed Garvey had the original," Ray said.

"It came out at Andy Miller's trial that Alex Patton had gone to see Ed Garvey after the robbery," Tony said. "I waited a few years, then sent four of my toughest thugs down to talk to him."

Ray chuckled and looked over at Carl. "And how did that work out for you, Carl?"

"Not that well, did it, Carl?"

"He broke my nose and two ribs," Carl growled, "and he dislocated my shoulder."

"And Carl was the lucky one," Tony said as he was seized by a brief coughing fit.

"We all wound up in the hospital," Carl said. "Vinnie was in a coma for two weeks. To this day, he has no memory of anything that happened before we met Ed Garvey."

"Did he beat you with a bat or something?" Ray asked.

"Tell him, Carl," Tony said.

"We jumped him on his front porch," Carl said. "He grabbed this, uh . . ."

"Broom," Tony said with a laugh. "He grabbed a broom."

"He beat all of you up with a broom," Ray said, suppressing a grin.

"Well, the broom part broke off over Vinnie's head," Carl said.

Ray couldn't help but laugh.

"It wasn't that funny at the time," Carl said, but a brief smile crossed his face. "I don't know where that dude learned to fight, but I'd never seen anything like it before or since. He was spooky fast. Two guys were down before I could even reach for my gun. I was on the ground before I knew what hit me. I never did get my hand on that gun. I'll bet that whole fight didn't last twenty seconds. After it was over, he looked down at us, just as calm as could be. He helped me and the other two up, and then he picked Vince up, carried him to the car, and shoved him into the back seat. After that, he helped us into the car and closed the doors, just like he was helping his elderly uncles go to a church meeting. We were so dazed, none of us got out again. I was the only one in good enough shape to drive. He leaned into my window and gave me directions to the nearest hospital. Then, before I started the car, he said if we ever came back, he wouldn't be nearly as friendly towards us."

"I did have Carl check up on Ed Garvey every so often for several years. Never let him get very close—I didn't want Garvey to beat Carl's ass with a floor mop or a feather duster," he said, chuckling.

Carl didn't find any humor in the remark.

"I'm convinced that Ed Garvey doesn't have that coin now," Tony said, "but I think he had it at one time—probably held it for Alex Patton."

Ray nodded in agreement. The cloth sack Joyce had mentioned was very similar to the jeweler's pouch he held in his hand.

"Ed's just a mechanic and tow-truck driver. I'm guessing Alex Patton got that coin back from Ed. I've thought for a long time that the fourth guy got that coin from Alex before he killed him and then disappeared, using the proceeds from selling it to live like a king. But that idea seems wrong now since there's only one person who would've wanted Andy Miller dead after he was released from prison."

"Our missing fourth bank robber," Ray said. "He never left."

Tony nodded and said, "He doesn't have the coin, or he'd be long gone. I'll tell you what I think now. I think Alex hid that coin, like my father did, where nobody is going to find it no matter how hard they look. Someday, it might roll out of the spine of a book or something. Who knows?"

"So unless Alex told the fourth bank robber about that coin, the robber still doesn't know what he robbed that bank for," Ray said.

"Right. But the murder of Andy Miller was never about the coin, Ray, since he never knew about it. He murdered Andy to protect his identity. Andy had either always known who he was or could've figured it out once he got home from prison. That's what scared our fourth bank robber. As far as the coin goes, I think if you burned down Alex Patton's house and sifted through the ashes, you'd find it. Otherwise, nobody is ever going to find it."

There was a long silence before Ray stood up.

"I want to thank you, Tony," Ray said.

"For not having you fitted for concrete shoes?" Tony said with a smile.

"That, too," he said, looking down at the old man.

"Anything else you want to know?" Tony asked.

"I'd sure be interested in what else is in that safe," Ray said with a chuckle.

"I don't think the world is ready for the secrets that are contained in there," Tony said with a weak smile. Ray could tell their conversation had taken a lot out of the old man. "You want to put that coin back in there?"

Ray looked down at his hand. He'd forgotten he was still holding the pouch. He walked over, placed it back on the shelf, and shut the door. A few seconds later, he heard the electronic bolt lock.

"Thanks again, Tony," Ray said as Carl opened the bedroom door.

"I'd be very interested to know who that fourth bank robber is,"

Tony said.

Ray paused. Suddenly, he realized that the fourth bank robber could know something about the Chicago men he was actually working for—he could've learned something during the planning of the robbery with Bruce Franklin. Tony O'Malley had a reputation for making witnesses disappear.

"You wouldn't take the law into your own hands now, would you?" Ray asked.

Tony waved his hand dismissively. "If you find out, he'll go to prison for the rest of his life. That's good enough for me. We won't be paying him any social calls since it's unlikely he knows anything that could hurt us. Plus, I'd be hard pressed to find any of my thugs who'd volunteer to go to Twin Rivers again anyway. Well, Vinnie might . . ."

"Only because Vinnie doesn't remember going the first time," Carl said with a chuckle.

"If I find out and you're still around, maybe I'll let you know," Ray said. "I'll have to think on that a little bit."

"I don't blame you," Tony said. "I've got a reputation—perhaps you've heard."

"That I have. Thanks for talking to me, Tony. I do think confession is good for the soul," he said as he followed Carl to the door. He paused and looked back at Tony O'Malley. "And thanks for letting me live."

"You haven't left yet, Ray," Tony said.

Carl snorted as he guided Ray out of the bedroom.

Chapter Twenty-Four

It was late afternoon when Levi swung Old Blue into Chief Craig's driveway and parked next to his Chevy Silverado. He pushed Rosco off his lap.

"You have your own window," he said, scolding the dog.

Rosco jumped out of the truck behind him. The garage door was up. Craig was unloading fishing poles from the back of his truck.

"Hey, Levi," Craig said, laying the poles on a bench in the garage and leaning down to pet Rosco.

Levi took off his Panama and wiped the sweat from his brow. It was unseasonably warm for the beginning of April.

"You talked to Ray today? He's missing in action."

"No, I've been out at the river junction since early," Craig said. "Hey, grab that cooler, would you?"

Levi walked over to the truck and pulled the cooler out. It was light. He heard empty cans sloshing around in what had probably been ice that morning.

"You in any shape to be driving," Levi said, holding up the cooler and shaking it.

"Well, unlike you Garveys," Craig said with a grin, "I don't drink. Never did. Those are pop cans."

Levi walked into the garage and set the cooler beside the workbench.

"Did you ask Ben if he knew where Ray went?" Craig said, opening the cooler and taking out a root beer. Levi reached in to help himself to the last one.

"Yeah," Levi said. "Ben said he was going out of town, but he'd be back by lunchtime. He didn't say where he was going. It's four, and he's still not back, and he's not answering his phone. Tori's worried. He was supposed to be over at the house earlier to meet the kids in the Young Authors program."

Craig shrugged. Leaning against the workbench, he opened his own can and took a long drink.

"I don't know. He never said anything to me about being gone today. Maybe he's looking for a house to rent."

"I'll bet you're right," Levi said as he looked around the garage.

He'd never been to Chief Craig's house before. The garage was typical for a three-car garage. Workbench. Lawnmower. Garden tools. But something on the workbench caught his eye.

"Hey, what's this?" Levi said, picking up the kind of cardboard tube posters are shipped in.

"I just got that," Craig said. "I've got to get it framed. If you're very careful, go ahead and have a look."

Levi slid what looked like a very old poster out of the tube, laid it on the workbench, and unrolled it carefully.

"Oh, that's very cool," Levi said.

It was antique theatre poster, probably from the 1920s. It featured a man in a top hat with red eyes and lightning bolts emanating from his fingertips.

"The Amazing Toscanini," Levi read off the poster. "You like magicians?"

"I sure do. I've been collecting for years," Craig said with a smile. "When I was a kid, that's what I wanted to do—be a great magician."

"Really?" Levi said, unable to picture Chief Craig as a kid—ever.

"It's true," Craig admitted. "When I was about five, I fell out of a tree and broke my leg in three places. I was in the hospital for six weeks in a body cast. This Shriner from Peoria came to the hospital to entertain the kids. They rolled me down to the cafeteria in my hospital bed so I could watch the show. Hospitals were a little different back then. Anyway, he did this magic show for us. I was hooked after that. That was more than sixty-five years ago. I still remember every trick he did, and I know how to do all of them now."

Craig dug into his pocket and pulled out a quarter. He held it up between his thumb and index finger. He waved his other hand, and in the blink of an eye, the coin was gone.

"Wow, that's good," Levi said.

With another wave of his hand, the coin was back.

Levi chuckled. "You never cease to amaze me."

"Now you know why I'm so fascinated by your little stunt," he said. "You did one of the best magic tricks I've ever seen—not once, but twice. And there isn't one single scrap of evidence about how you did it."

"Ah, the bikini on the statue."

"Exactly. You see, what I've learned from magic is that the trick seems impossible to those watching it," he said, holding up the quarter again. With a flick of his hand, it disappeared. "But for the person doing it, it's actually quite simple."

He turned his hand around. The quarter was wedged between his index and middle finger—invisible from the front.

Levi sighed. "Now you've ruined the trick for me, Chief. Aren't you afraid if you find out how the bikini got up there, it'll ruin the magic for you, too? Isn't it more fun not knowing?"

"I'm willing to take that chance. I won't tell Ben. Come on, Levi. How in the hell did you get up there?"

"I'll give you a hint," Levi said. "I didn't get up there."

"You did it from the ground?" Craig said.

Levi shrugged.

"You piss me off," Craig said, looking at him from under his heavy gray eyebrows.

"Did you say you collected?" Levi said, changing the subject.

"Wanna see?" Craig said, his dark scowl vanishing.

He cocked a thumb toward the corner of the garage. There was a concrete staircase going down towards a basement.

"Absolutely," Levi said, carefully rolling the antique poster up and easing it back into the tube.

Taking his poster tube, Chief Craig led Levi and Rosco to the staircase. At the bottom, he opened a door and flicked on a light that illuminated a beautifully finished full basement. Each of the four walls had posters of magicians, lit up with canister lights, as well as display cases filled with hundreds of magic artifacts. The back wall of the basement was dedicated to Harry Houdini. Levi spent a long time looking at the old posters and items in the display cases on the Houdini wall. Obviously, the Chief had been collecting most of his life.

"Houdini is your favorite," Levi said.

"How can you tell?" Craig said with a laugh. "He was one of the greatest."

One of the display cases was full of mostly Houdini event fliers and ticket stubs from performances, but one item caught Levi's attention.

"Those aren't . . ." Levi said, tapping on the glass.

"You've got a good eye. That's the best piece in my entire collection. Those are a pair of handcuffs that Houdini escaped from—they were actually on his wrists. He'd invite people to bring cuffs with them to his performances. As a member of the audience snapped the cuffs on him, he'd tell the audience about the reward he'd pay if he couldn't get out of them. And while he was talking about the reward, he'd get out of them and then hand them back to the disappointed guy who'd brought them—usually the local constable."

Levi laughed. "He was a great magician. And I think he was a Freemason, too."

Craig nodded. They stood looking at the posters for a few moments.

"Hey," Levi said suddenly. "Why don't you show me how to do that coin trick?"

Craig smiled as he walked to the center of the basement where a magician's table was set up. Craig spent the next hour showing Levi, unsuccessfully, how to tuck a quarter between two fingers. Levi dropped the coin over and over again. Levi didn't seem to possess hand-eye coordination.

"Well, just keep working on it," Craig said finally.

Levi's phone rang. It was Tori. After a brief conversation, he said, "Our missing chief of police has surfaced. Thanks for the tour, Chief Craig. This has been really fun."

"Well, feel free to come back if you want help learning that trick," Craig said. "Those kids from the library would love stuff like that. Just don't do that trick until you've got it down pat. If you screw it up, even little kids will know how you're doing it, and they'll never be fooled by it again."

"I'll work on it," Levi said. "Come on, Rosco. Let's go."

He'd gotten to the door when Craig called after him, "Just go ahead and keep that quarter."

Levi stopped and looked down at the quarter in his hand. He turned suddenly.

"What, this quarter?" he said with the quarter held between his thumb and index finger. He waved his other hand theatrically in front of it.

"Yeah, that's my quarter."

Craig knew what Levi was going to do before he did it. With a flick of his hand, the quarter suddenly vanished from Levi's hand. Smiling broadly, Chief Craig clapped. He was just about to congratulate Levi when the quarter rolled down Levi's arm and bounced across the floor.

Levi's face fell. "Your quarter is over there somewhere if you want it," he said glumly as he started up the stairs.

"Keep working on it, Levi! You'll get it," Craig shouted as Levi headed towards Old Blue with Rosco at his heels.

* * *

As they rolled Evelyn Miller into the back of the ambulance, one of the medics, Duane Washburn, walked over to where Stevie Miller was standing in the front yard.

"She's going to be fine, Stevie," he said. "I think she may have broken her hip. That's very common, and it's nothing life-threatening."

Stevie nodded but said nothing.

"You okay?" Duane asked. They'd known each other since grade school.

Stevie nodded slowly, but he still said nothing.

"You want to ride over to St. Anne's with us?"

Stevie shook his head.

"You call me if you need anything, okay?"

Stevie began walking up the driveway towards the house. As Duane watched him, he couldn't help but glance over at the bullet hole in the center of the picture window. He knew Stevie had been through a lot lately.

As the ambulance rolled out into the street, Stevie glanced down at his phone. He didn't know what to do. He was out of money. His mother's care had broken them financially. He'd sold off what securities they had, and piece by piece, the meager acreage his mother owned had also been sold. Dr. Jackson said his mother could live for years yet since, other than having Alzheimer's, she was physically in very good shape for her age. But Stevie couldn't leave her alone anymore, and he couldn't afford the in-home care anymore either. He had few choices left besides the county nursing home. The thought sickened him.

Maybe there's another option, he thought as he glanced down at the phone.

His brother Andy had been insanely drunk the night he was killed. He'd ranted and raved for hours about Ed Garvey after he'd returned from the Beer Chaser. He'd ranted about the bank robbery. He'd ranted about how unfair it was his life had turned out the way it had. But one interesting thing had come out during his brother's drunken rampage— the identity of the fourth bank robber. When Andy was murdered that same night, there was no doubt in Stevie's mind who'd killed his brother.

Stevie sat down on the bottom step of the staircase in the living room. He could still see the bloodstain on the carpet from his brother's murder. He glanced down again at the phone, steeling his resolve. Reaching into his pocket, he pulled out a scrap of paper on which he'd written down the number. Even then a vague plan had been forming in his mind. Now he needed for the plan to become reality. He punched the number into the phone and listened as it rang on the other end. When the voice he recognized answered, he nearly hung up.

But he didn't have much choice now if he wanted to keep a roof over his head.

"This is Stevie Miller," he said, his voice trembling slightly. "I thought I'd tell you that I know exactly who killed Andy. And I know what you did forty years ago, too. Andy told me all about it."

Stevie listened for a minute. Then a tight smile crossed his face as relief washed over him.

"Of course, I haven't told anybody else." He paused to listen, then added, "That sounds fine. You have nothing to worry about. We'll work it out when you get here."

Stevie shut off the phone and stood up. He walked into the kitchen to put on a pot of coffee. He was expecting company—somebody who just might be able to help him out of the financial mess he was in.

Chapter Twenty-Five

"THAT WAS REALLY STUPID, RAY," TORI SAID WHEN RAY FINISHED telling his story.

She was leaning against the porch post, stroking the head of a puppy, as the sun dipped below the horizon. Thunder rumbled in the distance, and a cold wind gusted through the trees as the darkness set in. A storm was coming.

"You're telling me," Ray said with a forced grin.

He finished his beer, set the can down on the porch rail, and reached into the cooler for another. Ray was still rattled from the experience.

Ed was sitting on the porch swing, stroking a sleeping puppy in his lap.

"So you actually drove right up to Tony "The Shotgun" O'Malley's door in your cruiser and questioned him."

Ray nodded.

"You dumbass," Ed said, shaking his head in disbelief.

Ray rubbed the stubble on his chin. It'd been a long day.

"So what do you think?" Levi asked.

He was sitting in one of the low Adirondack chairs that had originally been on his porch in Savannah. He picked up the last puppy from the porch deck and placed him in his lap. The puppy let out a long breath, rested his chin on Levi's knee, and closed his eyes. All three puppies were winding down as it got dark.

Ray sat down on the swing beside Ed, stretched out his legs, and rested them on the porch rail as they rocked back and forth.

"I was thinking about that on my way back. I don't think we're ever going to solve the murder of Andy Miller."

"You think it's over?" Tori said with obvious relief on her face.

Ed snagged a beer out of the cooler and cracked it with a hiss. "You think he came back to kill the last person alive who could identify him?" he said.

Ray nodded. "He's not going to hang around. And if you ever had that coin, and I think you did at one time, you don't have it anymore. I'm guessing you gave it back to Alex Patton at some point. He probably hid it somewhere nobody will ever find it, and besides that, nobody is looking for it anyway. You don't have it, and the bank robber most likely never knew it existed to begin with. "

"So it's over then," Ed said as lightning flashed up in the clouds in the distance. "It's going to rain like hell in a few minutes."

"Let it rain," Tori said. "I couldn't care less."

"They get the roof on the lodge today?" Levi asked.

She nodded. "They did."

Ray yawned.

"You should go to bed," Tori said. "You've had a big day."

"You're right," Ray said, standing and stretching. "That's exactly what I'm going to do."

A sudden bolt of lightning ripped across the sky over the Garvey house. The immediate explosion of thunder made them all jump.

"Holy shit," Levi said. "That was close!"

"I think I'll try to get home before the monsoon rain hits," Ed said as he handed the sleeping puppy to Tori. "I think these little guys are ready for bed, too."

Tori scooped up the other two puppies and took the wiggling armful into the house. The screen door clacked shut behind her.

Leaning over to scratch Rosco's ears, Ed said, "Let's start painting Pappy tomorrow."

"What color?"

Ed glanced into the foyer to make sure Tori was gone.

"We agreed on red, right?"

"We agreed on red if you're willing to take the blame for it," Levi reminded him. "Otherwise, you'd better get used to the idea of a purple Ford."

Ed laughed.

Ray leaned against the porch post as Ed turned to walk down the steps. Ray stopped him.

"You're not going to drive home with that open can of beer, are you?"

Sighing, Ed said, "I'll just take a few more sips and leave it here, Chief—"

"You hear that?" Levi said, holding up his hand.

Ed stopped half-way down the steps. They all froze for a moment. In the rising wind, they could faintly hear a siren.

"Fire truck," Ed said. "I hope the lightning hasn't set something on fire."

Suddenly, another crack made them jump, but it wasn't thunder. A huge sliver of the porch post splintered off inches from Ed's head.

"Get down!" Ed shouted as he dove off the steps behind the bushes in front of the porch.

Ray and Levi hit the porch floor, breathing hard and trying to see through the slats of the porch rail, where the shot had come from.

"What was that?" Tori said from inside the house.

"Don't come out. Call 911," Levi snapped.

"Could you tell where the shot came from?" Ray said.

"Directly across the road," Ed answered from somewhere below them.

"You hit?" Levi asked.

"I don't think so," Ed called back, "but either the ground is wet down here, or I pissed my pants."

"I can't get through to the police," Tori called out after a minute. "No cell signal. Probably because of the storm coming."

Ed stood up and brushed himself off. "Oh good, I landed on my beer," he said, looking down at the wet spot on his thigh.

"Get down, you idiot," Levi said angrily.

"Relax. He's gone. He missed, and he's not going to hang around,"

Ed said.

"You sure?"

"I'll tell you in a minute," Ed said as he climbed up the porch steps and looked at the damage the bullet had done to the porch post.

"When he shoots you, you mean?" Ray said.

"Exactly," Ed said, holding out his arms and turning around in a circle. "See, it's perfectly safe now."

Ray climbed to his feet and joined Ed. They both examined the hole in the post.

"That was close," Ed said, reaching up and touching the top of his ear. He had blood on his fingertip. "The bullet nicked my ear."

"You've got a splinter from the post in the back of your neck, too," Levi said.

It was small and not deep. When he pulled it out, Ed winced.

"What the hell is going on?" Ray said.

"I'll tell you," Ed said. "We were wrong. This thing ain't over yet. Come on, Ray."

"Where are we going?"

"We're going to find where he fired that rifle from before the rain comes along and washes everything away, and I got a good idea where to look," he said, pointing across the road from the Garvey house.

In the flicker of lightning, Ray saw an old corncrib in the center of the field.

"I'm coming, too," Levi said.

"No, you're not," Ed said. "You stay here with Tori and keep trying to get the police over here."

* * *

CHIEF CRAIG ROUNDED THE CORNER IN HIS CHEVY AND PARKED behind Deputy Walker's cruiser. There were half a dozen fire trucks parked in front of the Miller house. The entire street was bathed in flashing red, white, and blue lights. The house was fully engulfed in flames. Deputy Ben Walker was taking statements from the neighbors.

As Craig walked to the pump truck, he knew there wasn't much the fire department could do to stop the fire. The fire department's efforts were instead focused on wetting down the shingles and siding on the houses on either side and the ends of the Miller house. Even from the street, the heat from the fire was intense. He saw the fire chief hollering instructions at the firefighters.

"Jack!" Craig shouted over the roar of the fire and the pump trucks.

Jack looked over at Craig, gave a few more orders, and then walked up to him.

"What have we got?" Craig asked. "Lightning?"

"I don't think so," he said, wiping sweat off his face and leaving a long black soot smear. "The fire is just breaking through the roof now. It started inside the house. There's no saving it."

As Craig looked up at the house, he noticed the bullet hole still in the front window. A few seconds later, the front window exploded out, and flames licked up the front of the house.

"Where's Stevie Miller?" Craig asked.

Jack shrugged. "I hope he's at work."

"Oh, no," Craig said. "What about Stevie's mom? Evelyn?"

Jack smiled. "She wasn't here. She fell and broke her hip this afternoon. She's safe at St. Anne's Hospital."

Craig sighed.

"I gotta go," Jack said. "This house is going to burn to the ground. I only hope when it goes, it collapses down and doesn't fall over."

Craig knew what he meant. The Miller house was on the last street in Twin Rivers, so there were fields across the road, but the houses on either side were very close. That's why the firefighters were focusing their hoses on the neighbors' houses and the ends of the Miller house. They wanted the center of the Miller house to burn first, encouraging the house to collapse in on itself.

"Chief!" Ben yelled, running up to Craig, his cell phone in his hand. "I just got a call. Shots fired at the Garvey house!"

They both ran to their cars.

* * *

THE THUNDER ROLLED AND LIGHTNING STREAKED ACROSS THE SKY as Ray and Ed walked up the grassy lane. The corncrib loomed in front of them. As they reached it, Ed shined his flashlight across the front of it.

"There it is," Ed said.

Leaning against the corncrib was Ed's rifle.

Ed handed the flashlight to Ray and glanced back towards the Garvey house as if he were trying to get his bearings.

"He'd have fired from the ground like last time, right around in this area," he said. "See if you can find the spot."

Ed walked over to the corncrib and reached for the rifle.

"Don't touch it," Ray shouted.

"In about five minutes, it's going to rain so hard no evidence is going to be left on it," Ed said, picking up the rifle. "And our killer isn't stupid enough to leave anything on it anyway. We've got to move fast. Find that spot, Ray."

Ray began scanning the ground with Ed's flashlight. Within seconds, he saw the spot where the dry grass was matted down.

"I got it!"

Ed walked over, snapped out the bi-pod, and set the rifle up on the ground where the marks from the bi-pod were left. "Give me the light," he said.

Ray handed him the flashlight, and Ed knelt on the ground and examined the scope carefully. Then he chuckled.

"What?"

"Lay down on the ground like you're the shooter and look through the scope," Ed said.

Ray looked at him for a moment, then did as Ed said.

"You see the house?" Ed said as a couple of large, cold drops of rain splattered down. "Hurry, Ray."

The house was brightly lit from the lights on the porch and the light coming from the windows.

"Yeah, I see the house," Ray said.

"Line that scope up with the bullet hole in the porch post," Ed said.

"What are we doing?" Ray asked.

"Whoever fired this rifle doesn't know anything about rifles," Ed said. "The scope is still set exactly the same way it was when I last fired it at about 400 yards on a windless morning."

"I'm not following you, Ed."

"Bullets don't travel in a straight line for very far. At different ranges, you use the scope to adjust the aim up and down. You're basically lobbing the bullet into the target. The wind will push the bullet, too, so when it's windy, you have to adjust for that by adjusting the scope into the wind."

"I knew that," Ray said.

"Well, this guy either didn't know that, or he wasn't familiar enough with the scope to adjust it, so he just used it as I'd left it set. I suspected as much at the Miller house."

Ray nodded. "That's right. Andy Miller was hit in the throat, but the shooter was another hundred yards out from where you'd set the scope."

"So the shooter was actually aiming at his head," Ed remarked, "but because he was further out than the scope was set, the bullet dropped ten or twelve inches further down and caught Andy in the throat. The shooter lucked out. If it'd been windy, he'd have missed Andy by a mile."

"And I'd guess we're a little further out from that here," Ray said.

"I'd say 550 yards," Ed said, holding his thumb up to the house. "And it's windy." Ed picked up some grass from the ground and tossed it in the air, watching it with his flashlight. "I'd say about 20 miles per hour wind, but it's gusting. I'll have to guess on that."

"So what are we doing?" Ray said.

"We're going to back into that shot," Ed said, "to find out what the shooter was actually aiming at with that scope set wrong. It's not real scientific because we don't know the exact range and wind speed, but I think it'll give us a good idea."

"How will we do that? It's dark as pitch."

"You can see the porch through the scope, and I can adjust the scope with the flashlight. We don't have very long before that rain hits."

Ray nodded.

"We know where the bullet hit," Ed said. "So I'm going to have you aim at that bullet hole with the scope set wrong. Then I'm going to have you close your eyes while I adjust the scope correctly for distance and wind. When you look through the scope, you should be looking at what the shooter was looking at when he pulled the trigger."

Ray nodded. "Let's do it," he said looking through the scope.

"Are you on sight?" Ed asked.

Ray aimed on the bullet hole. "I'm on it."

"Now, hold the rifle as steady as you can. When you've got it held steady, close your eyes while I fix the scope," Ed said. "Tell me when you're ready."

Ray looked through the scope again, held the rifle steady, and closed his eyes.

"Ready," he said.

Ed reached over and gently adjusted the scope for the proper range and wind speed.

"Okay, Ray," Ed said, "open your eyes and tell me what you're looking at."

When Ray opened his eyes, he couldn't believe what he was looking at through the scope. After a few moments, he sat up on the ground and let the rifle rest on its butt. He frowned as he shook his head slowly.

"You knew, didn't you?" he said.

Ed nodded.

"He wasn't shooting at you," Ray said. "He was shooting at me."

"I know this rifle pretty well," Ed said, climbing to his feet.

He reached down, picked up the rifle, and snapped the bi-pod down.

"Our killer is still out there, Ray, and I'm not the target. You are."

Chapter Twenty-Six

"So it was an arson," Ed said to Ray, who was sitting on the other side of the booth.

Ray nodded and sipped his coffee. He smelled strongly of wood smoke. He'd gone to the scene of the fire after leaving the Garveys. The Miller house had burned to the ground.

"They find Stevie?" Ed asked.

Ray sighed and slowly nodded. "Badly burned with a bullet hole in his skull."

"You okay?"

"Since I took this badge two days ago, I've got on my hands two murders and the attempted murder of me, no less," Ray said as he glanced at Ed uncomfortably.

"Never been shot at before, huh?" Ed said.

Ray shook his head.

Ed chuckled. "You get used to it."

Ray looked back at him blankly. He didn't see the humor.

"Obviously, you've gotten used to it—the way you stood up last night and did that little twirl after he took the shot at me."

Ed chuckled again. "I knew he had only two rounds, Ray, the two he took from the back of my gun cabinet when he stole the rifle. There's no way he would've bought another box of shells for that .308. You've got to show your I.D. to buy ammunition in Illinois. There would've been a record. And I knew he wasn't familiar with that rifle because if he had been, he wouldn't have shot Andy in the throat—he sure didn't own a .308 himself. I knew there wasn't going to be a third shot."

"I'll bet you never explain that to Levi," Ray said. "You'd probably prefer he always believes his uncle is just an incredibly brave man."

Ed laughed. "If it makes you feel any better, he missed you by a mile and nearly got me," Ed said as he pointed to the wound on the top of his ear.

A small glimmer of a smile appeared on Ray's face. "You know, that does make me feel better," he said. "I hope you're with me next time he takes a shot at me."

Ed laughed again.

"What's your gut telling you about this, Ed?" Ray said.

He hadn't known Ed long, but he knew him well enough to trust his judgment. Ed shook his head as April came by to refill his coffee cup.

"I'm not positive about this," he said, "but it fits. I think Tony O'Malley lied to you. I think he sent one of his goons down here to plan that robbery, probably one of his four most trusted lieutenants—those four who came down here to rough me up some years after the robbery and who wound up in the ER. Tony's men were called The Four Horsemen back then."

"As long as Andy Miller was safety tucked away in prison—" Ray started to say.

"Tony wasn't very concerned about him," Ed said, finishing the thought. "But when they learned he was being released, Tony was afraid Andy just might stir things up and get people thinking about that bank robbery again."

"So it was a professional hit," Ray said with a nod.

"Yup."

"And then I went up there asking questions," Ray said, shaking his head.

"That Horseman was probably in Twin Rivers for awhile setting up the robbery," Ed said. "Stevie could've seen him. He was about ten years old at the time."

"So Tony had one of his goons follow me home yesterday. He killed Stevie and then tried to kill me."

Ed nodded. "That's what I think. But I've got a little problem with the timing. I can't believe Tony sent more than one Horseman down to kill Stevie and then you. But our Horseman couldn't have been in two places at once. Somebody killed Stevie and set his house on fire. Then he went to the corncrib, set up, and took a shot at you in a very short amount of time. That doesn't make sense unless we're dealing with two Horsemen."

"I thought the same thing. It seemed that way," Ray said, "but the fire chief told me something interesting. The murder of Stevie Miller most likely happened much earlier—it could've been hours earlier. The killer set that fire inside a closed house, and it could've smoldered a long time, starved for oxygen. The neighbor noticed the glow from inside the house after it started getting dark and called the fire department. Then he went over to see if anybody was in the house. Of course, he didn't know any better, but he made a big mistake. He opened the kitchen door."

"And gave the fire a big breath of fresh air," Ed remarked.

"By the time the fire department got there ten minutes later, the whole interior of the house was a burning inferno, and it wasn't long after they got there that the fire broke through the roof."

"So our killer was set up at the corncrib for some time, just waiting for the perfect shot at you," Ed said.

"He'll be back to finish the job," Ray said, swallowing hard.

"Not likely."

After looking at Ed for a long moment, Ray leaned back in the booth.

"Why do you think that?"

"Stevie was the last possible witness," Ed said. "The gunman meant to murder you, but instead he managed to send you a powerful message."

Ray nodded. "Message received. Being shot at makes a person think. But what about that coin? I know all about the robbery."

"First of all, you could never make that case, Ray," Ed said. "Tony knows that, and that's why he told you. You have no evidence that coin ever existed and not one scrap of evidence to tie him to it. And if you try, you know the killer will come back."

Ray nodded. He knew Ed was right.

"I got Stevie killed," he said quietly.

"No, Andy got Stevie killed by coming back here," Ed said. "Andy knew who he was working with."

"What do I do now?" Ray asked.

"You have to decide that," Ed said, "but know one thing. If you decide to go after Tony O'Malley, you'd better remember that not one witness has ever testified against him. Witnesses against the Chicago Outfit have a strange way of coming up missing."

"He won't be alive in another month," Ray said. "If I start digging into this, I could put a lot more people at risk. I nearly got you shot last night. Even if I could make the case, Tony will be dead before the case ever sees the inside of a courtroom."

Ed nodded. "Your case would die with Tony O'Malley, but your problem won't. If you open this up, you'll be going up against the whole Chicago Outfit whether Tony is alive or not. They'll hunt you down, Ray. The mob would turn Twin Rivers into Normandy Beach."

"I've already put a lot of people at risk. Levi could've been hit last night, too."

"What are you going to do, Ray?"

"I'm going to investigate two murders and an attempted murder," Ray said. "Then if I find anything concrete linking them back to Tony O'Malley, I'll do what I have to do—that's my job."

"You won't find anything."

"I know I won't," Ray said. "They're professionals. There hasn't been any evidence so far, and there won't be any at Stevie's house or the corn crib either. That's what really bothers me. I know the truth, but I just can't prove it. And if I push too hard on it, there's a good chance the body count will rise."

Ed looked at him and smiled. "You did do one good thing, Ray."

"What's that?"

"I now know why my friend Jim Mathis was killed," Ed said, "and

I know who did it. That's what I really wanted to know."

Ray knew Ed was trying to console him, but it didn't make the fact he was giving up any easier to accept. There wouldn't be a scrap of evidence, but he wondered how hard he'd pursue it if there were—with innocent lives at risk.

* * *

LEVI WAS SITTING AT THE TABLE IN THE KITCHEN NOOK WITH THE morning light streaming in through the windows. He was sipping coffee as he looked down at photos in an old family album. He rarely looked at the album since it was full of pictures from his childhood— not that he hadn't been happy growing up in the Garvey house with his Grandma Lucille. But at the same time, it was hard to look at the pictures because so few of them in the pages and pages of the album included his parents. Even before they left for good, they hadn't been a part of his life. It wasn't easy to grow up, knowing he was a mistake.

There was a picture of him going to school on his first day—he and his Grandma Lucille standing beside the school bus in front of the house. There was a picture of him and Uncle Ed on the porch swing, back when Uncle Ed looked a lot like Levi did now with his blonde hair and blue eyes. Levi was holding up his science fair award, and Uncle Ed had a can of Schlitz in his hand.

Levi smiled. At least the beer has gotten better over time, he thought.

Levi finally found the picture he was looking for—his fourth birth-day Wearing striped pants and a shirt with a collar so wide it looked like it was borrowed from the wardrobe of *The Brady Bunch*, he was standing in the driveway in front of the carriage house beside his new red bicycle. There were also several pictures of him riding up and down the driveway on his new bike. One, in particular, made him smile. He was lying in the driveway with the bike on top of him. It wasn't easy to flip a bike with training wheels, but he'd managed it. There was a blur at the edge of the photograph—Grandma Lucille rushing over to help him after his crash as Uncle Ed, no doubt, laughed and snapped the picture.

He remembered that entire day clearly. There was a party later. His friends from Sunday school came. Later many of those early friends became his friends in grade school. By high school, they were members of the Zoo Crew—Jerry, Jim, Tammy, Robin, John, and Vince.

There were pictures from the party, too. He was opening his gifts at a picnic table beside the house. In one picture, Uncle Ed could be seen off to the side tying Doug Malone's shoe. In another, Levi and Alan Haig were squirting each other with the water guns Uncle Ed had gotten him for his birthday. Uncle Ed often bought him the gifts he wanted but that his grandmother disapproved of.

But the photos chilled Levi in another way. Who would've dreamed back then that nearly forty years later, Uncle Ed would kill Doug Malone at Kingery Pond, and Levi would kill Alan Haig inside this same house where he and Tori now lived.

Levi shook off those thoughts. He was trying to recall something as he stared at the picture of himself as a four-year-old boy with his new bicycle. As clearly as he remembered his birthday, the day before was a jumble of disjointed memories—some of which had come back.

He remembered sitting on the counter at the bank, looking at Miss Darby as she counted out his grandma's money. He remembered looking at the suckers on the counter and hoping she wouldn't forget. He remembered seeing how afraid she looked suddenly and hearing somebody scream.

He remembered his grandmother grabbing him off the counter. He remembered hearing feet running across the floor, a loud voice and an explosion, followed by white powder and pieces of wood falling around him. He remembered squirming because he couldn't breathe—his grandma was holding him so tightly.

Then the memories fell apart—like a dream so vivid and clear upon waking but that, within minutes, is lost except for a few fleeting pictures.

"Levi, what are you doing?"

Levi jumped. He hadn't heard Tori come into the kitchen. She'd left for the lodge earlier that morning. Now she was covered in plaster dust, holding a pair of heavy leather gloves and wearing his grandma's old Cubs baseball hat. She tossed the gloves onto the counter in a puff of dust, scooped one of the puppies up off the kitchen floor, and kissed his head.

"Embarking on a useless exercise," he said, pushing the album away.

Tori sat down across from him and opened the album.

"Oh, look at that cute little blonde boy," she said.

"I'm still kinda cute, don't you think?"

"Not really."

"What?"

"Now you're ruggedly handsome," Tori said, grinning.

"You know that sarcasm is considered the lowest form of humor," Levi said.

"Well, you should know. You're the master," she said, turning pages in the album.

She stopped suddenly. "You're trying to remember the robbery, aren't you? What happened the day before your fourth birthday. Right?"

Levi nodded.

"Remember anything?"

Levi shook his head. "Nothing useful. I remember what happened right before the robbery, and I remember the robbers entering. I remember some kind of explosion, I think. I just can't get a clear picture. But there's something nagging me around the edges—something I should be able to remember. I just can't put my finger on it."

Tori nodded. "I was there that day. I've been trying to remember what happened, too."

"You were in the bank?"

"No, I was up on Main Street. Dad and I were waiting for my mom to come out of the pharmacy. I think she was getting a prescription filled. She was already sick. It wasn't long before . . ."

Tori didn't finish the sentence. Her mother hadn't been sick very long before she died.

"Anyway, I was coloring in the backseat when this car banged into us," Tori said. "That's probably the only reason I remember it. We got hit by the getaway car. I remember Dad talking to the cops afterwards while I cried and cried even though I wasn't hurt."

"Isn't that odd?" Levi remarked.

"What?"

"We wouldn't meet for another six or seven years, but we traveled in the same circles."

Tori chuckled. "Sad really. Had we met when we were four, we could've been married by the time we were in second or third grade."

"Oh, shut up," he said. "You know what I mean. And if we'd met then, we probably would've been divorced by fifth grade."

Tori laughed.

"So what do you remember? Levi asked.

"I remember that car hitting us and then looking out the window. I didn't cry until later."

"What did you see?" Levi said, looking at her intently.

"I don't remember very much. It's just bits and pieces really."

"Like what?"

"After they hit us, they sat there for a second," Tori said, thinking back. "I could hear them shouting at each other. The windows in their car were down—ours, too. That's about it. Then they pulled away. Oh, and I remember they clipped another car before they went around the corner."

Levi sighed, pulled the album back towards him, and turned it around so he could see it.

"But you know what's weird, Levi?"

"No, what?"

"I was a shy kid, but I do remember waving at them," Tori said. "I've been thinking about that. Why would I wave? I was that little girl who'd hide behind my dad's legs whenever somebody would look at me. It took me a long time to warm up to new people."

"You think you knew somebody in that car?"

Tori shrugged. "I've been trying to remember the men, but I think their faces are gone now. I just remember waving."

"There's something about it that bugs me, too," Levi said. "Maybe I'm mixing things up, but it seems like Grandma left me alone in the bank—in an office."

"Why would Lucille do that?"

"She wouldn't," Levi said. "I can't believe she would've done that as scared as I was, but that's what I seem to remember—sitting at a desk with a Dr. Seuss book, the one with Thing One and Thing Two."

"That was *Cat in the Hat*," Tori said.

"I also remember the whole bowl of suckers that Miss Darby had at her checkout window was sitting on the desk in front of me, but I wasn't interested in them either. I was crying."

Tori looked at Levi with the same look on her face as he had. Sometimes it was spooky, trying to remember that far back.

"We're mixing things up," she said.

Levi nodded. "It's possible. We were four. I remember a lot of things that never happened. I distinctly remember Herbie the Love Bug being in our carriage house once when I was in kindergarten."

"I saw one of those gorillas from *Planet of the Apes* looking in my bedroom window one time," Tori admitted. "Is it just me, or do kids go through a period when their imaginations take off, and they have a tough time distinguishing between make-believe and reality?"

"And they don't understand about dreams either," Levi said. "I've been trying to remember, and the memories I have are from a four-year-old brain and how I understood the world then. That's been my frustration. How do you untangle that?"

"When was the last time you were at the First National Bank of Calloway?"

"Not sure I've been there since the robbery. Grandma kept banking there, but she never took me with her after that. When she'd go to Calloway, she'd leave me with Uncle Ed. Sometimes she'd even drop me off at the Beer Chaser if he was there. Uncle Ed would push a barstool up to the pinball machine—he'd supply the quarters, and Joyce would supply the root beer and M&M's."

"So that's where your love of root beer and peanut M&M's came from," Tori said with a smirk.

"And later Pac-Man, then pool," Levi said. "But I'm sure I haven't been in that bank since the day of the robbery."

"Well, as the bank's former president, I can tell you it hasn't been remodeled since it was built in 1942," Tori said. "It's the same exact bank it's always been."

"Maybe I'll take a little drive later," Levi said.

Chapter Twenty-Seven

"What are you doin', Chief Craig?" Ray said as he walked into the chief's office.

Craig had a box on the desk, and all the desk drawers were open. He looked surprised to see Ray.

"I'm going to get out of your hair," he said, putting a coffee mug that said "To Protect and Serve" into the box.

Ray sat down in the chair across from the desk. He knew better than to say anything. He took off his hat and glanced across the small office at the coat stand behind the door. He looked down at his hat, then back at the coat stand.

Craig knew what he was thinking and shook his head.

"No way."

Ray tossed the hat like a frisbee towards the rack. It bounced badly and landed upside-down on the floor next to Craig, who laughed as he leaned over to pick up the hat.

"I'll get it, eventually," Ray said.

The remark had a double meaning, and he knew from the look on Chief Craig's face that he'd gotten it. They weren't talking about a hat. They were talking about a job.

As far as the hat went, Ray had already heard the story about Chief Craig, who could hit that coat rack with his hat from anywhere in the office every time. Craig walked over behind Ray's chair and tossed the hat. It landed neatly on the hat rack.

"It's not that hard, Ray. Like anything else, it just takes a little time, a little trial and error, and a lot of practice."

Craig walked back to the desk and packed a coffee maker into the box.

"You got a receipt for that coffee maker?" Ray asked.

Craig smiled. "I'm taking the light bulbs, too."

Ray chuckled, then asked, "What's going on?"

"I've seen the writing on the wall. It's time to go. I seem to be three steps behind you. A few days into the job, and you're breaking new leads in a case that's been sitting cold on the floor of this office for decades," he said, waving a hand at a pile of cardboard file boxes along the wall. "They were sitting there when I retired the first time. Malone never touched them, and they're still sitting there now."

"Are those copies of the robbery files?" Ray asked.

Craig nodded. "All of them. Useless to me but probably useful to you. I'll leave them."

"You're being too hard on yourself," Ray said.

"No, I'm being honest with myself. I knew when I took this job back, I was past my prime. I'm a little slower than I used to be. I'm a little less willing to wade into a conflict. I don't know when it happened, but I got old. I realized it the other night at the Beer Chaser when Andy came busting in."

Ray tried to maintain his eye contact and tried not to let his face betray what he really thought, but he remembered Chief Craig cowering by the jukebox, far from the melee that night. Something on Ray's face must've betrayed him because Chief Craig sighed and looked down.

"I chickened out," he said. "You saw it. All of you acted like you didn't, but you did. You, Ben, and Levi jumped up and went after Andy. I backed myself into a corner and let you younger guys handle it. Hell, Tori was ready to jump in, too."

Ray didn't know what to say.

Craig sat down hard in his desk chair.

"What's been bothering me is what might've happened if I'd been there alone and that had happened."

"Chief—"

"No, it's okay," Craig said. "I know what would've happened. I would've pulled my weapon on him. I wouldn't have wrestled him like you guys did since I am past being able to do that physical stuff anymore. He wouldn't have complied, and I would've shot him. I wouldn't have killed him, but I would've shot him for sure."

"You'd have been justified to do so," Ray said.

"Only because I'm old. I have to lean more on the gun than on muscle. Aging is a part of life, and you'll get there, too. You'll realize one day it's time for you to go. I've taken my licks over the years and delivered a few as well, but it's my time to go, Ray."

"I was hoping you were going to stick around a while. I've made a big mess of things. I've put my friends at risk. Actually, I came over here to ask you a favor."

"What's that?" Craig asked.

"I need to get out of the Garvey house," Ray said. "I got shot at last night because of my own stupidity. Even worse, Levi or Tori could've been injured—or Ed. I need to go house hunting, and I was hoping you'd watch things today while I find some place to live."

Craig smiled. "I know of a nice three-bedroom, just a couple blocks away, that'll be going up on the market soon."

"Reasonable?"

"We'll talk it over," Craig said. "It's mine. I've got a house on Olton Lake I've owned for a long time, and I've been remodeling it for the last ten years. I bought it when retirement seemed like it was a hundred years away, but I've arrived, and the house I spent so many hours dreaming about in my cruiser is ready for me to live in. I'm moving as fast as I can get all my crap packed up. I can sell or rent my Twin Rivers house to you. If you don't mind a few house rules until I'm gone, you can move into the guest room as soon as you want."

Ray was stunned by what seemed to be incredibly good luck. He'd been dreading the hunt for a place to live. All he could think of to say was, "Is there room for a pool table?"

"The basement is finished and carpeted, 1,200 square feet with a high ceiling. You could put in a pool hall with a full bar down there if you wanted."

"When can I look at it?" Ray asked.

Craig snapped the lid on his box. "Why don't you come over after lunch. I'm going to take a truckload over to Olton Lake now, but I should be back in a couple of hours. It's 903 Ash Street."

"I'll call you before I come over," Ray said.

Craig picked up his box.

"Hey, aren't you going to take all the stuff hanging on the wall behind your desk?"

"Not mine," he said. "That stuff belonged to Chief Malone."

Ray walked over to look at the collection of photos and certificates. Most of the pictures were of the Twin Rivers football team. There was a commendation when he was a deputy in Calloway. It was a pretty thin collection, considering he'd been chief of police in Twin Rivers for nearly twenty years.

"He framed his high school diploma," Ray said.

Craig nodded. "I don't even know where mine is. Framed his baptism certificate, too, from when he was eight years old."

"It's sad," Ray said, looking over a few framed certificates.

Craig watched him, waiting for him to see it. Finally, Ray put a finger on the glass of a small picture on the edge of the collection. It was a black and white photo of two boys sitting on porch steps, each with a bottle of Pepsi in one hand and an arm around a German shepherd that was sitting between them.

"I know him."

"That's your friend Levi Garvey and his friend Doug Malone, sitting on the steps of the Garvey porch. And that dog is the very first Rosco. They were about ten years old in that photo. They'd been best friends since kindergarten. You wouldn't believe how much trouble those two got into." Cliff laughed as he thought back. "Those two climbed clear to the top of the radio tower in 1976—three hundred feet in the air. When they finally looked down and realized how far up they were, they froze. We had every cop car, every fire truck, and every ambulance in the county at the tower. The kids looked like dots up there. There was only one way to rescue them. Somebody had to go up and get them."

"Was that you by any chance?"

Craig nodded. "I climbed that tower twice that day. I brought them down one at a time, one rung at a time. I got over my fear of heights that day, but my legs were so sore, I couldn't walk the next day. Keeping up with those two was a full-time job for me. That picture was taken not long before the friendship ended."

"Is that when Tori showed up in Twin Rivers?" Ray asked.

"It was. When Tori and Levi met, things changed. My job sure got easier."

"Tori replaced Doug as Levi's best friend," Ray said.

"She did," Craig said. "I think Ed Garvey put it best. He told me one time that Doug Malone lost a best friend and a potential girlfriend in one day. I don't know exactly when the war started between Levi and Doug, but by high school, those two were after each other all the time. I don't know how many fights I broke up between those two. Well, I don't know if you'd call them fights. Levi was always on the losing side of those encounters."

"It's pretty obvious that Doug was in love with Tori, too," Ray said.

"Yup. You remember fifth-grade love, don't you? When you realize there was a little more to having a girlfriend than just kissing her behind a tree at recess. That's when boys and girls start to understand that people do a lot of the same things pigs and cows and goats do on the farm."

Ray grinned. He remembered well when he'd first noticed the new bumps and curves the girls in fifth and sixth grade were developing and how badly he'd wanted to check them out himself. Those observations had gone right along with some of the interesting changes that were beginning to happen in his shorts.

"When I came back after Doug was killed, I couldn't believe that picture was on the wall along with everything else that meant something to Doug. I thought about telling Levi since I knew he was writing the book about what had happened here, but I didn't. I wasn't sure how

Levi would react."

"I think you were wise," Ray said, taking the photo off the wall. "That picture was hanging in Doug's office while he was planning to murder Levi."

Craig shook his head. "It's damn peculiar. There was something deeply wrong with Doug—with that whole cursed family."

Ray glanced down at the photo as he remembered something, and sweat broke out on his forehead. He was thinking about the first night he'd spent in Twin Rivers—the night Andy Miller was murdered. He'd returned to the Garvey house at well after four in the morning, and Levi was still sitting in his chair in front of the roll-top desk. He wasn't working, but Ray knew he'd been drinking. Levi was staring at an old photograph framed on the top of his desk, and he recognized that look on his face. Levi was a million miles away in his own head.

That can't be right, Ray thought.

But Ray knew it was right. He'd never seen the photograph clearly, but somehow he knew Levi had been looking at the same photo.

"Ray?" Craig said.

Ray was suddenly aware that he'd heard Craig say his name more than once.

"Something wrong?" Craig asked when Ray finally looked at him.

"No. You got another box?" Ray asked as he laid the photo on the desk. "This stuff has got to go. It's time to turn the page on that chapter of Twin Rivers history."

Chapter Twenty-Eight

IT FELT STRANGE TO WALK INTO THE LOBBY OF THE FIRST NATIONAL Bank of Calloway. It was as he remembered it, though his perspective was different since he'd been a lot shorter last time he was there. The two heavy oak islands in the center, where customers filled out their deposit slips, were waist high. Last time he was there, they'd towered over him. He remembered swinging from them and kicking the pedestal underneath as his grandmother filled out her paperwork. Sometimes, she'd pick him up and set him on top to keep him from running around inside the bank. He'd liked to run full speed across the lobby, then stop suddenly, sliding on the mosaic tile floors in his Buster Browns.

The teller counters were the same—the same marble counters, the same frosted glass with brass dividers between them. He remembered the vault behind the counter with its huge locking mechanism on the front. The half wall with the little half door still divided the foyer from the teller area and the vault. He remembered Miss Darby opening that half door and following her into the vault when his grandmother needed to put something in her safety deposit box.

Levi looked up at the clear glass skylight with green and blue designs in stained glass around the edges. It illuminated the lobby now as it had done then.

It wasn't busy at the bank. There were two customers at the teller windows. Offices were along the edges, each with a window that looked out into the lobby. The largest one at the end of the teller counter was obviously the office of the bank president—it'd been Tori's office for about ten years. Levi walked toward the office. There was nobody there, but the door was open. Levi stood in the doorway, leaning on the frame as he looked at the massive oak desk and the leather chair. There was something familiar about it—something he couldn't quite place. On the wall opposite the president's desk was a wall-sized book case. As he stared, the memory finally surfaced from the fog.

When he stepped into the president's office, somebody behind him said, "No, it's all right. That's Levi Garvey!"

He walked over to the bookcase where there were toys and kids' books on the bottom shelf. His grandmother and the bank president had been talking and looking at papers as he leafed through those books and played with a collection of matchbox cars.

He pulled a book off the shelf—*The Cat in the Hat* by Dr. Seuss— and sat down in the leather guest chair. He was sure this office was where he'd been sequestered after the robbery. He glanced at the venetian blinds on the windows that looked out in the lobby. They were open, but on the day of the robbery, he knew they'd been closed.

"If you like that one, we also have *Green Eggs and Ham* somewhere," a voice said from the doorway.

A woman, wearing a blazer, was leaning against the door frame, grinning at him. She was in her late fifties with dark brown eyes and readers perched on the end of her nose.

Levi stood up, looked down at the book, and smiled back.

"Juli Logan," she said, walking into the office. "Bank president."

Levi shook her hand. "Levi Garvey."

"I know," she said. "You need anything?"

"I'm just poking around. Actually, is there anybody still working at this bank who was here in the early 70s?"

Juli shook her head. "Researching a book? We've heard that the bank robbery is part of what's been going on in Twin Rivers the last few days."

"That's right. But I'm not writing a book or anything. I was here that day when the robbery took place. I was just a little kid, but I remember a few things. I was trying to piece together a little more."

"Make yourself at home," she said.

Levi grinned. "I think I already have. I apologize for the intrusion.

I'm done in here now."

"No problem," Juli said. "You're free to look around the bank all you want. Let one of us know if you need anything. And tell Tori I said hello. She recommended me for this job when she left."

"I will," Levi said.

He walked back out into the lobby and crossed to the first teller station, where he stood and looked around the lobby in a full circle. He remembered somebody climbing over the teller counter at the far end. He remembered the explosion again—the dust and debris falling. Levi looked up at the smooth plaster of the ceiling ten feet over his head. It was several seconds before he noticed that at the right side of the skylight, the plaster seemed to have a circular ripple in it. The ceiling had undoubtedly been painted half a dozen times over the last forty years, but the paint couldn't cover the repair of a sizeable hole in the plaster above the first teller station.

Then what he'd been grasping for came to him—a sound, chunk-chunk. A shotgun, Levi thought. He remembered the dust and the hunks of plaster and the pieces of wood lath falling after the explosion and something else bouncing on the floor. Even as a little boy, he knew what it was—a shotgun shell casing.

He leaned against the teller counter, rubbing his chin. The details were beginning to fall into place, but there was still something else missing.

A few windows down, an old woman was finishing her business. She'd been glancing at him as she talked with the teller. When she was finished, she walked towards him. He knew he was going to have to talk to her, maybe sign a book. He had a few copies behind the seat in Old Blue.

"Hello," Levi said.

"It's been a long time," she remarked as she looked up at him.

There was something familiar about her face, weathered into a roadmap of deep wrinkles.

"Do I know you?" Levi asked.

She laughed as she reached for something over the teller counter he was leaning on.

"Grape, right?" she said as she held out a sucker.

Levi looked at her questioningly for a moment. Then he knew. The face was older, but the eyes were the same. He took the sucker.

"Thank you, Miss Darby," he said, smiling broadly as he unwrapped it. "I think the last time I had a grape sucker, you gave it to me."

"You're thinking about that robbery," Linda Darby said. "I read about Andy Miller, and I heard this morning that Stevie died in a fire last night. It's all related, isn't it?"

Levi nodded, the stem of the sucker sticking out of the corner of his mouth. "I don't remember much about it."

"Well, maybe it's good we ran into each other," she said. "I'll never forget it."

"He shot a hole in the ceiling, didn't he?" Levi asked.

Linda nodded. "Come on. I'll tell you the whole story, Levi."

* * *

A FEW DAYS EARLIER, CHIEF CRAIG HAD TOLD THE STORY ABOUT WHAT had happened after the robbers left the bank. Now Linda Darby was telling Levi about what had happened inside the bank. They were sitting in the bank's break room—a small kitchenette with a fridge, a microwave, and a table in the center with a few chairs—drinking Diet Cokes. Linda told the whole story, ending with the bank robbers leaving the bank. As she talked, Levi remembered more and more about that day. After she finished, Levi tossed the stem of his grape sucker into the trash can in the corner and leaned back in the chair with a troubled expression on his face.

"What is it, Levi?" Linda asked.

Levi frowned. "It seems like I was in the president's office for a long time. Maybe I'm thinking of another time."

"No, you were in there that day. Lucille put you there. You were terrified, Levi. And there was a dead body on the sidewalk in front of the bank that was clearly visible through the doors. It's one of the most horrible things I've ever seen—Jim Mathis lying there on the sidewalk, firing at that car until his gun was empty, pulling the trigger even after it was empty. Blood was everywhere. I knew that was the last thing Jim Mathis would ever do in this life."

She looked at Levi with her eyes full of tears.

"Lucille didn't think you'd seen that, at least she hoped not. But I think you did see some of what was going on outside. The police had a lot of questions, and she didn't want you involved with that either. I don't know if you remember, but Helen, one of the cashiers, went in and played with you after the police were done questioning her."

Levi thought about it for a minute, then nodded. "She read books to me. I do remember that. You and Grandma figured out it was Andy Miller. How did you figure that out? He used to do work around the house. I kind of remember watching him mow the front yard."

Linda just stared at Levi. Suddenly, he knew. The memory flashed into his mind like a lightning bolt.

"My God," Levi said. "I recognized him!"

Linda nodded. "It was right after they left the bank. You were crying, and your grandma was trying to console you. She told you it was over, but it wasn't over yet. Just seconds later, we heard shots being fired outside. I think you saw part of that through the doors. Maybe you saw Bruce Franklin get shot and Jim Mathis fall as well."

Suddenly, the room seemed very small and very warm as flashes of memory clicked into place.

"I did see that—and a green car. I saw the guy driving the car drop a gun on the ground and slump over."

"Lucille didn't want you involved," Linda said, "but when we heard those shots outside, you looked at Lucille and said, 'Why is Andy being so mean?'"

Levi gasped.

"I saw the ring," Levi said. "I'd seen it before when we were sitting on the porch swing after he was done mowing one afternoon. Grandma had made him some iced tea. He saw me looking at his ring, so he took it off and put it on my finger. It was huge, so I stuck two fingers in that ring to make it fit me. Andy was nice to me. I liked him. I recognized that ring, and then when I looked up, I recognized his eyes behind that ski-mask."

"Lucille and I both saw that ring, too," Linda said. "We knew that the bank robber was probably somebody we knew, especially when he wouldn't take Lucille's cash. Even if you hadn't said anything, it wouldn't have been long before we figured it out. Helen and Tom had also seen the ring, and Tom was able to see the graduation year."

"So Grandma put me in the president's office so I wouldn't see any more through those glass doors and wouldn't be further traumatized by having to talk to the police. Then you and Grandma put the police on Andy Miller's trail," Levi said.

"That's right."

Levi leaned on the table with both elbows and rubbed his forehead. More pieces were falling into place—the robber with the shotgun leaning over and scooping up the shotgun shell off the floor, Miss Darby hugging Helen who was sobbing, Helen, with tears still running down her face, reading *The Cat in the Hat* . . .

"Are you okay, Levi?" Linda asked.

Levi nodded. "It never ceases to amaze me the lengths adults will go through to protect their kids."

As soon as he'd said it, his face went pale. He scooted his chair back and stood up.

"Levi?"

"I've got to talk to Ray—our new police chief," Levi said as beads of sweat popped out on his forehead.

"What is it, Levi?"

"I saw the shooter."

"Of course, you did," Linda said. "He was standing right next to you. I was so afraid he'd—"

"No," Levi said. "Before the robbery. I saw him. I'd seen that green car before."

Levi stormed out of the break room door. As he rounded the corner behind the teller counter, Juli was waiting for him in front of the vault with a copy of his first book and a pen.

"I was hoping to catch you before you left," she said, holding out the pen.

He brushed past her, jumped over the half wall that divided the lobby from the area behind the counter, and ran across the lobby. He banged out through the bank doors and dashed across the street, causing a Honda Civic to screech to a halt, narrowly missing him. He jumped in Old Blue and fired it up.

"Hang on, Rosco," Levi said as he threw the truck into reverse and backed out of his space, causing another near collision on Main Street. He popped the clutch into first gear on the old Ford's three on the tree and did something he'd done in that truck only once before in his life. He floored it. Old Blue's tires spun as he left an impressive black rubber patch on Main Street in Calloway and rounded the corner towards Twin Rivers.

* * *

OLD BLUE ROARED UP MAIN STREET IN TWIN RIVERS, CAUSING A FEW heads to turn. Levi didn't notice the sedan he passed going the other way. He skidded into a parking space in front of the Twin Rivers Police Department and ran inside.

The sedan slowed and then turned around. It drove by the police department as the four men in the car looked at the blue truck they'd been searching for all morning.

"I'm starting the think this is a really bad idea," Darren said as he turned off Main Street and crept down one of the side streets.

They'd driven by the Garvey house half a dozen times that morning, but there'd been no sign of Levi Garvey or Old Blue.

"You know how those Garveys are," he added. "Levi's bad enough, but you throw his Uncle Ed into the mix, and we're taking a dangerous chance."

"And he's way too close to the police department," Dan chimed in from the back seat. "Hell, the new chief is living in his house. And the old chief is tight with the Garveys, too."

The men had been watching them closely during the last few days.

"And the deputy, too," Dennis said. "I agree with Darren. We should walk away while we can. We've only got one chance at it, and if we drop the ball, we won't stand a chance. There's too much that could go wrong."

"We don't have a choice," an old man said from the passenger seat. "I've got too much invested in this. We can't walk away now—and we won't. We'll catch him alone, and it'll go down quickly and easily, just like we planned. And even if we can't catch him alone, there are four of us. We could easily take both Garveys. We've got the element of surprise on our side."

When Darren glanced in the rear view mirror, he saw Dan and Dennis looking at each other doubtfully in the back seat. He sighed. The old man glanced over at him with his hawk-like eyes.

"Nothing this big is ever easy, but we will pull it off, and we'll all walk away wealthy men for the rest of our lives."

Darren glanced over at him again and said, "You sure about this?"

The old man chuckled. "I couldn't be more sure. Turn up here," he said, pointing. "We'll make one more pass to see if Garvey is still there. Maybe we can catch him alone today and get this over with. If not, we'll come back in a week or so and finish this."

* * *

As the sedan rolled slowly by the police department, Carl watched it and the men inside from the diner window.

I gotcha now, he thought as he sipped coffee.

"Anything else I can get for you?" April asked as she stopped at his table.

She'd never seen him before, but she'd noticed his fine suit, the expensive watch, and his manicured nails—things not often seen in Twin Rivers.

He smiled. "No, thank you. I'd heard about that pie. I think Levi Garvey wrote about it in his last novel. It was certainly worth the side trip to check it out."

"I believe he did say something about my pies in his novel," she said, smiling broadly as she ripped off a green ticket and left it on the edge of the table. "He's in here a lot. Maybe next time you're in town, you'll have a chance to meet him."

"I think I just saw him," Carl remarked, pointing through the window. "That Panama hat kind of sticks out."

"Yeah," April said. "That's Old Blue and his dog Rosco, barking his head off as usual. He must be at the police department or upstairs in the Masonic Lodge."

"I'm sure I'll meet him next time I'm in town," Carl said.

Chapter Twenty-Nine

LEVI BURST INTO RAY'S OFFICE, OUT OF BREATH, STARTLING BOTH RAY and Craig.

"Levi, what's wrong?" Ray said, standing up from behind his desk.

The wall behind him was blank. There were a couple of boxes and a stack of empty photo frames on the desk.

"I remember," Levi said, shutting the door and leaning on it heavily. "I went to the First National Bank of Calloway this morning. I kept remembering things."

"Take a breath, Levi," Craig said, offering him a chair.

Levi plopped down. "It wasn't Grandma Lucille who identified Andy Miller. It was me. She didn't want me involved, so she and Linda Darby put me in the president's office. Then they suggested to the police that one of the robbers was Andy Miller."

"It's pretty amazing you remembered that," Craig said. "You were only four."

"It didn't come right away, but I finally pieced it together, and Linda Darby helped fill in the holes. But that's not all. That's not the most important part. I remember seeing that green Impala that day. And I remember seeing that car before the robbery, too."

"Where?" Ray asked.

"At our house. Andy was mowing our yard one day. Sometimes I watched him from the front window. Anyway, that green car stopped at our house, and a man got out. Andy stopped the mower and went over to talk to him. They got into an argument, shoving each other. The man pushed Andy down. I ran to the basement where Grandma was folding laundry. By the time I convinced her somebody was fighting with Andy and we got back upstairs, the car was gone, and Andy was mowing again. Grandma didn't believe me. She reminded me that I'd been attacked by an elephant hiding in a closet just a week earlier. The elephant turned out to be the hose from the shop vacuum which fell out when I opened the door."

Ray and Craig both laughed.

Levi glared at them, then said, "But you know what I think?"

"You think that guy who knocked Andy down was the fourth bank robber," Craig said.

"I'll bet that was his car they used in the robbery," Levi said. "I've seen pictures of Bruce Franklin and Joe Bailey, and it wasn't one of them. I knew Andy Miller, so there's only one person left."

"There were a lot of Impalas back then," Craig remarked. "And you were a little kid. Do you even know when that happened exactly? It could've very likely been unrelated."

"You're right. But it's a hell of a coincidence, isn't it? I do remember that car."

Ray sighed. "So Andy did know the fourth bank robber. That's why he was killed after he was released from prison. And there's a good chance if that guy was hanging around prior to the robbery, Stevie Miller probably saw him, too. That's why he's dead."

"You remember anything about that guy?" Craig asked.

Levi shook his head. "Not much."

"You know, Ed has a theory about the fourth bank robber that makes a lot of sense to me," Ray said. "He thinks Tony O'Malley lied to me. He thinks the bank robbery was planned by the Chicago Outfit, and one of Tony's goons was the leader."

Craig nodded. "I never believed Andy Miller's story that he never knew who he was working for. He must've known the Chicago Outfit had planned that heist, and he probably also knew how Tony has always dealt with witnesses—even those in prison. It's better to shut up and spend your life in prison than be dead in the cemetery. That's not a tough choice to make."

"But then Andy got out," Ray said, "and he stirred up a bunch of crap right off the bat."

"I think Tony decided it wasn't worth the risk long before Andy got back to Twin Rivers. That plan wasn't last minute. Andy was dead before he got home. He just didn't know it," Craig said.

"So if Tony O'Malley behind all this, you're still a target, Ray," Levi said. "You got too close."

Ray curled the ends of his mustache with his fingertips and leaned back. "Ed doesn't think so, and neither do I. Even though the shot missed, Tony sent a powerful message. And there isn't one shred of evidence to connect the mob at this point."

"You think it's over," Levi said.

Ray reluctantly nodded. "There's just no evidence from years ago, and in all honesty, there isn't any now—not from the fire or from the corn crib."

"Unless there's an eye witness who could connect Andy Miller with one of Tony's goons," Levi said.

"That's true," Ray said. "It would be thin, but it's worth a try."

"So the guy we're looking for worked for or still works for Tony O'Malley," Craig said. "I'd start with Tony's Four Horsemen, but you need to be careful. There aren't many who've survived an encounter with the Four Horsemen."

"Ed Garvey did," Ray said. "He beat the shit out of the Four Horsemen on his front porch a few years after the robbery. I didn't tell you before, but I think I saw them when I went to see Tony O'Malley. Three armed men were outside posing as gardeners. But they are old men now—late sixties, early seventies, probably retired. Then I met one face to face, Tony's butler now. A big man named Carl."

Craig chuckled. "That's Carl Clayburn," he said, "and he's no butler. And he's certainly not retired. He's Tony's right-hand man and in line to take over the Chicago Outfit."

"You know what I think you should do, Levi?" Ray said. "Go to the library and look up pictures of known members of the Chicago Outfit. I'll call and see if I can't get some pictures of Tony O'Malley's known associates, and I'll bring them over to the library later."

"Good idea," Craig said. "I'll bet it's one of the Four Horsemen who's responsible for all this."

"You know what? If I can't identify one of Tony's goons as the man I saw, there may be another witness."

"Who?" Ray said.

"Tori," Levi said. "She was on Main Street with her parents the day of the robbery. She thinks she knew somebody in that car."

* * *

"Shit," Levi said, pushing a pile of photos across the table in the audio/visual room at the Twin Rivers Library.

"Nothing?" Ray said.

"Dead end," Levi said. "I have so little memory of the man. None of these faces look familiar."

"What exactly do you remember, Levi?"

Levi leaned back and rubbed his chin. "He was older than Andy. Seemed like a grown-up to me at the time. He was muscular but maybe shorter than Andy."

"Andy was about 5'10," Ray said, "so the other man wasn't very tall."

"He was wearing a plaid shirt with the sleeves torn off. That was a style that remained popular in this area until the mid-80s. You still see that sometimes. And he had long black hair, which he wore in a mullet—another local style that remained popular until the mid-80s."

"And I've seen a few since I've been here," Ray said with a chuckle.

"Welcome to the country where fads have a tendency to last decades instead of months."

"Anything else?" Ray asked.

"He smoked," Levi said. "I remember he flicked his cigarette into the yard before he shoved Andy down."

"Everyone smoked in the 70s, including me. Remember anything about his face?"

"I saw it, but it's fuzzy," Levi said. "I think he was wearing mirrored sunglasses. He might have had a mustache. I'm just not sure."

Ray flipped through the pictures. "None of these guys are even close. They don't have long hair or mullets, and most of Tony's known associates are wearing ties and jackets in their mug shots. Here's one—this guy is wearing a t-shirt," Ray said, turning the picture around for Levi.

Levi shook his head. "Short hair, and I can tell it's light-colored even in this old black and white photo," Levi said.

"We're at a dead end," Ray said.

In a way, Ray was relieved that Levi didn't recognized anyone because he knew what that could mean.

"It was worth a try."

"I'm going to have Tori look at these," Ray said. "Maybe something will click with her."

"We're at the end of the case here, aren't we?" Levi said.

"We've got nothing to go on," Ray admitted.

"You really think you're off Tony's radar now?"

"I've got nothing to tie him to any of this," Ray said. "He knows that, and he's dying. Ed's got it right. Unless Tori gets something from these pictures, we're done here."

"It's a shame," Levi said.

Ray nodded. "We'll probably never know who's responsible for all this, but Levi—"

"No need to say it," Levi remarked. "It's already occurred to me. They've taken some big risks to knock out the last two witnesses. If they found out Tori and I saw something—"

"The Chicago Outfit doesn't play around," Ray nodded. "Tony O'Malley has never given a second thought to taking out witnesses."

* * *

IT WAS NEARLY MIDNIGHT AT THE TWIN RIVERS POLICE DEPARTMENT. Ben was sitting on the edge of Amber's desk.

"You know my birthday is coming up," he said, grinning at her.

"You know I don't make much working here," Amber said, looking up at him innocently with her dark eyes. "I hope whatever it is you want, it's cheap."

"Oh, it's cheap all right."

Amber giggled. "Like what?"

Ben walked behind her and whispered in her ear.

Her face reddened as she listened.

"That's really cheap. I don't think so."

"Well then, how about . . ." He leaned over and whispered again.

She laughed and slapped his hand.

"There's not enough wine in the world to get that to happen!"

"But it's my birthday!" Ben said with feigned hurt in his eyes.

He paused to think, then leaned over and whispered again, "Okay, how about . . ."

"Oh my God," Amber said, spinning in her office chair and pushing him back. "That's worse than the first two suggestions."

"But intriguing, you must admit," Ben said with a grin.

"Maybe," she said, standing and wrapping her arms around his neck.

Suddenly, the door banged open, causing both of them to turn around quickly—guilty looks on their faces.

"Sorry. I didn't interrupt anything, did I?" Levi said with a wicked smile on his face.

Amber and Ben looked straight ahead, expressions blank but faces red.

Levi dug into his jacket and flung a pink bra onto Amber's desk. She gasped.

Levi chuckled. "It wasn't that hard to figure out. I'm disappointed in you, Ben. I've solved my mystery, and you're nowhere close to solving yours."

"I will," Ben said. "I'm breathing down your neck. You just don't know it."

"Actually, until a moment ago, you were breathing down Amber's neck," Levi said with a grin.

Ben's face grew even redder.

Tori stumbled into the door behind Levi, flushed and smiling brightly as she tucked her shirt in.

"Hi," she said, a little out of breath. "Nice evening."

Ben and Amber looked at each other, eyebrows raised.

"You've had every opportunity to solve it, Ben. You were even provided with a second chance, and you've come up empty again. I haven't gotten a citation or anything. Now don't expect another opportunity."

"I wasn't expecting a repeat performance, so you had the advantage, but you wouldn't dare do it again."

"Is that a challenge, Ben?"

Tori nudged Levi. "He's taunting you, Levi. You know unless he catches you red-handed, he has little chance of figuring it out."

"I'll figure it out," Ben said. "I'll have to because there's no way Levi has the guts to do it again."

"I could do it a hundred times. Then using his best Cagney impersonation, Levi added, "You'll never catch me, copper, never!"

As Levi and Tori turned to leave, Levi said, "Stay out of my lodge, you perverts."

Ben laughed.

At the doorway, he turned again. "Left a little something for you in your cruiser. You really should lock your doors."

They could hear Levi laughing even after the door closed behind him. Ben walked over to the window.

"That jackass," Ben said, laughing hard.

Amber walked up beside him to look at the cruiser which was parked right in front of the police department.

"What is that?"

"My guess is that's Tori's bra, hanging around my rear view mirror. I have to get him now—that's an act of war."

Amber giggled. "You still want that second thing you mentioned for your birthday."

He glanced out at the cruiser, then slowly shook his head.

"Not now."

Chapter Thirty

"WELL, THAT'S ABOUT IT," CRAIG SAID, WALKING THROUGH THE BASE-ment doorway. He tossed the keys to Ray. "You mind if I leave a few things in the garage until I can get back over to get them? Probably in a few days."

"Not at all," Ray said.

He looked around the empty basement, which had seemed large before but which looked massive now with all of Craig's things gone.

"You know, I could almost live just down here."

Craig smiled. "I've got Spiffy Clean coming by on Wednesday to clean this house from top to bottom and shampoo all the carpets."

"You didn't have to do that," Ray said.

"It needs it. I was never much of a housekeeper. When is your stuff arriving?"

"It'll be a few days," Ray said. "Bernice has been packing stuff up for me in Savannah. The moving truck will be there tomorrow."

"Who's Bernice?" Craig said.

"First wife," Ray said. "The only one I'm sorry got away."

"You sure that truck won't be empty when it shows up? I've heard about these ex-wives."

"I wouldn't trust any of my other ex-wives, that's for sure," Ray said with a chuckle, "but Bernice is different. I still trust her."

"Sounds like you'd kind of like it if she'd pack herself up, too," Craig said.

Ray smiled ruefully.

"If you need anything or have any questions," Craig said.

"I'll call you."

"I'm only fifteen miles down the road. You'll have to come over and see the lake house some time."

"I'd like that," Ray said as they shook hands.

Climbing the stairs to the garage, Craig called back, "Did I mention the roof leaks, the septic backs up, and the wiring is shot?"

"For what I paid for this house, that'd better not be true," Ray called after him. "I can find you, Craig!"

After he was gone, Ray looked around the huge room again. What the hell am I going to do with all this space, he thought. There were three bedrooms, a large living room, a huge kitchen, and two full bathrooms upstairs.

When Ray heard footsteps on the stairs, he expected to see Craig, but it was a man with a clipboard.

"Are you Ray Billings?"

"Yes."

"Got a delivery for you."

Suddenly, four men appeared on the stairway, easing a giant box down into the basement. They grunted under its weight.

"What the hell is that?"

"Didn't you order a billiards table?"

"A billiards table?"

"A nice one, too—the best we sell. The Embassy model with a slate top, red felt, leather pockets, and all the accessories you'll need."

"I didn't order a pool table," Ray said as the workmen gently eased the enormous box into the middle of the room and laid it over flat on the basement floor.

"I did," Tori said from the doorway. "It's a little housewarming present from Levi and me."

"You two shouldn't have done that," Ray said.

"Well, if you don't want it, you'd better say something now," the man with the clipboard said. "That was the light piece—the oak frame. If you think that looks heavy, wait until you see the slate slabs."

Ray chuckled and glanced at Tori. "Thank you both."

"Where do you want it set up?" the workman asked.

Ray looked around the basement and shrugged. "Right here in the middle, I suppose."

"I'll be back later, and I'll need some help," Tori said. "Just wait until you see the antique pool light I found."

"I think I'm going to need a fridge down here, too."

Tori nodded. "That's probably a good idea. I have a feeling Levi and Ed are going to be over here a lot."

Ray laughed.

"I think you're going to like it in Twin Rivers," Tori said, leaning up on tiptoes and kissing his cheek. "Levi would never admit it, but he sure is happy you're here."

"I know, but you're right that he'd never admit it. And I do like this town."

"I gotta go," Tori said. "The carpet layers are supposed to be at the lodge in an hour."

"Hey, Tori," Ray said. "Did you look at those pictures?"

"The mug shots?"

Ray nodded.

"I did," Tori said. "I got nothing."

Ray sighed. "That's too bad. I've got nothing left to go on."

"It's over then, isn't it?" Tori said.

"I'm afraid so," Ray admitted. "It's too bad. Stevie Miller didn't deserve to die. He wasn't involved. He was killed because he may've seen something nearly forty years ago when he was just a boy."

"Andy sure stirred things up again by getting out of prison," Tori said.

"And I didn't help by going to see Tony O'Malley."

"You couldn't have known."

Ray nodded. "If Levi hasn't mentioned it already, it might be a good idea for you two to keep what you saw so many years ago to yourselves.

"He mentioned it. Maybe one day, what we saw will click into place," Tori said hopefully.

Ray thought it was unlikely, but he hoped she was right. But for now, he was just relieved that it was over.

* * *

LEVI WAS FILLING UP OLD BLUE AT HILLBILLY BOB'S CONVENIENCE Store when Ben Walker drove up to the pump across from him and climbed out of his cruiser.

"Levi," he said with a glint of humor in his eyes as he lifted the pump handle.

"Deputy Walker," Levi said with a nod. "No hard feelings?"

Ben shook his head as he stuck the nozzle into his tank and began pumping. He walked over to lean on the canopy post. "I had it coming," he said, smiling sheepishly.

"We're even then?"

"For now." Then, his face becoming serious, he said, "Actually, there is something I want to ask you. How can I go about joining your lodge?"

Levi raised a finger and turned towards his truck. "Move over, Rosco," he said as he leaned in through the window and popped open his glove box.

"As we used to say, 2B1ASK1. This is a petition. Fill it out, and give it back to me," Levi said as he pulled a pen out of his pocket and signed the bottom of the paper. "You need the signatures of three Master Masons who will vouch for your character. I went ahead and signed it, even though I know a few things about you." Levi grinned. "I'm sure Ray and Uncle Ed won't hesitate to sign it. For that matter, half the members of the lodge who know you will sign it if you ask them."

"Can I just fill it out now?" Ben asked, looking over the petition.

After Levi handed him his pen, Ben walked over to the hood of his car and began to fill out the petition. "You know, my dad was a Mason," Ben said.

While Ben was writing, Levi watched one of the convenience store employees change the letters on the marquee sign next to the road. The kid had dropped the letters onto the driveway, and, one at a time, he picked them up with a long rod with a pincher on the end, swung them up and over, and hung them on the sign twenty feet over his head. The kid was a pro. He never dropped one letter on the far side, and he was now spelling out the same message on the ground for the near side.

When the kid began the second message, Levi's nozzle cut off. He walked over and hung it up. Ben was talking about his grandfather being a 32nd Degree back in the 40s as Levi ripped his receipt off the pump.

Levi was ready to go, but Ben was talking more than he was writing. Half listening, Levi leaned against Old Blue and watched the store employee, making a mental bet with himself that the young man would get every letter up without dropping one. Watching that kid hang those letter reminded Levi of something, and he was trying to remember exactly what it was.

Ben finally stood straight up from the hood of his car, looked over the petition, and stepped toward Levi.

"I think I got everything on there," he said, holding it out.

At that moment, the store employee dropped a letter, and Levi chuckled. Ben looked toward the sign and then back at Levi questioningly.

"I'll give you a call," Levi said, taking the petition. "I'm sure you'll have a few questions about . . ."

Levi stopped in mid-thought. He looked back at the employee quickly. Ben followed Levi's gaze again, a small frown line appearing between his eyes.

"Oh, my God," Levi gasped. "I've been such an idiot."

"What is it?" Ben said. "Are you okay?"

Levi stared at the sign. Then he took off his Panama hat and ran his fingers through his hair as he shook his head.

"It was right there in front of my face all this time."

Levi opened his truck door and started to climb in next to Rosco. Then he paused and said, "You got time for a cup of coffee, Ben?"

Ben was still standing there, looking first at Levi and then at the kid changing the sign.

"Yeah."

Levi nodded towards the convenience store. "Come on. I'll buy."

Chapter Thirty-One

LEVI WAS STANDING IN FRONT OF THE DRESSER, ADJUSTING HIS TIE IN the mirror, when Tori walked in. She'd worked at the lodge all day. The sunlight was fading from the bedroom window. She turned on the light.

"I thought you were home tonight," she said, stepping in front of him and fixing his poorly tied knot.

She knew what he was doing as soon as she saw the tie with the subtle square and compass motif woven into it.

"No, I told you we had degrees tonight," Levi remarked as he put on his blue suit jacket.

"Are you conferring the degree tonight, Master?" Tori said with a grin.

"I've told you before, you don't have to call me Master," Levi said with a chuckle. "Worshipful is just fine when we're alone. But I doubt I'll be conferring tonight. We're going to Chebanse Lodge this evening to help out."

"Where is that?"

"South of Kankakee."

"That's a long drive. What time will you be home?"

"By 2 a.m., if I'm lucky."

Looking disappointed, Tori said, "We haven't had a lot of together time lately."

"I did tell you," Levi said.

"Such is the life of the Masonic widow."

They heard the front door open downstairs.

"Levi! You ready?" Ed said, his voice booming up the stairs. "Let's go! It's a long drive!"

Levi wrapped his arms around Tori's waist and kissed her.

"Tomorrow night?"

"You make plans tonight for tomorrow night, and you're dead, Levi. I know how this works. They'll drag you into something else."

"No chance," Levi said, walking out onto the top of the landing.

Ed and Ray were standing in the foyer, both wearing dark suits. Tori grinned when she saw them. She'd told Levi he should limit the number of lapel pins he wore on his jacket to three. Ed Garvey and Ray Billings had no such limitations—they sported half a dozen lapel pins each. Tori knew you could tell a lot about a Mason by looking at either the lapels of his suit or the bumper of his vehicle.

"We going?" Ed said impatiently.

"Don't rush him," Ray said, elbowing him. "Give him a minute with his wife."

"It'd only take minute," Ed said as he chuckled.

"All right," Levi said, shaking his head as he came down the stairs.

"Be careful," Tori said.

"Don't wait up. I'll be late."

Tori sighed as they walked out the door.

* * *

CARL TAPPED TWICE ON THE LIBRARY DOOR, SLOWLY OPENED IT, AND walked in. Tony O'Malley was sitting behind the massive mahogany desk at the far end, thumbing through some documents. Tony was an old man, but he was far from death's door. His "nurse" was sitting on the edge of the desk, filing her nails. She was wearing a leather mini-skirt and a thin low-cut blouse that left little to the imagination.

Carl took off his fedora and tossed it onto the back of a chair. The nurse glanced at Tony, who flicked his eyes towards the door. She slid off the corner of the desk, adjusted her skirt, and walked to the door, her high heels clicking on the hardwood floors as she crossed the library and departed.

Carl plopped down in an overstuffed chair and propped his feet up on the front edge of Tony's desk.

"You were right," he said. "Our mystery gunman is still around."

Tony leaned forward in his chair and put his elbows on the desk. "He's shadowing Ed Garvey, isn't he?"

Carl shook his head. "He seems to be more interested in Levi Garvey."

"Levi?" Tony frowned, tented his fingers under his chin, and thought for a moment. "You know who he is?"

Carl nodded. "I don't know who he is, but I know where to find him. I followed him right to his doorstep."

"Hmmm," Tony said, leaning back in his chair. "This is a big problem. Why would our mystery gunman be interested in Levi Garvey?"

"It's obvious he's knocking off anybody who can identify him," Carl said. "He killed Andy Miller. Then he killed Steve Miller, probably because Steve had seen him at some point. He took a shot at our friend Chief Billings, probably because Billings was digging into the bank robbery again and was getting close to something that made him nervous. Billings is probably a lot closer than he knows to figuring out who he is."

"But why would he be interested in Levi Garvey?"

"When Levi was four years old," Carl said, "he was in the bank with his grandma the day of the robbery. I learned that at this little diner in Twin Rivers. Too bad you didn't go with me. You wouldn't believe the pie the lady in this place makes. I brought you back a piece. It's in the fridge. Anyway, his grandma is the one who fingered Andy Miller because she knew him. He did odd jobs for her."

"When little Levi Garvey was running around and playing," Tony said, "maybe he saw the gunman at one time or another. It's amazing what little kids can remember years later."

Carl nodded. The closest Tony had ever come to being gunned down was in a restaurant twenty years earlier. A woman in her forties walked up to the table, pulled a gun, and fired six shots at close range. She managed to wound everyone at the table except Tony, who'd killed her father decades earlier—when she was only five years old. She'd witnessed his death and had finally remembered. She nearly took out

Tony "The Shotgun" O'Malley—something many had tried but failed to do before.

"This is a big problem," Tony said, looking at Carl with an ice-cold gaze. "If something happens to Levi Garvey, that's national news, and it will become a high-profile case. This moron will wind up caught sure as hell, and he may very well know who hired Bruce Franklin. I should've listened to you forty years ago, Carl, and had you set up the heist, instead of having Bruce Franklin take care of it. If that gunman winds up getting caught, he could lead an investigation right to our doorstep. We can't have that."

Carl nodded as he took his feet down from the edge of the desk and rose. He walked over to a sideboard and poured himself a bourbon.

"Pour me a scotch, would you?" Tony said.

Carl poured scotch into a tumbler from the decanter. Then he said, "There's another problem, Tony. The guy stalking Levi Garvey isn't alone. He's got three young associates with him."

"Pros?" Tony asked as Carl handed him the drink.

"No, amateurs of the worst kind. They stick out like a sore thumb. I'm surprised somebody hasn't noticed them. I'm guessing he did Andy and Steve and took that shot at Chief Billings alone. But he probably knew that going up against the Garveys was a lot more dangerous, and he hired some help."

"Ed Garvey took down four of the best in the business years ago with a broom," Tony said as he chuckled and Carl's face hardened.

"I know about Levi, too," Tony said, flicking a finger towards the bookcase behind him. A voracious reader, he'd read all of Levi Garvey's books. "He's cut from the same cloth. Our mystery gunman was right to get some help going up against that family, but we've got to make sure nothing happens to the Garveys."

"What are you thinking, Tony?" Carl finally asked.

Tony glanced at him as a cold grin crossed his face. "It seems we have only one option here. That hillbilly hit squad needs to disappear. Sooner rather than later."

Carl nodded, set his glass down on the sideboard, and walked to the library door.

"And Carl?" Tony said.

"Yeah?"

"You want to send Annette back in here. I could use a piece about now."

Carl chuckled. "We're talking about that pie, right?"

"I'm ninety years old," Tony said. "I'm much more interested in pie at this point."

Carl smiled as he walked through the door and closed it behind him. Three old men were waiting in the foyer, sitting on the lower steps of the winding staircase.

"Well?" one of them said anxiously.

"Lock and load, boys," Carl said, suppressing a grin.

They'd been hoping that was going to be the verdict—it'd been a long time. One of the men jumped up and clapped his hands. "The Four Horsemen ride again!"

"When do we go?" another asked, rubbing his hands together in anticipation.

"We've got to do this quietly and quickly," Carl said, "as soon as we can come up with a plan and load the car."

"Do we get to shoot Ed Garvey?" Vince asked.

"I'm afraid not," Carl said. "We've got to make sure nothing bad happens to Levi Garvey or Ed by making a few of their enemies disappear."

Vince looked down at the floor with his vacant eyes and nodded. "That's too bad. I really wanted to shoot Ed Garvey. I don't remember him very well, but I sure don't like him much."

The other three laughed. Ed Garvey had scrambled Vince's marbles pretty effectively years ago with a broom handle.

"Come on," Carl said as he nodded towards a hallway that led back to the kitchen. "Let's go downstairs to the armory and break out the hardware. We've got a job to do."

* * *

Holding a big bowl of popcorn, Tori had just settled down on the couch in the den to watch some TV. She had three puppies and Rosco looking up at her. The puppies had learned a trick from their father. One piece at a time, she flipped kernels of popcorn to them. Not one hit the floor as they snapped each out of midair. Tori was laughing at the way they kept begging her for more when somebody knocked at the door. Rosco started barking, and the puppies followed suit.

Glancing through the glass side panel of the door, Tori saw the familiar shape of Ben Walker in the light from the front windows. She flipped on the porch light and opened the door.

"Hi, Ben," she said.

"Is Levi home?"

"No, he's gone for the evening. He won't be back until the wee hours of the morning. He's off being a Mason."

Ben sighed and then smiled. "That's good news. I'm tired of watching that damned statue. I could use a night off without worrying about it."

Tori grinned. "Is Amber off tonight?"

Ben shuffled his feet as his face reddened.

"Why do you do it to yourself?" Tori asked. "You challenged him again. He's not that stupid. He's not going to give you another shot at catching him."

"If I hadn't opened my big mouth, I'm thinking he would've done it again."

"There's no way he's going to do it now," Tori said.

"Do you know how he does it?" Ben said, looking at her with pleading eyes.

Tori shook her head. "I've known him for thirty years, and I can honestly say that he's never given me even one hint."

Ben pushed his flat-brimmed hat up on his head with one finger and scratched his eyebrow. "Doesn't it bother you that he doesn't trust you?"

Tori looked back at him. "Maybe there's a reason he's never told me. Are you so sure he actually did it? Don't you believe there's a chance it was somebody else as he's claimed from the beginning?"

Ben laughed. "There's no chance. Who else in town is smart enough to pull off a prank like that? I'll see you later, Tori. Sorry to bother you."

"Good night," Tori said.

She watched Ben descend the steps and climb into his cruiser. After he turned around and pulled out of the driveway, she flipped off the porch light.

* * *

LEVI WAS A MILE OR SO PAST HILLBILLY BOB'S WHEN HE TURNED OFF the slab onto a narrow lane. The three of them were sitting shoulder to shoulder in Old Blue with Ray in the middle.

As they drove down the bumpy lane with weeds growing in the center and the trees canopied overhead, Ray said, "Where the hell are we going?"

"Not to Chebanse," Levi said with a laugh.

"There's no degree tonight," Ed said.

"What's going on?" Ray said, looking at each of them in turn.

"It's on a need-to-know basis," Levi said, "and you don't need to know yet."

When Levi reached the end of the lane, he pulled up to what looked to Ray like the edge of a cliff. Then Levi turned around and backed up to the edge.

"Where are we?" Ray said even though he thought he knew. He'd read Levi's last book.

"Welcome to Kingery Pond," Ed said tightly as he swung his door open and climbed out.

It was pitch black at first. There was no moon. As they walked towards the back of the truck, Ray's eyes began to adjust to the darkness. Below the cliff was Kingery Pond, its black center visible in the faint starlight. It was the mineshaft where Doug Malone had dumped his victims.

Levi popped the tailgate down and sat down as he pulled a cooler towards him. Ed and Ray also sat.

"This must be the overlook," Ray said.

He heard a hiss as Levi handed him a beer. He heard another hiss come from Ed's side of the tailgate.

"It is," Levi said, opening another can. "Turn off your cell phones."

Ed pulled his out of his pocket, his face illuminated by the blue screen as he turned it off. Ray thought for a moment, then did the same. Ben was on duty and knew he was going out of town.

"So we just came out here to drink beer?"

"I might get a phone call, and I might not," Levi said.

"And you're not going to tell me what this is about?"

Ray couldn't decide if he should be amused or irritated.

"Nope," Ed said. "We run out of beer before we get that call, we'll probably go to the Beer Chaser for a few more."

"How many beers did you bring," Ray asked. "A case?"

Levi chuckled. "A six pack."

The beer count indicated they weren't likely to be there very long. Again, no one talked. Ray sat silently, sipping on his beer and looking down at the water below. As his eyes adjusted, he could see more and more. The little round pond below was edged by dead trees. The smell of sulfur was thick in the air. Of all the places he'd seen, which included the Okefenokee Swamp where he'd spent a lot of time in his younger days, there was nowhere he'd ever been that was as creepy as this place. He thought about that as they waited for the mysterious call. Since he knew all about Kingery Pond from Levi's last book, it seemed very strange that Levi and Ed had come here.

"So when you were a boy," Ray said, breaking the silence, "you and Doug found this place, and you almost drowned here."

"Yup," Levi said, "and Doug Malone saved me."

"And you and Tori used to come up here when you were in high school to do what we're doing now."

Levi nodded.

"Then twenty-some years later, you almost die here again," Ray said. "And Tori, too."

"Yeah," Levi said. "Instead of saving me from drowning in the shaft, Doug Malone wanted to drown me in it. I was saved by a single shot Uncle Ed fired and the fact that Tori is a really good swimmer."

"What I don't get is why in the hell either of you would ever come here again?"

Ed laughed in his distinctive way—the mule laugh.

"What?" Ray said.

"You can't go through life in fear," Ed said. "I know that from experience."

"Anything that doesn't kill you makes you stronger," Levi added. "I faced death twice here, and the second time, I decided it was better to die if it meant Doug Malone didn't live."

"And killing that son-of-a-bitch freed me from demons that had haunted me from Vietnam for decades," Ed said. "It was the hardest shot I ever made, not because it was particularly challenging but because I knew Levi was sacrificing his life so I could make it. It's the only shot I've ever made that I knew I couldn't miss."

"And yet you both survived," Ray remarked.

Ed sighed. "I saved Levi from Doug Malone, and Tori saved Levi from drowning in Kingery Pond with a slug in his shoulder."

Levi chuckled, but it was a humorless, chilling sound in the darkness.

"Why wouldn't we like this spot? We survived it and walked away stronger. I still have nightmares about what happened here, but because of those things, I can honestly say there is nothing that I'm afraid to face now."

"Me, too," Ed said.

"Well, I'm glad you like it," Ray said, "because I've got to be honest. It scares the hell out of me."

"It should," Levi said. "I've always believed there are places on this earth that are inherently evil. This is one of them—this has always been a place of death."

"But those who live their lives in fear," Ed said, "eventually succumb to it."

Levi's phone buzzed on vibrate, and the display lit up. He answered it but said nothing. He just listened. After a moment, he stuck the phone in his pocket.

"Let's go."

The hairs stood up on the back of Ray's neck as Ed poured the rest of his beer on the ground, tossed the empty back into the cooler, and slid off the tailgate.

* * *

THEY SLIPPED BACK INTO TWIN RIVERS, TAKING A BACK ROAD, THEN drove down the edge streets and up a few narrow alleys before pulling into a parking lot behind a large brick building. Levi stopped Old Blue and climbed out. Ray had no idea where they were. For a moment, he wondered if this wasn't some kind of lodge initiation.

Motioning Ed and Ray over, Levi whispered, "No talking. Be very, very quiet."

Ed and Ray followed Levi up an alley, through a copse of trees, and into a grassy area with large shade trees. It was dark, but there were street lights along the edges of the area. Looking back, Ray realized they'd worked their way around the brick building they'd parked behind. He recognized it from the front—the Twin Rivers Library. They were in the park. Glancing around to get his bearings, Ray saw the War Memorial Statue in the center and the dark form of the park pavilion fifty yards beyond.

Suddenly, Ray knew what this was about. The Bikini Bandit was about to strike again. Actually, there were two Bikini Bandits—Levi and Ed Garvey. It all fell into place now. Ray had been brought into the prank to provide the perfect alibi. He'd be expected to say, "Levi couldn't have done it. He was with me and Ed in Chebanse . . ."

"You've got to be kidding me," Ray whispered.

Levi chuckled and motioned towards a large elm tree. "Stand behind that tree until I signal you. Be ready. We'll have to move fast."

Ray took his station while Levi and Ed took their places behind two trees nearby. Then they waited.

Ray realized, as he leaned against the trunk of the elm, that he'd stumbled onto a conspiracy. There weren't just two Bikini Bandits. There were at least three. He remembered the phone call. There was a third Bikini Bandit somewhere—a look-out. He was probably watching out for Ben Walker, the deputy. He smiled when he realized it was probably Tori.

But then he remembered something. It can't be Tori, he thought. If it were Tori, they wouldn't have had to trick her by saying they were going to a Masonic degree. The third conspirator was somebody else. He began running through a list of suspects in his head. Ray chuckled when he realized he'd just been inducted into a conspiracy that went back three decades.

They waited a long time, so long that Ray began to wonder if they wouldn't abort the mission. They were obviously waiting for an "all clear" phone call. Ben Walker must be prowling somewhere, he thought.

The minutes ticked by. They'd been there at least half an hour. In the dim light, Ray could see Levi peering at his phone occasionally. He was still waiting for the call. When Ray looked at the granite façade of the library, something caught his eye. Something had moved along the front of the building, probably just shadows from the tree branches in the park. Then suddenly, out of the shadows for a brief second was the perfect outline of a man as he crossed from the building to a clump of bushes very near where the three of them were hiding—the outline of a man wearing a flat-brimmed trooper hat.

Ray's heart leaped into his throat. Oh crap, he thought. That's Ben Walker. It's a trap!

Ray couldn't get Levi's attention without giving away their positions. Ben was too close. Levi was thirty or forty feet away. Ed was further. Ray's heart thumped in his chest as he looked for a stick or a rock to throw to get Levi's attention. Then, from the corner of his eye, he saw something else moving in the shadows even closer to him.

Oh, we're screwed, Ray thought. Ben has figured it out. He's got us surrounded.

But, suddenly, the second dark figure stepped out from the edge of the trees and walked out into the open area of the park. He stopped and looked around, just a few feet away from where they were hiding. After a few moments, he began walking towards the statue, staying within the shadows of the trees, stopping a few times to look around. Ray thought he was looking for a place to conceal himself when they sprang the trap to finally catch the Bikini Bandit.

Ray glanced over towards Levi, but he wasn't paying attention to the center of the park. His face was lit up by his phone display. Ray knew Levi had just gotten the all-clear, but it wasn't all-clear. They were doomed.

Ray lost track of the second man for a minute, figuring he'd found a place to hide, but then he saw him step out of the shadows and begin walking quickly towards the statue.

Suddenly Ben Walker stepped out from his hiding place behind the clump of bushes in front of the library and began to run towards the statue.

"Stop! Police!" his voice rang out.

The dark figure spun around and began running back towards the shadows, right next to where the three of them were hiding.

Levi shouted. "Now!"

Ed and Levi stepped out from behind their trees, and Ray, confused, did the same thing.

The Bikini Bandit saw them, quickly skidded to a stop, and changed direction. He was running back towards the statue, hoping to make his escape through the pavilion on the other side of the park, but Ben Walker had closed the distance and stopped him right at the base of the statue.

"I got you now," Ben announced as Levi and Ed ran up with Ray close behind.

They all saw the Bikini Bandit freeze in the dim light. He knew he was surrounded. He dropped a thick object he had in his hands.

"Hands up!" Ben yelled. "Put your hands on the statue and spread 'em."

Ben hadn't pulled his gun, but the Bikini Bandit reluctantly complied. The Bandit was wearing black clothing and a stocking cap. Quickly, Ben frisked him. Giddy with excitement, he spun the Bikini Bandit around.

"Now we're going to find out who you are," he said as he pulled his flashlight from his belt and snatched off the stocking cap.

Ben's face fell when the long locks of kinky blonde hair fell out from under the cap.

"Tori?" he said.

He never had a chance to react when the fist shot out and connected with his jaw. He tumbled over backwards onto the grass.

Rubbing his jaw as he looked up into Tori's blazing eyes, he sputtered, "You can't hit me, Tori. I'm a cop!"

"You touched my butt, you pervert," she said, pointing down at him.

"I didn't know you were a girl. I was frisking you! That's my job!"

When Ben started to get up, Tori stepped towards him.

"You get up, Ben, and I'll hit you again."

"I don't believe it," a voice said.

The man walked up to Ben and offered him a hand. Reluctantly, Ben took it and rose from the ground.

"Thanks, Chief Craig," Ben said sheepishly.

Craig sighed and rubbed his chin as he looked at the scene before him. "I can't believe I had it wrong all these years. Tori Buchanan is the Bikini Bandit."

"I fooled you, didn't I? I fooled everyone, but you tricked me, Ben," she said, taking a step towards him. "That's not very nice."

Ben quickly stepped behind Chief Craig.

"I had help," Ben said, pointing towards the three men who'd managed to stay in the shadows.

Levi stepped into the dim light from the distant street lamps. She recognized the shape of his Panama hat in the shadows.

"Levi," Tori said, "how could you?"

"How could I what? Bust you?" he said with a laugh. "You framed me twice in thirty years, left me clueless, and had me thinking all these years it was Jerry or Jim pulling this off. But I figured it out."

Levi leaned down to pick up the object she'd dropped—an aluminum tube about six feet long.

"Yeah," Ben said angrily from behind Chief Craig. "And thanks for clueing me in, Levi. When we talked this over at Hillbilly Bob's, I thought I was busting Jim or Jerry."

"What is that?" Craig asked, pointing at the object in Levi's hand.

"It's a sign changer. Tori got damned good at using one of these when she worked at Hillbilly Bob's back in high school. She rarely dropped a letter when changing the sign. I watched her many times."

Craig laughed as Levy began unscrewing the end, extending the pole, section by section, and tightening each section down.

"Chief Craig," Levi said. "If you check Tori's jacket, I'm sure you'll find a bikini top in there."

"Don't bother," Tori said, pulling it out.

"Yellow polka dots this time," Craig remarked. "Nice, Tori."

Tori tried to hide the smile.

"I haven't figured it all out," Levi said, "but Tori is going to show us how she did it—all of us."

Tori looked at him sharply.

"Do it," Levi said, handing the pole to her.

Tori huffed as she snatched the pole out of Levi's hand. She pulled a roll of duct tape out of her pocket, ripped off a small piece, looped it over on itself, and stuck it to one of the side straps on the bikini. Then she tied the straps that went behind the neck and tossed in on the grass.

She walked a few feet away, turned, and picked the bikini up with the pinchers on the end of the long pole. With one sweeping motion, she raised it, looped the tied neck straps over the statue's head, then grabbed the side strap with the duct tape on it, stuck it to the side of the statue, and released it. She carefully grabbed the loose strap with the pinchers, dropped it behind the strap stuck to the statue, and pulled it tight. With a few deft grabs with the pinchers on both straps, she pulled it snug. Finally, she pulled the piece of duct tape off the strap with the pinchers. She lowered the pole hand over hand, pulled the duct tape off the pinchers, and stuck it into her pocket.

"So simple," Chief Craig said, chuckling and shaking his head. "And how long did that take? Less than a minute? No ladder truck, no mountain climbing gear . . ."

"No helicopters or UFOs were involved," Levi said with a grin.

"Well you're under arrest, Tori, for assaulting an officer," Ben said, still rubbing his sore jaw.

"Oh, don't do that, Ben," Levi said. "You'll ruin the party."

"What party?" Ben asked.

"The baby shower," Levi said.

Tori's eyes widened. Levi raised two fingers to his mouth and let out a shrill whistle.

Fifty yards away, the lights in the park pavilion came on, revealing blue and pink ballons and decorations. Half the town who'd been hiding in there yelled out in unison, "Surprise!"

And Tori certainly was.

As they all walked towards the pavilion, Tori's eyes blazed, but a faint glimmer of a smile played at the corners of her mouth.

She whispered to Levi, "In eighteen years, when our child graduates from high school, let it be a reminder to you."

"A reminder of what?" Levi asked.

"The last time you had sex, more than eighteen years earlier," Tori said.

"Am I in that much trouble?"

"Oh, you're in more trouble than you can't possibly imagine," Tori replied.

Reaching over to take her hand, Levi said, "You can't stay mad at me."

A broad smile crossed Tori's face.

Chapter Thirty-Two

"How did you figure it out?" Tori asked as the sunlight streamed in through the window sheers and painted the interior of the small bedroom in golden light.

Levi was sitting on the floor of what was quickly beginning to look like a nursery, looking down at the instructions for the crib he was trying to assemble.

"It was at the Beer Chaser," Levi said. "When you didn't punch out Andy Miller after he attacked Uncle Ed, I knew something was up. Then I got thinking that even if you were dehydrated, you were following the doctor's restriction on coffee and beer way too closely."

"So you've known almost as long as I have," Tori said as she folded tiny little t-shirts she'd gotten the night before at the shower. She was sitting on the bed that was pushed against the wall, waiting to be dismantled and removed.

"I was suspicious at the Beer Chaser, but I wasn't sure until the next morning. I had a bit of a hangover, so I was looking for aspirin in the kitchen and found some giant ones. I'd taken two of them before I looked at the label. They weren't aspirins."

"Ah," Tori said with a grin, "the pre-natal vitamins Dr. Jackson gave me."

"Then I knew I was right," Levi said with a chuckle. "By the way, those pre-natal vitamins kicked the hell out of that hangover. We should keep those around."

Tori laughed.

Then suddenly serious, she asked, "You scared?"

"A little," Levi said. "Are you?"

She nodded. "Most people don't start families when they're in their early forties."

"Only start?"

Tori shrugged. "We'll see how this goes. I grew up an only child—so did you. More than one might be nice."

Levi looked at her for a minute and grinned. "We'd better work fast if you want more than one. I don't want to be the dad at the high school graduation that people mistake for the grandpa."

Tori laughed.

The blare of a horn came from the driveway.

"That would be Ed," Tori said.

"We're ready to begin painting Pappy today," Levi said.

"Thank God. I don't mean to be insulting, but you've got this crib assembled all wrong. Go paint my truck," she said, snatching the instructions out of Levi's hand.

Levi climbed up from the floor. "Are you sure? I could put together the changing table?"

"Go," Tori said. "I'll do it. It's very important that this furniture doesn't collapse under its own weight."

"I know how to build stuff," Levi shot back.

"Yeah," Tori said. "Trucks. Stick to trucks, okay?"

"Maybe you're right," Levi said.

When he looked at the mess he'd made on the floor, he had no idea why what he'd put together so far didn't look anything like the picture in the instructions. He turned towards the door.

"And Levi?" Tori said, stopping him.

He looked back at her.

"What color are you painting that truck?"

Levi quickly turned away.

"It's going to be my truck right?"

Levi sighed, looking at a spot on the floor. "Tori, I know when Uncle Ed first brought the truck here, you said—"

"It'd better not be purple," Tori said.

Levi looked at her—his face blank.

"I only said purple to screw with you two," Tori said with a wide grin, "and obviously, it worked beautifully."

Levi let out a long breath. "It was never going to be purple, Tori."

"It's probably not going to be my truck for a while either," she said. "It wouldn't be safe to put a car seat in an antique truck."

Levi nodded. "It's going to be red. But what are we going to do with it now? We're so close to finishing it. Maybe a week away."

"Old Blue was on blocks for twenty-five years," Tori said. "I'll get around to driving my truck eventually, and you can drive it every once in a while on your daily travels."

Levi shook his head. "Old Blue would get jealous. Remember when I took your Impala to Grand Lodge in Springfield?"

Tori laughed. "Yeah, a week later Old Blue's clutch croaked."

"Old Blue is very sensitive," Levi said, grinning.

"We'll figure out what to do with Pappy later," Tori said.

Levi paused in the doorway for a minute.

"What?" Tori said.

"I don't say it very often," Levi said. "But you know, right?"

"Know what?"

"I love you, Tori Buchanan. I always have."

That was not something either one of them said easily or often.

"Me, too," Tori said.

"You love you, too?" Levi said, toying with her.

"Don't you have a truck to paint," she said.

Levi chuckled. That was close enough. He could live with that.

* * *

"THAT LOOKS GOOD," LEVI SAID, STANDING BACK TO ADMIRE THE flawless coat of red paint he'd just applied. He set the spray gun down and pulled off the breathing mask.

As they'd done years before, they'd sealed the whole area under the lumber loft in the carriage house with sheets of plastic. They'd even covered the flagstone floor. They'd hung Pappy's doors from the rafters of the loft and started with those. Pappy was up on blocks in the make-shift paint room, stripped of all the major pieces.

"That's the first coat on the doors," Ed said. "We'll do the hood and tailgate next. Let's take a break since we've got plenty of time—at least five years before Tori needs this truck."

Levi pulled back the plastic and stepped out into the carriage house. Ed followed him.

"When we get done with Pappy," Ed said, "I think we ought to touch up Old Blue."

"Good idea. Old Blue has a few rock chips I've noticed. We might as well do that while we've got the paint room set up," Levi said as he jumped up to sit on the edge of the work bench.

"Anybody home?" somebody called from the sliding doors.

"We're in here," Ed shouted back.

Old Blue was parked just inside the carriage house. Ed's tow truck was parked in the center of the massive floor. They'd also opened the back sliding doors of the carriage house to help with the ventilation while they painted.

A man, wearing jeans and a plaid shirt, walked in. He had gray hair sticking out from under a St. Louis Cardinals baseball cap.

"Help you with something?" Levi asked.

"Yeah," he said, "I think we're lost."

Three young men followed him into the carriage house.

He looked down at a piece of paper in his hand. "We're looking for the Anderson place. Got a job there."

Levi glanced at Ed. The name wasn't familiar to Levi.

"Doesn't ring a bell with me," Ed said, scratching his chin. "There's Don Anderson, but he's way west of here. What kind of work are you doing at the Anderson place?"

"Cutting down and hauling off a tree that was damaged in a storm."

The other three men were spreading out across the carriage house floor, casually looking around.

When Ed looked out through the window at the sedan parked

at the end driveway, he knew something was wrong. You don't drive a sedan to haul off a tree you just cut down. He glanced at the other three men, who, although trying to seem nonchalant, were quickly surrounding them.

"You got a first name?" Levi asked.

The man shook his head as he walked up next to the workbench Levi was sitting on.

"Oh," Ed said, as if he'd just remembered. "I know who you're talking about now. You're looking for Rick Anderson's place."

Levi looked at Ed questioningly since he'd never heard of Rick Anderson.

"Who the hell is Rick Anderson?" Levi asked him.

"They moved into the old Webley place," Ed said, looking at Levi intently.

Levi glanced up at Ed quickly, then at the man standing next to him and the other three who were slowly surrounding them. Ed knew that Levi had finally realized they were in deep shit.

"Old Mr. Webley," Levi said. "I'd sure like to see him again. Where is he staying these days?"

"Directly south of here," Ed said.

Levi glanced at the tow truck, which was directly south of where Ed was standing. "Does Webley live alone now?"

Ed sighed. "Unfortunately. He's got no friends. Just him."

"Probably because he's always loaded?" Levi asked.

Ed nodded. "Yep, he's always loaded."

Levi had never seen the old man before, but he knew exactly who the man was. He was the right age, and there was a hard edge visible through the fake smile on his face. Levi was looking at the face of the fourth bank robber. The gunman.

Levi's face suddenly lit up as he snapped his fingers together. "Hey, you know what? I got a map in my truck," he said, sliding off the workbench and taking a step toward's Ed's tow truck.

"Don't worry about it," the old man said, stopping him with a hand on his shoulder.

He hadn't noticed that when Levi slid off the work bench, he'd grabbed the large socket wrench they'd used earlier to take off Pappy's doors and fenders.

Levi swung the wrench savagely, catching the old man on the side of the head with a solid blow. When he went down, Levi knew he wouldn't be getting back up again—ever. Ed dashed towards the tow truck as Levi took another savage swing, missing one of the other men by inches. They were caught off-guard. As they fumbled for their guns, they ran for cover. One of them dived behind the riding lawn mower as the other two found refuge behind Old Blue.

Ed was able to make it to the tow truck, but when the first shot rang out, breaking the window next to Levi's head, Levi was left in the open. He backed up next to the work bench and crouched behind it as best he could, but it provided little cover. Two more rounds slammed into the wall just over his head.

Ed popped up over the hood of his truck with the old Webley revolver and fired two shots. One blew the driver's side window out of Old Blue and the second caught the guy who was shooting at Levi in the shoulder. He grunted and fell behind Old Blue.

"Get over here. I'll cover you," Ed shouted at Levi. "Ready?"

"Do it," Levi shouted back as another round, fired by the guy hunkering behind the mower, slammed into the wall over his head.

But before Ed's started to fire, a fifth man stepped through the sliding doors in the back of the carriage house.

Crap, Ed thought.

Ed decided to take him out first since he was open and exposed in the entrance. But when Ed swung to take aim, he paused. The man was wearing a suit and tie and had a fedora on his head. Even though it had been many years since Ed had last seen him, he recognized him instantly.

"We've got trouble," Ed shouted.

Levi glanced towards the carriage house door as the man slowly raised an AK-47.

Oh shit, Levi thought when he saw the rifle.

Carl stared at Ed for a long moment, smiling tightly, with the rifle pointed at him.

Ed knew he was dead. This man had been waiting for this chance at him for decades.

But the man winked at him as he turned the barrel of the gun away and unloaded a massive barrage towards the three taking cover in the carriage house.

The sound was deafening as the bullets slammed a trail across the interior walls, blew holes in the riding lawn mower, and filled the air with dust and wood splinters. As Carl fired, three more men took advantage of the cover he was providing. They raced in behind him and took positions on either side of Ed behind the tow truck.

Levi had started to make a dash for the tow truck when Carl's ammo ran out, and he paused to snap in another clip. One of the men behind Old Blue rose and fired two rounds at Levi, causing him to back into his previous cover behind the work bench. The one behind the mower rose, too, and took two shots at Carl in the entrance, missing both times. Levi had no idea who the four were who'd just rushed in through the back door of the carriage house, but it was obvious they were on their side.

Ed reached over and grabbed the gun out of one of the gangsters' ankle holsters as Carl let loose with another barrage. Ed slid the gun across the flagstone floor of the carriage house towards Levi. It stopped six feet away from Levi as Carl's second barrage ended, and he went for another clip.

Levi glanced at Ed as another round hit the wall inches over his head, showering him with splinters. Levi didn't have a choice. He made a dash for the gun.

Ed saw the top of one of the men's heads round Old Blue's hood in a crouch. He didn't have a shot, and he knew Levi couldn't see him from his angle. He suddenly realized with sickening clarity it was the same trick the fourth bank robber had used to surprise Jim Mathis all those years ago.

"Levi, watch out!"

* * *

TORI HAD JUST FINISHED PUTTING THE CRIB TOGETHER WHEN SHE heard a couple of loud explosions come from the direction of the carriage house. They startled her, but she chuckled. She'd been hearing that for two weeks.

They'll never get that V-8 flathead running smooth, she thought. She could imagine Ed and Levi arguing as the truck backfired.

But when she heard the AK-47 open up, she dropped the clothes in her hand and dashed towards the bedroom door and down the stairs. Through the screen door, she saw the gray sedan in the driveway and a black Escalade parked behind it. She reached for her cell phone, but it wasn't in her pocket. She couldn't remember where she'd left it, but there was one thing she knew the location of. She opened the closet door in the foyer.

* * *

AS LEVI REACHED FOR THE GUN, HE SAW THE MAN HOLDING THE GUN leveled right at him.

"Shit," Levi said as he looked down the barrel of the gun. The man grinned as he squeezed the trigger. The gun clicked. Empty.

Levi snagged the revolver off the floor and shot him in the head. The man collapsed forward on the flagstones, his eyes staring blankly off to the side. Levi dashed towards Ed's tow truck as the man behind the mower rose. The Webley roared as Ed fired at him twice. The second shot caught him in the chest, and he folded over backwards as his gun clattered onto the flagstone floor.

"Is that all of them?" Levi yelled as he took cover behind the tow truck.

He looked at the other three men who were taking cover on either side of Ed—apparently friends rather than foes. But who?

"I think so," Ed said as he stood.

Suddenly, the first man Ed had hit, the one he'd shot in the shoulder, popped up from behind Old Blue and fired at Ed. Carl's rifle opened up again from his position, ripping a path down the inside wall towards him, as the last gunman decided it was time to go. He dashed from behind Old Blue and escaped through the carriage house door. Through the window, Ed saw him running down the driveway towards the sedan.

"Get 'em!" Carl roared from the back doorway.

Before any of Carl's men could react, they heard a massive explosion, followed by a blood-curdling scream.

All six of them raced towards the carriage house door. The man who'd just tried to escape was rolling on the ground, screaming over and over, "I'm on fire! I'm on fire!" The back of his blue jeans were pocked with holes.

Standing calmly on the corner of the porch, Tori loaded two more shells into Lucille Garvey's ancient 10-gauge double-barrel shotgun, which they used to call "Granny's Howitzer."

"Oh, suck it up. You're not on fire," Tori called from the porch as she snapped the shotgun closed. "But if you try to get up, so help me, I'll give you another one."

Levi smiled as he remembered what Ray had said about Tori. "That's no ordinary girl."

"Damn, that's got to burn like hell," Ed said to Levi. "Those shells are loaded with rock salt."

Levi winced.

"Who is that?" Vince asked, walking up next to Levi and staring at Tori.

"That is my wife, Tori," Levi said with a grin. Then he looked at the four old men that surrounded him. "The better question is who in the hell are you guys?"

"I think I can answer that," Ed said. "Meet Tony O'Malley's infamous Four Horsemen."

Levi's face fell. "You've got to be shitting me."

"Hello, Ed," Carl said, extending his hand cautiously. "It's been a long time."

Ed looked at his hand. "You scared me there for a minute."

"Good, I meant to," he replied. "And the name is Carl."

"I know your name. I'm not going to have to beat your asses again, am I?" Ed said, taking his hand. "It's already been a long day."

* * *

THE DRIVEWAY OF THE GARVEY HOUSE WAS FILLED WITH FLASHING lights and emergency vehicles. Chief Billings was standing in the center of the carriage house with a perturbed look on his face. He was staring at a line of large caliber bullet holes, one of several, that traced a path down the wooden interior wall of the carriage house.

There were two dead, one in front of the workbench and another facedown on the ground at Old Blue's hood. There were two wounded— one found screaming in the yard with a slug in his shoulder and an ass loaded up with rock salt and the other behind the lawn mower. According to the paramedics, it was unlikely the second man would survive the trip to the hospital.

Ray turned around to look at the Four Horsemen who were leaning against Ed Garvey's tow truck. Ed was sitting on the tailgate. Levi was crouched beside Old Blue, seemingly more concerned about the bullet holes in Old Blue than the chaos around him.

Cocking a thumb towards the wall, Ray asked, "Anybody want to tell me what made these holes?"

The Four Horsemen glanced at each other and shrugged.

"We'd rather not," Carl said.

"Probably wise," Ray snapped. "So let me get this straight. Tony O'Malley really doesn't know the identity of the fourth bank robber, so after our meeting in Chicago, he sends Carl down to shadow Ed Garvey, figuring the fourth bank robber probably means to take Ed out, too."

Carl shrugged, "That's not exactly right but fairly close."

"And you realize somebody is watching the Garveys, but it isn't Ed they're watching. It's Levi," he said.

Carl nodded.

"So Tony, the good Samaritan he is, sends you down here to warn the Garveys," Ray said.

Carl nodded again.

Ray looked at him for a long moment. "Okay, I don't believe that for a minute. You couldn't pick up a telephone and call? You had to come down here and warn him in person, heavily armed, and toting—judging from the bullet holes—some kind of anti-aircraft gun."

Ed chuckled.

When Ray glared at him, Ed stopped abruptly.

"That's what Tony wanted," Carl said. "I do what Tony says. I told you that before."

"That's bullshit," Ray said. "I think you four were sent down here to kill all four of these guys, but before you could get here to do it, they'd already launched their assault on the Garveys. And you four jumped into it."

Carl's face was as unreadable as that of a stone statue. "That's an interesting theory," he said.

Ray walked over to the old man lying on the floor in front of the work bench. "So this is our bank robber. The man who killed Deputy Jim Mathis back in '71. The man who shot Andy Miller and framed Ed. The man who took a shot at me the same night he murdered Steve Miller and burned his house to the ground. And he was here with his young friends to kill Levi and Ed, too."

"We'd have been in big trouble if these four hadn't turned up when they did," Levi said, rising to his feet and leaning against Old Blue.

"It'll be interesting to find out who this guy is," Ray said, looking down at the body on which they'd found no identification.

The man Tori shot was the only one able to speak, but he wasn't saying anything at all.

"He's not who you think he is," Ben Walker said, walking into the carriage house. "And this wasn't a hit either."

Ben tossed a plastic bag over to Ray. He examined it, shook his head, and tossed it to Levi. The plastic bag contained a white rag. Frowning, he glanced at Ray.

"Open it," Ray said.

Levi opened the top of the bag then pulled his head back quickly. The fumes were overpowering.

"What the hell is that?"

"Probably chloroform or maybe ether," Ray said.

"There were handcuffs and duct tape in the car, too," Ben added.

"Oh, my God, this was a kidnapping attempt," Levi said. "And I was the intended target. I thought they were just lousy shots, but they meant to take me alive from the beginning."

"You get an I.D. on any of these guys yet?" Ray asked.

Ben nodded. "You're going to love this. We just ran the plates on the sedan. The old man is Frank Malone."

"Malone?" Levi said angrily.

"Yeah, Doug Malone's uncle," Ben said. "And his three helpers were his sons—Doug's cousins. They don't live near here but over around Peoria."

"So this wasn't just about ransom," Ed remarked. "There was revenge involved here, too."

Levi's face was pale as he looked around at the destruction inside the carriage house.

"Good thing we stopped them," he said finally. "Even if they'd gotten the ransom, I've got a feeling I wouldn't have been walking away in the end."

"Not likely," Ray admitted.

"So this has nothing to do with the bank robbery," Carl said. "Not one damned thing."

He paused, then added, "I'm sure there was nobody else following Ed or Levi besides these guys."

"Which means our bank robber has gone underground," Ed said. "Probably went underground after he took that shot at Ray. We're unlikely to ever see him again since he's wiped out all the witnesses."

When Levi looked up, Ed's gaze told him not to say anything. Ray knew, but there was no reason to send that information back to Tony O'Malley—just in case they still had this all wrong.

"That should please Tony O'Malley," Ray Billings said snidely. "You go tell your boss that the '71 robbery case has officially gone cold. There are no leads, and he needn't worry himself anymore about the goings on in Twin Rivers."

"So we're not being detained?" Carl asked.

Ray flicked his hand at them. "I have your statements. You four didn't wound or kill anybody. In fact, it's kind of odd that three of you never fired a shot, and one of you fired around two-hundred rounds and never hit a damned thing."

Carl looked at him blankly.

"Interesting, isn't it?" Ray said glaring at him. "You really didn't want to get involved at all, but you knew your boss would be furious if something happened to the Garveys because you got here too late to take the Malones out quietly. You just kept their heads down, and let the Garveys pick them off one at a time when they popped up—didn't you? I'll bet you told your boys not to shoot or kill anybody unless it was absolutely necessary to save the Garveys."

Vince was nodding in agreement. Carl shot an elbow into his ribs.

"Are we free to go?" Carl said gruffly.

"If I have any other questions, I'll call you."

The Four Horsemen began walking towards the back door of the carriage house.

"Hey, Carl," Ed said.

Carl paused and looked back at him.

"I owe you one."

Carl rubbed the bridge of his crooked nose, the nose that had been straight before Ed Garvey remodeled it with a broom handle. A brief smiled flitted across Carl's face.

"I think I still owe you one, and I'm still going to beat your ass one day, Ed," Carl said over his shoulder as the four disappeared around the side of the building.

Chapter Thirty-Three

THE BELL OVER THE DOOR JINGLED AS BEN WALKER WALKED INTO Harv's Diner. When he spotted the Garveys in their usual booth, he walked over.

"Mind if I join you?" he asked.

Levi slid over to make room for him. "Please do."

Ben glanced at Ed, Levi, and Tori, who were unusually quiet, as April set a cup of coffee in front of him. Ben wondered if he hadn't interrupted something. No one spoke for several seconds.

Finally, Tori said, "Is there something on your mind, Ben?" She had plaster dust in her hair.

"Have you talked to Ray?"

They all shared a glance.

"We've just been talking about that," Ed said. "We've seen him, but we haven't talked to him since the kidnapping attempt last week. He seems to be avoiding us."

"I've called him a couple of times, and he hasn't called back," Levi said. "What's going on?"

"I don't know for sure," Ben said, "but I think he's going to resign."

The three of them didn't indicate their agreement, but they'd come to the same conclusion.

"Why do you think that?" Tori said.

"His stuff arrived from Savannah just before the deal in your carriage house," Ben said. "He brought a big box of things he was going to hang on the office walls, but it's still sitting there untouched. Then last night, I drove by his house, and the garage door was up. All the boxes that came in the truck are still sitting unpacked in there."

"I don't think he's going to stay, Ben," Levi said. "You can't blame him, can you?"

Ben shook his head. "Four dead bodies, an arson, an attempted murder, and a kidnapping attempt in a couple weeks."

"It's not just that," Levi said. "He's got a very strict ethical code, and he violated that code."

Ben nodded. "He let the Four Horseman go. He knew they were there to murder those four kidnappers but arrived too late to do that, so he let them go because they'd saved you and Ed and possibly Tori."

"That's not the only reason," Ed said. "He knows Tony O'Malley was behind the original robbery, but if he digs more deeply to prove it, it's likely Tony will have him killed and anybody else who knows anything about the crime. That's all of us. And it's possible there are still a few around we aren't even aware of who may know something about it."

"Ray is letting a man go who's responsible for the deaths of dozens over decades," Levi added. "It's something he's having a tough time reconciling."

Ben nodded. "But I think his decision to let it drop is the right one."

"Maybe you should tell him that," Tori said. "He needs to hear it. I think he believes he's settling on the lesser of two evils."

"He is," Ben said. "But like it or not, the Four Horsemen, as bad as they are, helped Ed and Levi out of a situation that could've ended very badly."

"That's not the way Ray sees it," Levi said. "He's thinking beyond that. He's thinking of all the lives that have been shattered in the past by the Chicago Outfit and the lives that are going to be impacted in the future by the Chicago Outfit."

"It's tough to live with when you view it like that," Ed said. "He thinks he's missing an opportunity to take down some really bad guys, and, in the back of his mind, he's wondering if it isn't just because he's afraid for himself and his friends. Every bad thing that happens because of the Chicago Outfit from here on out, Ray is going to feel responsible for. I know a little something about it."

"What do you mean?" Ben asked.

Tori nodded at Ed, encouraging him to continue. Levi didn't think he would because he rarely spoke about the topic he was referring to. Ed sat for a moment, then sighed.

"You probably know this, but I was a Marine sniper in Vietnam," Ed said.

Ben nodded. "I read Levi's book."

"I hadn't been in Vietnam long when I missed a shot," Ed said. "I was stalking a sniper who'd badly wounded two Marines in my unit. I found him, hidden in some tall weeds about four hundred yards from my position. I knew I had one shot at him, or he'd have me. But I got in a hurry because I thought he was about to take another shot at my unit, and I missed. I knew it wouldn't take him long to find me. I'd been trained to stay alive above all else and never take two shots from the same location, so I backed off my position slowly on my belly. By the time I found another position, he'd fired twice more from that position and then disappeared.

"Over the next week, that sniper took out several more Marines and wounded a few as well. He was good, but I finally found him again and killed him. I'd let him go the first time to save myself. I knew that's what I'd been trained to do, but it didn't help. I felt responsible for the Marines who were killed and wounded after he got away that first time. I felt guilty for a long time, but then a wise old Marine told me to start thinking about all the Marines that were still alive because I hadn't taken that second shot. Some had died, but many more had lived because I was still alive and still in the fight."

Ben smiled. "Maybe Ray will get a second shot at Tony O'Malley."

"When it's safer to do so," Tori added.

"But he can't do it later if he gets killed now, taking a long shot at him," Ed said.

"I think I'll go talk to Ray," Ben said, sliding out of the booth.

The Garveys were quiet for awhile before Levi said, "I don't think that's going to help. I think Ray's mind is made up."

"Unfortunately, I think you're right," Ed said.

* * *

"Hey, Chief," Russ Martin said as he stuck his head into Ray's office.

"Hello, Russ," Ray said, waving the young locksmith in.

"Moving in or moving out?" Russ asked, glancing at a large box sitting on the corner of the desk.

Ray didn't answer as he sipped his coffee. Russ wondered if he'd said something he shouldn't have.

"I'm over here to install a new lock on the Masonic Lodge, but I can't find Tori," he said, his tattooed arms crossed, his eyes big behind his thick glasses.

"I think she's lunching at Harv's."

"How's the hand?" Russ asked.

Ray flexed it and forced a smile. "It's mending. Pinkey finger still hurts like hell."

Russ laughed.

"Glad you're getting so much enjoyment out of my discomfort," Ray said, looking at him with his steely blue eyes as he curled up the corners of his mustache with his fingertips.

"Actually, I dropped in for a reason," Russ said. "I noticed something weird yesterday morning. It's not a big deal, but driving down here, I was thinking about all the questions you were asking that day in my shop."

"What is it?" Ray said, leaning forward.

"I think somebody broke into my shop."

"You think?"

Russ shrugged. "I noticed something was missing yesterday. I didn't report it because . . ."

"Because it's kind of embarrassing, considering your trade," Ray said, finishing Russ's thought.

"Yeah," Russ said. "A break-in can kind of make people think twice about trusting you to keep their stuff secure. Besides that, what they stole was worthless."

"Tell me about it."

"It's weird, Ray. Did you get a bunch of rain over here the other night?" Russ said, seeming to change the subject.

Ray nodded. People in the Midwest were obsessed with the weather. Of course, it changed a lot more in the Midwest than it did in Savannah. He'd seen his first tornado the other night.

"I think I heard somebody say we got over two inches in under an hour," Ray said.

"Well, we got four inches in about two hours. It was a downpour like I've never seen. A lot of basements in Calloway that had never gotten wet before wound up with water standing in them. The Home Depot sold out of sump pumps in an hour."

"I heard about that," Ray said. "Is this story going somewhere, Russ?"

"I'm getting there," he said. "So I checked the basement at the shop the next morning, just in case. There's nothing much in the basement, but I didn't want standing water down there."

"It's not like you could buy a sump pump," Ray said with a chuckle. "Home Depot was out."

Russ looked at him sharply. "You want to hear this story or not?"

Ray held his hands up, leaned back in his chair, and crossed his arms.

"Water was creeping in on one side. There was nothing down there but an old wooden table and two boxes of old records on the floor in the far corner."

Ray leaned forward. He was beginning to get interested.

"I put those two boxes on the table, so they wouldn't get wet if the water continued to seep in."

"Did it?"

"No, just a little came in on that one side and that dried up quickly, so I forgot about it," Russ said. "But yesterday morning, my grinder blew a fuse, and I went down to the basement to replace it. Old wiring in the building. It happens all the time. Sometimes my coffee maker blows a fuse. It's about the only time I go down to the basement."

"And?" Ray asked.

"Those two old boxes of records are gone, Ray," Russ said. "That's it. Nothing else is missing. I've got a fortune in tools in that shop, but the boxes are all that's missing."

"You got any idea what those records were?" Ray asked as a shiver went down his spine.

Russ shrugged. "They were down there when Dad bought the shop. Really old records in a couple of wooden soda bottle crates. I only glanced at them when I put them up on the table."

"So what did you see?"

"I didn't look too closely. They were pretty nasty. The mice had chewed the hell out of them, and they were covered in dust, but they looked like old business records, back before computers. There were a couple of ledger books in one box and tons of old cancelled checks. That's all I really noticed. I didn't even look at the other box."

"Anybody else have a key to the shop?" Ray asked.

Russ shook his head. "I'm a one-man operation. Dad doesn't even have a key anymore. I replaced the locks at the shop about a year ago—front door and back."

"You sure you didn't forget to lock the door?"

"I'm a locksmith, Ray," he said with the emphasis on *locksmith*. "I never forget to lock anything. I've got some very sensitive information in that shop, locked up in those safety deposit boxes in the back. Locking up is an engrained habit."

Ray sighed and rubbed the side of his head.

"Something wrong?"

"I didn't ask you the right questions the first time, Russ," Ray admitted. "I didn't know it at the time, but what I was actually looking for was probably in those boxes in your basement. You look at your locks?"

"In detail," Russ said. "I replaced them, but I had a good look at both of them inside and out. There was no sign of any tampering. I still have them if you'd like to have a look. They were good quality deadbolts. I just don't get it. Those aren't easy to open without a key."

"It would have to be somebody who knows locks," Ray said grimly.

Ray now knew exactly why somebody had tried to kill him. He hadn't realized how close he was. The man who broke into that safety deposit box in 1971 was a locksmith. There was little doubt left in Ray's mind that he had a connection with C & S Locksmith in Calloway, and his name was in those old records—probably on old payroll checks. Ray kicked himself for not thinking of it before. The other three bank robbers were locals, so why hadn't it occurred to him that the fourth bank robber was probably a local, too?

But how do I prove it now? Ray thought. How do I get that name without tipping him off?

* * *

"Wonder what Russ Martin is doing over at the police department?" April remarked, glancing out the window of the diner as she slid a piece of pie in front of her customer and refilled his coffee cup.

"Don't know," he replied as he looked out the window for a long moment.

"You know," April said with a smile, "Ray Billings hurt his hand when Russ was teaching him how to break into safety deposit boxes."

As he looked out the window at the C & S truck parked across the street, his pulse raced and his stomach knotted, but he smiled as he said, "I heard that."

"I'm sure we'll find out. Maybe he's over there to find out if Ray's hand healed up. I think he felt bad about that." April stepped away from the booth, then turned back. "You okay?"

"Yeah," he said. "Why?"

April picked up a napkin and dabbed the sweat on his forehead. "You're covered in sweat," she said.

"My blood sugar gets a little low sometimes."

"You're sure you're okay?"

"I'm fine," he said, smiling wanly. "I shouldn't have skipped breakfast this morning."

"Let me know if you need anything else," she said.

"I will, April."

After she walked away, he looked out the window. He could hear his heart thudding in his ears. That was really stupid, he thought. I should've left it alone. I shouldn't have taken those records the other night. Chief Billings is going to figure something out.

He tried to calmly eat his pie since April was watching him. She thought he was ill. Suddenly, he realized he'd made another stupid mistake. He hadn't skipped breakfast, and if April thought about it, she'd remember that he'd eaten breakfast there that morning as he usually did.

I'm making too many mistakes, he thought. I'd better leave it alone.

By the time he finished his pie, Russ still hadn't come out of the police department. He never hung around long after he finished his pie. If he did it now, April would notice.

"Hey, April," he said, pointing at his plate.

She pulled another piece out of the pie carousel on the corner of the coffee counter and brought it to him.

"You're looking a lot better," she said, sliding the piece in front of him.

He rubbed his hands together and picked up his fork. In truth, he didn't know where he was going to put more pie. He was stuffed. But he had to know how long Russ talked to Chief Billings.

"That hasn't happened for a long time," he said, wiping a hand across his forehead. "I get a little shaky all of a sudden and break out in a sweat."

"You should see Dr. Jackson about that. Blood sugar isn't something to mess around with. Ask Harv. He's right on the border, and if he doesn't lose weight, he's going to wind up insulin dependent. You were confused, too, and that's another bad sign," April said, walking away. "You seem to have forgotten you ate breakfast in here this morning."

He forced a smile as another layer of sweat broke out across his forehead.

As he struggled to find room for the pie, he saw Russ Martin walk out of the police department. He'd started to turn up the alley when Tori pulled her Impala into a parking space nearby. They talked for a minute on the sidewalk and then walked down the alley between the buildings together.

He glanced at the clock over the coffee counter. He'd been there no more than ten minutes, even though it'd seemed a lot longer. He felt a little better about what he'd seen. Maybe it was just a social call. Russ had probably come over to Twin Rivers to do some work for Tori. Maybe he hadn't even noticed those records were missing. They'd been down there in his basement for decades.

He picked up his ticket and paid Harv at the register. The bell jingled over the door when he left. As he crossed the sidewalk to his truck, Chief Billings walked out of the police department and spotted him.

"Hey," Chief Billings hollered across the street. "Is today lemon or butterscotch?"

"Lemon," he yelled back. "You'd better hurry if you want a piece. I just made a hell of a dent in the supply."

Ray chuckled as he climbed into his cruiser.

After the man got into his truck, he hesitated for a moment as he watched Ray Billings in his rearview mirror. After Ray was gone, he fired up his truck and slowly backed out.

This is probably a dumb idea, he thought, as he followed Chief Billings at a distance.

He hadn't gone far when Billings turned right off Main Street, just past the Comet Theatre. Sweat broke out on his forehead again as panic set in. He knew exactly where Ray Billings was going. There wasn't much down that street but houses, but once it left town, it turned into the road that Ed Garvey's junk yard was on.

He knows. I've got a feeling Chief Billings knows.

Chapter Thirty-Four

RAY PULLED INTO GARVEY USED AUTO PARTS, PARKED BEHIND ED'S white tow truck, and stepped out of the cruiser. The business operated out of an old metal shed with a rusty roof and two large garage doors. Behind the building were acres and acres of dead cars, many stacked one on top of the other with tall weed growing everywhere. Surrounding the property was a rusted chain link, which sagged in several places.

"Dammit," Ed said from somewhere down a narrow, weed-lined lane.

Ray couldn't see him, so he headed in the direction from which he'd heard the cursing. He found Ed, standing in front of mid-90's Dodge Ram pick-up, his finger in his mouth. He was in the process of removing the grill and headlight housings from the truck which had obviously been rear-ended.

"You okay?" Ray asked.

Ed spun around. Then, realizing he had his finger in his mouth, he pulled it out and looked at Ray as his face reddened.

Ray laughed.

"Smashed my finger. Happens all the time," Ed said, holding up his other hand which had bandages on three fingers.

"You sure that's okay?" Ray said when he noticed blood dripping off his fingertip.

"It's fine," Ed said. He pulled a bandage out of his tool box and leaned against the truck. "So when are you leaving, Ray?"

"I'm not. Ben Walker told me the most inspirational story I've ever heard. I've decided to stay."

A brief glimmer of humor appeared in Ed's eye.

"You should write that story down," Ray said. "They might make a

Hollywood movie out of it like they do with Levi's books."

Ed didn't say anything as he carefully wrapped his finger.

"In fact, I think they did back in the early 80s," Ray said with a smile. "I can't remember the name of it, but I watched it on television the other night. Maybe you saw it, too. In fact, I'll bet you did since it was still so fresh in your mind."

A sly smile appeared on Ed's face. "You didn't know that movie was based on a true story, did you?"

Ray chuckled. He sure hadn't expected Ed to stick with the story.

"No, I had no idea that movie was actually *The Ed Garvey Story*. So that story you told Ben was just part of the story—the opening sequence."

Ed grinned.

"Boy, that must've been something to have lived through. The way you broke into that POW camp later and rescued that prisoner, and then the two of you blew up the whole camp and released all the rest of the POWs and escaped into the jungle as the entire Vietnamese Army pursued you. You must've gotten a medal for that, huh?"

Ed rubbed his chin. "I never would've survived that alone, but I lucked out. I had no idea the guy I was rescuing from that POW camp was Chuck Norris."

Ray laughed loudly as he walked over to the truck and leaned against it next to Ed. "You have no idea how hard it was to keep a straight face as Ben told me that story."

"Well, it worked, didn't it?"

"That wasn't it," Ray said, suddenly serious, his voice low. "I'm very close to the fourth bank robber."

Ed's head snapped towards him.

"I talked to Russ Martin earlier. Somebody broke into C & S Locksmith in Calloway the other night and stole two boxes of old records from the basement."

Ed shook his head and looked at the blood soaking through the pad on his finger. "We're not very smart, are we?"

"Apparently not," Ray said. "We never seriously considered he could be a local, too. He could've worked at C & S at any point previous to 1971, but I'm sure that's where he learned about locks. That's got to be it."

"You're right. That's it, but we've got to be damn careful," Ed said. "If he's a local, he never left. He's been here all along. It could be anybody. You figure he's probably between sixty-five and maybe seventy-five?"

"Or he could be older than that," Ray said. "He seemed to be the leader. Everyone agrees on that fact. He could've been older than the other three. He could be in his eighties now."

"So he could be anybody in Twin Rivers or Calloway between the ages of sixty and eighty," Ed said. "That's half the men in this town."

"We say nothing to anybody except Levi and Tori until we figure this out," Ray said. "He's willing to kill to keep his identity a secret. And you're right. He's closer than we think."

"And people in small towns talk," Ed said. "They don't do it maliciously. It's just a fact of life. We've got to keep a tight lid on this, and don't assume that Russ Martin isn't going to repeat the story he told you earlier. It will get around. You just can't let on that it means anything to you. If he's a local, he'll find out you know. You've got to act as if you know it but that it's meaningless."

"How do we figure out who worked at C & S in the 60s and 70s without it hitting the grapevine?" Ray asked.

Ed shrugged. "IRS maybe? We can't really go to the courthouse in Calloway and pull the business records. That would get around. And those wouldn't tell you much. You're not going to find out who worked there from the courthouse records."

Ray took off his hat and wiped the sweat off his brow. "So how do we find out?"

"I'll bet Levi would know," Ed said. "He's a very good researcher."

"You want to run over there with me?" Ray said.

Ed glanced at his watch. "I've got a guy coming for this grill in about twenty minutes. Can you wait?"

"You haven't got that off yet, and you're about out of good fingers," Ray said.

"I don't know how you and Levi got to be friends because you're kind of a jackass," Ed said, glancing at his most recently injured finger. "You want to hand me that long handled screwdriver, Chief?"

"My pleasure," Ray said, leaning over to reach into the toolbox.

* * *

"So he never left," Levi said, sitting on the porch rail and leaning against a post.

Ed was also sitting on the porch rail and leaning against another post a few feet away. Ray and Tori were sitting on the porch swing. They'd been talking about what Russ Martin had told Ray earlier.

"You're right about one thing," Tori said. "You can't go asking questions about C & S."

"But how do we find out who worked at C & S years ago?" Ray asked as he rubbed the ears of the puppy in his lap which was wrestling with his hand.

Levi was deep in thought as he stroked the head of another puppy in the crook of his arm. "It's a long shot," he finally said, "but I can't think of any other way."

"What?" Ed asked.

"Census records," Levi said. "I think the library has them for the county going back a hundred years."

"What'll that tell us?" Ray asked.

"Maybe nothing," Levi admitted. "Or we may be able to tell who owed C & S at different points during the sixties and seventies. I've looked at the River County census records a few times. I looked up Grandpa William once when I was younger. Those records told how old he was, who he was married to, and the number of dependents living in his house."

"That's not going to help us," Tori said.

"It also recorded that he was the owner of the Garvey Brick Company back in the fifties."

Tori grinned as she followed where he was going. "By name?"

"Yes," Levi said. "I asked Grandma about it. I didn't know the family had once owned a brickyard. It was out by the river somewhere."

"I know exactly where it was," Ed remarked. "The current location of Garvey Used Auto Parts. The family already owned that piece of property, so I bought it and started my business there. The brickyard had burned down in the mid-sixties, but it'd been closed for years before that."

"You'd have to go through every record," Tori said. "You've got to figure there are probably tens of thousands of names in those records."

"I may not have to go through all of them," Levi said. "I'll start with last names that start with 'C' and names that start with 'S'. There's only one census every ten years. I'll start with 1980, then go back through the decades."

"It's a needle in a haystack," Ray said. "Russ Martin's father never changed the name when he bought the shop because it was well-established. The previous owners could've done the same thing."

"True, but it's all we've got," Levi said. "I just might get lucky. If I can find the owner, we might just have an idea of how to identify our missing gunman."

"It could work," Ed said. "And nobody will think twice about Levi researching obscure facts in the library. He's there almost every day."

When a truck drove by, Ed glanced up and waved. It honked twice. Levi also waved.

"Somebody want to give me a ride over to the library," Levi asked.

"Why don't you borrow the Cadillac until we get Old Blue patched up," Ed said.

"It's a Chevy," Levi hissed.

"Watch your mouth—that was your grandma's car," Ed said, giving him a sidelong glance. "She loved that car."

"That Chevy," Levi muttered.

Ed chuckled. "You can just walk then. It'll be good for you, Tubby."

"Okay, I'll borrow it," Levi said. "Let's go get it."

Ed and Levi slid off the porch rail. Levi set his puppy down on the porch floor and started down the steps. Ray stood up and started to hand his puppy back to Tori.

"Why do you keep leaving him here?" Tori asked. "You always grab the same puppy. He likes you, and you like him. Take him home, Ray."

Ray looked at Tori and then down at the puppy. He held him up to his cheek.

"You want to go home with me?" he asked as the puppy licked his face and messed up the curly waxed ends of his mustache.

Ed laughed like a mule. "Well, that seems settled."

"What's that phrase you Masons use?" Tori asked. "So mote it be?"

Ray laughed, tucked the puppy under his arm, and said, "So mote it be."

* * *

TORI WAS DOZING IN THE DEN. SHE'D FALLEN ASLEEP TOWARDS THE end of a Humphrey Bogart movie and awakened in the middle of a Clark Gable one. She was waiting for Levi to return from the library. Rosco was snoring on the floor in front of the recliner, and two puppies were sleeping in her lap. She glanced at the wall clock. It was nearly midnight. Mrs. B. would've left Levi there after the library closed. He had a key.

She was thinking about going to bed when the Cadillac pulled into the driveway, and the headlights flashed across the wall of the den. A minute later, Levi opened the back door. Tori heard the rattle of bottles in the refrigerator. Moments later, he crossed the den and plopped down on the couch. Sighing, he twisted the cap off a beer with a hiss and took a sip.

"Nothing?" Tori asked.

Levi rubbed his eyes and shook his head.

"Damn," she said.

"I had no idea how many Calhouns, Carters, Cessnas, Colemans and Cashs there were in River County. Not to mention the Smiths, Snyders, Sloans, Spurlocks, and Stewarts."

"It was a good idea and worth a try," Tori said.

Levi smiled tiredly at her.

"So now what?" she asked.

"I think I'll run over to the library in Calloway tomorrow morning," Levi said. "I still think if I saw that face again—the guy I saw arguing with Andy Miller when I was four—I'd recognize him. He was older than Andy, I think, but he wasn't old. I don't remember a lot about him. But he had to be in his late twenties, maybe early thirties."

"Calloway High School?" Tori asked.

Levi nodded. "They should have all the yearbooks. We've made a connection to Calloway since we know he worked at C & S."

"So where do you start?"

Levi took another sip of his beer. "I'm going to start with 1950 and work my way forward."

"That's a lot of faces," Tori remarked.

"It's a small high school. Maybe a hundred graduates a year," Levi said.

"If you go up through 1970, that's still 2,000 faces," Tori said.

"And he'd probably been out some years before he robbed the bank, so he may've changed a lot. It's another long shot," he said, glancing at the television and sipping his beer.

"I can't watch this," Tori remarked.

"I was wondering about that. You can't stand Clark Gable."

"I never understood the attraction. He's got big ears and buck teeth."

"Oh, but this is a great movie. *It Happened One Night* with Claudette Colbert," Levi said. He was a huge classic cinema nut.

"It's not the movie I can't watch," Tori said. "What I'm having trouble with is watching you drink that delicious ice-cold beer."

"Sorry," Levi said. "That's got to be rough."

"Thanks to you, I can't have a beer or a cup of coffee until Thanksgiving," she said.

"Hey, I wasn't alone when this happened. You were there, too."

Tori stood up. For the first time, Levi noticed a slight change in her shape as she picked up the puppies to put them to bed.

"Don't stay up all night, Levi."

"I'll have another beer and watch the end of this movie," he said.

"You'll fall asleep."

"No, I won't. I'll be up right after this is over. Another forty-five minutes."

Tori looked down at him and smiled. She knew better. The problem with the old movie channel was that it ran 24-hours a day. There was always another old movie on. Levi would get hooked into the next one as he always did. She knew he'd be asleep in that very spot when she got up in the morning.

* * *

He'd been working in the basement for hours when he pushed away from the workbench and looked down at his work. He set the soldering iron to the side and carefully studied the connections. The device was crude but effective.

Part of him was trying to talk himself out of using it, but the other part knew he had little choice. When he'd seen Chief Billing's cruiser parked at Ed Garvey's junkyard after his talk with Russ Martin, he'd known Russ wasn't there for a social call. Russ had noticed the records were missing, and he'd decided to tell Chief Billings.

Then when Ed Garvey and Ray Billings had made a beeline to see Levi and Tori, he'd known they weren't far away from the truth. He'd seen the serious expressions on their faces as he'd driven by. And since that meeting, Levi had been parked at the library in Lucille Garvey's old Caddy. The library had closed, but Levi had stayed.

Levi's got to go first, he thought. He's the most dangerous. If anybody figures it out, he will. He just might find something in that library that jogs his memory, and it will all fall together for him.

And Tori saw me that day, too.

When the getaway car had banged into a parked car, he'd seen her little face in the back window. She'd waved at him. A few months earlier, her father had put a new roof on his family's house, and Tori had come along since her mother was sick and her father had nobody to watch her. He and Tori had watched Scooby-Doo cartoons while her father hammered away on the roof above.

He didn't have a choice. Levi and Tori had to go. He'd worry about Ed Garvey later.

Planning was the easy part. The Garveys, for the most part, were predictable. They seldom varied their routine much from day to day. Most days, they were up early. Tori would join Levi on the porch for coffee and then go off to work on one of her projects. Levi would go for pie and more coffee and then run errands. He'd usually wind up at the library for a few hours by mid-morning.

Ed was the only part of the plan that worried him. If anything happened to Levi or Tori, Ed Garvey would find him. And another problem was Chief Billings. He had no idea how close the chief was to him. There was a good chance that unless this plan went off flawlessly, Ray Billings would knock something loose. He'd already linked him to C & S.

It was a huge risk, and he knew it. But there was no other way.

He picked up the device he'd made and carefully placed it into his old olive drab duffel bag. He'd carried that bag the day of the bank robbery with the thumper inside—the locksmith tool he'd used to open that safety deposit box thirty-eight years earlier.

He glanced at his watch. It was just past midnight.

Sighing, he wiped sweat off his forehead with the back of his hand. It was going to be a long night.

Chapter Thirty-Five

"AND WAIT UNTIL YOU SEE WHAT I'VE DONE WITH THE LIGHTING," TORI said as Levi sipped coffee on the porch swing and watched Rosco chase squirrels around the yard.

"I can't get a little preview?"

Tori was absolutely beaming as she talked about the Twin Rivers Masonic Lodge. If she was excited about the lodge, it would be beyond his wildest expectations.

"Two weeks," Tori said, "then you all can see it. No peeking. We're down to paint, carpet, and refinishing the old chairs and altar. I've also got a lot of work to do in your new bathroom. Then you Freemasons can have your lodge back."

"Well, it would be kind of hard to take a peek since you had Russ rekey the door, and you have the only key."

Tori kissed him on the cheek and skipped down the porch steps. She paused at the bottom. "Free for lunch?"

Levi nodded. "Going to the Calloway Library, but I'll see you at Harv's at noon."

Levi stood as Tori backed down the driveway in her Impala. Then he walked to the carriage house with Rosco on his heels, slid the door open, and walked over to the Cadillac. He'd never say it out loud, but he kind of liked his grandma's old ride, even if it was a Chevy.

Rosco jumped in before Levi climbed in behind the wheel. He turned the key, but the ignition just clicked. The engine never turned over.

"Chevy," he said simply.

When he reached down to pop the hood, he glanced at Old Blue, which looked like hell. They'd repaired the bullet holes, but one side was covered mostly in gray primer paint. As soon as Pappy was finished, they planned on giving Old Blue a brand new paint job.

"Oh, what the hell," Levi said. He opened the Caddy door, and Rosco bailed out over his lap. "Let's take Old Blue. I'm tired of bumming rides and dealing with loaners."

Rosco jumped in with Levi right behind him. As he pulled the door closed, he noticed the faint smell of gas fumes. He leaned over the seat to unroll Rosco's window on the passenger side. Because the carriage house always smelled faintly of gas and oil, especially since the mower had been shot to hell with an AK-47, he didn't think much of it.

Levi fired up Old Blue and left the carriage house. As he was driving by the porch, he realized he'd forgotten his laptop in the den.

"You stay here," he said to Rosco as he mashed the clutch down, popped it out of gear, and set the brake. "I'll be right back."

There was a deafening bang behind his seat, and in a brief second, Levi felt heat behind his head. He glanced down. To his horror, he both saw and smelled the gasoline running across the floor of the cab from the truck's gas tank behind the driver's seat.

He knew he had only seconds.

He threw the door open, grabbed Rosco's collar, and bailed out of the cab. Flames licked up behind him as he sprinted away. Feeling the intense heat, he realized his shirt was on fire. Resisting the urge to keep running, he dived onto the ground and rolled in the grass, still wet from the morning dew. He heard the fire sizzling in the damp grass as he rolled.

Finally, he sat up and looked around. His Panama hat was on fire a few feet away. The back of his neck and arms were burned—how badly he didn't know—but the pain was intense. The entire cab of Old Blue was engulfed in flames. His stomach sank at the sight, but another thought put him into a panic.

He looked down at his hand. He was still gripping Rosco's collar, which had slipped off over his head when he'd tried to yank him out of the cab.

Oh no, he thought. I can't lose another dog.

"Rosco!" he yelled as he struggled to his feet.

All that answered was the roar of the flames and the crack of glass as the windows broke due to the tremendous heat. When Levi ran around the front of the truck towards the porch, he saw Rosco running towards him.

"Oh, thank God," Levi said, falling to his knees.

Rosco licked his face over and over again. Levi felt both sides of Rosco as tears blurred his vision. His fur was singed, but they'd both survived. As Levi reached for his phone, he heard the fire trucks in Twin Rivers. Somebody had seen the smoke.

As he waited for the fire department, Levi hugged Rosco and watched Old Blue burn. Tears ran down his face as what had just happened finally soaked in. Levi and Old Blue had been together a long time.

"I just killed my truck," Levi said as Rosco licked the tears from his face.

* * *

ED GARVEY WAS HAVING HIS BREAKFAST AT HARV'S. IT WAS BUSY THAT morning with all the farmers there. They were hoping to get some work done. It looked like it might be the first day dry enough to start preparing the fields for planting.

Harv was whistling in the kitchen as eggs and bacon sizzled on the grill, and April hustled orders back and forth and refilled coffee cups.

Suddenly, shrill alerts went off in several places in the diner as the emergency radios carried by the members of the volunteer fire department sounded with the garbled language translatable only by fire fighters.

"What is it?" April asked one of the men with a radio when the siren of the fire truck wound up as it left the station a few blocks up the street.

He glanced at Ed.

"Fire at the Garvey house," he said as he headed for the door.

Ed set down his coffee cup and ran after the firemen as they quickly left the diner. One firetruck slowed to a stop in front of the diner. The firemen jumped onto the back—Ed, too. A second truck was close behind. As they reached Elm and roared out of town, Ed's gut wrenched. Clouds of black smoke drifted up and over the road in front of the Garvey house.

* * *

"I THINK HE'S OKAY, LEVI," THE PARAMEDIC SAID, RISING FROM HIS knee next to Rosco, as another examined Levi, who was sitting on the bumper of the ambulance, "but keep in mind, I'm no vet. The fur on his haunches and tail is singed pretty good, but I don't think it got down to his skin. I'd have a vet check him out."

Levi nodded.

"What about Levi?" Ed said impatiently.

"He's lucky he dropped and rolled when he did. His shirt was on fire, and so was his hat." Turning to Levi, the paramedic said, "Your hair is singed, too. You're lucky it didn't catch fire. You've got some second degree burns on the back of your neck and the backs of your arms. It'll be like a really nasty sunburn, and it'll blister. You'll be uncomfortable for a week or so. You should go in with us and get checked out more thoroughly."

"I'll go see Dr. Jackson later," Levi said, shaking his head.

The fire department had put Old Blue out quickly, but the truck was still ticking and pinging as hot surfaces do when they cool down. Levi and Ed walked over to Old Blue.

"What the hell happened?" Ed asked.

"Your stupid Chevy wouldn't start, so I took Old Blue," Levi said. "I smelled gas when I climbed in, but I thought it was from the mower."

"I just don't get where the leak could've come from. I checked the fuel line and the gas tank after the shoot-out in the carriage house, and I didn't see any damage at all," Ed said.

"I checked, too," Levi said. "We must've missed something. One of those bullets obviously did more damage than we saw. I shouldn't have started Old Blue, smelling the gas like I did. I killed my truck."

Ed rubbed his chin as he looked over the damage. "The cab is toast, but I'll bet that engine is fine."

Levi glanced at him doubtfully. "With that kind of heat? Hard telling what kind of damage the fire did underneath. The frame even."

"I've still got the Frankenstein trucks," Ed said, referring to the fact that Old Blue was the best parts of about four Ford trucks.

"You serious?"

"Pappy is about done," Ed said. "A few more hours maybe, and we'll be done. Tori won't be able to drive Pappy with a baby, but you could while we rebuild Old Blue."

"I don't know," Levi said, shaking his head.

"Listen," Ed said. "We'll either rebuild this one, or if we find we can't do that, we'll find another one just like it. Then we'll take every salvageable part off Old Blue and build Old Blue II."

There was a hint of a smile on Levi's face.

"See, don't you feel better now?" Ed said with a grin as he leaned against Old Blue's door.

The metal hissed as Ed jumped away quickly, rubbing the back of his pants.

"Son of a bitch!" he shouted.

Levi laughed. "I do feel better now."

Turning towards the ambulance, Levi yelled, "Medic!"

Two paramedics ran over.

"I think Uncle Ed just burned his ass."

"I'm fine," Ed said as the two medics took his arms and guided him towards the ambulance.

"Now why would you do that, Ed," one of the medics said. "You knew that truck had just been on fire, didn't you?"

* * *

It was a good lock Russ Martin had installed on the door of

the Twin Rivers Masonic Lodge. The man was impressed. It took him a full minute to open it as he looked nervously up and down the alley. When the deadbolt finally yielded to his expert touch, he slipped in.

He stood at the bottom of the long staircase that led up to the second floor. As he ascended the stairs, he could hear the loud music echoing upstairs. When he reached the Tyler's room on the first floor, he looked into the massive lodge room. It was empty.

Tori was in the bathroom just off the Tyler's room, wiping down the wall behind the new urinal, with her back to him. Boxes of pale blue tiles lay on the floor nearby. Guitars from her boom box sitting on the sink screamed 80s metal.

He climbed the stairs to the third floor and glanced into the small kitchen upstairs. It was empty as well. Tori was working alone. Quietly, he returned to the second floor.

He wasn't sure how he was going to do this since he hadn't planned yet. He thought it would come later, but when Tori didn't show up at the fire, he'd wondered why. Now he knew she hadn't heard the firetrucks because of the loud music—or her phone, which was lying on top of the boom box nearby. Tori had no idea her husband was dead.

Slowly, he crept into the bathroom behind her and picked up her cell phone. He thought about the revolver in his pocket, but the police department was downstairs. If they heard a shot, and they probably would, he'd never get out of the building since there was only one way out—back down the staircase.

As he eased out of the bathroom, he surveyed the collection of construction equipment in the Tyler's room. A red gas cylinder caught his attention. It was a tank full of CO_2, which is used to blow out filters and remove drywall dust from electric boxes. CO_2 is safe in small quantities but deadly in high amounts in closed quarters.

He pulled the spray nozzle off the bottle, leaving just a long rubber hose attached. He glanced into the bathroom. Tori was still tiling, oblivious to anyone being there, probably never even considering the possibility with the brand new deadbolt on the door downstairs. He swung the bathroom door closed and wedged it shut with a metal chair. Then he slipped the hose under the door.

It would happen quickly. The gas would sneak up on her in that small space. She'd get dizzy, then pass out within a few minutes, and finally asphyxiate. He reached down for the valve on the bottle but paused.

This is Tori, he thought. I'm killing Tori Buchanan.

But it was too late to stop. He'd already killed Levi. Tori knew too much.

Slowly opening the valve on the bottle, he heard the gas being released. Rising, he glanced down at the hose under the door.

That's two down and one to go. Ed Garvey is next, he thought. Then I'll see what Chief Billings does.

He knew there was a good possibility Ray Billings would have to go, too.

* * *

ED AND LEVI WERE SITTING ON THE PORCH, WATCHING THE FIRE CHIEF, Jack Hooper, examine Old Blue in detail. The fire had been out less than an hour, and the truck was still hot. He was wearing heavy gloves as he sifted through what was left in the cab. Ed and Levi said little to each other as they watched him try to determine the cause of the fire.

Ray Billings pulled up in his cruiser, got out of the car, and strode up to the porch.

"Everybody okay?" he said, climbing the stairs.

"Uncle Ed burned his ass," Levi said with a snicker.

Ray smiled, looking down at his feet. "I'm sorry I wasn't here sooner, Levi. I was over at C & S Locksmith with the CSI. Jeff went over the basement and the locks."

"Let me guess. Nothing," Levi said.

"Nothing," Ray said. "You call Tori?"

"Tried," Levi said. "She's not answering. Probably has the music blaring up in the lodge room. I'll tell her at lunch."

"Sorry about Old Blue," Ray said.

"It was my fault," Levi said.

"We're going to rebuild Old Blue," Ed remarked.

That didn't surprise Ray one bit.

Jack Hooper, still wearing his yellow helmet and fireman's gear, walked up to the steps and joined them on the porch. He was holding something in his gloved hand.

"What's that?" Levi asked.

He looked down at the object in Chief Hooper's hand—a small metal tube about three inches long, blackened by the fire. Levi didn't know what it was, but it wasn't a part from Old Blue that he recognized.

"This wasn't an accident, Levi," he said with a sigh.

Staring at the object, Ed said, "I haven't seen one of those in a long time."

"What is it?" Ray asked, peering over Ed's shoulder.

"It's a blasting cap," Ed said. "You shove that into a stick of dynamite and wire it to a detonator. Then when you push down the plunger, the blasting cap shoots hot sparks into the dynamite, causing it to explode."

"Where did you find that, Jack?" Levi asked.

"Sticking out of a hole somebody drilled in the top of your gas tank," he said. "There was a battery under your seat and a switch under your clutch pedal. We checked out the Cadillac in the carriage house. It was intentionally disabled."

Levi's face went pale. "How is it I'm still here?"

"You're lucky it didn't go up in the carriage house," Jack said. "My guess is you didn't push the clutch all the way down when you started Old Blue and put it into gear to pull out of the carriage house."

Levi nodded. "I never do. You don't have to push the clutch in too far to get Old Blue in gear."

"But I'll bet getting her out of gear is a little different," Jack said.

Levi nodded. "All the way to the floor, and that's when I heard that loud bang behind me."

"Let me tell you what saved your life, Levi," Jack said. "Probably two things. The tank was nearly full, wasn't it?"

"I'd just filled it the day before the shoot-out in the carriage house," Levi said.

"Since it was full of liquid fuel, there was a minimum amount of gas fumes in there to ignite. That was important. The second thing was that gas tank had a weak seam, so when those fumes ignited and expanded, the tank ripped open, dumping gas across the floor of the truck. It gave you just enough time to realize what was happening and get out before the fire consumed the cab. If that tank had been stronger or the tank had been half full, it would've exploded like a bomb instead of rupturing and burning as it did. You would've never known what hit you."

Levi sat down hard in the porch swing. My God, somebody just tried to kill me, he thought.

"This just happened," Ed said suddenly. "I moved Old Blue yesterday afternoon. I backed it up into the center of the carriage house to do more sanding on those doors. And I always clutch it to the floor."

"Why would somebody want to kill me?" Levi said.

"I think you know why," Ray said. "He knows you saw him, and he knows we're close."

Levi's face snapped towards Ed.

"Tori!" he gasped.

In an instant, Levi and Ed were running down the porch steps. They stopped at the bottom and looked around. Neither of them had a vehicle. Jeff, the CSI, had just pulled in behind Ray's cruiser, blocking it in. They raced across the yard towards the fire truck closest to the road.

"Hey," Jack yelled. "You can't take that!"

Levi jumped in and fired it up as Ed pulled the passenger door shut. As they roared down the driveway, Ed reached up and flipped on the lights and the siren.

Jack stopped running halfway across the yard when the firetruck swerved onto the road in front of the Garvey house and headed towards Twin Rivers. Ray Billings ran up next to him, out of breath from the sprint.

"The Garveys just stole my freakin' fire truck," Jack said, resting his hands on his knees, breathing heavily. "In thirty-five years, nobody has ever stolen my fire truck."

Turning, Ray ran back towards the house. "Move your car, Jeff! I gotta get out!" he yelled.

* * *

WHEN THEY REACHED THE TYLER'S ROOM, ED AND LEVI IMMEDIATELY saw the bathroom door wedged shut with the folding chair and the red tank on the floor in front of it.

"Oh, no," Levi said.

Ed dashed over and threw the chair across the room as Levi pulled the door open and rushed in. It was like a fog bank in the bathroom. The air was full of drywall dust, and the music was thumping loudly. As the air cleared, Levi reached over and yanked the boom box cord out of the wall. It went suddenly quiet. Ed cranked the valve on the tank closed.

"Tori?" Levi yelled, squinting through the dust.

"Hey, look at this," Ed said, pointing at the hose that had been run under the bathroom door from the tank.

The hose had been folded over in half and clamped shut with a pair of vise-grips. As the air continued to clear, they realized Tori wasn't in there.

"The window," Ed said.

The small bathroom window was open. Levi looked out. There was nothing outside the window but a narrow ledge—and a long drop to the alley below. Suddenly, they heard loud banging coming from the lodge room. Levi rushed from the bathroom into the lodge room.

A large piece of plywood, which had been used to seal the window when the stained glass had been removed for restoration, came flying out of the window frame. Tori was standing on the ledge outside. She stepped in through the window hole and hopped down onto the lodge floor.

"What the hell is going on, Levi?" Tori said, her eyes wide. "Somebody just tried to kill me."

"Me, too," Levi said, hugging her.

Then he held her away at arm's length, "You okay?"

"I'm fine," she said, "but what happened to your shirt? And your hair?"

"I got a little singed, so don't hug me too hard," he said, holding her tight again. "But if you think I'm in bad shape, you ought to see Old Blue."

Ed was leaning against the doorway of the lodge room, trying to catch his breath. As he watched Tori and Levi embrace, he thought about how very lucky they'd been that day. Suddenly, he heard footsteps running up behind him. Before he could react, somebody shoved him hard from behind.

He fell into the lodge room. Levi and Tori spun around and saw him lying on the floor.

"Ed," Levi said, running up to him.

"Go," Ed said, holding his knee. "He's still here!"

Levi heard feet running down the steps and rushed to the top of the stairs. Ray Billings was halfway up the stairs as the man was running down.

"Stop him, Ray," Levi shouted.

Ray barely had a chance to look up before the man caught him in the throat with an elbow. Ray lost his footing, and as the man fled the building, Ray tumbled down the steps—landing at the bottom in a motionless heap.

Chapter Thirty-Six

"Ow," RAY SAID, SLAPPING AWAY THE HAND OF THE PARAMEDIC. "I don't need much more of that."

"You're going to need a couple stitches in that eyebrow," the paramedic said, standing back with a swab in his hand. "And I'm a little concerned about that shoulder."

"Stop," Ed said, pushing away a second medic who was looking at his knee. "I've had about enough of you today, Duane. That knee didn't bend like that even before it was injured!"

They were both sitting on the back of the ambulance on Main Street while all the regular lunchtime diners at Harv's stood on the sidewalks, watching from across the street.

Tori was telling Jack Hooper what had happened to her at the lodge as Ray listened. Levi was holding her hand, his face pale and drawn.

"So it was the dust?" Jack asked.

"Yeah. I'd just finished sanding all the drywall seams yesterday, so the whole bathroom was covered in dust. I was going to tile around the urinal, so I was wiping down the walls with a damp sponge when all of a sudden, it started getting cloudy in there. I didn't know why, so I went to the door but found I couldn't open it. Then I felt the compressed air blowing my pants legs. When I saw that rubber hose sticking out from under the door, I knew I was in trouble. I grabbed the hose, folded it over, and clamped it closed with my vise-grips."

Levi looked at her. "So why did you climb out the window onto that narrow ledge? You could've fallen, Tori."

"I wasn't sure how much gas had gotten into the bathroom, and I wasn't sure what kind of gas it was either."

"What do you mean?" Ed said.

"There was a welding tank out in the Tyler's room, too," Tori said.

"So you were thinking it might be flammable gas, and there could be an explosion," Jack said.

Tori nodded. "The dust was thick in the air. The music was blaring. I opened the window to air it out, but after I opened the window, I could see our house—all the black smoke—and then I heard a fire truck," Tori said. "I thought his plan wasn't to smother me, but to burn me up in a fire, like he did Stevie Miller."

Tori stopped as a sob escaped. Then with tears running down her checks, she said, "I knew he'd already been to see Levi."

"He had," Levi said.

"But I knew you were okay," Tori said. "I just knew."

Levi nodded—he knew what she meant.

"But I wasn't hanging around to wait for the explosion," Tori said.

"The fire truck you heard probably wasn't us going to the fire," Jack said. "It was probably Ed and Levi in the fire truck they stole rushing to rescue you."

"You stole a fire truck?"

"It was Uncle Ed's idea," Levi said defensively.

"And we didn't steal it," Ed said. "We borrowed it."

"They didn't have much of a choice," Ray said, glancing at Jack, "and it's a good thing they did."

Jack reluctantly nodded. "No harm done."

"What about Old Blue?" Tori asked.

"Oh, he'll be fine," Ed said. "He'll just be out of commission for a while."

But Tori caught the pained look in Levi's eyes. He knew the truth, and now she did, too. Old Blue was gone.

A fire truck made its way up the street towards them. For all the world, it looked like a German shepherd was driving with his head hanging out the driver's side window. As the truck rolled to a stop in front of Harv's, a firefighter appeared in the window behind the giant dog.

"Would you get off me?" he shouted as he tried to push the dog off his lap.

It was a losing battle. Levi grinned, and Tori laughed out loud.

"Hey, Levi," the firefighter called over. "Can you call this damn dog? He jumped in when I was leaving."

Levi smiled, and let out a shrill whistle. Rosco's ears popped up and his head snapped towards Levi. "Come on, Rosco!"

The firefighter opened the door. Rosco bailed out, ran over, and jumped up on Levi, nearly knocking him over.

"I know," Levi said as Rosco licked his face. "It's been a hell of a day, and it's not even noon yet."

* * *

"That's better," Ed said, looking at the target several feet away.

Tori loaded three more rounds into the Webley. They were standing in the yard beside the carriage house, shooting at playing cards stapled to a large piece of cardboard which was leaning against a tree.

"You nail the first shot dead center, but your second and third shots get progressively worse."

"It's the recoil," Tori said. "It kicks like a mule."

Ed chuckled. "Don't think about it. Squeeze off all three exactly the same way. You've got to focus on the target and where you want that bullet to go. Don't think about the recoil. Try the ace of spades up in the right corner this time."

Tori leveled the revolver using a two-handed stance and slowly squeezed the trigger. The first shot hit dead center.

"Do it again. Think about the target. You've got to be the bullet."

"That's very Zen, Ed."

He shrugged.

Tori took a deep breath. As she reached the bottom of her exhale, she began squeezing the trigger. The Webley roared.

Tori looked at the target and shook her head at Ed. "I missed it completely that time."

Ed laughed. "No, you didn't. You put the second round in the same hole. Bet you can't do it again."

Tori leveled the Webley again. After the gun fired, she smiled. The third shot had hit less than an inch from the first hole.

Ed let out a low whistle. "You're pretty good for a beginner."

"The target is only twenty feet away, Ed."

"That's the range you want to get good at. If you can hit that every time, you know you can hit something closer, and to be honest, you wouldn't want to take a shot at anything much further away than that with a handgun."

"Twenty feet," Tori said looking at the target, which seemed very close to her. "You sure this is necessary?"

"It's better to be prepared, Tori."

"We're not done yet, are we?"

Ed knew she wasn't talking about target practice. He glanced at her and then at the target. After a long moment, he slowly shook his head.

"He's going to make another attempt, isn't he?" Tori said.

Ed nodded. "It'll be sooner rather than later. He's desperate. He took a big risk today. He attacked you in broad daylight on the spur of the moment. He'd planned to kill Levi today, but I don't think he'd planned on killing you. He simply saw the opportunity and took advantage of it. He could've gotten caught a hundred different ways—almost did."

"He won't make that mistake again," Tori remarked.

"You're right about that. Next time he comes after us, he's not going to be taking any chances. Levi knows that, too," he said, nodding towards the house. Levi was sitting on the swing, staring at what was left of Old Blue. "He never flinched when I suggested his pregnant wife ought to learn to fire a handgun."

She looked over towards Levi. "I've never seen him like that before."

"Like what?"

"Depressed," she said. "I don't know what he's more upset about. The fact somebody tried to kill us today or the fact that somebody killed his beloved truck. Can Old Blue really be restored, Ed? Honestly?"

Ed frowned and shrugged. "I doubt it."

"I didn't think so," Tori said.

"It's just a truck, Tori. And they made a lot of trucks like that."

"But they aren't that truck," Tori said. "You could fix up another one and paint it the same, but Levi would always know. That truck is a part of him. He's had it since high school."

Ed flinched when she said it.

"What?" Tori said, looking at him closely.

"That's not Old Blue."

Tori's eyes widened. "What do you mean?"

Ed sighed and rubbed the side of his head. "You can decide whether or not to tell Levi. I'd never ask you to keep something from your husband, but that's not Old Blue—the original anyway. The real Old Blue is well hidden in the weeds behind my shop. I wrecked that truck in '96 coming back from a poker game in Olton. It was snowing and blowing like hell. I slid on some ice, crossed the center lane, and got hit by a county plow truck going the other way. I got two broken ribs and a DUI out of the ordeal. But other than a few parts, like the radio and the steering wheel, there's not much of the original Old Blue in that truck."

"You built another truck?" Tori said.

Ed nodded. "Actually, it was several years later—after I ran into you when you were working on the Comet Theatre. I saw what you were doing, and I knew why. I decided to build a new Old Blue. I knew he'd come back to find you, Tori. I wasn't sure I'd still be around when that happened, but I wanted to leave something behind that I knew he loved."

Tori smiled. "We grew up in the Comet Theatre. I just couldn't let something both of us loved so much go. He still loves that old theatre."

"That's kind of spooky, Tori. You brought back the theatre, and I brought back the truck, and in the back of our minds, we were both thinking the same thing . . . he'll be back."

Tori smiled. "And when Levi came back, he found his favorite place and his favorite thing waiting for him—and his favorite people, too."

Ed smiled. "If you build it, he will come. What movie was that from?"

"*Field of Dreams*," Tori said. "The Comet Theatre ran it again about six months ago."

"I've got an idea," Ed said.

"Oh, no," Tori said.

"I think Levi needs a distraction," Ed said. "If not, when he's done doing his thinking, he's going to start doing his drinking. He'll wind up drunk tonight, and considering that we're being stalked by a killer, I don't think that's such a good idea."

Tori nodded. "What are you thinking?"

"I think that if you and I spend three or four hours in the carriage house, Pappy just might be ready for a debut. At least, Levi will have something to drive while we build another Blue."

"Really?"

"The painting is all done. We just need to bolt it back together," Ed said. "You up to it?"

"It's Wednesday," Tori said. "I could take him out on a date to the Comet Theatre. They're running a Tony Curtis tribute all afternoon and night."

"I don't think Levi is a huge Tony Curtis fan," Ed said.

"No, but he's a big Marilyn Monroe fan," she said with a smile. She glanced at her phone, which she'd found on the staircase at the lodge. "Can we be done in three hours? *Some Like It Hot* starts at 7."

"We'll have to move fast. Let's go," Ed said, motioning her towards the carriage house.

"He'll know what we're doing . . ." Tori said, nodding towards the porch where Levi was sitting.

Ed glanced up at him and shook his head. "Maybe. And if he does, he'll come and help us, and we'll get done faster. But I think Levi is about a million miles away right now. When he gets like that, a marching band could go by the house, and he'd never notice it."

* * *

Ray was sitting on his back patio in a deck chair, watching the cardinals at the bird feeder in the back yard. He could hardly move. The fall down the stairs had left him bruised from head to toe. He'd spent most of the afternoon in the ER, waiting for the twenty minutes of treatment he got. His head was throbbing, and as it turned out, the paramedic had been right. His shoulder had been dislocated. He could barely raise his arm.

His puppy was playing in the yard, trying to catch the birds feeding on the ground without much success, but he was getting a little better at it. Ray knew it wouldn't be long before he'd manage to grab one.

The sliding patio door opened behind him. When he tried to turn his head to see who'd come out, he winced.

"Just me," Clifford Craig said as he stepped out of the house onto the porch. "Good God, you look like hell."

"Took a header down a flight of stairs," Ray said.

"I heard. Are you okay?"

"I'm trying to decide what hurts the most, but I think I should wait until everything that's going to hurt starts hurting first."

"What are you, about fifty-five?"

Ray nodded.

"Wait fifteen years," Craig said with a rue smile. "I fell off a step stool, changing a light bulb last year, then spent two days in my recliner, and made three visits to the chiropractor."

Ray laughed but winced again.

"I came to get a couple of boxes out of the garage," Craig said. "I'll have the rest of my crap out of there tomorrow. Is that one of Levi's puppies?"

"Yeah," Ray said. "I've been sitting here, trying to come up with a name."

"That's a Garvey dog. You're not required to name him Rosco?"

"No, but I haven't got a name yet."

"I thought all you Southern boys named your dogs after Confederate generals."

Ray gave him a sidelong glance. The truth was that he'd just been considering Beauregard.

"That's a very insensitive and politically incorrect stereotype."

Craig chuckled. "Sorry, I know how sensitive you are. You need anything before I go?"

"I'm fine," Ray said.

"Just wondered because I grabbed this out of the fridge on my way through the house," he said, holding up a bottle of beer.

"Oh, that would be perfect," Ray smiled, "if you could open it first."

"I saw a full one sitting on the counter and figured you'd tried to open it and couldn't," Craig said with a laugh.

"I hurt all over," Ray said. "I've never been in such bad shape I couldn't twist the cap off a beer, but that's where I seem to be right now."

Craig handed it to him.

Ray shook his head. "Just set it there on the deck next to me. I'll get to it."

Craig set it down next to him. "I'll be going. Take it easy."

"Before you leave, would you open two more and leave them in the fridge?"

Craig smiled. "Consider it done. I'll open three just in case. You call me if you need anything, okay?"

"I will," Ray said. "And thanks, Craig. This is a great house and a great job."

"You staying then?" Craig asked.

Ray nodded. "I've got to admit, though, that this is way more than I expected when I got here, but it's surely not like this all this time, is it?"

"I'll have to admit, Ray, I've worn out a lot of shoe leather in this job, but most of it was on the heels of my boots where I rested them on the edge of my desk, napping in my office."

"Would you consider working part-time? Ben's doing a great job, but I'll need another deputy. Pick your shifts."

"I might just take you up on that one day," Craig said.

As Craig walked to the sliding door, he paused and looked back at Ray.

"You know a good name for a dog?"

"No, what?"

"Sherman."

"I don't think so."

"Ulysses?"

"Not likely."

"Ah! Abraham!" Craig suggested.

"I think you'd better leave now, Chief," Ray said.

"That's former Chief," Craig said with a chuckle.

"Or Chief Emeritus," Ray suggested.

"You know, I think I like the sound of that," Craig said as he slid the patio screen shut behind him.

Ray chuckled as he heard a few beers being opened in the house. He counted five hisses, not four, which seemed about right to him.

"I left them in the fridge," Craig called from inside the house. "Don't let them go flat."

"I'd never allow that to happen!" Ray shouted back.

The puppy made a sudden leap from his hiding place under the forsythia bush and just missed catching a sparrow.

"Come here, dog."

With some effort, the puppy climbed the three steps of the patio and bounded over to Ray, wagging his tail, waiting to be picked up.

"You're going to have to jump up here," Ray said. "I can't reach down there and get you."

Ray patted his lap. Three attempts, three fails.

"Come on. You can do it."

The puppy backed up a few steps, leaped, and landed on the lounger—knocking over the beer bottle.

"Oh, dog, that's a party foul," Ray said as the puppy licked his face, and the beer gurgled out of the bottle and ran through the slats of the deck to the ground underneath. "If you weren't so damned cute, you'd be in trouble."

The puppy looked at Ray. Then his head snapped around as a bird landed on the deck rail.

"Go on," Ray said. "Go chase those birds."

The puppy leaped off the lounger and bounded down the steps.

Your name is Beauregard, Ray thought. That's a good name for a dog. But I'm going to call you Bo.

* * *

Tori stood back from Pappy and smiled. "That's it?"

Ed was leaning against the workbench, wrapping a bandage around his knuckle.

"Yeah, that's it. Pappy is ready to roll," he said. "Just don't drive it too fast. A few of those bolts will need a little tightening up later."

"You got another one of those?" Tori said, looking at the blood oozing from the side of her hand.

"Small, medium, or large?"

"Medium," she said from around her hand in her mouth.

"You shouldn't do that," Ed said. "You know your mouth is full of germs."

"Oh please," she laughed. "I've seen you do this three times today. I saw my dad do it hundreds of times, and I've done it a thousand times myself."

"There are two gallons of hydrogen peroxide under the workbench you could use to clean that wound."

"That's for Rosco, the skunk hunter."

"Oh, I thought maybe it was for your hair."

Tori glared at him. "I'm a natural blonde, jackass."

Ed laughed.

"I'm starting to see why you and Levi argue constantly," Tori said. "You're not that much fun to work with, Ed."

"Well, at least he knows a passenger door from a driver's side door," Ed said. "You didn't break a nail, did you?"

Tori's eyes flashed. "If you'll remember correctly, Ed, I spent some time in the carriage house working with you and Levi on Old Blue back in the day. It seems like you gave me all the crappy jobs to do. 'Hey Tori, sand that fender. Hey Tori, climb under there and grease that joint.'"

Ed nodded. "Yes, you did spend some time on that truck, and yes, I did give you all the crappy jobs. Better you than me."

He reached into his pocket and pulled something out.

"I've been waiting to do this," he said.

"Do what?" Tori said.

Ed tossed her the keys. "It's all yours, Tori."

She beamed.

Levi had told her the story repeatedly. Barely a week after they'd finished Old Blue and Levi had earned his driver's license, Ed had tossed him the keys to Old Blue and said "It's all yours, Levi." He'd done the same thing a couple of years ago when Levi had returned home. Now, he'd tossed keys to Tori.

"Is it going to start?"

Ed shrugged. Then he walked over to the truck, snapped the tailgate down, and sat on it.

"That's a really good question. It might."

Tori glanced at her phone. They'd finished in time. It was 6:30.

"Thanks, Ed."

"Take him up to the Comet and have a good time."

"I will, and we will."

"But be careful, Tori," Ed said in a low voice. "I took the liberty of putting Mr. Webley in the glove box."

Tori nodded.

"I need to ask you a favor," he said.

"What's that?"

"I gave you a key and now I need one with no questions asked."

"What key?"

"The key to the lodge," Ed said.

Tori reached into her pocket and pulled out her keys. She removed one from her chain and handed to it him.

"Why?"

"No questions," Ed said as he dropped it into his shirt pocket.

Suddenly, she understood. Her face dropped.

"You've still got it," she said with a gasp.

Ed looked at her blankly.

"It's in the lodge, isn't it?"

Ed didn't react. "No questions, Tori."

"You've still got that coin," she said. "You never gave it back to Alex Patton. It's hidden somewhere in the lodge, isn't it?

"Tori—" Ed started.

"It's true, isn't it?" she said, pressing him.

Ed nodded.

Tori leaned back and thought about it. Where was it? There wasn't much left to do in the lodge besides stripping and refinishing the lodge furniture. Ed would've seen that she'd started on the altar when he was up there earlier in the day.

"You've hidden it, and you know I'm going to find it. It's in one of the pieces of lodge furniture, isn't it?"

"Didn't I say something about 'no questions asked?'"

"I just can't believe that somewhere in that lodge is a coin worth millions of dollars."

"Our problem now doesn't have anything to do with that coin," Ed said. "It's about what you and Levi saw, and it's about what Ray Billings is getting close to. The killer is doing this to protect his identity. He probably doesn't even know the double eagle exists since he probably never learned what that robbery was actually about. And if he ever did, he probably thought Alex Patton had cleverly hidden it where he'd never find it—the same conclusion Tony O'Malley came to."

"Why have you kept it all these years?" Tori said.

"I've never stopped looking for that bank robber," Ed said, looking at her with haunted eyes. "I always figured one day I'd figure it out, and I could use that coin to draw him out into the open."

"But he's not looking for it," Tori said. "Why do you want to retrieve it now?"

"I want to keep it close to me," Ed said. "Something is going to happen, Tori. Instead of using it to bring him out, maybe I can use it to make him go away."

Tori looked at Ed. She didn't understand at first, but then it dawned on her.

"He could live the rest of his life on what that coin could bring."

"I have a gut feeling he knows I'm still looking for him," Ed said. "I have a feeling he'll come after me first the next time around. And when he does, one way or another, he can use that coin to get away."

"But you'd know who he is."

Ed sighed. "He'll kill me, take the coin, and get away."

"Or kill you, take the coin, kill me, Levi, and Ray and then get away."

"It's not much of a plan," Ed admitted. "But it's all I've got. Like it or not, we're going to see him again."

* * *

FROM WHERE HE WAS HIDING IN THE SHADOWS AT THE EDGE OF THE old apple orchard, the man could see Levi sitting on the corner of the porch, staring at his truck. He'd sneaked onto the Garvey property from the back. He still couldn't believe Levi had managed to survive the explosion. But nothing about the Garveys surprised him anymore. Nothing. They were relentless. That's why he had to do this.

He wasn't sure if Levi was alone or not. He needed to know. If he was, there was no doubt in his mind he could get close to him. They knew each other well. Levi would never suspect him—at least not yet. But he knew that it was only a matter of time before one of them put all the pieces together.

He glanced over at the carriage house. The back doors were open. If there was anyone else at the house, their vehicles would be parked in there.

Working his way around the edge of the trees, he came up to the back of the carriage house. As he moved along the back wall to the doors, he bumped the woodpile. A large fireplace log rolled off the top and banged against the outside wall of the carriage house.

He stopped in his tracks to listen, his heart beating loudly. He could hear two voices inside. When he heard Tori laugh, he knew they hadn't heard the log fall.

He peeked in. Tori and Ed were talking on the tailgate of the red truck. It looked as if they'd finally finished Pappy.

He leaned against the door, trying to decide what to do. He hadn't planned on taking them all on at once. And then there was Chief Billings. He'd have to take care of him, too. After his fall down the stairs that afternoon, he was pretty sure Chief Billings wouldn't be out and about this evening.

Maybe it's better if I do this right now, he thought. Take them all out at once in one fatal swoop, instead of picking them off one at a time.

When he thought about how he might go about it, he realized it really wasn't that difficult. He'd just walk in and walk up to them, probably joking along the way. Then he'd pull the gun. He'd kill Ed first, then Tori before she had a chance to react. Of course, Levi would hear the gunshots and come running. He might be armed, but with Tori involved, he wouldn't be careful. He'll just react. I'll kill him the second he runs into the carriage house, he thought.

The man pulled the gun out of the holster and tucked it into the back of his jeans. Then he glanced in the door again. Ed and Tori were still sitting on the tailgate talking.

He took a deep breath and checked that he could reach the gun easily.

Just before he stepped into the carriage house, he heard a snippet of their conversation. It stopped him cold. He couldn't believe his ears.

Tori had just said, "I just can't believe that somewhere in that lodge is a coin worth millions of dollars."

The man quickly stepped out of the entrance. Wiping his hand across his mouth, he pulled the gun from the back of his jeans and holstered it as he continued to listen to Ed and Tori.

Until that moment, he'd never known what the robbery was actually about. He'd been hired and well-paid in advance just to open that safety deposit box. Bruce Franklin had told him they were after a ledger, but he'd never bought that. He'd always known it had to be something big. He was certainly right about that.

I think the plan just changed a little, he thought as a wide grin crossed his face.

Chapter Thirty-Seven

LEVI HAD BEEN THINKING FOR HOURS AS HE STARED AT THE RUIN OF Old Blue. Finally, he went into the house for a beer and then sat back down with it.

He knew this was going to get ugly, and he was scared—not for himself, but for Ray, Uncle Ed, and especially Tori. He'll be coming back for us, Levi thought as he took a long pull from the bottle. It's got to be somebody we know. He has every advantage over us. Will we even see it coming?

Levi understood the danger. The killer wouldn't make the same mistakes again. He'd leave nothing to chance when he came for them next time. He's going to make sure we don't walk away, Levi thought. He's going to pick us off one at a time, up close and personal, when we least expect it.

Levi was having a tough time accepting the fact that there was a good chance they weren't going to get out of this encounter alive.

Suddenly, he heard a motor start in the carriage house, followed by a loud backfire.

He knew they'd been working on Pappy because he'd heard them banging and thumping around in there and the occasional exchange of loud voices. Tori had made fun of him for his loud arguments with Uncle Ed in the carriage house, yet it hadn't taken her long to fall into the same argumentative habit when working with Ed, who knew exactly how to bring that out in those he worked with.

But Levi was surprised when the carriage house doors rolled open. He stood up. Surely, they didn't . . . he thought.

Pappy rolled out as the light from the fading sun winked off the chrome on the grill and sparkled around the headlights. The paint was gleaming over the high-domed hood, and the leaves on the trees over the driveway were reflected on the polished windshield. The truck was a thing of beauty.

Levi was amazed. A broad smile crossed his face as he walked down the steps. Pappy rolled up the driveway in jerks and starts. Tori was sitting behind the wheel, grinning from ear to ear, as she pulled up beside him.

"You're going to burn out that clutch before you get to the end of the driveway," Levi said with a chuckle as he rubbed the smooth paint on the edge of the open passenger window and looked up and down the sides of the truck.

"I'll get it eventually," Tori said.

"It's beautiful," Levi said.

"Want to go for a ride?" Tori said.

"Oh yeah," Levi said as Ed walked up the driveway from the carriage house, wiping his hands on a rag. "Come on, Uncle Ed. Let's take Pappy for its debut appearance."

"You two kids go and have fun," Ed said.

Levi jumped in next to Tori and pulled the door closed. "Where are we going?"

"Oh, I've got an idea," Tori said as the truck lurched forward and nearly stalled.

"You know," Levi said. "I don't want to tell you how to drive your truck, but I find if you start out in first gear, it goes a lot smoother."

Ed walked to Tori's window. "How did you get to be your age—"

"Watch it, Ed," Tori said, cutting him off. "I haven't forgotten that peroxide remark."

"How could you grow up in a rural community," Ed said, "and never learn to drive a standard transmission?"

"Oh, shut up," Tori said.

The gears ground loudly as Tori looked for first gear. Levi and Ed winced. When she finally found it, she looked at them both proudly.

"Ah! There it is! Ready?"

Ed rolled his eyes as Levi gripped the door tightly.

"I'm going to miss you, Levi," Ed said.

"I'll miss you, too, Uncle Ed."

"Say hello to Mother for me."

"I will," Levi said.

Tori glanced at Ed. "You're going to see her first, Ed, when I run you over with this truck."

Ed exploded into his distinctive mule laugh as Pappy lurched forward and turned at the end of the driveway towards Twin Rivers.

Suddenly, Pappy skidded to a stop, and the passenger door opened.

"Rosco! You coming?" Levi yelled.

Rosco was lying on the porch with his head down, looking depressed since he'd been forgotten. His head popped up, and his tail wagged as he jumped off the porch, ran across the yard, and leaped into the truck.

Ed grinned. Even at that distance, he heard Levi grunt and then let loose with a stream of foul language as the dog landed on him. The truck lurched forward again, and Rosco's head appeared in the passenger window. Ed couldn't even see Levi anymore.

Ed walked over to the burned out shell of Old Blue. He rubbed the paint on the hood which was spider-webbed and peeling off from the heat of the fire.

"Don't worry, Blue," he said. "You're next. Let's get you in the carriage house and find out just how badly you're hurt."

He patted the hood a few times before walking back towards the carriage house for his tow truck.

* * *

As the house lights at the Comet Theatre came up and the curtain closed over the screen, Levi said, "One more?"

Tori laughed. "I assumed when we got here to watch one movie that we'd wind up watching them all."

The Tony Curtis tribute had started at three that afternoon, and the last movie would get out about one in the morning. Since the theater was almost full, they'd been lucky to find two seats together when they'd showed up for the third picture. Tori had looked at Levi several times during *Some Like It Hot.* He was laughing as the images from the screen flickered across his face—just like when they were kids. Levi could lose himself so easily in an old movie. As he was so fond of saying, "All the best movies are in black and white."

Levi held up his empty popcorn bucket and shook it. It was empty. "Really?"

"I know you have to pee."

She sighed. He was right. She took the popcorn bucket and got up. "Rosco, do you need to go outside?" she asked.

Rosco glanced at her from the floor and put his head down on Levi's lap. He didn't. If he had, he'd have wagged his tail and followed her out.

Levi stroked Rosco's head as Rose Daley began playing the Wurlitzer organ off to the side of the stage. As she played a medley of movie themes, Levi looked around the massive interior of the old art deco theatre—the gilded trim around the stage with the comet motif around the corners, the red velvet seats, the stained-glass wall sconces. He still couldn't believe Tori had brought it back to its original 1920s splendor. The theatre was so different now from what it had been when they were kids—a run-down firetrap with sticky floors and long rips in the screen.

Every time they'd visited the Comet Theatre since he'd been back, he saw a new detail about the old theatre he hadn't noticed before, and he knew it was a tiny detail Tori had spent hours bringing back.

It wasn't long before Tori returned and handed him the refilled popcorn bucket. She smiled as Levi tossed a few pieces of popcorn to Rosco, who snapped them out of the air. It didn't matter how or where you threw it. If it was anywhere near his head, Rosco would never let a kernel of popcorn hit the floor.

"So what's on next?" she asked.

Levi shrugged and looked around.

Floyd was sitting behind them, snoring in his seat.

"Floyd!" Levi said loudly.

He jumped awake, looking confused. When he finally saw Levi, he said, "What?"

"What picture is on next?"

"*Some Like It Hot*," he said.

"That was the last one," Tori said with the chuckle.

"Oh," Floyd said, rubbing his face, "I must've dozed off for a while."

"Two freakin' hours," Levi said.

Rose finished her medley with a flowing rendition of "As Time Goes By" from *Casablanca*. As the last notes echoed through the theatre, the lights dimmed, the curtain opened, and the cartoon began. Levi's face lit up when he realized it was his favorite—an old black-and-white cartoon where all the characters from fiction classics come out of the books after the library has closed to sing and dance. Tori never understood why he liked it. It was such a dorky example of early Warner Brothers cartoons, but Levi loved it, and she knew it.

Levi grinned over at her knowingly. She knew what the smile meant. Sometimes Levi thought he was the luckiest man on earth. The fact that the cartoon playing was his favorite confirmed the luck he carried around with him.

You're not nearly as lucky as you think, she thought as she suppressed a chuckle.

When she'd gone for popcorn, she'd made a little trip up to the projection room with a request. The Comet Theatre always accommodated Tori, the woman who'd saved it from the wrecking ball. Her portrait hung prominently on a wall in the lobby behind a red velvet rope, surrounded with photos she'd taken during various stages of the long restoration process.

* * *

ED GARVEY FLIPPED ON THE LIGHT IN THE LODGE ROOM AND STOOD in the entrance for a moment, marveling at the job Tori was doing. He really hadn't noticed much that morning. There'd been a lot going on.

The black and white mosaic tile on the floor around the altar was new. So was the lighting along the top edges of the walls that shone up on the vaulted ceiling, which she'd painted dark blue and studded with bronze stars. At the center of each star, a tiny LED light shone faintly. It reminded Ed of the night the lodge had met without a roof and with the night sky above them. That was obviously Tori's inspiration for the ceiling treatment. The letter G over the Master's chair was a massive antique bronze piece Tori had found, green with verdigris and stunning against the parchment colored wall.

Tori wasn't done yet with the Twin Rivers Masonic Lodge, but Ed could sure see where Tori was going with it. He couldn't believe the room was nearly one hundred years old.

Nice work, Tori, he thought.

He walked across the lodge towards the Master's chair in the East and climbed the three steps up the dais. Levi's chair was a massive piece of oak furniture that stood over seven feet high and weighed more than six hundred pounds. It had three majestic seats padded in blue velvet built into it with the Master's seat, which was the widest and tallest, in the center. The chair was original to the lodge.

Embedded into the back of the Master's chair was a more modern addition although it looked original. It was a three-inch bronze medallion with a depiction of the Master's working tool—the simple square, a tool used to determine right angles. Over it, faintly depicted, was the All Seeing Eye, one of the most misunderstood symbols of Freemasonry. The symbol, however, wasn't original to Freemasons. For thousands of years, in many cultures, the symbol had represented the eye of God, watching over His creation.

The medallion was the work of the talented jeweler, Alex Patton. There was a medallion with a different working tool depicted embedded into the back of every officer's chair in the lodge.

Reaching into his pocket, Ed pulled out the penknife he'd carried since he was a kid. He put his knee down on the seat of the Master's chair and began to gently work the bronze medallion loose. After it fell into his hand, he placed it on the seat cushion next to the Master's seat and peered into the smaller recess he'd bored out behind it nearly four decades before.

He reached into the hole with his fingertips, grabbed the string on the small velvet jeweler's bag he'd hidden there, and pulled it out. When the coin fell out of the bag and into his hand, he marveled at it—so small yet so valuable. He hadn't seen it for thirty-eight years, but he'd always known exactly where it was.

He'd started to slide it back into the bag when he heard the floor creak behind him. He froze. He knew he'd locked the door. Closing his eyes, he dropped his head. He hadn't expected it so soon.

I won't be getting out of this one, Ed thought.

Two years ago, it wouldn't have mattered to Ed because he hadn't had much to live for then. What a difference two years could make. He only hoped that Levi and Tori weren't stupid enough to name their child Ed in his memory.

As he stood, his back to the man he knew was behind him, fear crept into his heart—something he hadn't felt in a long time. His hand holding the coin was trembling slightly. You only know fear when you've got something to lose, Ed realized. But I'm not going out a coward. I'll do what I have to do to protect Levi and Tori. I'm not going to make it easy for him.

Ed chuckled as he rose with the coin in his hand.

"I always knew this coin would bring out the fourth bank robber," he said, "that cowardly murderer that killed my friend Jim Mathis."

There was no response.

For a brief moment, relief washed over Ed. He thought maybe he'd imagined somebody was behind him. Maybe that creak was just the settling of a hundred-year-old building. But when the floor creaked again and a shadow moved across the dais, Ed's heart sank.

He knew he wasn't alone.

Chapter Thirty-Eight

"Oh, this is a good one," Levi whispered to Tori as the title screen came up. "It's not a very accurate depiction of his life, but it's a good film. And it's even more interesting to watch when you realize Tony Curtis is starring in this film with his wife, Janet Leigh. And of course, the guy he's portraying was a Freemason."

"Of course, he was," Tori said.

There was always a Freemason connection with Levi. They'd yet to watch a John Wayne picture or a Tom Mix western or a Clark Gable film that Levi didn't mention they were Freemasons. Or the director was a Freemason. Or the writer. Or the guy who owned the studio. She thought back. Jack Warner of Warner Brothers was, but his brother wasn't. Louis B. Mayer was. His favorite cartoons were voiced by Mel Blanc, who was.

She only hoped Levi didn't know a lot about the film, or she'd get one of his running monologues throughout. It wasn't always fun to watch a movie Levi, especially an old black and white. Fortunately, he didn't seem to know much about this film. Tori leaned back in her seat. Levi did the same. The group in front of them had left after the last film, so they propped their feet up on the row of seats in front of them. They'd spent so many hours watching movies at the Comet that being there felt like home.

Levi had been right. It was a good film. Tori was soon lost in it, but when she glanced at Levi, she thought that maybe he didn't like the movie. The strange look on his face was the same one he got sometimes when he was watching television but was thinking about something else. That little line he got between his eyebrows when he was thinking made her nervous. And he wasn't eating his popcorn.

As the movie played, the look on Levi's face got tighter. Tori was spending more time watching Levi than watching the movie. During the scene where Tony Curtis locked himself in a large vault, Levi made a grunt. She glanced at him just as his face went slack. She reached over to touch his arm. Suddenly, he sat straight up on the edge of his seat.

"Hey, down in front," Floyd whispered behind him.

"Shut up, Floyd," Tori whispered. "What is it, Levi?"

There was confusion on his face. He was still working something out.

"Oh, my God," Levi said.

The look of dawning realization on his face made gooseflesh stand up on her arms.

"What, Levi?

"Harry Houdini," he said, looking at her with panic on his face.

She didn't understand.

"I've got to go," Levi said, standing suddenly and dumping the popcorn bucket on the floor.

He scooted his way to the aisle and made a beeline for the exit. He was half running across the lobby when Tori burst out the door with Rosco on her heels.

"Levi!" she shouted as he reached the glass doors of the outside entrance.

He stopped.

"What is it?" she asked, running up to him.

"I know who it is," Levi said.

"The fourth bank robber?"

Levi nodded. "It was right there in front of my face the whole time. Why didn't I see it?"

* * *

RAY SHIFTED IN THE RECLINER, FINDING ABSOLUTELY NO COMFORTable position. He was watching his third episode of *Matlock* reruns of what was apparently a *Matlock* marathon. The remote was sitting on the coffee table ten feet away, but for three hours, he'd decided to watch Andy Griffith rather than suffer the pain of getting up for it. As the third episode ended, he hoped something else would come on, but as the music began for the fourth episode, he knew he'd have to get up.

"Scoot over, Bo," he said, shifting the sleeping puppy from his lap and slowly rising from the chair.

The pain wasn't as bad as he thought it would be as he stood and carefully stretched. He'd been given a prescription for Vicodin and a muscle relaxant at the emergency room, but he'd opted not to take them. He'd had a bad experience with that pain killer a few years before, so he usually stuck with what he knew—good old aspirin.

He reached down slowly, picked up the remote, and tossed it into the seat of his recliner next to the sleeping puppy, who was twitching—no doubt dreaming about chasing birds in the yard.

He went to the kitchen to get one of the cold beers Craig had opened for him. They were sure to be flat by now, but he didn't care. They were cold. As he took a sip, he remembered seeing his heating pad in one of the boxes in the garage he'd been unpacking—the pad he'd gotten a few years earlier about the same time he'd had his bad experience with Vicodin.

He'd been chasing a shoplifter up River Street in Savannah when the guy cut up one of the narrow alleys that led up from the low landing along the Savannah River—an area popular with tourists for its shops and bars. The old alley, like so many that went down to River Street, had been there for a couple hundred years. It was paved in smooth river rock, which was slick on a good day and treacherous on a foggy night like that one. The shoplifter had gotten away when Ray fell on the jarringly hard surface and fractured his tailbone. He was off work for only a week, but the painful recovery had lasted months.

Ray took a long drink of the flat beer and set it on the counter. He opened the kitchen door that led down into the three-car garage, which was half-filled with Craig's stuff and half-filled with the stuff Ray had yet to unpack. He flicked the light switch at the top of the stairs—nothing.

I'll need to get that fixed, he thought as he made his way to the bottom of the stairs in the dark.

At the bottom, he was groping along the wall for the switch when he bumped into something that fell over with a crash. His hand finally felt the switch, and he flipped the light on.

The fluorescent lights bathed the three-car garage with blinding brilliance. As his eyes adjusted, Ray realized he'd knocked over one of Craig's totes which were stacked against the wall. Ray reached down to put the things that had spilled out onto the garage floor back into the tote—a bunch of stuff from Craig's huge collection of magic memorabilia. There were handcuffs, a straight jacket, and something that looked like antique ankle restraints from the turn of the last century.

The things people collect, Ray thought as he tossed them into the tote.

The last item on the floor was a small pouch which he tossed in before closing the lid. He set the tote on top of the stack, minding his back, which was already screaming from the effort, and walked over to his side of the garage to find the heating pad.

He was rummaging through his boxes, looking for the heating pad, when he suddenly stopped. Something he'd seen had just clicked. He walked back over to Craig's tote, reopened it, and took out the leather pouch.

I've seen something like this before—recently, he thought. When he opened the pouch, it suddenly struck him like a bolt of lightning.

"Oh, shit," Ray said aloud, dropping the pouch back into the tote. As adrenalin pumped through him, he dashed up the stairs to get the keys to his cruiser. As he reached the top of the stairs, he was wracked with a sudden sharp pain that bent him over double. He leaned over the counter on his elbows, waiting for the sharp pain to ease.

He was reaching for his cruiser keys on the hook next to the door when a second wave, even more intense, struck, and he fell to his knees, gasping. The world became fuzzy around the edges. Ray knew he was about to lose consciousness. As he opened his cell phone, the final wave came. His phone clattered across the kitchen floor as he fell over, unconscious.

* * *

ED WASN'T SURE HE WANTED TO SEE WHO WAS STANDING BEHIND HIM because it was probably somebody he'd known for years—somebody who'd overheard his conversation with Tori earlier, somebody who'd likely gone to the carriage house to kill all of them. It was the only way he could know where Ed was going.

The shadow on the dais shifted again as the man walked up closer. Ed's only advantage was being three tall steps over the man's head. Whatever happened—and he was pretty sure he knew how it was going to end—he wasn't going down without a fight.

He heard the metallic chunk-chunk of a pistol being cocked behind him.

He dropped his head. He knew.

That distinctive sound of the weapon being cocked was all he needed. Nobody had more knowledge about guns than he did. He knew exactly what kind of pistol was aimed at him, and he suddenly realized who held it.

"That'd be a nine-millimeter Glock," Ed remarked. "A cop's gun. Why is the bad guy always the last person you'd suspect?"

"Where's the Webley, Ed?" Clifford Craig said.

"I don't have it. I'm unarmed. But you'll see it. I promise you that, Craig. Mr. Webley might just be the last thing you'll ever see."

"Turn around slowly," Craig said.

"You're not going to shoot me in the back?"

"Turn around!" he yelled.

Ed turned and looked down at Craig from the top of the dais.

"Another dirty damn murdering Twin Rivers cop. It's no wonder we wound up with the likes of Doug Malone after you retired. It seems to be a town tradition."

"I was a great police chief," Craig snapped back.

Ed laughed, a humorless laugh. "You only took that job so you'd know everything going on in this town, so you'd know if anybody ever started wondering who that fourth bank robber was. Bet you didn't have any interest in law enforcement before you got involved in the bank robbery and murdered Jim Mathis on the street in Calloway."

"You'd better shut up, Ed," Craig warned as he pointed the Glock at him.

"You're going to kill me anyway, so I might as well say what's on my mind. How can you say you weren't a dirty cop. You were already a murderer when you took the job. You've murdered two more since and attempted to murder three more. That's not even mentioning two arsons and several breaking and entering. You're dirty," Ed said. "You always have been. But you've put on a really good show all these years."

"I'm warning you," Craig said, his hand trembling slightly.

"You probably thought you were free and clear—that you'd sail off into retirement and nobody would be the wiser. Then the state of Illinois went broke and started releasing their "rehabilitated" criminals, like Andy Miller. The prison called you, didn't they? They told you they were going to release Andy Miller, but you just kept that to yourself."

Craig's face tightened.

"You had a couple of days to plan it. You figured you'd murder him and frame me since I was a suspect the first time around. Andy Miller couldn't just run around town again because he knew you from the bank robbery. You knew the second he saw you he'd recognize you. You knew he'd either blackmail you or rat you out. But you sure never figured he'd get to work as fast as he did—charged right into the Beer Chaser first thing and knocked my ass off that stool. That's why you backed into that corner. You've never been afraid of a fight. You were afraid he'd recognized you, and he did. When he saw you, he kind of snorted. I remember that now. You killed him that same night with my rifle, knowing I'd be at the bar as I usually am until last call."

"Well, as it turned out, it wasn't Andy who tried to blackmail me. It was his little brother, Stevie," Craig snapped.

"So that's why you killed him," Ed said, shaking his head.

"What have you got in your hand, Ed?"

Glancing down at the fist which contained the coin, Ed said, "Why don't you come up here and see?"

"I think you'd better come down."

Craig backed a few steps away. He didn't like the idea that Ed had the high ground. He might be unarmed, but his hands were close to a heavy oak mallet, the Master's gavel. Ed was a dangerous man. He'd taken down Tony O'Malley's Four Horseman with a broom handle. Craig wasn't going to give him a chance to get the upper hand.

"I don't think so," Ed said. "I see this going down two ways. You either come up here and get it, or you shoot me now and take it."

"I can work with that," Craig said, leveling the pistol.

"Fire away," Ed said as he sat down in the Master's chair. "But don't you think I knew you'd come? I didn't know who you were, but I knew you were coming. Are you so sure this coin in my hand is what you think it is? Or did I set you up? You think I didn't know you were listening to Tori and me at the carriage house. You dumbass. You're about to get a big surprise when you pull this gold coin out of my cold dead hand and learn it's not the priceless 1933 gold Double Eagle but a worthless Sacagawea dollar."

Craig's face tightened as Ed's laughter rang out.

"With this," Ed said, holding up his clenched hand, "and another twenty-seven cents, you can buy a cup of coffee at Hillbilly Bob's."

Craig's face twisted. Things had just gotten a lot more complicated.

* * *

"Levi, stop!" Tori yelled as she ran out of the Comet Theatre to where they'd parked along the street.

Levi paused as he pulled Pappy's door open. The entire street from Harv's Diner to the post office was lit by the three-story neon lighting and canopy of the restored Comet Theatre.

"Where are you going?" she said.

"I've got to find Uncle Ed," Levi said. "He'll go after Ed first. He knows Ed is his biggest threat. He'll kill him and then come after us."

"Who is he?"

Levi shook his head quickly as he climbed into Pappy. "You can't go where I'm going, Tori. You're—" Levi glanced at her and couldn't finish.

"I'm what?"

"The last Garvey," he said as he pulled Pappy's door shut. "Actually, the last two Garveys."

She reached through the window and grabbed Levi by the collar.

"I have no intention of being known as the widow Garvey. We're a family now, Levi. You're not going to pull this hero shit on me. I saved your ass from Kingery Pond, and I saved your ass from Alan Haig, too. You and I will go after Ed together. You take on one Garvey, and you get us all. That's how it's going to be. So get your ass out of my truck. We don't need it, anyway. I know exactly where Ed is."

Levi stared at her. He'd never loved her more. When he opened the door, Rosco jumped in.

"Before you get out," Tori said, "you might want to pop that glove box."

When Levi reached over to do what she asked, he felt the familiar shape of the holster in the darkness.

"What the hell did you and Ed talk about today?"

"Give it to me," she said. "There's a box of shells in there, too."

He handed her the Webley and the shells.

"Let's go," Tori said.

Levi watched her as she started down the sidewalk towards the Masonic Lodge, loading the Webley as she walked. He glanced at Rosco, who licked him from his chin to his forehead.

"Thanks," he said, wiping his face on his sleeve as he climbed out of the pick-up. "Let's go, Rosco. You heard Tori. If you take on one of us, you get all of us."

Chapter Thirty-Nine

"I GUESS THAT COIN DOESN'T MATTER THAT MUCH," CRAIG SAID. "You've either got it in your hand, or you don't. I planned on killing you, anyway. But I have the feeling you're bluffing. Last chance, Ed."

Ed shook his head and leaned back in the Master's chair.

Craig was leveling the pistol when he saw Ed's eyes flick with recognition behind him.

"Oh, please," Craig said with a frown. "Is that the best you've got?"

"What?" Ed asked.

"You're trying to trick me, Ed. You're trying to make me think there's somebody behind me so I'll turn around and look. And the second I do, you'll grab that heavy oak gavel and brain me with."

Ed shrugged. "It was worth a try."

Craig leveled the Glock at Ed from the bottom of the dais and took aim. The conversation was over.

"I'll see you in hell, Clifford Craig," Ed said, glaring at him.

The look on Ed's face made Craig's heart beat faster and sweat break out on his forehead.

"And you'll be about two minutes behind me," Ed added as Craig started to squeeze the trigger.

* * *

LEVI AND TORI HAD QUIETLY CLIMBED THE STAIRS IN THE DARK. THE lights were on upstairs. They could hear voices as they got closer to the top. They crept across the Tyler's room and peeked into the lodge room. Ed was sitting in the Master's chair, and Clifford Craig was holding a gun on him.

Tori's eyes widened when she realized he was the fourth gunman.

She looked at Levi, who nodded. She shook her head. It'd been right there the whole time, and neither of them had seen it. Levi motioned for her to stay there as he started to enter the lodge room. Tori put her hand on his shoulder to stop him. She held out the Webley.

He paused, then took it. He tucked it into the waist of his pants in front and pulled his shirt down over it. Tori and Levi looked at each other for a long moment. This was bad. Craig was desperate. Tori stepped up to him and kissed him.

"It'll be fine," Levi whispered in her ear. Tori knew he didn't really believe that.

Then Levi stepped into the lodge room.

"Good evening, Worshipful," Ed said, rising suddenly.

Craig nearly turned to look before stopping himself. Ed had almost bought himself the opportunity he needed.

"What the hell are you doing in my chair?" Levi asked, sounding annoyed as he strode in.

Craig's face twisted in anger as he glared at Ed.

"If you shoot me in the back, Levi, you'd better take careful aim," he growled, "because the last thing I'm going to do on this earth is kill your Uncle Ed."

"I'm not armed," Levi said.

"Bullshit," Craig said, his hand trembling as he maintained his aim on Ed.

Levi walked along the edge of the lodge room. Craig backed away from the dais in order to see Levi, who had his hands out to his sides.

"See," Levi said. "Not armed."

"It's stuck in the back of your belt. I read your book. I know that old trick."

Levi turned slowly around and pulled up his shirt so that Craig could see he wasn't armed.

Craig pointed the gun at Levi and flicked the barrel towards the dais.

"Over here," he demanded. "And you come down here, too, Ed."

Ed climbed down the three steps as Levi walked to join him in front of the dais. Craig covered them both as a small smile crossed his face.

"You might as well come in, Tori," he called, "and bring that Webley with you. If you try anything, I'll shoot your husband dead where he stands."

Before walking into the room, she reached over and flipped a switch labeled "meeting light," which turned on the small blue globe two stories up on the front of the lodge building. Only a Mason would likely notice it, and even then he might think nothing of it—but it was something.

As she walked in, Craig said, "Where's the gun?"

"I don't have it."

"You can stop worrying about that Webley, Craig. It's in my glove box," Ed said. "I'll have to admit that you got the drop on me. I didn't think I'd need it this soon."

"Then come over here, Tori. Slowly," Craig said.

She did as she was told. As she reached Levi, her knees buckled and she nearly fell. Levi caught her arm.

"What's wrong?" Levi said.

Her face was pale. "I don't feel well. I think it's the baby."

Ed grabbed her under her other arm.

"Put her in that chair," Craig snapped, waving the Glock towards the Senior Deacon's chair.

Levi and Ed helped her over to the chair.

"Are you okay?" Levi whispered, his face lined with worry as he leaned over her.

The pain in her face suddenly vanished. She looked up at Levi with her green eyes and winked. Levi glanced up at Ed. They had a whole conversation in a single glance.

Ed touched her forehead. "My God, she's covered in sweat."

"She needs a doctor," Levi said as Tori grabbed her side and let out a sharp cry of pain.

"Not for long," Craig said coldly.

"So you're going to kill a pregnant woman?" Levi asked.

Craig nodded. "You haven't left me with much choice. I'm going to kill you all, I'm afraid. But I am curious about one thing."

"What's that?" Levi said.

"Ed didn't figure it out, but you did finally," Craig said. "What was it?"

Levi glared at him. "You should've gone to the movie this evening. You would've really enjoyed one of the films. Great picture. It was Tony Curtis and Janet Leigh starring in *Houdini*."

Craig smiled grimly.

"I'm watching that movie, and I'm remembering that day we were down in your basement, and you showed me your collection. You had a whole wall dedicated to Houdini, who wasn't so much a magician as he was an escape artist. In fact, as a boy he was an apprentice in a locksmith shop. That's where he learned his skills—opening just about any kind of lock he had to get out of."

Craig chuckled.

"We've been looking for a bank robber who's good with locks," Levi said. "He broke into a bank vault. He unlocked and relocked a gun cabinet. He opened a brand new deadbolt on this lodge when he tried to kill Tori this morning. He even broke into C & S and stole a box of old records. I'm watching that movie, and I'm thinking about C & S Locksmith. Then it all tumbled together. Suddenly, I knew what the C in C & S Locksmith stood for."

"Craig & Sorkin," Craig admitted. "Three generations of my family ran that shop. I grew up there, and I learned a lot."

"And a little boy who wanted to be a magician instead of a locksmith might just idolize somebody like Harry Houdini," Levi said.

"Mystery solved," Craig said. "A little too late but you figured it out."

"Maybe not," Levi said, suddenly grinning as he looked over Craig's shoulder.

Craig laughed as he recognized the ploy. "Do all of you Garveys take your plays out of the same book? Now who do you want me to believe is standing behind me, Levi? Maybe Ray Billings?"

Levi nodded. "Yeah, it's Ray. He's standing there behind you with his Glock."

Craig shook his head and laughed. "Not likely. I hate to be the one to tell you, but there's a good chance Ray Billings is dead. I dropped by to see him earlier. The poor guy was in so much pain he couldn't even open a bottle of beer. I helped him out—opened a few beers for him. I guarantee that after he drank that first one, he didn't feel any pain at all."

The Garveys looked at each other in shock.

Craig chuckled humorlessly.

* * *

FLOYD COULDN'T SEEM TO FOCUS ON THE MOVIE. HE KEPT DOZING off. After the Garveys had left so suddenly, he started to wonder if something was wrong. He knew somebody had tried to kill Levi and Tori that day. He knew they were helping Ray with his investigation into the deaths of Andy and Stevie Miller.

Floyd stood up and worked his way to the end of the aisle, amid the muttering of the other movie patrons. When he walked out of the theatre, the first thing he noticed was the beautiful old Ford truck parked right in front of the Comet Theatre canopy.

That must be Pappy, he said to himself as a smile crossed his face.

Ed and Levi had been talking a lot about the truck they were restoring. He touched its smooth red surface, admiring it under the glaring lights of the canopy.

Hearing a car screech around the corner, he glanced up. A Twin Rivers police cruiser locked its brakes and came to an abrupt stop at the end of the red Ford pickup. Ray Billings leaned out the window, his face ashen and covered in sweat. Floyd walked to the window.

"Levi and Tori in there?" Ray asked.

Floyd shook his head. "They left a few minutes ago—very suddenly."

"I've got to find them," Ray said as he put the car back into gear.

Something caught Floyd's attention up the street. "Wait, Ray," he said as he stepped out from under the blinding glare of the canopy and squinted up the street. There was a tiny blue light shining on the front of the Twin Rivers Lodge. "Why do you suppose the meeting light is on?"

Ray glanced up the street and then pulled his cruiser in next to Pappy. Slowly, he climbed out of the cruiser, breathing heavily. He started to pull his Glock out with his right hand, then winced. He reached for it with his left.

"I don't know what's going on, Ray," Floyd said. "But you aren't in any shape for it. You can't even use your good arm. Let me come with you."

"I'll be fine," Ray said. "You stay here. I don't need or want your help—you hear me?"

Floyd nodded as Ray turned and walked unsteadily up the street towards the lodge. When he disappeared into the mouth of the alley, Floyd looked at the cruiser. Mounted between the seats in a locked stand was Ray's police shotgun. After glancing up the street where Ray had vanished up the alley, Floyd opened the cruiser door and looked at the gun stand.

"Sorry, Ray. I never was too good at followin' directions," Floyd mumbled to himself as he fished his penknife out of his bib overalls pocket.

* * *

"YOU POISONED RAY BILLINGS?" ED SAID.

Craig nodded.

"Well, that doesn't make any sense," Levi said.

"I had to. He was about to figure it out, too," Craig said.

"No, that's not what I meant."

"Then what did you mean?" Craig said angrily.

Craig's face went pale when he heard somebody behind him rack the slide on a Glock.

"I didn't drink that beer," Ray said. "My puppy, Beauregard, knocked it over."

Craig backed up a few steps until he could see Ray.

Ray was holding the Glock in his shaking left hand. His shirt was drenched in sweat.

'You'd better put that down, Ray," Craig said. "You won't be able to hit anything in the shape you're in."

"I'll manage," Ray said.

"I'm going to count to three, and if you haven't put that gun down, I'm going to shoot somebody."

Ray noticed Tori's hand slowly moving from the arm of the Senior Deacon's chair. She wrapped her fingers around the seven-foot rod in its holder beside the chair.

"You want to test me?" Craig said.

"I know you'd do it," Ray said as he lowered his gun.

Craig smiled broadly. "Now you're being smart."

Ray looked at him with his cold steely blue eyes. "No, it's just that right now, I'm not your biggest problem."

"What do you mean?" Craig said.

His eyes widened when he heard somebody rack a shotgun behind him.

Floyd was standing in the open door of the preparation room with the shotgun pointed at the back of Craig's head.

"I think we've been skeet shooting together enough that you should know I won't miss," Floyd said.

When he recognized the voice, Craig's face reddened, and a look of desperation came into his eyes. Levi knew he had seconds to do something before the bullets started flying. He thought about the Webley in his waistband, but with Craig's Glock aimed right at him, he knew it was unlikely that he'd be successful at reaching it in time. Suddenly, he had a thought.

Levi glanced at Ed's hand. "Hey, is that the coin that started all this crap?"

"Yup," Ed said, tossing it to Levi.

Craig's face twisted as he glared at Ed. "Thought that was a worthless Sacagawea dollar."

Ed shrugged. "I lied. Too bad you didn't shoot me when you had the chance. You'd have been gone before anybody else showed up."

Levi looked down at the coin and whistled. "This little thing is worth millions?"

"That's what they say," Ed remarked.

"Hey, want to see something cool?" Levi said.

He held up the coin between two fingers and waved his hand in front of it.

"Don't, Levi," Craig warned. He knew exactly what Levi was going to do.

"Chief Craig showed me this," Levi said with a forced grin. "I've been practicing."

"Do you not get that I have a loaded gun," Craig shouted.

"Then either shoot somebody with it or shut up," Ed said. "I want to see this. Go ahead, Levi."

"But remember, Craig, I'm going to blow your head off if you do," Floyd said from behind him.

"Watch closely," Levi said, shifting the coin from hand to hand.

Finally, he held it up between two fingers and waved his other hand in front of it a couple of times. It vanished.

Ed laughed. "Whoa! That's excellent. How'd you do that?"

"I know," Craig said, taking a couple of steps towards Levi and pointing the Glock in his face. "Turn your hand around, Levi."

He knew the coin was wedged between two of his fingers, just like he'd taught him. Levi had mastered the trick very well.

Levi sighed. "Dammit, Chief. You're not supposed to reveal the trick. You're going to ruin it for everyone now."

"Turn your hand around," Craig shouted, his face even redder yet.

Slowly, Levi turned his hand. Craig's face fell. The coin wasn't there.

"Where is it?" he shouted, the gun shaking visibly.

Levi shrugged. "I don't know. It's magic."

Craig knew that when he was teaching Levi that trick, more often than not, Levi dropped the coin. It must've fallen to the floor. He couldn't help but glance down.

The second he did, Levi smacked the gun in his hand. It went off—the bullet imbedding itself in the wall beside Ray's head. Tori lunged out of the chair with the Senior Deacon's rod in her hand, gripped like a bat. It whistled through the air, catching Clifford Craig in the back of the neck with such force that the end of the rod snapped off with a loud crack.

Craig went down hard and lay motionless.

Levi kicked the gun away from him and glanced at Tori.

"Batter up," he said, his face relaxing into a wry smile.

Ed sighed. "That was easier than I thought it was going to be."

"Sorry," Tori said, looking at the rod in her hand. "I broke your little stick."

Levi laughed as he looked at his beautiful, pregnant wife.

"I've got to tell you, Tori," Ed said. "That's not standard rod work in any Masonic lodge I've ever visited."

Tori shrugged as she smiled weakly.

"How did you figure it out?" Ed said, looking over at Ray, whose face was gray.

"Long story, but I suddenly put it together when I found a set of Craig's lock picks in one of his boxes in the garage. I'd have been here sooner, but I had a little problem," he said, wiping sweat off his face. "I dashed up the stairs, which was a little more activity than I should've been undertaking. My back seized up, and I passed out cold on the kitchen floor."

"Then how'd you get here?" Tori asked.

"Little puppy named Beauregard," Ray said with a weak smile. "I woke up because that little guy was licking my face. I was able to get up and find that prescription the doctor gave me. Powerful stuff. Within a few minutes, I was able to walk. It's a damn good thing Floyd noticed that somebody had left the lodge meeting light on, or I'd still be looking for you."

"Good thinking, Tori," Levi said.

"And it's a damn good thing I didn't listen to you, Ray," Floyd said from the doorway.

"Thank God, this is over," Ray said. "I don't know how much longer I can stand upright. I don't react real well to pain killers as I—"

Ray froze. Carl had suddenly appeared standing behind Floyd with the muzzle of his revolver pressed into the back of his neck.

Ray started to raise his Glock.

"I wouldn't," a second Horseman said, pressing his gun into Ray's back. He'd slipped in unnoticed, Carl providing the distraction.

Ray flipped the Glock over, and the Horseman took it from his hand. The other two armed Horsemen walked in and took positions on either side of the altar in the center of the room.

"All clear," Carl called over his shoulder as he took the shotgun from Floyd.

An old man, dressed in a gray suit, walked slowly into the center of the lodge room, looking at each of them in turn. He nodded at Ray Billings. Ray nodded back.

"You're looking a little better than you did the last time I saw you," Ray said.

"You're looking a lot worse," the old man said with a chuckle.

"Tony O'Malley, I presume," Levi said.

The old man stared at Levi for a long moment, a stare that chilled Levi.

"I recognize you from your book covers," Tony said. "I've read them all. They're very good."

"Always good to meet a fan."

Tony smiled. "A great author once wrote that sarcasm is the lowest form of humor."

A brief smile crossed Levi's face as he recognized his own words.

"I really wish we could've met under better circumstances," Tony said.

"Are these bad circumstances?" Levi asked.

"It depends," Tony said, glancing down at Craig on the floor. "Is this our boy, Ray?"

"It is," Ray said. He knew why they were there.

Tony nodded to two of the Horsemen, who holstered their weapons and walked towards Craig.

Ed took a few steps forward. "Wait a minute. What are you doing?"

Tony O'Malley pulled a revolver from his shoulder holster and raised it. Ed knew from the cold glint in his eye that he wouldn't hesitate to kill him without a second thought. He stopped short.

"He's caused us a lot of grief," Tony said. "I'm afraid we're going to have to take him with us. You can accept that fact, or you all can join him."

"At the bottom of Lake Michigan perhaps?" Ray said.

Tony shrugged. "I made a big mistake not taking Andy Miller out in prison. I'm not going to make that mistake again."

"Let me put him in prison, Tony," Ray said. "He doesn't know anything."

"Yeah, I thought Andy Miller was harmless, too," Tony said, "and here we are forty years later because of him. If I knew for sure he didn't know anything, I'd consider that. But he's had a long time to work it all out. He's got to know our connection to the crime. If he didn't back then, he certainly does now. And I've got a feeling he's the kind of coward that wouldn't think twice about trading information for better treatment or accommodations."

"Maybe we could make a trade," Ed said.

Tony's eyes narrowed in on him. "Like what?"

"I'll trade you a 1933 $20 gold Double Eagle for Clifford Craig," he said, motioning towards the man on the floor.

A slow smile crossed Tony's face. "You've still got it . . . I knew it."

Ed looked at him sharply. "Interested?"

Tony looked at him for a long moment and then holstered his gun.

"On two conditions," Tony said. He glanced at Ray. "The investigation ends here."

Ray shrugged. "You leave Craig here. I don't have one shred of solid evidence to link you to anything else and no desire to ever see any of you in Twin Rivers again."

"And what about the Garveys?" Tony said, glancing at the three of them.

Ed, Levi and Tori exchanged glances.

"Clifford Craig is the cause of all this as far as I'm concerned," Ed said. "You may've planned the robbery, but it was Craig who killed Jim Mathis. I believe the story you told Ray—you never meant for anyone to get hurt. And Craig didn't stop there. Craig's the man I hold responsible for all this."

Tori and Levi both nodded in agreement.

"And what about this guy?" Tony said, glancing over at Floyd.

Floyd shrugged. "I don't know a damn thing. Ask anybody."

"You can trust Floyd at his word," Levi said. "He's a jackass, but there are few men I've ever met that are more honest."

"That's so sweet," Floyd said.

Tori glared at him.

Floyd raised a hand, "No need to say it, Tori. I know what you want to say."

"What's the other condition?" Ed asked.

"If he gets off on a technicality or if he gets to be a problem later on in prison . . ." Tony said.

"I'd say that's his problem," Ray said.

"We got a deal then?" Ed said.

Tony nodded.

Ed elbowed Levi. "Give him the coin."

Levi looked back at him with a troubled expression on his face.

"Give it to him, Levi," Ed said impatiently, nudging him towards Tony O'Malley.

"I don't know where it went," Levi said nervously.

"What do you mean?" Ed said.

"I usually drop it," Levi said, glancing around the floor.

Tori snickered. "That's a good trick, Levi. Not even you know how you did it."

Ed glared at her. This wasn't a particularly humorous situation in his opinion.

"Let's look for it," Ed said sharply, glancing around on the floor. "It's got to be around here somewhere."

"Are you telling me you kept that coin safe for nearly forty years and then lost it in the last five minutes?" Tony said, suspecting a trick. "You think I'm that stupid?"

The Four Horsemen took a defensive stance. They were prepared for Tony's order, whatever it might be.

"It's got to be around here somewhere," Tori said nervously.

Suddenly realizing the trouble they were in, she began looking around the dais and under the chairs. Levi leaned over to look under the Chaplain's chair.

"Oh wait," he said, standing up with a grin on his face.

"What?" Tony said.

"I think I just found it," he said.

He raised his arm over his head. Then he began to shake his shoulders and move his hips. As he gently began shaking his leg, the gold coin slipped out of his pants leg and rested on top of his tennis shoe.

Tony laughed, and the Four Horsemen relaxed a bit as they looked at each other and grinned.

"Must've rolled down my shirt sleeve," Levi said, smiling sheepishly.

"That's a great trick," Tori snorted. "I'll bet you can't do it again."

Levi plucked the coin off the top of his tennis shoe as Clifford Craig stirred on the floor. His eyes fluttered open. He sat up on his elbow and looked around, rubbing the back of his neck. When he saw Tony O'Malley and the Four Horsemen, his face blanched.

"Do you know who I am?" Tony asked as he cocked his revolver and aimed it between Craig's eyes.

Craig swallowed hard and nodded.

"So we have a deal?" Ed said.

"We do," Tony said.

"We keep the coin, and you take Craig, right?" Ed said.

Tony looked at Ed questioningly. Then, after a moment, he understood what Ed was doing. He motioned towards two of the Horsemen, who picked Craig up under the arms and began dragging him to the door.

"Wait," Craig yelled. "You can't do this? Ray? Ed? They'll kill me!"

With a flick of his hand, Tony stopped the two Horsemen.

"Like you killed Jim Mathis? And Andy Miller? And Stevie Miller?" Ed said coldly.

"And tried to kill just about everybody else in this room?" Levi said. "Goodbye, Craig."

"Ray!" Craig pleaded. "You have a duty!"

"Don't talk to me about duty, Chief," Ray snapped. "We're all about to become wealthy men. They've offered us a fortune for your worthless hide. I've got no sympathy for a dirty cop. Consider yourself lucky. I'm sure it'll be quick when it comes."

"I wouldn't be so sure about that," Tony said. "Put him in the trunk and make sure he's unconscious when you do."

The two thugs began dragging Craig towards the door again.

"Wait!" Craig said. They stopped again at Tony's signal. "I'll never say anything. I promise. Not one word ever. I'll admit to the whole thing. I'll even admit I planned it with Bruce Franklin. That's the truth! I never knew who was behind any of this until recently."

"I don't know," Tony said. "What do you think, Ed?"

"I'd like to him suffer a little more," Ed said. "A bullet in the back of the head is too quick for the likes of him."

"Maybe you're right, but there's something I want to know," Tony said, glaring at Craig. "Did you kill Alex Patton?"

Clifford Craig's face revealed the truth.

Anger flashed across Tony's face, and for a minute, Levi thought he was going to raise his gun and shoot him right there. Tony walked over to Craig and leaned inches from his face.

"You have no idea how badly I want to kill you. If I actually let you go with Chief Billings here, don't think I can't get to you any time I want to. You double cross me, my friend, and I'll find you. Just give me a reason." Craig shook his head emphatically. "I give you my word. I'll confess everything and take what the law dishes out. You'll never come into it, I swear. I'll tell it the way I knew it until a few weeks ago."

Tony glanced at the two men who were holding him and nodded. They released him, and Craig crumpled to the floor.

"Take him, Chief," Tony said to Ray. "And do it before I change my mind."

"You want to give me a hand here, Floyd?" Ray said.

Carl glanced at Tony, who nodded almost imperceptibly. Carl handed the shotgun back to Floyd.

As they hauled Craig up from the floor and headed towards the door, Tony said, "And don't forget to read him his rights, Ray."

"I won't. But I'm not promising you I won't ask Floyd to shove his ass down the stairs. We'll see how he likes that," he said, rubbing the back of his neck.

Seconds after Ray disappeared from the door, his head popped back in. "Hey, there's somebody out here who wants to see you, Levi."

Levi chuckled when Rosco ran into the lodge. Levi sat down on the bottom step of the dais as Rosco put his front paws on his knees and began licking his face.

"Boy, you were a lot of help," Levi said as he tried to escape the tongue. "Did you hide out there or something?"

"Smart dog," Tony remarked.

"I don't know if you were aware of this, Tony," Levi said with a grin, "but when you take on one Garvey, you get us all."

"Well, in all honesty, I was a little concerned about taking on the Garveys, but I'm not very concerned about that dog," Tony replied.

They all shared a laugh

Then Tony looked at Ed and said, "That was pretty clever."

"I thought I'd give you a chance to scare the living shit out of Craig.

I've got to admit you kind of scared me, too."

"Years of practice," Tony said, a hint of humor on his face.

"I guess that just leaves us with one piece of business left," Ed said, nudging Levi.

Levi handed the coin to Tony.

"It's such a small thing. What does it weigh? Maybe an ounce?" Tony said, looking down at it.

"I'll bet Alex Patton knew precisely what it weighed," Ed remarked.

Tony nodded. "We both lost friends because of Clifford Craig. Alex Patton was my friend. He was such a gifted artist and a gentle man. I never should've brought him into my world. I regret that."

"But he stole from you," Ed said.

"We all make mistakes," Tony said. "He knew the coins he made were perfect. He made an extra and then decided he might as well keep the original. Since he'd worked on that project for years, I guess he felt he deserved it. I don't know why he did that, but I should've just let it go. I think if I'd paid him a little visit and talked to him, none of the rest would've been necessary—the bank robbery and what's happened since."

"You're right," Ed said. "He would've given it back to you. After the bank robbery, that's exactly what he was going to do, but he never got the chance. I never knew the details, but I was to hold that coin until he could work something out with the rightful owners. I never knew who that owner was until your Four Horsemen paid me a little visit some years later. I figured it out then.

"But before Alex could work it out with you, he got beaten up, and then before he recovered from that, he was dead. I held onto the coin because I figured the rightful owners would get around to me eventually—and you did, finally. I knew early on that the rightful owners of that coin wouldn't have killed Alex Patton because he was going to hand it over to them, so the man who killed Alex was the fourth bank robber. Alex wouldn't have given it to him any more than he'd have given it to Andy Miller when he beat the hell out of him. Alex was much more afraid of the rightful owner—you."

"You know what I don't get?" Tori said looking at Ed.

Ed shook his head.

"Why did you nearly beat Andy Miller to death the first time he attacked you at the Beer Chaser?" "When he charged in there and kicked me off my stool, claiming I had something that belonged to him, I knew he was one of the four bank robbers who were responsible for the death of my friend Jim Mathis. When I saw the blood on his knuckles and on his shirt, I knew where he'd gotten his information. I figured he'd killed Alex Patton, too, so I was going to give him what he had coming to him. If Joyce hadn't shot me with her .22, I would've killed him for sure."

"What?" Levi said.

"Oh, I didn't tell you that part," Ed said. "Joyce shot me. She stopped me from killing Andy Miller and probably saved me from going to prison, too. She went to jail but wasn't charged with anything in the end. Thanks to Joyce, I went to the hospital instead of jail, and by the time I was released, they'd decided I'd acted in self-defense. I was never charged with beating up Andy Miller. It's a good friend that will shoot you for your own good."

Levi chuckled.

Tony looked down at the coin again. "So much death and destruction caused by such a tiny thing. My father died because of this coin, too, and I doubt he was the first."

"He wasn't the last either," Ed said.

"It's too bad some good couldn't come out of all of this," Tori said suddenly.

Tony glanced at her and then down at the coin in his hand. "What would you do with it, Levi?"

Levi thought for a minute. "You mean the coin that Tori stumbled upon when she was restoring this old lodge building—the coin we later learned was worth a fortune?"

Tony's gaze narrowed in on him, and he nodded.

"Hard telling how that coin wound up here or where it came from originally," Levi remarked. "It must've belonged to a Mason with a guilty conscience. He probably left it hidden in this lodge seventy or eighty years ago, hoping that one day somebody would find it and do some good with it. Money like that could sure help a lot of people who need it."

Tony glanced around the lodge room. "And I'll just bet you know people who could do the most good with money like that," he said, looking back at Levi.

Levi grinned. "I know a lot of people who could—they wouldn't waste a nickel."

After looking down first at the coin and then at Levi, Tony tossed the coin to him. When Tony turned towards the door, the Four Horsemen followed. Then he paused in the doorway and looked back at Levi.

"We're going across the street for a piece of that famous pie, and then we're leaving Twin Rivers," Tony said. "We won't be back."

He began to turn when Levi called after him, "Hey, Tony."

"Yeah?"

"Your Four Horsemen saved our lives in the carriage house. I can never repay that debt."

Tony chuckled. "Don't worry, Levi. I won't be calling on you for any favors. But there is maybe one or two small things you could do for me . . . if you'd be willing to."

Levi's mouth went dry. "Like what?"

"How about signing a book for me?"

Levi relaxed a bit. "I can do that. What else?"

"Maybe you'll show me that gun you've got shoved down the front of your pants," Tony said. "It's the Webley, isn't it? The one from your book—the one your great-grandpa brought back from World War I."

Levi smiled, and nodded. "Tell you what, after I sign that book, I'll even shoot a hole in it with Mr. Webley."

It was a joke, but Levi knew, from the look on Tony's face, that before the evening was over, he'd be signing and then shooting a copy of his book for one of the most notorious Chicago gangsters in American history.

Chapter Forty

It was the first week of June. The sun was shining, and a cool breeze was blowing through the oaks and maples at Oak Hill Cemetery. Standing near the head of the casket, Levi delivered the final prayer of the Masonic Funeral Rite as the officers of Reverend Guy Garvey's Prince Hall Lodge stood in formation around him, wearing their dark suits, gold jewels, officers' aprons, and white gloves.

The family was arranged around the foot of the casket, and down either side stood several lines of Master Masons, both white and black, wearing white aprons. Behind them was one of the largest assemblages of uniformed Knights Templar Levi had ever seen—the handles of their swords gleaming in their sheaths in the bright morning sunlight.

Levi had never seen a Prince Hall Masonic Funeral Rite before. Many of the Masons in attendance probably never had either. Even though the African-American Lodges had started before the Revolutionary War, they had always remained separate and independent. It was only in recent decades that the two organizations had begun to recognize each other. That day, just about every lodge in five counties, regardless of affiliation or origin, had turned out for the funeral of the Illustrious Reverend Guy Garvey, 33°. Nearly the entire town of Twin Rivers had turned out as well.

Levi felt greatly honored to be asked by Reverend Guy's lodge to do the Chaplain's part. When Levi had told the men he didn't know the Prince Hall version of the ritual, they'd simply told him to do it the way he knew it. But as Levi finished the sentence he was on during the rite, he realized he had a problem—he couldn't remember the next line.

As he struggled to recall the words, he felt a hand on his shoulder. It was the Junior Warden, who was standing behind him. His low, deep voice whispered the first few words of the next verse in Levi's ear. It was a voice he knew well—the voice of Guy Garvey's son, Hank, who'd been one of Levi's teachers in high school.

Levi nodded and finished.

"And now, O God, we pray for Thy hand to lead us in all the paths our feet may tread, and when the journey of life is ended may light from our immortal home illuminate the dark valley of the shadow of death, and voices of loved ones, gone before, welcome us home to that house not made with hands, eternal in the heavens, where no discordant voice shall arise, and all the soul shall experience shall be perfect bliss, and all it shall express shall be perfect praise, and love divine ennoble every heart and hosannas exalted employ every tongue. Amen."

"So mote it be," the Masons said in unison.

The service was over. The Masons formed a line and filed past Guy Garvey's family, shaking hands and giving their condolences.

Tori, who was by now very obviously pregnant, walked over to Levi.

"You want me to wait?" she asked.

Levi shook his head. "I'll stay a while. I'll be home in a little bit."

"You did a really nice job," Tori said as she leaned up and kissed him on the cheek. "I think Reverend Guy would've been proud of you."

Levi smiled as he watched Tori, weaving her way through the headstones to her car.

Levi leaned against a tree trunk nearby as others walked to their cars and the crowd thinned. It was a tradition in some lodges for a member to stay until the casket was covered. Levi intended to see to that duty. While he waited, one of the stones near the Garvey family mausoleum caught his eye. He wandered over to it. It was his great-grandfather's stone. Levi had never known Abe Garvey, but his gun, the Webley, had certainly come in handy a few times during the last couple of years.

"I remember Abe," a voice said beside him.

It was Hank Garvey—his dark face solemn and what hair he had left more white than dark. He was no longer the young man who'd been

Levi's favorite teacher thirty years ago, but he had the same gleam in his eye and the same passion for life he'd helped to instill in a young Levi Garvey.

"I helped him change a tire on his Cadillac one Sunday after church," Hank said. "It wasn't long before he died. I was about ten years old at the time, but I'll never forget because he gave me a five-dollar bill. That was a fortune back in 1965 for no more work than it took to change a tire."

"Abe was a Chevy guy, too, huh?"

Hank nodded. They stood silently for a moment.

"Thanks, Levi," Hank said finally.

"Your dad meant a lot to me," Levi replied.

"That's why I asked you to be Chaplain. You meant a lot to him, too."

"He went easy?" Levi asked.

Hank nodded. "Massive heart attack. He'd been diagnosed in March with a serious heart condition. At his age, the family knew it was only a matter of time—a few months at best. He refused to retire early, and he didn't want anyone to know. We spent a lot of time with Dad the last few months of his life."

"I wish I'd known. We had a little unfinished business. He was going to tell me a story about our families. I guess I'll never know that story now." Levi paused, then added, "Unless you know it?"

Hank shook his head. "I'm assuming it was the answer to the question we've all had at one time or another."

Levi glanced at him as a wry smile appeared on his face.

Hank chuckled. "Sorry, Levi, but he never told me either. He did ask me to give you something though," he said, reaching into his pocket. "Dad said it might point you in the right direction. You know how he loved a good mystery."

Levi smiled. "I remember. We used to love it when our Sunday school teacher was sick and Reverend Guy would fill in. He'd give us a break from our lessons. He made us promise not to tell, but more often than not, he'd read us a Sherlock Holmes story."

"Yeah, that was my dad," Hank said as he handed something small to Levi.

Levi looked down at a small pin—a white enameled cross with rose vines growing over it. Levi recognized it immediately.

"That's a Scottish Rite pin—the Rose Croix," Levi said.

"That's right. It's just a $3 pin," Hank said with a shrug.

"Did he say anything else about it?"

"Not a word," Hank said. "Thanks again, Levi. And if you'd thank your lodge for turning out, I'd certainly appreciate it."

"I'll do that."

"You don't need to stay, Levi. The funeral director is a member of our lodge. He'll be here until the burial is complete."

Levi nodded as they shook hands. Then he watched Hank walk across the cemetery.

Looking down at the pin again, he muttered, "Well, this doesn't tell me much."

He stuck the pin into his pocket and headed towards Pappy. He was driving up the narrow cemetery lane towards the church when he suddenly locked the brakes.

"Wait a minute," Levi said aloud.

Thinking back to when he'd gone through the Scottish Rite, he remembered something about the Chapter of Rose Croix degree he'd received. The Chapter had given each of the members of his class a couple of gifts after the degree.

He took his phone off the belt and punched in a number. Tori answered.

"You at home?"

"Yeah."

"Do me a favor. Go into the den. On the shelf over my desk, there is copy of the New Testament with a Scottish Rite eagle on the cover. I think it's bound in red leather."

He waited as Tori went to look for the book.

"I've got it," Tori said.

"Inside that Bible is a rose pressed between the pages. What chapter is the rose pressed into?"

"Corinthians I: 15," she said after a moment.

"That's what I needed to know," Levi said. "Thanks."

Levi climbed out of Pappy and walked briskly towards the church. He tried the doors, but they were locked. He walked around to a side door and rattled it, too, but it was also locked.

"Damn," Levi muttered.

As he began walking back towards Pappy, he smiled. Reverend Guy had meant to see him in church again, and if he couldn't do it in life, he'd make sure it happened after he died. Levi was climbing back into Pappy when he heard somebody call his name. Eva Sinclair was standing in the doorway of the church.

"Did you want something, Levi?"

"Yes! You mind if I have a look at the altar Bible?" he said as he dashed past her into the church.

Eva grinned as she watched Levi run up the aisle between the pews and bound up the steps of the dais.

"Sure, Levi, go right ahead," she said.

Levi thumbed carefully through the Bible as Eva watched from the bottom of the dais steps. His face fell as he closed the Bible.

"Looking for something?" she asked.

"Yes, well, no. I guess I was wrong," Levi said as he walked down the steps past her. "I thought maybe Reverend Guy had left me something."

"Well, the Bible he preached from he kept on the pulpit."

Levi paused, then turned back around. He walked back up on the dais. He smiled when he saw the large well-worn leather Bible on the pulpit with all manner of notes and papers and bookmarks sticking out of it. Carefully, he turned the pages to Corinthians I. A broad grin crossed his face.

"What is it, Levi?"

He held up the white envelope with a single word written on it in Reverend Garvey's meticulous handwriting—Levi.

"I guess you found it," Eva said.

Levi walked down the steps and planted a big kiss on her cheek. "Thank you, Eva!"

* * *

Levi sat on the bench he and Reverend Guy had shared that spring and looked down at the envelope. As he'd walked over to the bench, he'd had the feeling that the envelope wasn't going to contain what he thought it did. The sun was warm on his face. The cemetery was almost empty. Everyone, except the funeral director and the backhoe operator, had left. He looked again at his name, carefully lettered in Guy Garvey's exceptional handwriting. He turned the envelope over and opened it carefully. After he read the first few lines, he knew his feeling had been right.

> Dear Levi,
>
> I promised you a story about the Garveys. I have been regretting that promise ever since. I should have never brought it up. I have been thinking a lot about this as my time has grown short. As I told you, Lucille knew part of the story, but I left things out of what I told her. I regret having told her what I did because it changed our relationship forever. She questioned me about some of the details, and to be honest with you, I lied, and she knew it. I am a terrible liar—I guess it goes with the job. I believe she knew there was a good reason for my deception, at least I hope she did. In hindsight, I do not think any good came from her knowing what I did tell her.
>
> But I know how you are, Levi. You would never accept at face value the same story I told Lucille, and that is the one I would have told you. You would start dig-

ging into the past to find those parts I left out. I know that now, and thinking about it since has kept me up nights. There are things buried in the past that should remain buried in the past. I am afraid I have opened Pandora's box. That was a foolish mistake.

By the time you read this, I will be gone from this Earth. If you get it into your head to know the past, I have no doubt you can learn all the things I know about the Garvey family. It will not be easy, but the Garveys are like pit-bulls, and once they grab onto something, they never let go. That story I wanted you to know is about your great-grandfather Abe, and it is a wonderful story, but there is no way to learn that story without learning the rest. You have always trusted me, Levi. You have come to me for guidance and advice.

I am going to ask you to trust me just one more time. Leave it alone, Levi. Let it rest.

Guy Garvey

Levi looked up from the letter—the funeral director was lowering Reverend Garvey's casket into the ground with a hand crank—and then back down at the shaky handwriting. Levi felt sure that letter hadn't been easy for Guy Garvey to write. Levi was torn. He really wanted to know that family story. He wanted to write another book, and after months, he still didn't have an idea for it. He'd been banking on Reverend Guy's story to give him the idea for his next novel.

But Levi had also learned something about the past since he'd come back to Twin Rivers. Old secrets had twice nearly destroyed everything he had. In Levi's experience, the past had a way of jumping up and biting him right in the ass.

As he looked at the letter again, he realized the decision before him was a big one. If he went against Guy Garvey's advice, he might dig up something he might very well wish he hadn't. But if he took Guy Garvey's advice, he might never write another book.

He carefully folded the letter and returned it to the envelope. Guy Garvey had been right just about every time he'd sought his advice.

Levi arose and walked over to Guy Garvey's grave. The back-hoe operator paused with the first bucket of dirt poised over the hole. Levi stared first at the vault below and then at the letter in his hand. Tears welling in his eyes, he tore the letter in two and tossed it into the grave. Turning quickly, he walked away as the first bucket of dirt clattered onto the vault.

Blinking back the tears, Levi realized that Guy Garvey had been absolutely right. Levi had enough money so that he didn't have to ever write another book. Eventually, he would get another idea if it was meant to be. There was no reason to dig up the family skeletons, and he had no intention of doing so. Let the past remain in the past.

Smiling, he fired Pappy up and headed toward the present and all that he loved—the woman, the home, the baby who'd be there soon . . .

* * *

"I wonder where Levi is?" Ed said, reaching into the cooler for another beer and then leaning back in the porch swing.

It was the first day that was beginning to feel like fall after an intensely hot summer. The breeze was rustling the dried corn in the field across the road from the Garvey house. Within the week, they'd be harvesting. The stiff breeze also caused the flag on the Garvey porch to occasionally pop. Ed's dog, one of the shepherd puppies, was alternately chasing squirrels in the yard and his own tail.

"I'm more concerned about what's keeping Ray," Tori remarked from the Adirondack chair. "He should've been back a long time ago."

As big as she'd gotten, Ed couldn't believe she still had nearly two months to go.

"Try calling Ray again," Ed said.

Tori shook her head. "I'm sure his phone is off."

Suddenly, Rosco bounded up the porch steps and lapped water noisily out of his water dish beside the door.

"Well, where the hell did you come from?" Ed said as he glanced in the direction from which Rosco had come. Levi was walking across the yard—his face looked like a thundercloud.

"Oh, boy," Ed muttered as he glanced at Tori. They both knew what had happened—again.

He stomped up the porch steps, reached into the cooler, cracked a beer, and leaned on the porch rail, taking a long sip.

"Where's Pappy?"

Levi glared at him. "Dead as a hammer in front of Harv's."

"Did you check the . . ." Ed started to say.

"No, I didn't check anything. I'm tired of tinkering with that damn truck every time I want to start it. I just decided to walk," Levi growled. "That's the third time in a month that stupid truck has left me stranded. I'm buying a new truck tomorrow—brand spankin' new. They've got a beautiful Ford F-150, electric blue, over in Calloway. I'll be driving it home tomorrow afternoon."

"Don't do that," Ed said. "Let me work on Pappy again. Once I get it adjusted right, it'll be fine."

Levi glared at him again. "I don't like that truck."

"You will," Ed said. "Give me another shot at it. I'll get it ironed out."

Tori and Ed both knew what the problem was. Pappy wasn't Old Blue.

Levi sighed as Ed's dog ran up the steps and jumped up on him, leaving muddy footprints all over his pants. Tori suppressed a grin.

"Get down, Luke," Levi said, pushing the dog away.

"Go lay down," Ed said sharply.

Luke plopped down at the top of the stairs next to Rosco, who growled at him.

"You and Rosco seem to be in the same mood," Tori said with a chuckle.

Levi shot her a look.

"Has Ray called?" he said, changing the subject.

Ed and Tori shook their heads.

"Something is wrong," Levi said.

Seconds later, Ed stood as the Twin Rivers police cruiser turned into the drive. Levi stood, too. Tori struggled to get up.

"You want to help me here?" she snapped.

Ed cackled as he took one arm and Levi took the other, and they hoisted her out of the low chair.

The three of them stood at the porch railing as the cruiser pulled to a stop in front of the porch, but it was Ben Walker, not Ray. They all laughed when they saw the head of the German shepherd hanging out the window. When Ben climbed out, the dog bailed out after him and ran up to Tori. Ben's dog was the last puppy they'd found a home for, and Tori had gotten very attached to her.

"Hello, Daisy," she said as the dog licked her face while she rubbed the dog's ears.

"So Twin Rivers finally has a police dog," Levi said.

"Two, actually," Ben said with a smile. "Bo rides with Ray all the time."

"You heard from Ray?"

"Nothing," Ben admitted.

"Chief Craig's court date is the biggest news this county has had for years," Ed remarked.

"We'll know soon enough what happened," Ben said.

"You want a beer?" Ed asked.

"No, actually, I'm on official business I'm sorry to say." He pulled out his citation book, ripped off several sheets, and handed them to Tori. "I kind of forgot about it, but you'll need to pay these within thirty days."

"$75?" Tori said as she realized she was finally being ticketed for her vandalism of the war memorial statue. "At $25 a pop, it should be only $50. I never got it done the third time."

"But you punched me in the face," Ben remarked.

Ed chuckled. "That's true."

"Pay the damned tickets, Tori, or I'll set my dog loose on you," Ben said, pointing at her.

Laughing, Tori tucked the tickets into her shirt pocket. "You know, Levi, you never told me how you figured out I was the Bikini Bandit."

"It was a couple things actually, but it all came together at once. I used to watch you change the sign at Hillbilly Bob's when you worked there in high school, and that's what finally cinched it for me. You got so good at it, you never dropped a letter. I was watching one of the employees change the sign one afternoon while Ben and I were getting gas, and I suddenly knew it wasn't Jim or Jerry. It was you. I also remembered you'd stolen one of those sign changers."

"Me?" Tori said with a grin.

"Yes, you," Levi said. "I saw you use it at your house. You and your dad used it to put Christmas lights on that big blue spruce in your front yard, and that was after the first Bikini Bandit episode. I'm surprised I didn't figure it out then."

Tori smiled broadly. "You weren't nearly as smart as everyone thought you were."

"But that wasn't the only thing that cinched it for me," Levi said.

"What else was it?"

"When I got back from the lodge the evening the Bikini Bandit struck again, I kept hearing this weird noise outside," Levi said. "I couldn't figure out what it was, but there was something very familiar about it, but I just couldn't place it."

Tori smiled again. She knew what he'd heard.

"You went out of the bedroom window and climbed down the rain gutter," Levi said, looking at her.

"We'd climbed up and down that rain gutter a million times," Tori said with a shrug.

Levi laughed. "We never got caught either, but that rain gutter used to make a very distinctive sound when we climbed on it. I hadn't heard that sound in years, but there was something familiar about it—it just took a little while for me to place it."

"It still makes that same sound," Tori said with a smile.

"I can't believe you did that, at our age," Levi said curtly, "and in your condition."

"Actually, I didn't," Tori said. "I changed my mind once I got outside the window and started to go down. I realized it was a long way to the ground. I lost my nerve, so I climbed back in the window and decided to sneak out the back door instead. But I knew you'd heard me. I saw you looking out the window in the library while I was still on the edge of the roof. By the time I'd gotten back in the house and made my way down the stairs, Rosco was awake. I knew there was no way I'd be able to open the back door without Rosco alerting you, so I kicked over the baby gate and released the hounds."

"Ah, the classic diversion tactic," Ed said with a chuckle.

"It worked," Tori said. "I went out the back door, made it over to the park, and was back within half an hour. Levi was still outside the backdoor, trying to get the puppies back inside after they'd peed in the yard. I tiptoed in the front door, went up the stairs, and was back in bed before he was any the wiser. I stashed the sign changer under the bed."

Levi laughed. "You're a criminal genius."

"It was still under the bed when I went to make a third attempt," Tori remarked.

"Makes me want to go upstairs and look under the bed."

The four of them laughed.

The laughter stopped when Ray Billings' cruiser pulled into the driveway, Bo's head hanging out the passenger window. Ray stopped in front of the porch and climbed out slowly.

"We expected you back hours ago," Levi said.

"Took a lot longer than I thought, and then I stopped to get Bo," Ray said as the dog jumped out of the cruiser and ran out into the yard to play with his siblings.

"Everything okay?" Ed asked, but he already knew from the dark look on Ray's face that it hadn't gone well at the Calloway Courthouse.

Ray shook his head. As he climbed the steps, he stopped to scratch Rosco on top of the head. Then he reached into the cooler and grabbed a beer. The can hissed when he opened it. Levi, Ed, and Ben followed suit, each reaching into the cooler and grabbing a beer as they took their usual favorite seats on the porch. Tori eased herself back down into the Adirondack chair. Ray took a long drink from the can and sighed.

"Well?" Levi finally said.

"There will be no trial," Ray said. "It had all been prearranged. He pled guilty to four counts of first degree murder, four counts of attempted murder, and I don't know how many more charges were read off, but he pled guilty to all of them, just like he'd promised Tony. He waived his rights to a jury trial."

"I'm not surprised," Levi said, sipping on his beer.

"The judge required him to give a full accounting of the crime in open court, which he did at length—standing stock still, his voice flat. It took him over an hour, and he told every detail from how he'd gotten involved in the robbery to begin with, to how he'd killed Alex Patton, to how he'd built the devise he thought would kill Levi."

Levi glanced at Tori, whose face had gone pale.

"Tony O'Malley's name never came into it, and once Craig was done, the judge accepted the story. He sentenced Craig right then and there—life in prison without the possibility of parole. I thought it was odd, but Craig almost looked relieved. He kind of nodded as he stared down at his feet. He was handcuffed by a deputy . . ." Ray said, his voice trailing off as he took another sip of his beer.

"So that's the end of it," Ben said.

Ray shook his head. "That's not the end of it. The judge snapped his gavel and stood. He started to walk towards the door to his chambers, and those in the gallery were getting up to leave. I was kind of rattled by the whole thing, so I was sitting there, wondering how I'd missed so many little signs about Clifford Craig that I should've seen sooner. The deputy was leading Craig out of the courtroom when there was this loud noise—sounded like somebody had dropped something heavy on the wood floor of the courtroom. Everyone, including the judge, turned to look."

"What was it?" Ed asked.

"Craig's handcuffs," Ray replied. "Before anybody could react, he grabbed the deputy's gun and fired off two rounds. Both hit the wall three feet over the judge's head."

"Oh no," Tori said.

"The bailiff shot Craig," Ray said.

They didn't have to ask. The answer was written on Ray's face—Clifford Craig was dead. There was a long silence as they all thought about it.

"Getting out of handcuffs was a piece of cake for Craig," Levi remarked. "He gave me a little demonstration with a pair of cuffs Houdini had escaped from the day he taught me that coin trick. He was out of those cuffs seconds after I clapped them on him. He'd practiced for years. He told me there wasn't a pair of cuffs in his entire collection he hadn't learned to escape from."

Ray nodded slowly. "He used a paperclip today—probably one taken from the defense table in the courtroom before he even stood to allocute."

"He never meant to kill that judge," Ed said.

"Of course not," Ray said. "He'd have needed only one hand free to do that, but he freed both hands."

"He did that so he could drop those cuffs," Tori said, her eyes wide. "He wanted to draw attention to himself, so everyone would turn and look in his direction—including the bailiff."

"It was suicide by cop," Ben said.

"All those years he spent learning and practicing how Houdini escaped," Ray said. "In the end, it enabled Craig to escape from prison."

There was another long silence.

"Strange," Levi said finally.

"What?" Ray asked, glancing at him.

"You know he saved my life when I was a kid. He climbed the

radio tower and rescued both me and Doug Malone. I drove the poor guy crazy with the crap I used to pull. Never would've dreamed he was capable of the things we now know he did. I have a tough time reconciling the Chief Craig I know now with the man I knew before."

"What did he say that night on the porch—the night Andy Miller knocked Ed off that barstool?" Tori said, thinking back. "Something about the mistakes of youth."

Levi remembered. "It's often said the mistakes of youth are soon forgiven. Some aren't. Just ask Andy Miller."

"That was it," Tori said.

"I think he understood that better than anybody," Levi remarked. "Do you think he was talking about Andy Miller, or was he talking about himself?"

"He knew when he said that what he was about to do," Ray said. "He didn't want to do it, but he left us early that evening, knowing he was going to kill Andy Miller that same night. Once he did that, he knew there was no going back."

"How do you know he didn't want to do it?" Tori asked.

"After he was arrested, we searched his house on Olton Lake. We found two letters addressed—both stamped and ready to be mailed—but he'd never mailed them. He just couldn't bring himself to do it. Those letters were dated a few days before Andy Miller was released. The prison had notified the Twin Rivers Police Department that Andy Miller was being released, and Chief Craig had taken the call—we suspected that, and the letters prove it. Craig had typed up a letter of resignation to the Twin Rivers Village Board with a copy to the River County District Attorney. It was a four-page letter in which he admitted to being the fourth bank robber. It was a full confession of all the things he'd done up to that point. When he wrote it, he was planning to turn himself into the River County Sheriff the next morning."

"But he couldn't do it," Tori said.

"It would've ruined the life he'd made here over the last forty years," Levi said. "He wasn't that criminal anymore. He'd become something different. I can't believe the things he did as police chief all those years was an act—what he'd done as chief was the real Clifford Craig. I have no doubt he regretted what he'd done back in '71, but he just couldn't stand throwing away forty years of decency over the likes of Andy Miller."

Ray shook his head. "I can't believe you just said that, Levi. He tried to blow you up in your truck. He tried to shoot me in the head and later tried to poison me. He tried to kill Tori, too."

"If you and Tori had shown up at the lodge a minute later," Ed said. "I'd have been dead."

"And there's Andy and Stevie and Alex Patton," Tori said.

"And Jim—" Ed said.

"You're wrong, Levi," Ray said. "If he was the man you thought he was, he would've mailed those letters—that would've been the right thing to do. But he didn't do the right thing in the end. He decided to kill a man instead, and it didn't stop there. He was never the man you knew. Just look how quickly he went back to being the man he was forty years ago—the man who robbed the Calloway Bank and murdered Deputy Jim Mathis. He never regretted what he'd done. If he had, he wouldn't have gone down that same road again."

"We'd all be dead right now if Clifford Craig had succeeded," Tori said. "We had something he didn't—and it's a damned good thing, too."

"What?" Levi said.

"Friends," Ed said.

"And luck," Ray added.

There was a long moment of silence.

"Life goes on," Levi finally said as he reached over and took Tori's hand. "I don't think we'll ever understand all this. Maybe it's best we just thank God we survived it and put it behind us."

Tori looked at him. A small smile crossed her face, even as tears filled her eyes.

"Beer Chaser?" Ray said, ending the brief moment of sentimentality.

"I got a better idea," Tori said. "We've never had a chance to break in that great pool table you have in your basement."

"That's an excellent idea," Ben said, jumping up.

"And we won't talk about this tonight," Ray said. "We'll talk about all this later, I'm sure, but tonight, let's celebrate those things we have and all the wonderful things that are coming."

Ray held his hand out to Tori, who smiled. Then she grunted as Ray and Levi pulled her up out of the chair with some effort.

"Holy crap," Ray said as he rubbed his shoulder.

Tori reached over and flicked the end of his nose with her finger. "Watch it, Ray."

Rubbing his nose, Ray said, "Let me get one thing clear right now, Mrs. Garvey. If I'm going to be chief of police here, you're going to have to stop assaulting the officers in my town."

"Your town?" She chuckled as she rolled her eyes.

Then her face fell and her green eyes flashed when Ray reached over and flicked the end of her nose.

Levi and Ed looked at each other with wide eyes.

"My town," Ray repeated.

Nobody moved as Tori rubbed her nose.

"Your town, Chief Billings," she said with a nod as a smile crossed her face.

As they all walked down the porch steps, Ed whispered to Ray, "Unless you want to walk with a limp for the rest of your life, I wouldn't ever do that again. They never found the last guy who did that—well, not all of him, anyway."

Ray looked at Ed, and they both erupted into laughter.

CONCLUSION

LEVI WAS SITTING IN THE LIBRARY IN A WINGBACK CHAIR, HIS FEET propped up on the ottoman as Adam lay on his legs, trying to focus his eyes on the bright white lights and the colorful decorations on the Christmas tree behind his father's head. He was a month old, blonde-haired and blue-eyed and perfect, Levi thought. He was just beginning to look toward voices and sounds in that vague way tiny babies have.

Rosco was sitting on the floor, his muzzle resting on the arm of the chair, on guard duty as he'd been since the baby had arrived. The library floor was covered in gift wrapping paper. Tori walked into the library and sat down on the settee, sipping a cup of coffee and smiling broadly. She handed Levi a warmed bottle for Adam.

"How did I do?" Levi asked, cuddling Adam in the crook of his left arm.

"Oh, Levi," she said, taking another sip. "Nine months without a cup of coffee. I have to admit that coffee maker makes coffee almost as good as April's."

"It's okay to say it," Levi grinned. "It's better than April's."

"I don't know about that," she said, unwilling to say such a statement out loud—there were rules in small towns.

"That's your fourth cup," Levi said with a chuckle.

"I've got some catching up to do. And did you like your gift?"

"Are you kidding me?" Levi said, looking down at the gold Mason ring on his hand. "How could I not like it. It was my great-grandfather Abe's."

"Your great-aunt Margaret over in Olton had it. I've had it for over a year. I met her when I restored the Majestic Theatre. The ring is from the 1920s—a beautiful example of art deco jewelry, but it was in bad shape. Abe must've worn it a lot. I couldn't find anybody locally who could restore it, but Ed knew a Mason in Champaign who did an amazing job."

Levi shifted Adam to his chest and started to gently pat his back.

"Uncle Ed always knows a guy. It looks brand new," Levi said as Adam let out a huge belch.

"Just like his father," Tori said with a grin.

Levi grunted. "You have a rag? He just spit-up on my shirt. Just like his mother."

Tori tossed him a rag. "I only did that once, and I've never had peppermint schnapps since."

Levi laughed. "As fast as he's putting away bottles, there's a little Uncle Ed in him, too."

They both heard a honk come from the driveway.

"Speaking of which," Tori said.

They listened as Ed walked up the porch steps, stomping the snow off his shoes, and crossed the porch. It'd finally a snowed a little bit, just enough to powder the ground.

"You know who's coming?" Levi said, looking at Adam. "It's Uncle Ed."

"Uncle Ed is here," he boomed from the library door.

His German shepherd, Luke, was at his heels, wagging his tail.

"What the heck is that?" Ed said.

"What?" Levi said.

Ed shook his head as he pointed at the fireplace. He grabbed the fireplace poker and tossed a couple of logs on the fire.

"You've got five ricks of firewood out there, Levi Scrooge," he said. "Why don't you build a decent fire. It's Christmas!"

"Why so cranky, Uncle Ed?" Levi said. "Oh, that's right, you don't sleep very well on Christmas Eve, what with all those ghosts visiting you all night."

Ed waved him away as he walked over behind Levi's chair to look at Adam. Rosco growled.

"What's wrong with that dog?"

"I don't know," Levi said. "He's gotten real protective of Adam. Just don't walk up too fast. He snapped at Harv Jenkins yesterday."

"You're a good dog, Rosco," Ed said, dropping to one knee and rubbing Rosco's ears.

Then rising, he said, "I got you something, Levi."

"I got you something, too."

"Yeah?"

"It's under the tree," Levi said. "That big box."

Ed walked over, picked up the box, and shook it. Then he sat down next to Tori on the settee.

"I wonder what it is?"

"It's something you can use," Levi said.

Ed began to unwrap it, glancing up at the smug look on Levi's face every so often. When he was finally done, he looked at Levi and smiled.

"Hey thanks, this something I can use," he said.

The look on his face, however, gave away the fact it wasn't what he'd thought it might be. It was a first aid kit—funny but not very thoughtful.

"Oh, it's better than that, Uncle Ed. That's no first aid kit. That's a Garvey emergency kit, which I put together myself, just for you!"

"You did?"

When Ed opened the lid of the metal box, a smile crossed his face.

"There must be a thousand band-aids in here."

Levi chuckled.

"I've got Dora the Explorer," Ed said, "and Spiderman, Hello Kitty, My Pretty Pony, The Smurfs, Scooby-Doo, and SpongeBob SquarePants. Oh, and there's also a beer in here, too, and a map—of River County. And a compass."

Levi laughed. "All things you can use. I figure that's only about six months worth of band-aids for you, but I'm sure going to enjoy the next six months. There's also six Batman condoms in there—I figure that's a lifetime supply for you. And they glow in the dark."

"At my age, that actually might come in handy."

Ed looked down at his emergency kit, an odd look on his face.

"What's wrong?" Tori said. "You don't like it?"

"No, it's not that. It's just, well . . ." He held up his hand. Blood was running down the side of his hand. "I cut my thumb opening the box."

Levi laughed so hard, he nearly dropped the baby.

After Ed had used a sanitary wipe, which Levi had obviously stolen from Kentucky Fried Chicken, to clean his thumb, he dressed his injury with a Sesame Street band-aid.

"So what did you get me?" Levi asked.

Ed said nothing as he got up and walked into the foyer, returning a moment later with a small box, which he held out to Levi. Tori took Adam and sat back down on the settee.

"Don't shake it," Ed said.

Levi unwrapped it carefully, opened the box, and smiled as he pulled the object out.

"I used to build models when I was a kid," Ed remarked. "I hadn't done that in years, but I made that for you."

When Levi looked at the small model of the Ford pick-up, painted in blue, his vision blurred. He knew Ed understood how much he missed Old Blue and had spent hours making this little model of his truck. Levi just couldn't get used to Pappy. He probably never would. In fact, he'd considered buying a new Ford pick-up several times over the last few months. Blue, of course. He regretted how nasty he'd been with Ed in expressing his displeasure with the truck's lack of reliability.

"Thank you," Levi said. "I'm going to put this on top of my desk."

When he raised the model up to look at it more closely, he heard something rattle inside the model. A smile crossed his face as he shook the model gently from side to side. A loose piece was rattling around inside. Levi chuckled.

"What?" Ed said.

"Oh, nothing," Levi said, suppressing a grin.

"Is there something wrong with it?" Ed said.

"No, it's just that . . ." Levi paused to shake it again. "Well, I've built enough trucks with you to know that you must've had a few pieces left over."

Ed's face fell.

"Levi," Tori scolded. "Can't you ever just say thank you without making a joke? Ed spent a lot of time on that."

Levi glanced at the box of silly bandages sitting next to Ed. Suddenly, Levi felt like a huge ass. The model had obviously taken Ed a great deal of time to build.

"I'm sorry. Thank you, Uncle Ed. I love it."

Ed nodded, obviously still hurt.

"Sorry we couldn't save Old Blue," Ed said.

They'd tried, but Old Blue was dead. There was no saving the truck since almost nothing had survived. In June, they'd taken Old Blue out to Ed's junkyard and left it there in the weeds behind the shed. It was one of the hardest things Levi had ever done.

"I just wanted to give you something to remember Old Blue by."

Levi nodded.

"It's not the first time you've done that," Levi said. "Brought Old Blue back for me."

Ed and Tori looked at him suddenly, eyebrows raised.

"You knew . . ." Ed said, staring at Levi intently.

Levi smiled and nodded.

"You think I'm stupid? That truck I drove for the last two years was not Old Blue, but it might as well have been. I knew after I drove it the first time. I recognized a part here and there, but I knew what you'd done. You'd built another one. I didn't love that truck any less knowing that, and I don't miss it any less because it wasn't the first."

"Well, that makes this easier," Ed said.

"What?"

"That's not a model truck, Levi—it's a piñata."

"What?" Levi said.

"Don't you know what a piñata is, dumbass?" Ed remarked.

"Yeah," Levi said, looking down at the model truck. Slowly, he began to understand what Ed was saying. He stood and glanced at Ed, who nodded. Levi violently pitched the model truck onto the flagstone hearth of the fireplace where it exploded into tiny pieces. Gleaming in the light of the fireplace among the shattered remains of the model truck was a key attached to a chrome ZZ-Top keychain—a keychain just like the one that'd been attached to the key Ed had first tossed to him in 1982.

Ed's voice cracked as he said, "It's still yours, Levi. Tori and I put the tailgate and hood on it from Old Blue. But that's about all that survived the fire. I couldn't believe it when I found the truck in the classifieds. The kid we got it from had nearly finished the restoration, and he'd done a really good job, except it was red. We fixed that paint—and the engine still needed a lot of work. Tori and I've been sneaking off to work on it in my shed since we took Blue out there in June."

Levi stared at the key on the fireplace hearth, speechless.

"Merry Christmas, Levi," Ed said.

Levi picked up the key and dashed towards the foyer. Ed chuckled as he followed him out, Luke on his heels. After snagging a blanket off the back of a chair to toss over Adam's head, Tori followed them.

Levi froze at the top of the porch steps when he saw it—a blue 1960 Ford F-100 sitting in the driveway.

"Old Blue," Levi gasped. He couldn't believe it.

"Nope," Ed said. "That's New Blue."

"Hood and tailgate?"

Ed nodded. "Oh, and your beer cooler survived somehow. I tossed that in the back. I kept the plates of course—LEVIZ 60."

"It's Old Blue," Levi said resolutely.

"It's your truck," Ed said. "Call it what you want."

Levi turned, put his fingers into the corners of his mouth, and let out a shrill whistle. Rosco banged through the screen door, ears up and tongue hanging out.

"Let's go, dog," Levi said. "And no barking."

"Wait," Tori said. "Ray wanted to be involved, too. He's down in

Savannah right now, but I have a feeling he'll be coming back to Twin Rivers with his first wife. There was something he wanted to give you."

She passed Adam off to Ed and went back into the house. When she returned, Levi grinned when she placed the new Panama hat on his head.

"Ray said you couldn't go driving around in Old Blue without proper headgear. Now you're ready," Tori said, kissing him on the cheek.

"Come on, Rosco," Levi said as he walked down the steps.

Rosco bailed in, and Levi climbed in behind him. Ed chuckled as Levi leaned over the seat and rolled Rosco's window down.

"This is your window, Rosco," Levi said sternly, "and this one is mine. Got it, dog?"

Then he fired up New Blue. No, Ed thought, correcting himself, Levi said that's Old Blue.

They watched as Levi drove down the driveway.

"He's going to be pissed off when he realizes it's Christmas Day and Harv's is closed," Ed remarked to Tori, handing Adam back to her.

"He's got a key. Levi has a key to everything. And I'll bet you anything, April left a piece of chocolate for him."

Ed chuckled. Levi was trying to push Rosco off his lap.

"We did it again, didn't we?" Ed said.

Tori adjusted Adam on her arm. "We did. We're whole again."

"We needed a new Rosco after Rosco the Brave," Ed said.

"You took care of that. And then we needed a new Blue," Tori remarked.

"And we took care of that. We keep getting off easy, don't we?" Ed said.

Tori nodded. "We've been very lucky. All the things that really matter have survived," she said as she leaned over and kissed Ed on the cheek.

With the sound of Old Blue fading, Ed looked at Tori.

"What?" she asked.

"You think Craig and the bank robbery might've been our last adventure?" Ed asked.

"I sure hope so," Tori said. "I mean, how many secrets could this small town have? We've stumbled into two. I think we're done, especially since Ray's here now. Like they always say, nothing ever happens in Twin Rivers."

Ed looked out over the front yard, rubbing his chin. There might be one or two more secrets, Ed thought. He wasn't sorry that Levi had given up on the idea of digging through the family's skeleton closet after Reverend Garvey died. Levi was right to take Guy Garvey's advice. Sometimes it's best to leave the past in the past.

"Merry Christmas, Ed," Tori said.

Ed smiled as he looked at Tori and his great-nephew, Adam—the next generation.

"Merry Christmas, Tori," Ed said.

* * *

CARL WALKED INTO THE LIBRARY, TOSSED HIS HAT ONTO THE CHAIR, walked over to the sideboard, and poured himself a bourbon. He glanced at Tony, who'd been absorbed in a book all afternoon.

"You want a scotch?"

Tony glanced up from the desk and nodded.

Carl poured two fingers of scotch into a tumbler and set it on the desk next to Tony. Then he plopped down in the chair across from the desk and propped his feet up on the edge.

"You've been reading that old book since lunch," Carl remarked.

Tony loved history. His library was full of rare books. Long before he was the head of the Chicago Outfit, he'd participated in history—he'd been a survivor of the Japanese attack on Pearl Harbor. He collected old history books with a passion and read them with the same enthusiasm.

"I've read it before," Tony said. "I've had it for years. By the time it was published posthumously in the mid-1930s, there wasn't a lot of interest in Civil War memoirs. Americans were more interested in fiction by then—and movies. I've never seen another copy of it anywhere.

It's very rare. It's a memoir of a Union officer who served under General Hancock during the Civil War. It's interesting because it doesn't stop with the Civil War. He continued the story clear up to a few years before his death in the late 1920s. This guy, after the Civil War was over, went home, started a family, and built an empire in lumber, steel, brick, coal, and even ice. A whole town grew up around him."

Carl chuckled. "A diverse portfolio."

Tony smiled. It was a phrase often used when they talked about the various illegal enterprises the Chicago Outfit ran.

"And a good deal of this book talks about his son, too, who went off and fought in World War I—and you know what's interesting about that?"

Carl shrugged as he sipped his bourbon.

"We sat on his son's porch in that town he founded, and I've got a book written by his great-great-grandson with a slug in it from that same gun the captain's son brought home from World War I," Tony said. He nodded towards the edge of his desk where a book with a bullet hole in it lay. Levi's book had become one of Tony's most prized possessions. He kept it close by so he could show it off to the associates he met with.

Rising, Carl walked behind Tony and looked down at the book in his hands—*From Gettysburg to Twin Rivers: A Memoir of Captain William Garvey*.

"No kidding," Carl said. "That's why you were so interested in Levi's old Webley. You knew all about that gun from his great-great-grandfather's book."

Tony chuckled. "That's right. I know more about Levi's family than he does. Levi's book wasn't the first book I'd read that talked about the Webley. I thought I'd reread William Garvey's book. Levi gave me a book, so I'll send him one after I finish it. I'll bet Levi doesn't even know it exists. You know, Carl, it's important to know where you came from—to know your family history."

"The Garveys will never accept a gift from you," Carl remarked.

"You're right again, but I'd be willing to bet if a wealthy collector, who wishes to remain anonymous, donates a copy to the Twin Rivers

Library Historical Archive, Levi Garvey will hear about it within five minutes. That is where this book belongs, after all—in the library of the town this man founded."

"You're gettin' soft, Uncle Tony," Carl said with a grin.

Tony glanced up at his nephew sharply. They'd kept the true nature of their relationship a secret for good reason. Few of the O'Malley family had survived the brutal nature of the family business. His three sons picked off one at a time over four decades; his wife, Anna, killed by a car-bomb meant for him; his daughter and her groom shot down on her wedding day in '58—again in an attempt to murder him. The O'Malley cemetery plot was a testament to mob violence.

"Levi did me a favor," Tony said. "That coin was a curse. Now it's doing some good in the world after all the death and destruction it caused, including the death of my own father."

"That's not what I'm talking about," Carl said. "Didn't you already give Levi a Christmas present?"

"I don't know what you're talking about," Tony said, staring up at him over the top of his reading glasses.

"I'm talking about a 1960 Ford F-100 pick-up you had mostly restored, then painted red, and then sold through the classified ads in a tiny small-town newspaper by a young associate at a substantial loss back in June," Carl said. "Very clever how you pulled that off. I'm sure the Garveys have no idea who was behind their incredible bit of luck in finding a truck like that in such good condition."

Tony looked at his nephew coldly before a small smile appeared on his face. Carl knew the family business almost as well as he did, including the auto restoration business that fronted their illegal chop shop. He should since he'd been working at his uncle's side for more than fifty years and would soon take over in his place.

Carl looked at the book again for a long moment. Then he said, "Something tells me there's a lot more to this story, isn't there?"

Tony laughed as he raised his scotch. Tipping it towards Carl, he winked and said, "There always is, Carl. There always is.

About the Author

Todd E. Creason, the father of two daughters, lives with his wife Valerie, near his hometown in Illinois. He considers writing a hobby. *A Shot After Midnight* is his second novel in the Twin Rivers series. The first, *One Last Shot*, was published in 2011. He works full-time as a business manager at the University of Illinois. An active Freemason, and Past Master of his Masonic Lodge, he is the author of the award-winning *Famous American Freemasons* series. When he's not reading or writing, his hobbies include fishing and music. An accomplished piano player, he has spent more than twenty years playing everything from rock and roll to country and blues.

Visit the author's website at: TODDCREASON.ORG